JUNKYARD COMMANDOS

JUNKYARD PIRATE
BOOK 7

JAMIE MCFARLANE

PREFACE

FREE DOWNLOAD

Sign up for the author's New Releases mailing list and get free copies of the novellas; *Pete, Popeye and Olive* and *Life of a Miner*.

Click here to get started:

http://www.fickledragon.com/keep-in-touch

1

HUNTED

AJ - Earth

Albert Jenkins sat up and slipped his leg from beneath the blankets, setting his foot quietly on the unfinished floor. From the bedstand, he pulled his .45cal, 1911 pistol, which was hot-loaded, the familiar weight reassuring him of its full magazine.

"I heard it too." Beverly, his four-hundred nanometer Beltigersk sidekick appeared next to the closed bedroom door as a projection of a six-inch tall woman dressed in jungle combat fatigues.

AJ couldn't afford to respond vocally. Beverly's communication was entirely internal, as she lived within him and communicated by stimulating auditory nerves. As an eighty-year-old Vietnam war veteran, AJ had undergone significant physical changes upon accepting the tiny symbiote and was in top physical condition.

The scrape of flesh against the unfinished floor of the living room just outside his door alerted both AJ and Beverly of a presence.

"AJ, get down!" she yelped.

Even as Beverly warned her human host, she projected the outline of a tall humanoid form aiming a thick rifle at the closed bedroom door. Firing AJ's adrenal glands, she flashed a light in his peripheral vision, urging him toward the outside wall.

Heart hammering like the drummer in a rock band, AJ responded. Without the perfect union of symbiote and human, he'd have been too late. As it was, he didn't hear the flimsy wooden door blow inward any more than he felt the small shards of wood embed themselves in his back and legs.

"Window!" Beverly urged, outlining the window's frame with a pale blue light.

"Ah, shit!" he growled.

Churning his legs against the floor, he struggled forward. With the strength and agility of a much younger man, he grasped the windowsill and lifted just enough to carry himself into the window and through. Glass exploded, cutting into his skin as he tumbled onto his unfinished home's front porch.

An unearthly roar of anger preceded the staccato sounds of energy-based weapon's fire tearing through the fabric of his house. AJ's breath was knocked from him as he impacted a heavy wood post. Stunned, he couldn't decide which way to turn.

"Right! Stay low," Beverly urged, manipulating his vision to illuminate the path she indicated. Having worked together for a multitude of missions, he didn't have to think to understand the tiny alien who'd become so important to him.

Peeling himself from around the post, AJ contemplated the railing in his way. The momentary pause would have cost him his life if not for a sudden pinch in his side as Beverly tweaked a sensitive organ in his abdomen. Inches over his head, an energy bolt sheared off the thick wooden post.

With an abundance of anxiety fueling his movements, he leapt over the railing, twisting to get a look at the looming figure that followed him through the bedroom. The glance did little for his mood as he took in an alien standing six and a half feet tall and was wider than a linebacker.

A bright red reticle showed on the alien's shoulder. AJ's aim was unsteady, and required entirely too much focus to bring it true. At the last moment, the center of the reticle aligned with the alien's plated skin. He squeezed off two shots, but only one of the .45 caliber slugs found purchase.

A howl of pain and anger erupted from the alien. The sound was a mix between a goat's bray and a diesel engine. Bright red blood erupted from a wound as chips of its natural armor were violently removed. Unfortunately, this only seemed to further enrage the angry alien.

"AJ, that's a Togath. Its critical organs are low center mass," Beverly said.

The information became less useful when AJ's shoulder struck a rock on the way to the ground and his pistol flew from his hands. For a split second, he considered trying to grab the 1911 weapon, but the notion was set aside when a bowling ball-sized hole of rocky soil was displaced by another close miss.

"At least he isn't a very good shot," AJ grumbled, scrabbling for purchase on hands and knees. While his shoulder ached from impact with the rock and his backside from embedded wooden slivers, Beverly had muted the pain, which allowed him to continue functioning.

"Togath are hard to kill," she said. "They're genetically developed for the purpose of war."

"It's not a real alien?" he asked. As soon as the words were out of his mouth, he realized he wasn't making a ton of sense. Fortunately, Beverly could assess his question.

"Real enough to kill the both of us. Togath are slow, but they're very difficult to kill," she said. "They can't easily move sideways but have very quick forward movement."

"What's with that cannon he's carrying?" AJ had skirted around the corner of the house and discovered that sightlines weren't working for him. A gaping hole had been blown through the corner of his house. "Well, shit!"

"They're specially designed for Togath," Beverly explained. "But there's something more important you need to know."

AJ skidded to a halt. A much larger version of the alien that had been chasing him stood in front of him.

"Let me guess, they travel in pairs," he said.

"Mated for life," Beverly said.

"How fast do they run?" AJ sprinted into the junkyard.

"Faster than you, even when fully amplified."

"Good to know." He leapt at a stack of cars and kicked off to change directions. He felt the wind of a body race past him.

"Alpha One, this is Alpha Two, do you copy?"

AJ's ears perked at his callsign coming through his embedded communications hardware powered by Beverly's presence.

"This is One. I'm in a bit of a pickle here. Gonna need to call back," AJ said.

"We got the call and are six minutes out."

The voice belonged to his best friend, Darnell Jackson. While the idea of help was welcome, Darnell was hardly the guy to fight against a superior enemy. Softened by midlife, Darnell, who also carried a symbiote, had spent his tours in Vietnam in the cockpit of a helicopter.

"Bubba, you need to think again," AJ said. "I got a whole shit-pile of trouble here."

"I've got Three and Four aboard," Darnell said. "We're gonna drop fast ropes in four minutes thirty. Keep moving."

"What the hell?" AJ asked, scooting around the end of a tall pile. "BB, what're Lefty and Frenchie doing in town?"

Just then, a beam of light was interrupted by a figure passing between AJ and the moon. Heavy physical impact on his back tossed AJ forward and into a pile of uncrushed cars he'd been parting out. The pile was unstable, but not so much that a man's body would topple it. At least, he didn't think it would.

With his head slapping against a steel doorframe, AJ once again fought to shake off a stun. The now familiar sound of a Togath's charge alerted him just enough to roll out of the way. The impact of the three hundred fifty-pound alien into the stack of junk cars had a different result than had AJ. As a junker, AJ was used to assessing his stacks. He imagined the irony of being crushed by his own incompetent junkyard management.

"AJ, it's coming down," Beverly warned unnecessarily.

"Yeah, got that," he answered, crawling on hands and knees back toward the old F150 on the bottom of the stack. With wheels removed, there wasn't much room beneath the truck but that had been his big plan anyway. He'd hoped the massive Togath wouldn't be able to follow him.

As far as his plan went, he was right. Of course, when a massive, three-fingered hand wrapped around his ankle, AJ realized he was in trouble. Stomach sliding against rocky soil, he twisted until he could grab the truck's frame. That stopped his momentum, but the force exerted by the Togath was extreme. Even in his great shape, he couldn't resist for long.

"I need something, BB," he said, between clenched teeth. His fingers started to give and he twisted his head back and forth looking for anything that could help.

"There's a rebar rod, but you'll never have the strength to impale a Togath's armor."

"Never say never!"

AJ saw the rebar as it had been highlighted by Beverly's special link with his optic nerve. Not having other, better ideas, he released the truck's frame and reached for the four-foot-long bar, sliding it onto his belly to use as a prod that might give him some separation from the Togath.

Sliding free from beneath the truck, AJ pressed the rod forward into the Togath's chest. For a short moment, it did exactly what he'd planned. That moment was soon ruined by the Togath releasing his ankle to slap the bar away.

Movement from above made AJ's eyes widen even further and he dug his heels into the ground, pushing to re-insert himself beneath the truck. The Togath saw the move and brayed like an angry mule, reaching down to grasp his ankle again.

This time, however, AJ stopped and sat up, lodging the rebar into the Togath's stomach while at the same time bracing it against the ground. One look in the Togath's face conveyed exactly what it believed was about to happen as it drew back a clawed, three fingered hand with intent to impale.

"Look out!" he shouted, releasing the rebar. He pulled his legs back in a modified sort of crunch as he grasped for the bottom side of the old truck.

The Togath saw AJ's shout of surprise and hesitated. It was enough, as an old Subaru station wagon toppled onto its back, pressing the Togath down with deadly force, driving the rebar directly into its stomach.

Not one to count blessings early, AJ crawled away from the monstrous beast, his only objective to hide like the multitude of rats that lived in the ancient heaps piled by the three generations of Jenkins who'd owned the property.

"That might not have killed it," Beverly warned.

"How much to insertion, Big D?" AJ called out.

"Forty seconds," Darnell answered.

"BB, mark that Togath," AJ ordered. "There are two hostiles on the ground. Tough beyond measure. Take it slow, boys. Don't outrun your cover."

The heavy thumps of a helicopter's approach cut the still night air. It was an altogether familiar sound that transported AJ back to the jungle. Like most of the men he'd served with, he suffered from PTSD triggers. The stress of the attacking aliens did just that. Instead of disabling him, he rolled with it, knowing that to survive, he had to go back to war and embrace the junkyard's chaos just as he had embraced the jungle years ago.

Impossibly, the sound of bending metal and breaking glass warned of the big Togath's refusal to die. AJ scoffed at the thought. Nothing easy about the damn Togath. Importantly, he'd managed to drag himself far enough beneath the truck that he didn't expect the Togath to reach his ankle again.

The downside to being stuck beneath the truck was that he had no idea what the Togath was doing. A loud crash told him that somehow the beast had not only survived but had freed itself. Whether it had or not was an open question that was quickly answered when a fat arm swung beneath the truck, looking for him.

"Missed, you fat bastard!" AJ taunted as the arm came up well short.

Either as result of AJ's insult or for other reasons, the Togath responded with a quick series of sharp, barking sounds. It was obviously an attempt at communication, and that Beverly was unable translate concerned him.

The sound of screeching metal preceded movement of the truck over AJ's body. Spying beneath the truck, AJ saw two pairs of legs at opposite ends of the truck. He was good and screwed as the truck started to slide off and then was impossibly lifted away.

In a last-ditch effort to buy time, he grabbed the truck's exhaust and driveshaft, wrapping his hands and feet around anywhere he could find purchase. He was lifted into the air and the truck turned over as the pair of aliens lifted it overhead.

Recognizing he wouldn't get a better moment, AJ released his hold and climbed up the now vertical bottom of the truck and jumped onto another pile of rusty objects, most of which were well designed to rip into his soft skin.

"Grenades! Alpha One, take cover now!!!"

The sound of Lefty's command got AJ's attention and brought clarity to the moment. With no care for the minor injuries sustained, AJ scrambled for cover within the pile he'd landed on. He ended up settling for sinking behind a row of old rusted-out washing machines. It was a tight fit, but the tighter the better, given what would come next.

"I'm to ground, Two. Light those asshats up!" AJ called. "BB, can you get me some video?"

Like being immersed in a movie, the junkyard spread out in front of him. Using the video feeds from AJ's team's cameras, Beverly constructed a full battlefield view in real time. Three men in old jungle fatigues had spread out and were on approach with the Togath in their sights.

"Execute," Alpha Two ordered. Three contrails of rocket propellant trailed out behind fast-moving projectiles. For a moment, AJ wondered if the Togath armor could withstand the concussive impact of the RPGs. His question was quickly put to bed upon impact as the smaller of the two Togath received a pair of RPGS right at waist level. The damage was devastating, cutting the thickly muscled, biological construct in half.

Professional soldiers, the team didn't rest on their success or even wait to see the result of their work. Instead, they switched to M110A1 rifles, sending hot 7.62mm rounds into the chaos as they slowly advanced. AJ felt a certain pride at their no-nonsense approach. To underestimate the Togath would have been a giant mistake. But then, AJ's crew were to a man over seventy-five years and hadn't made it that far in life by taking shortcuts.

"Frags!" Alpha Three called. "Keep it down, Jenkins."

The din of bullets was suddenly replaced by a pair of closely matched explosions. And then there was nothing, which to AJ seemed even louder than had the firefight.

He watched the video as his team approached the fallen aliens. Not willing to take chances, the soldiers followed through with closely aimed shots and then stepped back.

"Jenkins, show yourself, I know you're hunkered down like an old swamp rat," Lefty called.

AJ tried to move but found that he'd slipped so far between the old metal machines he couldn't free himself without dragging skin across sharp metal surfaces that had seemed welcoming only a few minutes prior.

"I'm gonna need some help here, boys."

"Typical," Darnell said. "How long you been hiding back here?"

The washing machine against his backside started to move. Recognizing there was no longer a need for video, Beverly gave AJ his sight back.

"Did you not tell me to take cover?" he asked testily.

"Don't be getting all defensive. I just asked how long you been hiding. No offense intended," Darnell said.

With a few pulls, Lefty and Darnell moved the machine far enough from the pile that AJ rolled out onto the ground.

"Aww crap, he's pretty messed up. Three, grab a kit," Lefty ordered.

"Copy that, Two," Frenchie answered.

As the heat of battle diminished, Beverly allowed AJ's body to finally start acknowledging the wounds it had received. He groaned painfully as he discovered just how serious the wounds were.

"We're gonna need a litter, aren't we? You're not getting off the ground anytime soon, and with all this rusted metal. Shee-it, this isn't good." Darnell placed his hand over his ear for no better reason that it helped him focus on longer range communications. "Doc, AJ got hit tonight."

AJ couldn't hear the other side of the conversation but the look on his best friend's face told him it wasn't an easy conversation. "No. He's fine. This all got ahead of us. …. No, I know. We were here six minutes after the attack started. No, you're right. … Big suckers, Petey says Togath. Not even proper aliens, they're made in a factory. Probably better bring some blood, yeah. And, not sure about tetanus."

Darnell let go of his ear and raised his eyebrows.

"How'd that go?" AJ asked, wrestling with consciousness.

"I think it's fair to say she wasn't excited about our life choices," Darnell said.

"Do you want to explain how you three are on mission and I don't know anything about it?" AJ asked. "BB, were you in on all this?"

"No, AJ," Beverly said. She'd changed her clothing to that of a WWII nurse, complete with triangle hat and white dress. "Let's get you fixed up."

"What are the odds there are more of these guys?" AJ asked.

"Well, they're in for a bad night. We've got Rock, Bald Norm, Peppers, Chach and Birdie comin' in," Lefty said. "They should be here in an hour."

"All right, One, let's get you loaded," Frenchie said, setting a portable stretcher next to where AJ lay, still bleeding through the clothing he'd gone to sleep in, or at least what was left of it.

"I'm waiting for an answer, guys," AJ said, irritation the only thing keeping him lucid.

"That's my fault," Darnell said. "And I'm never gonna hear the end of it from Jayne. She said something like this might happen."

"You knew Togath were coming for me?" AJ asked, raising an eyebrow.

"Not specifically Togath, but we had intelligence that something was coming and it was probably aimed at you," he said. "My fault we let it get this far. We thought we'd see 'em coming, but they must have some new kind of stealth insertion or something. We had nothing."

"But you knew they were coming tonight."

"Not specifically. We've been on hot standby every night for the last week. Haven't you noticed how I've had something going every night?"

"I just thought you were busy."

"Can we maybe talk in the house?" Frenchie asked. "Doctor Jayne will arrive soon. I do not wish her to think this was my doing."

"Oh no, bub, you don't need to worry about that," Darnell said. "She's got her sights clearly lined up on me."

"Jayne knew too," AJ said. "Why the hell wasn't I read in on this? They were trying to kill me!"

"They had your place bugged nine ways till Monday," Darnell said. "We couldn't be sure they didn't have you bugged. Apparently, they have tech that does that stuff that nobody can follow."

"You wanted to catch them," AJ said, "and it nearly got me killed."

"Yeah."

"You know, I think you did me a favor. If I'd made that call, I'd be in deep shit."

2

I DO

DEKE - EARTH

"Move your gawd damn fat asses!" Second Lieutenant Kait Dekoster, or Deke, called angrily as her platoon of special infantry crested the hill and ran into the backside of another platoon run by Thad Kersey.

"We're pinned down. There are six Togath over that hill. They've already taken out Blake and Johns." Lieutenant Kersey's voice was high with excitement. Whatever command presence he'd possessed had run down his leg along with the contents of his bladder.

"They've got high ground," Deke yelled, closing on Kersey's position. "We can't let them advance. They'll overrun the base. Move, dammit. Shit!"

"Grenade!"

It was every soldier's worst nightmare to be bunched up with grenades flying. Worse yet, Deke tracked the grenade's flight and knew it would take out at least half a dozen who couldn't possibly get out of its way.

"Aww, fuck!" she cried, pumping muscular thighs built from a once promising rugby career. The plan she had in mind was equal parts insanity and heroism. As was her trademark, there was little time between thought and action. Closing the three steps between herself and Kersey, she leapt, planted a booted foot onto his shoulder against his neck, and sprang into the air. With the lift of her jump, she gained just enough height to grab the cantaloupe-sized Togath grenade and pull it against her armored chest plate.

With half a second to plan, she'd made the best choice available and targeted her landing in a small depression in the earth. That she'd gotten to step on Kersey's neck as a final fuck-you farewell seemed appropriate, although she had little time to appreciate the moment.

She never felt the impact of her landing as the explosive charge dumped its energy into the ground, the armored plate, the bottom of her chin, and tore through both shoulders, sending her forty feet into the air like a spinning blood-filled balloon rag doll. Not that she was conscious for any of it.

"Lieutenant Dekoster? Can you hear me?"

Deke tried to open her eyes. Nothing. The strange voice sounded off and the smell in her nose was one of cooked meat. Something about the voice bothered her. It was off.

"Your respiration has increased. You have nothing to fear," the voice continued.

"Why the hell can't I open my eyes?" she tried to say but words wouldn't form in her mouth and there seemed to be no breath in her lungs. "Shit! What's happening?"

With every attempt to speak, panic increased.

"Please calm," the voice continued. "You will not be harmed. Trust me."

Two of the worst words anyone could use under the circumstances. Deke trusted no one but her squad.

"I'll kill you!" she tried to growl. Even that yielded no results.

A warm sensation flooded her and sleep pushed at her consciousness. If the intended effect was to deescalate, it failed. She pressed her body into high gear, kicking out with her legs. This time, something *did* happen. A general clattering sound was followed by scuffling and indistinct commands.

Her world faded to black.

∼

"DEKE?"

The voice was familiar. *Did he just call me Deke?*

"Can you hear me, *Deke*?"

She tried to open her eyes. Still nothing. Fear gripped her and she lashed out. This time, her powerful legs were caught by straps and held in place. There was pain, but it felt good in an, *I'm probably dead, but if it hurts, maybe not,* way. She tried to move her arms since she was getting nowhere with her legs but there was no response.

"Shit," she breathed. Or at least tried to breathe. There was only pain.

Consuming panic caused her to thrash her head. This brought more pain and a return to the blackness.

∼

DEKE RECOGNIZED CONSCIOUSNESS RETURNING. She wondered if the strange man would talk to her again. He didn't and she simply existed in darkness. It was peaceful, a feeling she didn't often experience. She wondered about feelings, which seemed odd to her, but no more so than the dark universe she now inhabited.

Time passed. How much or how long was beyond Deke's ability to process. But finally, curiosity got the better part of her.

"Hey, are you there?" she asked. While her mouth didn't seem to work, the words formed in her throat, albeit with some pain. Maybe that wasn't enough.

"I am," replied the voice she'd become accustomed to.

"How long have you been sitting there?"

"Fourteen days, nineteen hours, seven minutes and six seconds, if you'll accept a certain lack of precision," he replied.

"We might define precision differently."

"I suspect that is correct."

"Am I dead?"

"No."

"Coma?"

"This word imprecisely encompasses your condition," he answered.

"Precision's a thing for you, huh?"

"We have yet to establish conversational norms that allow me to understand how precise you wish details to be presented."

"That's a good example of too much. Fewer words."

"I will make an effort."

"Good job," she said. "So, coma, huh? That tracks. What happened? Did I get run over in the field by a truck or something? I have a bad habit of running on the road."

"Your memory has been impacted by trauma. It is common. Can you try to recall prior events?"

"I don't know if you're allowed to know the stuff I've done," she said. "We're kind of a black label outfit."

"Do you recall your second-to-last assignment when your platoon took part in Operation Fire Ring?"

"I can neither deny nor affirm this information," she said, amused.

"You led a team of eleven into the Huangshan Mountains in the Anhui province, where you scuttled a Cheell trading vessel. You destroyed its cargo after engaging in a protracted firefight in which twelve Red Army soldiers were wounded or killed," he said.

"You shouldn't know about that."

"Do you remember the end of the battle?"

"I'm not sure. What are you asking me?"

"Do you recall being approached by a Cheell holding a weapon?"

"I wondered if that's where you were going," she said. "Sure. I put it down. That's my job. Gun pointed at my team earned him a trip dirtside. Attacking Chinese soldiers is pretty much something we shouldn't do, though, so let's keep that between us."

"Do you know why you were sent on a mission that could cause such escalation between your two great countries?"

"Not officially. Doesn't take a genius to figure it out. China was getting dirty tech. Our job was to stop 'em. Done. That's what we do. Did something happen at the end of that mission? I feel like I remember a plane ride back. Some new urgent sort of deal. They were bringing in a bunch of loose teams. Some new alien attack they had wind about."

"That is interesting," he answered. "What do you remember about the plane ride?"

"Pretty much like all of 'em – loud, cold, and uncomfortable. They had beer, though, so that worked."

"Do you remember getting off the plane?"

"Oh, so something happened after the trip, huh?"

"Best if you tell me."

"Gawd, are you a shrink?"

"There is irony in your question. No, I am no psychologist."

"Irony, huh? That's some sort of clue. Maybe I should noodle on that for a minute."

"Certainly."

Deke pondered the plane ride. She had images of walking down the wide ramp at the back of the plane, but wasn't sure if those images were of the same trip or one of the myriad, similar trips she'd taken.

"It's foggy," she finally said. "You know something you're not telling me."

"I know many things I am not telling you. Speech is an ineffective mechanism for transmitting large volumes of data. I believe you are referring to circumstances that brought you to your current state."

"Right," Deke said. "I don't care if you like milk or beer with your Cheerios, I'm pretty much interested in me in this moment. You know, since I lost memory and am living in some sort of dark hole."

"I understand. There is value in you testing your memory. I am pleased that you were able to recall your last trip. The damage is less than I anticipated. For diagnostic benefit, would you talk about your childhood with me? Name as many people, dates, and locations as possible. I'll validate this information and together we will discover how injured your brain is."

"They call that a TBI, right? Traumatic Brain Injury."

"A common diagnosis that covers what has occurred."

"How will talking about my childhood help?"

"It might not. Would you like a detailed analysis of why? You do not seem to tolerate long descriptions well."

"Touché," Deke replied. "Okay, what do you want first? Mom and Dad or shitty school memories? Oh, wait, I have a fun story about playing by a stream when I was a kid in a thunderstorm. I fell in and my sister jumped in and rescued me. That was super messed up. We could have drowned but it didn't seem so bad at the time."

Deke talked about her childhood, jumping between years almost randomly until she tired of the exercise.

"I see you have a diagnosis of ADHD. What do you think of this?"

"It's kind of obvious."

"Interesting. You do not feel stigmatized?"

"Look, pal. I didn't join the special recon for no reason. Might as well keep it real and own my shit."

"That is commendable, although I see that your promotions have suffered due to three incidences of insubordination. You have lost rank twice. How does this make you feel?"

"Oh, gee, Dr. Phil, let me see. I feel fucking fantastic. Besides, they wouldn't let me go on mission if I was still a captain. And on mission is when I feel alive. So, yeah, I have all the feelings."

"There is no need to be angry."

"I've been through enough psychological BS in my life. You're evaluating me," she said. "Truth time. What gives?"

"Are you aware of a gene discovered by Dr. Hamut Brown in 1993 coined *super*? I could give you the scientific description, but I don't sense you'd have interest."

"Maybe I would."

"Is that a request?"

"Nope. Just making sure you were listening. No idea about your *super gene*."

"You might want to spend time getting details. This gene is rare in humans. You have it. It is why the army saw fit to introduce us."

"You're Army?"

"I am not."

"That's mysterious," she said. "How am I doing on your psych eval?"

"Well."

"First time I've heard that. Most of the time, this conversation is followed by a minute in the brig."

"Have you not wondered why you are returned to active duty and given a team each time?"

"No. That part's easy. I kick ass. My teams kick ass. We get shit done when others can't because I just don't care what other people think. Do you know what I like about time in the brig?"

"I don't. Please tell me."

"I meet interesting people. You gotta do some messed up things to land in the brig in the army. Did you know that? Especially nowadays."

"Like killing a major's dog?"

"Oh yeah, that's definitely on the list. How does killing helpless animals fit with your psych eval?"

"It would be a disqualifying discovery."

"I didn't kill his dog," she said, feeling momentarily vulnerable. "He was an asshole and was hitting it. I just rehomed it."

"I know."

"Do you have a name?"

"Do you want me to have a name?"

"Don't do that. Answer questions like a normal person."

"Ah, yes, that."

"You're not a person," Deke said, understanding dawning on her. "Tell me you're not some sort of messed up Quarr spy."

"What do you know of Quarr?"

Deke stopped. The word Quarr had popped into her mind, but she had no reference for it. "I ... well, hell, I have no idea. Do you know what Quarr is?"

"I do. And no, I am not Quarr. Do you think I am an alien?"

"I'm giving it good odds," Deke said. "You don't know things you should know, but you cover well. You're way too smart to be human. Lying is tough business. People don't give good liars enough credit."

"I feel we'll want to get back to that."

"I thought you might like that one," she said thoughtfully. "Togath. That's another word that's next to Quarr. They're related."

"Indeed they are. They were also part of your last mission briefing."

"Last," she said. "As in, I'm done?"

"No. It is just the one before the next."

"That's very imprecise. I'm proud of you. Let's get back to the name thing."

"Might I ask that we delay that for a moment?"

"Oh, well, you've been polite in your request. I suppose I can return the favor. Sure, let's delay a super easy piece of information that would take a moment to communicate," she said dryly.

"It is not that simple."

"Fine. Your circus. Herd your monkeys already."

"I need to tell you difficult things."

"That's funny. I've had a lot of crap in my life. Difficult is where I live."

"I'll go slow. Stop me if it becomes too much. We have as much time as you require."

"Stop treating me like a baby, asshole. I'm a grown-ass woman."

"Your anger is understandable."

"Dude, you're starting to piss me off. Stop trying to manage me and just spit the hell out whatever you're trying to say."

"That is fair," he said. "On your last mission, you were grievously wounded."

"I feel like that's why we've been talking about memory loss," she said. "Not a big jump. It must be bad."

"How many details would you like?"

"Go broad brush and we'll work back from there."

"Your right arm and a portion of your torso were damaged beyond traditional repair. Your jaw and lower sinuses were vaporized, as was your left arm from just below the elbow."

"Damn, don't go slow on my behalf."

"Did I misunderstand? Did you wish less information?"

"No. So, I can't feed myself and my chest is so messed up I can't live a normal life. Feels like that's not going to be a good time for me."

"Ordinarily, you would have been allowed to pass away," he said.

"This is about the *super* gene thing, isn't it."

"You are quite perceptive."

"Hyper vigilant. It's a word worth checking out. It's a skill earned by growing up with trouble."

"Yes. I have information on this. And, yes, you have the mutation known as the *super* gene."

"Tell me about it. Do I have superpowers?"

"No, but you are receptive to stimulus that aids the body in repairing itself," he said. "You heal well."

"That's disappointing. I was kind of excited about flying."

"It is poorly named in that case."

"But still something you are interested in and might get my team back."

"There's more to it."

"There always is. What's the hook?"

"We need to bond."

"Fuck, seriously?" she groaned. "How do I always miss this? So damn lame. You're hitting on me when I literally have no hands? I mean, sure. Do what you need to."

"It is not as you imagine," he said. "I am not human."

"Great. I'm going to have an alien baby. Won't that make Mom proud?"

"There will be no procreation in our bonding," he said. "Why are you making this difficult?"

"You've read my disciplinary reports. I make everything difficult. It's kind of my thing. If it's not on the battlefield, I'm your worst nightmare. Of course, if I'm on the battlefield, I'm someone else's worst nightmare. I figure it evens out."

"I am Beltigersk," he said, pushing through the conversation. "My physical dimensions are less than that of a grain of sand by a considerable margin."

"I'm not sure I'll feel that. You'll need to do a lot of grunting."

"You are baiting me."

"A little."

"It will not work. I do not think of the world through the lens of someone with human hormones."

"We'll see."

"If we bond, I will use this *super* gene's capacity to repair your body."

"So it needs you to get it rolling?"

"It does."

"And you get to hang out in my body," she asked. "Why and for how long?"

"There is more."

Deke attempted a chuckle. It didn't work. "There's always more. You might not have male hormones, but you sound like every guy I ever dated."

"This is no date. The *how long* question should be answered. You should know, my removal can be difficult for both parties and there are occasions where one or both experience significant trauma, including death."

"Good information. It kind of gets back to why, again, then," she said. "Why would I do this? Why would you do this?"

"As to you, that is simple. Your body will be repaired to a state far superior to the excellent shape you had already achieved."

"That's not possible if my damage is as bad as you say. I'm missing my lower jaw. Is someone going to give me theirs? You can't regrow bone."

"That is partially true. If we are bonded, together and with technology beyond humanity's capacity, we will repair your body to full health," he said. "That is the incentive you are being presented with."

"Paying for you to bond with me," she filled in.

"At some level, yes," he said.

"That's become a theme in our conversation. Explain what you get out of it. And don't say my sparkling personality. We both know better."

"There is another mission. One of great importance to both Beltigersk and humanity."

"You're a soldier?"

"Not precisely. At four-hundred nanometers, Beltigersk have little capacity to impact the physical world around them without technology or other sentients," he said.

"Aside from upgrading my body, what are you bringing to the table, then? There are a million soldiers out there. You don't need me."

"Which question would you like answered? Why my interest in you or what is my value?"

"You're exhausting. Try to be flexible and just go with the conversation. You can answer both questions. It's just not that hard."

"There is a mission. It is dangerous. Perhaps more so than any mission you've participated in."

"Does it involve blowing off parts of my body? Because that felt like a decent level of danger was reached."

"It is not just dangerous to you," he said. "Failing this mission could impact humanity's chance at long-term survival."

"That's a lot to lay on a girl," she said. "Let me get this straight. You want to bond with me to save Earth."

"That is simplistic, but there is truth in your statement."

"But you're smaller than a grain of sand."

"Measured in nanometers, yes."

"And this isn't a sex thing."

"That is not possible between human and Beltigersk."

"And you need a name."

"I need a name."

"Keegs."

"That is an unusual name," he said. "Might I inquire as to its origin?"

"An old boyfriend. Someone I'd like to come back to when I get done with all this. Whatever all this is. That's if he's still around."

"I accept this name," Keegs said. "It is a fine name. I especially like that it is unique."

"Tell me how this bonding works? Do I have to say your name three times while looking in a mirror? That doesn't work, just so you know."

"Kait DeKoster, will you allow me to bond with you and take residence in your body? We will be joined in a way that I will gain insight into your most private moments. There will be no aspect of your life that I will not witness unless you specifically ask for me to stop observing. In exchange, I will enhance your bodily functions to repair and even enhance its natural ability. We will become stronger as one than is possible, individually, for either of us. You will give me the ability to interact with physical matter in a way I have never had before. There will be learning for both of us. I will commit to you that I will treat you with great respect."

"Damn, did you just take a knee?"

"It is an apt description."

"Well, then, I do."

3

RIDE OR DIE

AJ - EARTH

DARNELL'S HEAD whipped to the side at the sound of the front screen slamming shut. The team had pulled AJ's bed from the ruined bedroom and set it in the living room, with AJ atop a plastic tarp and a now, blood-soaked sheet.

"Jayne, I'm ...," Darnell started.

"I'll get to you later," she snapped. With fifty years of surgical experience that began in the war zones of Vietnam, Doctor Amanda Jayne took command of the room with an intensity none would challenge. "Nit, show me his back."

Like all of AJ's team, Jayne had a symbiotic rider, affectionately nicknamed Nit. Unlike Beverly, Nit was reserved in her communication and preferred not to project a human analog of herself, a behavior unique to Beverly.

"I'll join the patrol," Roland 'Frenchie' LeBeau said quietly.

"You'll wash your hands. Both of you will. Soap. One full minute of scrubbing to elbows," Jayne ordered, not looking up from the projected view of AJ's back. Her tone softened as she stepped closer to where he lay panting atop the sheets. "Hey, babe. How are you doing?"

"Had kind of a tough night," he said, reaching for her.

Taking his hand, she gave him the smile she reserved only for him. "This is my fault. I should have warned you. I'm so sorry."

"Kind of water under the bridge. Right?"

"You could have died, AJ," she said.

AJ squeezed her hand. "So let's not do that again."

"Never again."

"How bad?"

"Without Beverly, sixty percent chance of survival. If I support Beverly's efforts, you'll be walking by tomorrow afternoon," she answered honestly.

"You're going to scrub the crap out of my wounds, aren't you?"

Jayne smiled. "Yes. I'll use a local, or we can knock you out."

"I'd like to stay awake."

"Okay."

～

AJ'S EYES OPENED SLOWLY. By the position of the sun, he gauged it to be late afternoon. Turning his head to the side, he found Jayne propped against his bed, her hand on his arm. Emotion welled in his throat. He wasn't sure what he'd done to deserve her attention.

"How are you feeling?" she asked.

"Like I could eat a horse." AJ pushed against the bed to sit up. The sheets were clean. "How are you and Darnell doing?"

"Did I hear someone's hungry?" AJ smiled to himself as he heard Lisa Jackson, his business partner and Darnell's wife, call from the kitchen. He anticipated the next comment and wasn't disappointed. "Are you ready for the good stuff?"

"Is there lard involved?" he asked.

Lisa looked around the corner from the kitchen with a grin. "Oh, there's that and more."

"Wave it in," he said. "Biggest plate you've got."

With a lowered voice, Jayne continued, "We've got to be smarter in the way we deal with the army and all the alien factions we're in contact with. It is not reasonable you were put in the position you were. We ignored red flags. Darnell is no more guilty than am I. Our error is that we had warning of an attack and thought we were equal to what was coming."

AJ nodded. "Do we know why someone sent Togath? Do we know who sent them?"

"You're gonna love this answer." Lisa carried a heaping plate full of meatloaf, mashed potatoes, and beans, all smothered in a rich creamy gravy.

"The answer where I get to eat that? Or another one?" AJ asked, eyeing the plate. One of the side effects of the healing work done by Beverly was a considerable uptick to his metabolism.

"Do you recall hearing the conversation about the Quarr?" Lisa asked.

AJ, who'd already started digging into the meal in front of him paused to chew what he had in his mouth. Not coming up with the reference, he shook his head and took a long drink of water. "That's not familiar. BB, you got a picture for me?" he asked.

"To the extent it is helpful," she answered, appearing seated on his legs. She'd changed into her schoolteacher outfit, complete with long woolen skirt, horn-rimmed glasses, and a wooden pointing stick. "Like most species found across the great expanse of space, Quarr start out at birth with a basic humanoid shape."

A portable projector screen complete with tripod legs appeared on the bedspread. Beverly walked over to the screen as an image of a mottled gray humanoid with a wrap of cloth around its waist appeared.

"As the conversation of sexual organs isn't interesting, I'll draw your attention to average mass of one hundred kilograms for a male and eighty-five kilograms for the female. On average, ten to fifteen percent denser than human. This turns out to be insignificant, however," she said.

"They could pass for human in the right light," AJ said.

"I'm not sure that's right," Lisa said. "Check out those ears. Nobody has ears like that. They look like someone stuck cinnamon rolls on the side of their heads. And no hair. Are they always hairless?"

"Yes," Beverly answered.

"Hold on, guys, there's something Beverly is trying to get to," Jayne said. "Give her a minute."

Lisa and AJ quieted, which allowed Beverly to continue. "Lisa, thank you. You are correct. What this image fails to correctly convey is the Quarr custom of genetic alteration. A process that is as is engrained in them as wearing clothing is to humanity. With few exceptions, Quarr embrace radical changes to their bodies caused by millennia of genetic experimentation.

"So Togath?" AJ asked.

"If your question is that Togath are Quarr, the answer is no," Beverly said. "Togath are manufactured from cellular material they create through processes not shared with other species. Quarr consider the

Togath a disposable resource. Togath are their primary fighting force and are used as laborers."

"A slave class," Lisa said, angrily.

"Yes. Genetically engineered with minimal IQ, but with highly developed motor skills and tactical planning."

"That's immoral," Lisa said. "How are they allowed to do this?"

"Quarr are an ancient species, not part of the Galactic Empire," Beverly said. "They have the capacity to resist even the Tok. Much of that strength comes from their ability to manufacture Togath."

"And the Togath have never risen up or fought back against their slavers?" Lisa asked.

"There are references to early uprisings in captured data," Beverly said. "Please understand, this has been their practice for longer than humanity has existed."

"Let's get a little more practical," AJ said. "What would Quarr want with me?"

"Togath aren't exclusive to Quarr," Beverly answered. "We can't assume they are behind the attack, though Togath are exclusively created by Quarr. There is a system in the Contested Zone. Planet Gnorz, technically Gnorz-2, but commonly referred to as Gnorz as it is the only habitable planet in the system. Quarr interested in trade will do so on Gnorz."

"So – maybe Quarr, maybe not," AJ summarized. "Seems like we should try to locate whatever ship our buddies from last night came in. That seems like a good start, right?"

"Colonel Baird is on her way," Lisa said. "They're bringing a team to clean up the Togath. Apparently, the Army is very interested in getting a good look at these aliens."

The high-pitched sound of heavy diesel motor turbos drew AJ's attention. "I think they're here," he said. "Maybe help me put on some clothing?"

"You're not in good enough shape to be running around," Jayne said with minor irritation.

"But you'll help?"

"I will."

With her help, AJ managed to dress in jeans and a clean t-shirt. On the way to the front door, he got his first good look at the damage the Togath had caused to his house. There was a gaping hole surrounding the missing door to his bedroom and the bedroom was in even worse shape. The entire corner of the house and a good portion of a new dresser had been vaporized.

"It could have been worse," he said, shaking his head at the damage.

"Maybe," Lisa said. "That's some first-class structural damage and won't be cheap to fix."

"Gotta be cheaper than having a spaceship sit on it, doesn't it?"

"I suppose you're not wrong," she agreed. "Way to go glass half-full on me. You surprise me some days, AJ."

"I'll take the compliments where I get 'em," he said.

The damage looked even worse from the outside, with wind blowing through a sagging roof. Fortunately, the honk of a loud airhorn drew his attention to the front gate where Lefty and Darnell stood, holding their rifles, still dressed in jungle fatigues.

"Two, when's the last time you slept?" AJ asked.

"It's been a minute, AJ," Darnell answered.

"You guys are no good to me if you can't function," AJ said. "I think we can let Baird take the scene. Stand down the teams, there's plenty of room down in the bunker. I'll get food coming."

"Bubba, we need to talk. I screwed this up," Darnell said.

"Not the time, brother, and we're good. I'm that guy you don't need to say shit to." AJ stood in front of Darnell. "You were doing what you thought was best. Lesson learned. New day."

"Okay. We can work it through another time if you want."

"Yeah, that sounds like me," AJ said sarcastically.

"You can be an asshole, you know that?"

"That hurts," AJ said with a faked flinch backward. "Now get out of here. We're about to be overrun by testosterone-filled youth."

"You should be madder," Jayne said as he walked back the gate.

"It's not a matter of being mad," AJ said. "I gotta work through how my team was subverted to leave me out of something this important. That's a leadership problem, Amanda. That's on me."

"Only you could turn this around on yourself."

"You're a brilliant woman. Tell me where that's fucked up."

"You know I don't like it when you use that language."

"Don't deflect."

"You're definitely getting better at arguing."

"I'll take that as agreement with my position," AJ shouted over the line of trucks rolling through the gate.

"I'll think about it," she said.

After the lead truck stopped in front of the house, a woman with a silver eagle on her modern combat fatigues jumped out and jogged over to the pair.

"Looks like you got that promotion, Colonel Baird," AJ said, offering his hand.

"Congratulations, Jackie," Jayne added, also shaking the woman's hand.

With hat in hand, Baird looked at the ground. "We screwed that up, AJ. That's on me."

"Sure. Move on. Tired of the conversation already," AJ said. "Who sent 'em?"

"We have no idea. We only found out about it because of a tip from the Tok," she said. "We kept the circle small because other than you, we didn't know who'd been exposed."

"How was I exposed?"

"You have trackers all over you," she said. "Sergeant, come get this man cleaned. I want this entire property clean by 0600 tomorrow. Do you copy?"

A woman in fatigues jogged up and saluted. "Yes ma'am. We're on it," she said crisply. "Corporal Tuggs, on the double, please."

Tuggs carried a small backpack with a wand sticking out from the top. Slinging the device onto his back, he held the wand in hand and swept it along AJ's body. Like fireflies emerging from an evening lawn, small, bright dots of light emerged from AJ's skin, burning up as they were extracted. The process took a couple of minutes, and he continued until none remained.

"Sir, I'll need you to stand still so we can continue with the rest of the group. These bugs are adept at reproducing," the young corporal said, "but we can beat 'em."

"Those were all bugs?" AJ asked.

"Cheell," Baird explained. "Not that different from our own nano technology. They replicate in the skin of hosts after landing on a DNA profile they've targeted. Splash one person in a city of a million and within a few days, the trackers will have found the host they're looking for by passive transference."

"Someone was looking for me. Why?" AJ asked.

"This isn't a conversation to be had in your front yard," Baird said. "There are security concerns. I request that you and your team accompany me back to the base."

"First, you assemble my old team without telling me. And then you nearly get me killed because you don't tell me what's what. Now you want to take me back to the base with no explanation," AJ said, the expression on his face hard. "You're about to make a big ask and you've got no ground to stand on. I like you, Jackie, I do, but I don't trust you or the Army."

"That's a good starting position," she said. "The reality is that like it or not, you're in this. It won't hurt to hear me out. If you don't like what you hear, you can walk away."

"What, and the next time an attack is coming you won't tell me?"

"I did not say that," she said. "Apart from the good you've done this country with your service, I like you too. If there's anything within my power to do to keep you this side of the grave, I'll do it. You've certainly earned that from me."

AJ scratched his stubbly beard as he inspected Baird's face. She had an intensity he liked and not for a moment did he distrust her loyalty to the country they both had defended with their lives. "All right, Colonel," he said. "We'll hear you out."

"Transpo leaves at 2030 for a 2100 meeting. I'd recommend packing for a few days TDY."

"We haven't even heard what's going on and you want us to pack up and leave?"

"It'll be your call," she said, "but that's exactly what I'm saying."

"Will there be beer?"

"No. I can arrange for food."

"My boys haven't had a break since this fired up last night. Make sure that food is worth it."

"See you at 2100." She turned on her heel to address a corporal awaiting her orders.

"I don't have a good feeling about this," Jayne said as they walked off.

"Talk to me," AJ said.

"She's already two steps ahead. I'm not sure she didn't let last night play out to get your attention. That's paranoid, I know, but it feels about right."

"I got a whiff of that too," AJ said, sighing. "It's not an excuse, but that's the way cake eaters think. Stick or carrot. Good ones know how to use both. Last night was stick. She's going to offer carrot. We might be reading it wrong, but I don't think so."

"Why attack only you?" Jayne asked. "Why not all of us?"

"Cut the head off the snake with the least amount of collateral damage. Nobody's gonna miss an eighty-year-old junkyard operator," AJ said. "Kill a prominent surgeon and humanitarian activist and people will talk."

"You're more notable than you believe," Jayne said, "but I understand your point."

"As much as I don't trust Baird to prioritize our lives above national interest, I think her heart is in the right place," AJ said. "She's a patriot and I don't say that about many cake eaters."

"I'm fearful of where this leads, but I'll try to keep an open mind."

"Talk to me about that."

"You're a first-class curmudgeon, Albert Jenkins. Your first answer to anyone who asks, no matter the question, is no. Your second answer is hell no. Your third is get the eff off my porch," Jayne said. "Sound familiar?"

"Well, sure," he agreed.

"Good. You don't have the same response to big asks from the Army," she said. "All they need to do is touch the flag and tell you it's national security and you're suddenly jumping over spike pits in the jungle. Does this help you understand why I'm concerned?"

He nodded. "It's who I am, Jayne."

"I know. I just need you to know there's collateral damage when you're hurt or worse."

"I'm sorry."

"You don't need to be sorry. And I don't need you to be someone else. I just need you to come back to me."

AJ turned and pulled her into a hug.

"When do you want to wake the team?" Lisa asked softly, approaching the pair.

"Give them a couple more hours," AJ said. "I don't suppose you have any more of that meatloaf, do you?"

Lisa smiled. "Darnell thought he got the last of it, but I made my lean version and left it out for him to find. There's plenty more of the good stuff. I'll get you good and taken care of."

The sound of a big diesel firing up across the yard drew AJ's attention. Someone had started his big loader. Ordinarily, he'd have been looking to knock their head off for messing with his machines. This time, however, he shrugged it off. Life was moving too quickly.

Two hours later, his team assembled in the machine shop, all looking worse for the limited hours of shut-eye. AJ opened his refrigerator to display rows and rows of chilled beer.

"Boys, it sure feels good to see you all and I wish it was under better circumstances," he said.

"What's this all about, AJ?" Frenchy asked, leaning against the steel frame of the large sliding door to the building.

"We've been asked to meet with Colonel Baird's team to discuss the current situation," he said. "I think it's bigger than that. Baird is angling for something."

"You think last night was just the beginning," James 'Rock' Barnes said in his deep baritone.

"I do," AJ said. "Baird didn't need to call you guys up. She could have put defenses at my house."

"Did you see those boots out there?" Steve "Birdie" Turner asked. "Don't know their butts from a latrine if you ask me."

"Here's the deal. I'm gonna roll out to the base and get the skinny on what's happening. You're all invited to come along. Just know, I think the Colonel is leading up to something. If you get read in, you probably won't be going home. Think about that before you get in line. No hard feelings if you stay back."

"Ride or die," Scott 'Chach' Magliano said, holding up a beer.

"Ride or die," echoed around the room.

"Let's see what they've got, One," Lefty said. "Not one of us came to Arizona because we were lookin' for a tan. Let's get to work."

4

SPA TREATMENT
DEKE - EARTH

"I don't feel any different," Deke said. "You said you're small, but I was expecting something."

"I am small. I have questions."

"So do I."

"Please, ask questions. Trust can be established only with mutual understanding."

"First, I need you to stop with all the word salad," she said. "Do I get a ring? I figure if you're going to bond with a girl, she should get a ring."

"I cannot tell if you are serious. Even with our bonding, your emotional responses are complex. I have not had enough time to recognize subtle changes."

"Welcome to every woman, ever. You'll need to expand your emotional range," Deke said. "Yes, I'm serious and no, I'm pimping you around. The answer is both. You get to wade through the crap and find the right answer on your own."

"There will be no ring in the short run."

"Why?"

"You have no hands."

"Fair," Deke said. "What now? I just lie here in the dark?"

"What would you like to see?"

"That's an odd question. If I could at least stare at the ceiling, that'd be a change."

"That is not possible. The corneas of your eyes were destroyed in the explosion."

"Then how can I see anything?"

"At the risk of over-describing and breaking our compact, human brains process images captured by your cornea on the visual cortex. It is a wonderfully complex evolution. The detail of images produced is well beyond any other sentient species."

"Neat, but not really an answer."

"You did not let me finish."

"Go on."

"When our bonding is complete, I'll have the ability to place signals directly onto your visual cortex. The connection is weak yet, but I have enough that I am capable of limited projection," Keegs said.

"Like TV?"

"I will demonstrate."

"This should be good."

At first, the changes Deke noticed were subtle. It was as if she'd been on night patrol beneath a cloud-covered sky, deep in the wilderness. The thought brought back memories of missions where she was required to remain still in the pitch black. Dim ambient light filtered into her consciousness.

"I'm seeing something," she said as dim shapes started to resolve. "Are those trees?"

"Yes. Very good," Keegs said.

A dark, rectangular object, only a few feet from her position came into focus. "I'm on a beach. Those are palm trees and there's a TV. It's off."

"I am being careful not to overload the connection. Your brain needs time to accept the input I'm providing," he said.

"Oh! Did you just turn that on?" she asked when a still image appeared on the screen. It was a simple scene, a figure lay on a hospital bed with a myriad of tubes, wires and monitoring devices connected to and surrounding it. "That's me, isn't it?"

"Is it disturbing? Your blood pressure has increased as has your perceived respiration rate."

"You use a lot of weasel words. Did you know that?"

"I don't believe rodents have the capacity for speech."

"Weasel words means that you make partial statements. Essentially lies, like perceived."

"I see. Your lungs do not respond to your brain's requests. Your respiration rate does not increase as it is being controlled by medical devices. You experienced an emotional response," he said.

"Fair enough. I don't look that good. Are you sure I'm worth all this effort? I mean, my goal has always been to get my insides to match my outsides. I was thinking of that going a different way."

"I don't understand your reference."

"It's a therapy thing. Getting the emotional stuff to be in agreement with how I act is what that means. I was being ironic. My life is a shit show, my body now looks the part is all I was saying."

"Yes, your body is in poor shape. I would venture that your persona is in better shape than is your physical body."

"This will be a day of firsts, then. How long will it take to get me back in the teams? You said something about a mission and saving humanity and all that."

"Perhaps we could suspend that conversation. There is nothing to hide but we have much work to do," he said. "Focus will be required."

"I suppose. Maybe a different picture on the TV, then. I'm not loving the view."

"Do you have a favorite sporting team?"

"You're kidding, right?"

"No. It is a real question."

"I missed a bunch of women's World Cup soccer," she said. "Is that something you can do?"

"Do you have a favorite team?"

"Duh. US."

"They are no longer ..."

"Whoa! Stop! Don't tell me what happened. That's most of the fun," she said. "Do you have game one? I know the score, but I was going to watch, anyway."

"Yes."

The TV in Deke's view blinked on, and an announcer's voice sounded in her ears. Her attention was drawn to the field as her favorite players took the field and the game started. The reprieve from the heavy moments of that morning was welcome and she sighed with relief.

Changes to the scene around her were at first subtle and she brushed them off as things she hadn't observed. A light breeze wafted across her skin and she glanced above the TV to see the palm trees gently swaying.

"That's more than visual cortex," she said. "I felt that."

"Yes, our bond has deepened. Like most things, we're able to achieve eighty percent effectiveness with relatively light effort. Reaching full connection will take several days. I initially focused on your visual cortex as human brains process this information most efficiently. Initial connection to your nerve complex, however, allows for stimulation of more complex senses."

"The breeze is a nice touch," she said. "How do we get to work, though? I don't think I'm going to like watching soccer games forever."

"This depends on you to some degree," Keegs said.

"How is that? I don't even have hands."

"I am blocking your pain receptors," he said. "This limits my ability to connect with your body's unique regenerative capability."

"Regenerative, huh? You didn't use that word before."

"I did not know the strength of your genetics prior to bonding," he said. "We must never talk about what I've learned to anyone. The extent of your *super* gene is well beyond what others might have believed possible."

"And to get this going, I need to feel pain," she said.

"That is correct."

Deke shrugged and was gratified when it felt as if her shoulders moved. Glancing down, she found she was sitting on a chaise lounge, wearing a one-piece bathing suit with her legs basking in the sun. With her observation, the heat of that sunshine suddenly became evident.

"This is nice."

"You should know what you'd be giving up," he said. "With the pain, you will lose this illusion."

"How much faster would I heal? How long before I'm ready to go if we keep the spa treatment?"

"An order of magnitude," he said. "I do not currently have estimates. Your corneal implants are constructed, though. I would like to make you unconscious while human surgeons do the work I will coordinate."

"That doesn't sound painful."

"None of this needs to be painful," he said.

"It'd just be faster," she filled in for him. "Screw it. Do the pain thing. Just make sure there's an end so we can talk. Also, I want a view of what's happening to my body. I don't know how that will work out with me being unconscious."

"I will wake you after the surgeons have completed their work with your eyes. There will be pain. You will need to be honest with me about how you are coping. It will not do us either any good if we cause emotional damage."

"Don't worry about me, pal. I'm tougher than you can possibly imagine."

"I hope that is true."

Deke blinked sleepily as the ambient lights around her dimmed. The sensations of the sun's warmth and the light breeze faded and then there was nothing.

Time passed. Just how much she had no idea. When she awoke, it was not the same gentle moments she'd experienced falling asleep. Instead, it was with sharp pain in her jaw and a headache the likes of which she'd never experienced.

"What in the hell?" she tried to say.

"Welcome back, Kait," Keegs said. "I see that your nervous system is responding well to the assault on your body. Are you capable of maintaining this level for a time?"

"Fuck, there's an elephant sitting on my head and rats chewing on my chin."

"Tell me you wish to stop. I can reduce the pain considerably."

"Oh, shit, it hurts so bad!"

"I will stop."

"No," she said, closing her eyes, trying to shut out the pain. Of course, her attempt was ineffective as she had no eyelids, nor did she have control of any of her musculature. "Damn, it's so much. Don't stop."

"I am concerned about your confusing message," Keegs said. "I do not wish to hurt you. I believe you are asking me to stop and keep going in the same moment."

"Yeah! Deal with it," she growled. "I can take it. Fuck. How long? Let me see what's happening."

"Are you certain? It is quite grisly."

"Dammit. I can't ask twice."

A top-down view of the medical suite suddenly appeared. Unlike the soccer match displayed on the TV, the view was fully resolved. Deke felt as if she was floating above a veritable horde of nurses and doctors all hunched over her face.

It was a lot.

"What's going on with my jaw?" she grunted through pain which she was able to match up with surgeon's movements. Initially, she'd thought they were working on her eyes, but in fact, one had a stainless-steel drill and was digging around on the side of her face.

"Your eye surgery was successful. I decided to have your surgeons install the jawbone lattice upon which we will affect repairs."

"That's not bone," she observed after a time, struggling to manage the pain.

"No. That is a matrixed alloy of titanium and other elements. When complete, a mesh of this same alloy will surround your entire skull."

"That's going to mess up my hairline, isn't it?"

"How much do you want to know?"

"I'm pretty sure I'm all in. Hit me with your best shot."

"Over the next seventy-two hours, we will remove and replace the entirety of the skin around your skull to implant this mesh."

"You're scalping me."

"Think of your skin as a dress shirt. We're going to take it off and place a t-shirt beneath," Keegs said.

"You need to work on your analogies."

"Did you not understand?"

"Aaargh," she answered as a chip of bone caught on the drill bit and flung off. "Watch it, you damn hack!"

The surgeon seemed not to notice beyond nodding to the nurse next to him to catch the chip with a vacuum wand.

"Understand what?"

"The analogy."

"Oh hell, Keegs, I have no idea what we're even talking about."

"The drilling is almost complete," Keegs said. "This should be the most intense pain for the next few hours. Can you continue to bear it?"

"Do I look like I'm not handling it?"

"You look like you can't move."

"Fair point. Don't stop."

"You are strong. I am gratified that I placed my faith in you."

"That's an interesting way to put that," she grunted through the pain. "Did you have other choices?"

"Yes, Kait."

"Could you call me Deke?"

"Of course."

"Why me?"

"This."

"I'm not following."

"Your strength in this moment. We probably won't survive the mission that is to come. I want the best possible chance. The stakes are too high."

"Way to sell it. Want to tell me more?"

"Certainly. I considered four thousand possible candidates. Most of them were not wounded. My leadership questioned the value of someone with your past."

"But the *super* gene tipped the scales for you?"

"Yes, at some level. Mental toughness isn't unique to you," he said. "Proven mental toughness is less common. I need to trust that when we are in the darkest moments, I can rely on my partner to not give up."

"I'm not smart enough to give up. Oh, fuck, what in the hell are they doing?" she asked, staring down at the side of her face. As she focused, her viewpoint shifted until she could see exactly what was happening. "Oh, no, that's not something I want to see. I hope you can stop me from puking. Nobody should see themself do that."

"I don't think it is necessary for you to watch the skull mesh installation," he said. "I've placed game two on the wall. Perhaps you would enjoy watching it. There is a chair available."

Deke glanced at a leather recliner that appeared in the surgical suite's alcove. Focusing on it caused her to float over and settle into it. While the pain was just as intense, the distraction of moving and finding her place buoyed her spirits.

Turning to the TV, the sound of the match filled her ears.

~

"You had to knock me out, didn't you? Was I screaming? I remember screaming," she said. The headache was still present but had dimmed significantly. Her head felt like it was being roasted over a low flame, intense but just short of overwhelming.

"There was no reason for you to experience the physical act of degloving your skull. You will be pleased to know your mesh has been installed and we are five percent complete in integrating that mesh."

"Is that the burning?"

"Yes. I can reduce the pain."

"But it'll slow us down."

"That is correct."

"I'll deal. How's my jaw regrowth coming? Does it make sense that I'm starving?"

"Yes. This is why we focused on your jaw and trachea," he said. "You did not have significant fat reserves. I am being forced to budget your caloric output. It would be much easier if you were able to directly ingest calories."

"Doesn't seem like something I can help with. Can I see my jaw?"

"Certainly."

Deke's *eyes* opened and while she was still seated in the leather chair, she no longer sat within the surgical suite. For a moment, she considered the seamlessness in which Keegs integrated consistency in her physical experience. "Nice touch, leaving me in the chair."

"Your brain would invent a story as to what happened, otherwise. If I can give it clues, there is less cognitive dissonance."

"Well, it's helpful."

"That's the idea."

Deke willed her virtual self from the chair and moved to the bedside. Bandages covered her entire head to her collarbone. She reached for the bandages and found a ghostly arm acting just as she'd have expected her own arm to move. The bandages moved and when laid to the side she was set back a moment as her own face stared back at her.

"That's disturbing," she observed passively.

"I imagined that would be the case. Take it slow."

"Good advice," she said, reaching to touch the metallic structure that was in place of and shaped like her lower jaw. A white film covered the structure. "Is that bone growing over my jaw lattice?"

"It is," Keegs answered. "When complete, the same alloy lattice will be integrated into your spine, ribs, hips, legs, etc. Essentially your entire skeletal structure. It's a tremendously expensive surgery and your government argued against the investment."

"I bet. I'm not exactly a rising star. How's that going for you?"

"I have persuasive diplomats navigating on our behalf. We will not survive what is to come without the investment. Politicians are bothersome but, in the end, we will be successful. Your response to this first series of surgeries has solidified our position. You are, in fact, a rising star."

"I'll believe that when I see it."

"You will believe."

"How can you have so much faith in me?"

"Would you be interested in watching your final moments in your last battle?" Keegs asked. "I believe it would be useful for this conversation."

"That sounds interesting," she said. "Let's do it. I've been wondering about all that."

A TV screen flickered to life and the camera's perspective showed Deke's platoon from the small observer drone that followed every combat team, at least as long as that team kept from entering combat, as most combatants were quick to take down all reconnaissance drones.

"Your team landed at the Normanville Base thirty minutes prior to this moment," Keegs explained. "You were flown in specifically to deal with the influx of several Togath teams."

"Togath are the aliens we learned about, huh? The name is familiar. I'm not clear on what they look like," she said.

"You've never seen one," Keegs said. "They are large, humanoid, and bred specifically for combat. In that you were not directly exposed to them, their description is not particularly important, other than one-for-one, humans are no match in combat."

"What's that even mean? We have guns. They have guns. It's a fair fight, right?"

"Not at all. Togath have the ability to shrug off attacks that would kill other sentients. They are constructed at a genetic level to thrive in combat."

"The tungsten lattice you're installing on my skeleton is starting to make a bit more sense," she said.

"That is a logical and intuitive leap, Deke."

While they'd been talking, Keegs had frozen the video. He started the video again and Deke listened to her own, calm, authoritative voice directing her platoon to advance toward the front line, which she understood to be over the next hill.

"Shit's about to get real, isn't it."

"We're pinned down. There are six Togath over that hill."

The voice belonged to Lieutenant Kersey, a man Deke had served next to and around for much of her career.

"Shit, not Kersey," she said.

Her platoon crested the small hill, and she scanned a swale that led to another, taller hill. Tall figures stood just behind that next hill. If it had been Kersey's team, she'd have felt much better. To her horror, she found that Kersey had dropped his team into the lowest point between the two hills and was trying to find cover in the low ground.

"This can't be real," she said, immediately seeing the tactical disadvantage for what it was.

Fat blobs of energy streamed into the shallow valley from the high ground as impossibly thick humanoids hoisted equally impossibly heavy weapons and rained fire down upon the trapped team.

Blood pounded in Deke's head as she watched the slaughter that was about to happen. Kersey had given up the high ground and trapped his people. She had no other choice but to send her team in to rush the hill and try to clean up. Her platoon was battle hardened and unreserved in their valor. Kersey had likely killed them all with his cowardice. She gritted her teeth and watched as the men and women she'd trained with, fought with, and would likely now die with raced forward.

"Shit, grenade," she said, as a football sized object was hurled from the Togath's position. That she used Kersey as a springboard to personally intercept the grenade made her chuckle darkly.

The drone caught her final act of pulling the grenade into her chest and blinked out a moment later with a bright flash.

"That tracks," she said. "Tell me Kersey didn't make it."

Sixty seconds after your bravery, Army Apache helicopters arrived on the scene and drove the Togath team back to their transportation. "Lieutenant Thad Kersey survived and is in line for a special promotion for bravery in combat."

"Tell me that's not true."

"It is true."

5

PRIORITY KILL
AJ - EARTH

"At least we're traveling incognito," Tony 'Peppers' Salazar said, pulling back a canvas curtain to climb into the back of the Army's eleven-ton MTT (medium tactical truck). Pepper's dry wit drew a couple of quiet chuckles as the team of old vets joined a smaller team already loaded.

The two teams couldn't have looked more different as the Vietnam era warriors still proudly wore jungle fatigues that hadn't been in service for decades and were in stark contrast to the desert fatigues of the significantly younger soldiers.

"Uh, sir, you can't carry that weapon into base," a young corporal said nervously.

"Good to know," Peppers said and accepted an M110 from Lefty as he climbed in behind. Without further comment, Peppers walked to the front of the truck bed and sat on the inward facing bench with a rifle in each hand.

"I don't think he heard him," another young soldier offered.

Duffle bags were tossed over the tailgate, handed forward, and stacked as the team loaded. All the while, Peppers sat quietly, holding both weapons.

"Dude, are you too good to help?" the corporal finally asked.

"Might want to take a step back there, son," Birdy said, sitting next to Peppers. "Everybody has a job. Peppers here is just keeping Two's weapon hot and handy."

"You can't have weapons where we're going."

"I guess you'll need to decide how you want to deal with all that," Birdy said. "Keep chirping in his ear and it's not gonna go well for you. Do you read me, Diapers?"

The comment caused others in the corporal's team to chuckle, which did not improve his mood. He stared sullenly at Peppers, who was leaning his head against the canvas tarp.

Loading last, AJ sat at the back of the truck next to Jayne, who along with Lisa were the only women and the only people in street clothing.

"You know, I don't have a change of clothes if we're getting pulled out," Jayne said. "I'm not wearing fatigues."

AJ grinned. "I suppose not."

Just then the truck lurched to life as it backed through the junkyard's main gates. The movement stirred old memories for AJ as the smells of diesel, canvas and sweaty team members melded together.

"Are you okay?" Jayne asked, running her hand beneath his as the truck rocked to a stop and then started moving forward.

"A whole lot of bad journeys started in the back of trucks like this," AJ said, adjusting the grip on his rifle in one hand and squeezing Jayne's in the other. "These kids don't even know enough to be nervous."

"Maybe we shouldn't be in a hurry to take that from them."

AJ chuckled darkly. "That probably won't be up to me."

"Good."

"We're not headed to the airport," Jayne observed. "We're headed east."

"Well, that's something," AJ said.

"Do you know where we're going?"

"No, but the boys up front are pretty keyed up for a simple transport," AJ said. "Diapers has orders that are in conflict."

"How do you know that?"

"He's not hard to read. For someone worried about us carrying a few rifles, he seems oblivious to the crates beneath these benches. Either he's dumb, which I doubt, given the detail, or he's been given orders to keep hands off my team, but knows something about the security posture of a base that nobody knows about."

"There are a lot of crates under these seats," Jayne whispered. "What's in them?"

"Enough ordnance to end a war on a small Mediterranean island," AJ said. "They were expecting something big at the junkyard."

Suddenly, and without warning, Peppers yelled, "Frag. Take cover!"

Without hesitation, AJ swept his arm across Jayne's back, knocking her to the aisle between the rows of seats before landing atop her. He had just enough time to look up at the young, inexperienced team who, in the confusion, had not reacted instantly as had the old guard.

One moment, the corporal was staring at AJ's face in confusion. The next, he'd pitched forward, his body contorted by an explosion which ripped through the man's torso as easily as it had the canvas cover. The truck rocked as two additional blasts struck its side.

"We're going over!" Chach called. "Grab your asses!"

With a single, violent lurch, the side of the truck lifted and pitched to the side, throwing the contents and occupants into a blender of mad pandemonium.

"AJ, we have contact with an antigrav propelled aircraft at five-hundred yards," Beverly said, using her considerable control over his adrenal system to tamp down the attack's initial shock.

With preternatural grace provided by Beverly's fine tuning. AJ moved through the truck bed's interior, even as it twisted, bumped, and fell onto its side. The same unnatural grace was provided to his entire team by their symbiotes as they fell into a dance of simple movements that allowed them to adjust to the constantly changing environment.

Before the truck had stopped rolling and was scraping metal against pavement, AJ started execution of an action plan he'd worked out in advance. While he hadn't fully expected an attack, he expected its possibility. That his team hadn't gone up in a puff of smoke due to overwhelming firepower by the as-yet unknown enemy was a chance he wouldn't squander.

"Two, Three, get those damn crates open. I need two RPGs standing up before they get a second look at us. Four, Five, Six, you're with me. We'll lay down suppressing fire and buy Two and Three a minute," AJ snapped. "Lisa, Doc, get clear of this truck. It's not gonna make it through a second attack."

Pulling the KA-BAR knife from where he kept it strapped to his calf, AJ sliced open the canvas roof which was now oriented as a wall. With the long barrel of his rifle forward, he stepped out onto the road's gravel shoulder. The truck continued to slide as he stepped free, and AJ dropped to a knee.

"Four, are you up?" he demanded. Even as he spoke, he scanned the horizon for the enemy aircraft.

"No. Not Up. My damn leg messed up," Bald Norm answered. "Trying to get into the ditch."

"I'm coming," Jayne answered.

AJ grimaced. He hated Jayne getting into the middle of a fight but there was nothing he could do. She'd never turn her back on someone she could help. It was how she was built.

The staccato pops of 7.62mm bullets announced the team's first response. Tracking the position of a target Beverly identified, AJ swiveled and joined the attack. While it was unlikely the weaponry would take down the attacking spacecraft, there was some chance, that with highly accurate fire, they could inflict enough damage to keep it at bay until stronger measures became possible.

"Missiles incoming. Take cover!" Peppers cried out.

It was a message long engrained in each of the old soldier's DNA. Each flung themselves to protective cover, most using the steep embankment to carry them away.

"BB, get Baird on the damn line," AJ angrily shouted. His volume was unnecessary, in that Beverly could hear him under any circumstance.

Two twumps were followed by explosions. A fraction of a moment later came the painful searing of the heat caused by resultant fireballs. A fragment of truck body sailed past, slashing AJ's side.

"This is Baird," came a reply in his ear.

"Who the hell knew our route?" he shouted, trying to maintain some level of composure.

"What do you mean?" Baird answered. "Shit, I just got word. You're under attack?"

"Yes. What the hell? Can't you guys keep anything secret?"

He climbed up the opposite side of the ditch and flopped onto his stomach once he had a view of the approaching spaceship.

"I've scrambled fighters. One minute forty-five seconds. Can you hold on?"

AJ shook his head as he started firing his weapon again. "Might as well be an hour, Baird. This guy's about to pick us off all personal like."

"You need to hang on," she answered.

"Mute her, BB," AJ growled. The alien spacecraft was closing, and it quickly became obvious that the 7.62mm rounds were minimally penetrating. "Boys, we're not getting through this bastard. Find weak spots. Make your shots count."

"He's lining up for another missile. One, Five, you've gotta move, now!" Peppers called.

With Pepper's new information, a small virtual window appeared in his vision. It showed the alien spacecraft's new overhead position and the trajectory of a missile strike about to occur.

Grabbing the earthen bank in front of him, AJ drove his legs into the loose soil embankment and crawled like a wounded animal, flipping himself over the crest just in time to allow the bank to shield him from the next missile strike.

"Baird, we need help, dammit! It's right on top of us," AJ called, looking up at the spacecraft above him as it slowly turned, orienting directly on him. This time, no maneuvering would save him from the next missile to fly. "Aww, shit."

"One, stay down!" Lefty called over comms. "Keep your damn head down!"

It wasn't like Lefty to repeat himself and while AJ would have liked to believe he'd have listened to Lefty the first time, he recognized that his head was indeed raised. Rolling over, he placed his hands over the back of his head and tried to commune with the soil beneath the grass.

"Hooah, bitches!" Chach cackled over comms a split second before the sounds of a fifty-caliber machine gun rattled off super-hardened bullets downrange and danger-close to AJ's position.

Unlike the M110A1's 7.62mm payloads, the fifty-caliber machine gun was punching in an entirely different weight class. Metal on the spacecraft, which had only seconds ago been providing resistance to small arms fire suddenly started screeching horrifically as it was peeled from the spaceship's frame.

"Put a damn frag in that hole," Lefty ordered.

The sounds of twin RPG launches caused AJ to question his current position. If the spacecraft were directly overhead, he could be killed because of a million different things, not least of which was the concussion from exploding grenades. But like many things, he knew better than to try to move while so deeply in the crap.

Fortunately, the spaceship's captain realized the momentum of the battle had shifted. Sliding away from the onslaught, the vessel continued to take damage as it attempted to exit the battle.

"We have a positive lock on gray bogey one. Please confirm mission termination order."

The voice that crackled to life was not one AJ recognized. Pulling to his knees, he faced the direction in which the spacecraft had fled.

"Termination order is confirmed."

That voice belonged to Colonel Baird.

"How'd you get on this channel, BB?" AJ asked.

She appeared with an old-school radio pack on her back as she knelt in the grass and mimicked playing with the dials. She smiled as she turned to him. "I'm pretty good with comms. I think you know that."

"Oh shit, they're lighting him up!" Peppers cried.

From a pair of interceptor jets flying high overhead, a pair of sidewinder missiles launched and streaked through the evening sky, beautiful as the setting sun's rays illuminated their contrails. AJ wondered if the missiles would find their home. Twin fireballs erupted. They did.

Nothing more than an empty husk fell from the bright blue Arizona evening sky into the rugged desert terrain. AJ sagged as the adrenaline which had been driving him suddenly dried up.

"That was close," he said, mostly to himself, turning to assess the damage his team had taken. "Jayne, talk to me."

"I'm up," she answered wearily.

"Lisa?"

"I'm here."

"Count 'em down, boys," AJ said. Beverly showed statuses on each of his team members, but it was critical to reconnect with his team.

"Three of the boots are done for," Birdie said. "I'm patching up the blonde kid."

"Jayne, how is Bald Norm's leg?"

"He won't be dancing for a few days. He needs fluids and probably a cheeseburger," she said.

"Damn, Doc, that's what I call bedside service," Bald Norm said.

"Careful, Baldy," AJ said. "You're talking to my girl."

"I guess we'll see how that goes," Bald Norm answered with a laugh.

Sliding down the embankment, AJ climbed to other side of the road. His team had already moved to aid the fallen soldiers. AJ joined them, helping to move the bodies of the young men who'd only minutes previous seemed too annoying to be near. Now, in death, they occupied a special place of honor where the cost of entry was the ultimate price. Never again would the young corporal be called Diapers.

"AJ, can you talk?" Baird asked over comms. "We have a detail coming your way at high speed. I'm leaving those jets in the air and we're locking down the airspace."

"We lost three of your team in the opening attack," AJ said somberly. "We're setting things right here."

"We're thirty-two minutes out," she replied.

"We'll dig in." AJ muted his call with the colonel. "Two, set up a perimeter. Backup is thirty-two minutes out."

"Copy that, One," Lefty answered.

The men fell to the familiar work of securing their location. In that the transport truck was burning, they moved two hundred yards up the road, not interested in discovering if they'd retrieved all ordnance carried by the vehicle. The loss of life climbed when they discovered the drivers of the truck had been thrown clear.

"BB, any idea what kind of ship that was? Who built it? Maybe you got a registration off the tailfin?" AJ asked.

"The ship is a common Vred spaceframe. Given their ubiquity, we can make no assumption about the occupants," Beverly said. "Also, there was no obvious transponder signal. I say obvious, because while I tapped into those Air Force jets electronics, there wasn't much time to adjust frequencies and fully test."

"So much for keeping their attack on the downlow," AJ said. "I can't imagine someone didn't video some part of that. We're not that far from civilization."

"Both local police and fire department have been redirected," Beverly said. "This suggests that a member or multiple members of the public witnessed the conflict and called it in."

"Any way to know if it those were Togath?" AJ asked.

"Unlikely, but possible. Flying a spaceship an extended distance is within the capacity of a Togath team, but without oversight, there is potential for significant error. Unkindly said, they are not given enough reasoning capacity to deal with the moments between battles. It is their primary weakness," Beverly said.

"So long space flights and planning sneak attacks are outside of their core strength," AJ said. "Maybe they arrived on that spaceship and whoever was in charge stayed behind."

"Strategically, it was a poor decision," Beverly said. "It is well known that humanity strongly defends its territory, especially near military installations. Human fighter jets, while not sophisticated vessels by most measures, are quite focused on destructive tasks. The outcome should have been considered."

"I feel like you're talking in circles. Now maybe you think it was Togath because they didn't make good strategic decisions?" AJ said.

"No, I don't think that's the case," Beverly said. "I think it is more likely that the occupants of that Vred spacecraft were under significant pressure to complete a task. The failure of the Togath, which are expensive assets, would have been devastating to their mission."

"And they probably didn't expect us to roll out a fifty-caliber machine gun," AJ said. "Nobody wants to run into that."

"One, we have a column moving this way," Peppers said twenty minutes later. "I'm sending up some eyes."

"Good call, Five," AJ said. "Thanks for the warning."

"Copy that, One."

Twenty minutes later, they were loaded into the back of an MTT and rolling down the road. It was a somber group that finally arrived at an installation in the rolling hills to the east.

"Boss, there's something you need to know," Peppers said, making room next to AJ.

"What's going on, Peppers?"

"This base has an unusual airstrip. It's too long," he said.

"I imagine they land cargo here," AJ said.

"Maybe. But there's something else. Check out all these F-35s. Something big is going on." Peppers shared video from high overhead on a virtual screen between them.

"Hmm, that does seem suspicious."

The truck ground to a halt at the gate just as Pepper's video blinked out. "Darn it, they have active drone defenses up. There sure is a lot of hardware out here where nobody knows about it."

"I'm not loving where this is headed," AJ said.

His words caught Lisa's attention, who to that point in the drive had been sitting tight in next to Darnell, decompressing from the evening's events. "What are you thinking, AJ?" she asked.

"It feels like we're getting set up for something," he said. "Secret bases with extra security."

Before he could finish his conversation there was a rap on the tailgate and an older Army sergeant climbed up to open the back flap of canvas, tying it off. "We'll need to offload here so we can get through security," he said. "Please leave any personal weapons on the seat. They'll be collected and returned after your meeting this evening. Our next stop will be a security check point."

"Gunny, what's going on here?" AJ asked.

"Mr. Jenkins, you need to know I'd like nothing more than to tell you exactly that," he said. "You're one of my personal heroes. Thing is, this shit's so far above my paygrade they'd never find my body if I started talking. You know what I mean?"

"I think I do," AJ said and then turned into the truck. "Okay boys, all weapons on the seat and we'll follow Sergeant Blaise to the security checkpoint. We've all had enough excitement for the evening, so let's keep it professional."

"Thank you, Mr. Jenkins," Blaise said. "On the other side of the checkpoint, I'll run you over to quartermaster and set you up with clean fatigues. Sorry that we don't have any of the green left over, that's been a couple of minutes."

"Days like today makes it feel like it was hardly yesterday," AJ said, offering his hand to Jayne as she climbed from the truck.

The trip through the security checkpoint was subdued, the team reflecting on the events of the day.

"Boss, you need to take a look," Peppers said when they stepped onto the tarmac and started loading into electric personnel transports.

"What's up?" AJ asked, following Pepper's pointed finger.

At first, he couldn't make out what he was looking at, but with Beverly enhancing his view, he finally found what his old friend was pointing at. High over the sandy plains, a massive civilian jet was on approach, flanked by no fewer than six F35 fighters.

"See it, now?"

"We're screwed," AJ said, shaking his head. "Could this day get any worse?"

Peppers laughed darkly and sent a captured image of none other than Air Force One, inbound, to the rest of the team. "No, probably can't get a lot worse."

6

UP CLOSE AND PERSONAL
DEKE - EARTH

"That's totally messed up," Deke said, rubbing a skeletal hand over the thin red skin that had formed over her jaw. "I can't believe this was all just missing three days ago. Now it looks like I was on a bad diet. What's on the docket for today?"

"During your sleep cycle, I instructed your body to rebuild your pharynx, trachea, and esophageal tract. There is work yet to be done to strengthen those tissues, but I am confident you are capable of ingesting nutrition which has simple physical structures or has been pulverized."

"I think the word you're looking for is puree," Deke said, her stomach growling approval at the conversation. "And I could eat a horse right now."

"I do not believe horse meat is available in local markets," Keegs said. "There is an importer not far away, however, if this is a strong desire."

"Uh, no. Sorry about that. Human idiom. Totally not eating horse. And if we're doing the puree thing, I feel like lots of things I'd like are off the table," Deke said.

"Do you have an example?"

"Pizza, hamburgers, French fries, steak. I mean, really all the major food groups."

"Would you be willing to start with milk products? Your body is in dire need of calcium, which we'll be adding to all your meals. Your body will process natural sources most efficiently."

"Let's take a pivot on that," Deke said, "and talk milkshakes. Specifically, strawberry with a giant spoonful of caramel. And when I say giant spoonful, I'm thinking maybe one-third."

"That is reasonable," Keegs said. "You will struggle to swallow today as we must train muscles that are a fraction of the size needed for efficient operation. We will start slowly."

"When do you suppose I'll be able to talk for real?" she asked. While she'd gotten used to acting like she was talking during simulated conversation with Keegs, the process felt limiting and unnatural.

"Fortunately, we will train your new tongue so you may swallow. While not perfectly suited to the task of speaking, it is a preliminary step. Also, you should know, your voice will sound different due to numerous changes in the structure of your throat, larynx, and mouth."

"I'm getting tired of lying around. When can I get moving?"

"That depends on your actions," Keegs said.

"Tell me what I can do."

"Try to open your eyes."

With Keegs simulating a constant feed of visual stimulation, Deke had little sense that she wasn't using her own eyes. That her own eyes and lids had been burned off in the blast was something she thought about, but didn't directly relate to her current condition. "I ... I'm not sure how."

"I have blocked the nerve pathways and will now make it possible," Keegs said. "Go slowly. I have the lights at minimum in the room, but it could be startling."

"Are you ready?" she asked.

"Yes."

Impatient for progress, Deke urged her eyes open. Her mind was flooded by sensations and stimuli. Instead of being overwhelmed by brightness, it was the complexity of the images she faced that was her undoing.

"I'm gonna barf!" she said, her stomach roiling with grief.

"I'll manage this," Keegs said. "Try to partially close your eyelids. You are suffering from information overload."

"What the hell, Keegs? That's not right," she said, closing her eyes completely. "There's too much. It's like I had binoculars."

"Ah, yes, I should probably have warned about this," he said.

"You think?"

"I do. Your eyesight was significantly improved. I thought you'd be pleased."

"You wanted to surprise me with that?"

"Perhaps a mistake."

"Yeah. That's a mistake. What part of me sounds like someone who likes surprises?"

"I apologize."

Deke slowly opened her right eye, and this time allowed the image in front of her to resolve. She was lying on her back and facing the ceiling. The ceiling tiles were a common grid pattern she'd seen before. She became aware of the texture as details became even clearer as her focus remained on one location.

"It's like I'm zooming in," she said mostly to herself.

"This is a feature of the cybernetic implants I integrated into your replacement cornea," Keegs said. "If it is too much, it is possible to remove this feature without surgery."

"Let's not get hasty," she said, bringing her left eye open again. "Can you dial back the default detail setting, at least for now?"

"Yes, fine tuning is possible."

Her vision blurred and then snapped back into focus. While she could still see the textured ceiling, details were no longer as pronounced. As her focus remained in place, those details started to return.

"That's really cool," she admitted after shifting her attention around the ceiling, which was all that was possible given her unmoving head.

"I am glad that you approve. Improved vision is a significant advantage in combat situations," Keegs said.

"Aww, you say the most romantic things."

"Lieutenant Dekoster, you do understand that our relationship is purely platonic, do you not? We are not the same species and our physical size differences would make anything else very difficult if not impossible," Keegs said, his voice suddenly professional.

"Are you blushing?" Deke teased. "I think your cheeks are red."

"That ... I ... I do not even have cheeks," Keegs said awkwardly.

"Oh relax, little man," she said. "I'm just screwing with you."

"Interspecies romance is not strictly forbidden. I just don't believe it would be advisable given our upcoming deployments. Also, physical engagement would be impossible."

Deke blinked a couple of times at Keegs' continued confusion. A smile broke on her face when she realized her words weren't making sense to him. "Buddy, I didn't mean *screwing* with you. I meant I was messing with you ... kidding ... it's a joke. I don't bend that way. I need more than a couple of nanometers, if you know what I mean."

"Oh ... well, that is a relief," Keegs said. "I can understand why you would be grateful to me. I just think an entanglement would not be productive."

Deke attempted to shake her head even as she smiled, imagining all the deliciously awkward conversations she would enjoy entertaining in the future.

"Okay, so I opened my eyes. How's that getting me out of this stupid bed?"

"I have given you a small amount of control of your neck and trapezoid muscles. Try to turn to your right and tell me what you see."

With significant effort Deke turned her head. It was the first moment that she got a good look at the room where she lay, and her eyes flitted around as she took in the details. There was a low window several feet from the end of the bed, although the curtains were drawn. An uncluttered, low counter sat atop cabinets. Suddenly, it struck her that she'd completely glossed over a figure seated in a chair next to those cabinets.

"What the fuck?" she exclaimed, although all that made it to her throat was a sort of choked gurgle.

"Lieutenant Dekoster, welcome back."

Deke focused on the seated woman wearing Army uniform with full-bird colonel silver eagles. That the woman was in her late thirties told Deke much of either her connections or competence ... probably both.

"Keegs, are you going to do the talking for me?" Deke asked.

"Speak as you have been with me, I will do as you request."

"It was a question."

"I understand."

"Smartass."

"I await your input."

Deke attempted to roll her eyes and was gratified when it mostly worked out. That her head swam with the additional information, and she almost became sick was an acceptable price for her first ability at self-expression.

"Can I take it by your eye movement that you are able to hear me?" the woman asked. "I am Colonel Jacklyn Baird of US Army Intelligence."

"Are you behind all this?"

"Did I select you for extraordinary, life-saving means?" Baird asked. "No. That was the Beltigersk envoy who I understand has taken residence within your body and is seventy-two percent bonded."

"Keegs," Deke explained. "That's what I call him."

"That seems rather informal for such a distinguished guest of honor," Baird said. "I hope you understand the high honor our Beltigersk friend has bestowed upon you. You were selected from tens of thousands of applicants that at least on paper significantly surpass your qualifications in every appreciable way."

"Nice to know. Apparently, there's this thing called a super gene. I've got it," Deke said flatly. "So, pound sand with your *every appreciable way*."

"There were hundreds with this gene in the pool."

"Well shit, Keegs. You do have a crush on me."

Deke blinked a few times when suddenly a muscular, well-tanned man wearing desert combat fatigues appeared on the counter next to

Baird with hands clasped behind his back. Most striking about this man was probably the fact that he was only a foot tall. "You are baiting me."

"Good that you figured that out. It'll make things more interesting in the future for us."

"Are you talking to him now?" Baird asked.

"Yes. We're having kind of a first date sort of argument," Deke said. "He's a little shy."

"I don't think that level of informality is appropriate under the circumstances."

"Well, I guess that's something we'll need to talk about, then," Deke said, challengingly. "Or maybe you'll cut the shit and tell me why you're here."

"I read that you have a difficult time with authority while off-mission," Baird said. "You have been cited for insubordination at an alarming rate and your career has suffered greatly."

"Are you kidding me? I'm a shit-kicker from the git-go. Promotions would only hold me back. I assume someone like you would have already figured this out. Keegs did. He's my boy."

Baird closed her eyes and shook her head, trying to tamp down irritation. "Please don't push me. I understand you're a firebrand. I'm certain this is why your Beltigersk companion chose you."

"Keegs. He's fine with the name," Deke said. "You're here to take my temperature about a mission. You want to know if all this investment is worthwhile. You don't like that I'm insubordinate and you're trying to ease your mind. How am I doing?"

"You are not wrong."

"So, just get it out, already. What's this mission that's got you all tied up in knots? Trust me, I couldn't tell anyone about it if I wanted. So, there's no security risk. I literally can't talk without Keegs' help."

"The mission is extraordinarily dangerous and will likely fail," Baird said.

"Well, don't sugarcoat it for me, give it to me straight already."

"That is the sugarcoated version."

"This should be good. Do tell."

"Fimil Prime is a mineral poor, land diverse, poorly populated planet in the Fimil Prime system. To sail directly to Fimil Prime through normal means is a multi-week journey."

"That sounds uninteresting."

"The Galactic Empire has offered humanity full recognition as a sentient species if we are able to colonize and hold this planet for a period that works out to forty years, give or take," Baird said.

"That's a longer-term mission than I usually take," Deke said. "I suspect the whole colonization thing is harder than us just loading up Noah's Ark with sheep, monkeys and some cows."

Baird raised an eyebrow but let the oddness of the conversation go. "There is competition. Fimil Prime is close to a contested region of space. Thirty months ago, another mission was dispatched to defend the planet against an invasive species that had decided to make Fimil Prime a toehold in Galactic Empire space."

"But we took care of business."

"There was no *we* in this. Unbeknown to any Earth government, the Tok Supremacy utilized a group of Vietnam war veterans to achieve what was arguably an impossible mission."

"Vietnam? Wouldn't those guys be pretty old?"

"Yes. But they had an advantage."

"I'm not sure any advantage gets you over being eighty years old," Deke said.

"That is where you're wrong," Baird said. "Albert Jenkins' team is one of the finest fighting forces in human history. They are adaptable due to forged relationships with Beltigersk symbiotes. They have the wisdom of decades of life after living through one of our most contentious wars. And they have the strength of men and women in their mid-twenties."

"So why are you talking to me, then. Go get this Jenkins dude."

"He is not employed by the US Army and would not be interested in a long-term mission off-world."

"You totally asked, didn't you? He told you to go screw yourself," Deke said. But that wasn't exactly what she said, having chosen a less appropriate word. "Keegs, are you editing my words?"

"Colonel Bird is critical for our mission," he said. "There is no reason to challenge her authority."

"Albert Jenkins and his team declined. You are correct," Bird answered, unaware of the sub-dialogue between Deke and Keegs. "They are also a smaller team than is needed for this mission."

"I'm a platoon leader, how much smaller does it get?"

"Yours is not the only platoon we intend to send," Bird said. "I must be clear with you. The survivability of this mission is less than fifty percent. There is an entity that does not want to see humanity on Fimil Prime. The recent attack at Normanville was in response to leaked intelligence. The entire base was lost in the attack."

"Those Togath overran the base? Shouldn't we have had some bigger weapons to defend against a ground assault?" Deke asked.

"The Togath were successful at navigating our defenses."

"Damn, how bad was it?"

"Sixty percent casualties," Baird answered.

Deke attempted a whistle. "Sixty percent? That's unheard of."

"In the end, all military discipline was lost. Our soldiers, who in their defense, were young and undertrained, ran from the field."

"No way," Deke said, scandalized. "Our people don't do that."

"The Togath do not fight in traditional ways. They cause damage beyond that of weaponry. They do not recognize the Geneva convention and lean into animalistic brutality. It is like nothing we have seen since ..."

"Vietnam," Deke filled in. "And you're telling me this because you want me to sign up."

"I am."

Deke's attempt to shrug her shoulders was ineffective. "I'm a wildcard. You've said it yourself. Why would you put your faith in me?"

"Because you never back down. On the battlefield, you're thoughtful, focused, and make instinctive decisions that most commanders take years to develop – if they ever do. You have almost no hesitation between thought and action. You are strong, and with Keegs' help, you will be stronger."

"Wait, back the heck up," Deke grimaced at Keegs' edit of her words. "What does strength have to do with anything? We were told those Togath were beyond our physical capabilities. I'm not gonna get into a fistfight and win."

"Togath warriors are capable of sustaining considerable injury before they are incapable of battle. When they meet our troops, it is often the case that our defenses are overrun and it is in fact an in-person fight."

"Oh, well, now we're talking." Deke smiled darkly. "You should have led with that."

"Are you serious?"

"Up close and personal is my jam. How many of my team made it?"

"Sammy Bing," Baird answered. "But you're thinking too small. I'll put you in charge of Zebra Company. You'll be promoted to O-3."

"Captain? I'm a Second Lieutenant."

"You were a First Lieutenant sixty days ago. I've already overridden that demotion and purged your record of all past offenses of insubordination. Take this assignment and you'll have your silver bars."

"That's dumb."

"Pardon?"

"If you take me out of the field, I'm just a paper pusher. I'm no good with paper."

"Zebra will be the smallest company in the theatre," Baird said. "You'll have two firsts reporting directly to you with a total of eighty soldiers. Even with that, we expect losses to be twenty percent in the first two weeks."

"That's cold."

"You'll either figure out how to fight Togath or the first month could be your last," Baird said. "We're sending big hardware, but you need to understand, every pound we send costs several thousand dollars. This mission's expense has required Congress and Potus to work together."

"That never happens. And our success rate is less than fifty percent?"

"If you're able to get the base set up, you'll have a chance," Baird said. "We're sending enough ordnance to end a world war. Unfortunately, Togath are warriors like we've never encountered."

"They have big grenades," Deke said. "That's a fact."

"I need to know if you're a volunteer."

"Had me at up close and personal," Deke said. "I'm going to want some say in our loadouts."

"Like what? We're sending the most advanced weapons we can either procure, manufacture, or steal," Baird said.

"Really? Steal?"

"You didn't hear it from me."

"I feel like we could be friends."

"I'm not coming."

"Something tells me we'll be in touch."

"Can I tell Potus you are committed?"

"Sure. When do we leave?"

"We'll transfer you to a rehabilitation suite aboard *Angry Ark* in twenty-four hours when the mission officially launches."

"You don't exactly screw around, do you? I'm an invalid," Deke said. "How am I supposed to train my team if I'm flat on my back, getting meals through my nose?"

"I expect you to overcome this challenge like you have every other challenge you've faced," Baird said.

"Well played. Make it my problem."

"Is it not your problem?"

"I take it back. I'm glad you're not coming. You're an asshole."

Baird's smile was self-satisfying. "I'm glad we are communicating effectively."

"When do I get to meet my commander?"

Baird stood and when she did, pulled a tall metal cup from a bag next to her. She placed the cup on the table beside Deke and stretched a long straw to her. "Good luck, Captain Dekoster. Try to avoid a demotion in the first couple of days if you could. Humanity is counting on your success. It's time to think beyond yourself and consider what's good for a bigger group."

"I guess we'll see how that works," Deke said. "Not like I can actually talk and when I do, Mr. Keegs removes the juiciest parts."

"I wondered," Baird said pushing the end of the straw against Dek's lips. "The conversation was quite a bit more civilized than I'd expected."

"Hmm," Deke said, applying light suction to the straw. The taste of coffee sweetened by caramel filled her mouth. She blinked, not having expected the intense flavor, especially since she hadn't tasted anything for a time.

"Thank you, Kait," Keegs said. "I am sorry for changing your words."

"If you ever do that again, we're done," Deke said, her voice smoldering with anger. "I'll dump your fucking ass into a petri dish and toss it into an airlock. Do we understand each other? And before you answer. I'm not having this conversation twice."

Keegs' small figure stared at Deke for a moment and then he nodded. "I understand. I will show you the respect you have requested."

"Demanded."

"Yes."

7

OPPORTUNISTS

AJ - EARTH

"Well, that's something you don't see every day," Darnell said. "Is she coming to see us?"

"I'm not sure what the alternative might be," AJ said, shrugging. "Why else would we be at a top-secret base after being attacked twice by unknown aliens?"

"I suppose that's a reasonable point."

"Maybe the better question is what would POTUS need to fly all the way out here to talk to us about? It can't be good. Especially after we've gotten our asses handed to us a couple of times," AJ said.

"You'd think they wouldn't even let her come out this way after all that," Lisa added, catching up to the two men.

"File that in the 'this conversation's about to suck' folder," AJ said, grimacing.

"You know you can turn her down," Jayne said. "We could pack up and head back to Xandarj. There's no reason we need to stay in this mess."

AJ stopped and looked at Jayne for a moment, pulling her hand into his own. "I'll do that if that's what you want after hearing her out."

"I think we both know better than that," she said.

"Don't hang that on me," AJ said. "You're not being fair. Which conflict would you have turned away from? Was it the one where you universally cured cancer and the common cold after we got locked away in a container ship? Was that the one we needed to step away from? Or how about when we stopped the invasion on Fimil Prime and saved the entire population from being wiped out?"

"You can stop," Jayne said softly. "I hear you. I'm just scared. One of these times, one of us isn't going to make it back."

His expression softened. "I know."

"Today wasn't our best day with that, but we can put a pin in it for now," Jayne said. "We're causing the good sergeant stress. We should get going."

AJ glanced in the direction Jayne was looking. They'd stopped forty yards from the main building while the rest of the team had continued. Sergeant Blaise stood outside the door and looked back at them with practiced patience.

"That I'm sure of," AJ said, resuming their walk across the paved courtyard.

Sergeant Blaise smiled professionally as AJ and Jayne approached. As soon as they were within a few yards of the entry, he turned to the pair of Military Police, who stood at guard on opposite sides of the door. "These are the last of our visitors," he explained. "Albert Jenkins, Doctor Amanda Jayne."

"Thank you, Sergeant," one of them answered, checking two names from his list. "I'll need to verify IDs."

AJ frowned. He'd already had his ID checked at the security checkpoint. Jayne caught his irritation and put a hand on his arm. "Fight the battles worth fighting."

He sighed and extracted his wallet, handing over his Arizona driver's license.

"Thank you, Mr. Jenkins."

Once they were through the door, Blaise offered, "Everyone is on edge with big brass showing up. Appreciate that you're taking it easy."

"Not my first impulse," AJ said.

"I imagine," Blaise said. "Our first stop is to get you both some fresh clothing. My apologies in advance for the limited selection. I have a laundry detail ready to see if they can salvage your civvies."

Looking down, AJ realized he was covered in grime from crawling in the ditch and blood from working with the dead and wounded. Jayne's clothing was in even worse shape.

"I don't think there's much hope," she said, seeming to read his thoughts.

"You're probably right, ma'am," Blaise said. "But if we're good at anything in the Army, cleaning up messes is something we've some experience with."

Jayne chuckled at his response. "I suppose that's right."

Blaise led them to a room where the rest of the team were in some level of undress, either taking advantage of the row of shower stalls or pulling crisp new tan fatigues and trying on the flexible, breathable boots modern soldiers were equipped with.

"I guess we're regular Army now," Rock grumbled.

"Like hell we are," Birdie said.

A murmur of grumbles passed through the team as Rock's irritation was mirrored.

"Fellas, we're here to listen. That's all," AJ said. "Something big is going down. I, for one, want to know what it's all about. You know the stakes of the game."

"We know, One," Rock said. "Just seems like the same shit we saw in 'Nam. Cake eaters keep the intel to themselves and we pay the price."

"That's why we've got Lisa along," AJ said. "She was plugged into the MI team under Colonel Baird last go-round. We'll make sure that's part of the conversation. Less confusion on what data comes our way."

"They gonna accept that?" Birdie asked. "Seems like they're keeping a lid on it all."

"Can't know what brass will do," AJ said. "Thing is, I'm too old to play games."

"Cost those boots their lives," Chach said. "Someone had to know there was an enemy craft hanging around. They used us as bait."

"Guys, stop," AJ said. "Everything you're saying is true, but I can't do shit about it. Let me get the skinny and I promise to tell you everything. First, though, a shower and a shave."

A knock at the door was followed by Sergeant Blaise stepping in.

"Can you be ready to go in five?" he asked, noticing that AJ was still in his filthy clothing.

"Make it ten and my boys need food," AJ answered, locking eyes with Blaise. "We're coming down from combat and my team's welfare comes first. Read me clear on this, Sergeant. I don't care if POTUS has to sit on her hands while we wait for a pizza delivery. I'm not moving until that's done. Do we have a good copy?"

Blaise closed his eyes and shook his head. "Not the best time to be digging in."

"Tell that to the men who were being shot at all afternoon. I'm sure we're all worried about timing." AJ stalked toward the bank of showers.

With hot water coursing through his hair, AJ watched blood and dirt stain the white floor of the shower beneath his feet. It required every effort to tamp down the residual anger and adrenaline common after combat engagements. Twenty minutes later, he emerged from the shower and toweled off. With neither haste nor dawdling, he shaved and changed into the fresh clothing.

Entering the main room where his team had been sequestered, AJ was pleased to find that someone had taken to heart his demand for food. A table had been set up and a pair of hosts were setting plates and trays in place.

"You need to eat, AJ," Lisa said, stepping between him and Sergeant Blaise.

"Fatigues are a new look for you," AJ said, grinning at Lisa while making eye contact with Blaise. "Five more minutes, Sergeant. I know bosses are waiting and all, but trust me, they'll appreciate my blood sugar being in a decent range."

"I assume you know who our special guest is and why there's a sense of urgency," Blaise said.

"I do and if she's taken the time to come this far, she can cool her jets for ten more minutes," AJ said.

"Ten minutes and then you'll come with me?" Blaise asked.

"Ten minutes," AJ said. "And make sure they know I might bring a handful of the team along. Depends on who wants to hear what's going down."

"The request is for you alone."

"You'll work it out."

"You could make this easier," Blaise said.

"No, I really can't," AJ answered. "I know what I need to make this conversation successful. Do your job, I'll do mine. We'll save the world, or whatever it is we're doing this time."

Lisa's eyebrows shot up at AJ's increasing vehemence and waited for the sergeant to walk off before addressing him. "That whole cynical thing is something you might want to get a handle on. Maybe start with a couple of Oreos or a lemon bar."

He shook his head. "If they think I'm asking any of these men to risk their lives without an opportunity to hear why from the horse's mouth, they're crazy. I owe … no, our country owes each of these men more than we could ever pay them. A little respect seems a small price."

"So that's a no on the Oreo?" Lisa asked, handing him a lemon bar on a napkin.

"Did you know you're a jerk somedays?"

"Only way to get through to you."

"That tracks," AJ bit into the lemon bar. "You know, these aren't bad."

"Most people like them."

"What's the plan, AJ?" Lefty asked, approaching the table.

"We're going to meet with POTUS and Baird. I imagine there will be a dozen other stuffed suits in the room, too. They'll ask for something dangerous and horrible and offer that we'll be given the opportunity to serve our country like nobody in history," AJ said.

"That's what I was thinking," Lefty agreed. "Do you think they'll actually stand in front of a flag while they do or just have a lapel pin?"

AJ laughed. "I bet there's a flag."

"I've talked to the team."

"About?"

"Who wants to go."

"What'd you come up with?"

"We're hanging back."

"There's no reason."

"You said it yourself. Some random act of violence that serves a purpose greater than the value of the lives of the men and equipment deployed," Lefty said.

"I'd want to do that math for myself," AJ said.

"Which is why we want you in that room representing us. AJ, you have a knack for coming back from tough missions. Or have you forgotten how we met?"

"If I recall, you're the one who rescued my ass from that hellhole," AJ said.

"Doesn't change the facts, pal. Every time you get into the shit, you find a way out. We've all seen it. We've all survived because of it. None of us understand how to deal with the cake eaters. They just piss me off."

As they were talking, several team members were hanging close trying to act interested in the food, but AJ wasn't remotely fooled.

"Frenchy, Peppers, Rock? Is that how you see it?" AJ asked. "Do you really want to hitch your wagon to mine?"

"Do your job, One," Rock said in his deep baritone. "We'll do ours."

"That is right, One," Frenchy added. "I have only one request."

"Oh?"

"If we are using mechanized suits again, I do not wish to use Rock's. He has a smell that resists cleansers."

"Are you serious?" Rock asked after a moment of stunned quiet. "You wear that god-forsaken aftershave. At least I smell like a man."

"I don't know what suits you're talking about," AJ said, giving them meaningful looks. The use of the mechanized infantry suits was illegal in most of the universe. That AJ's team had secreted away a stockpile was a highly guarded secret, the integrity of which AJ was starting to question.

"Lisa, are you coming?" AJ asked, stuffing the remainder of a croissant filled with a sweet, chocolaty filling into his mouth.

"As opposed to allowing you to decide my fate? That's not a thing, AJ," she said. "You'd be lost without me."

"You'll get no argument from me. Jayne, are you coming?"

"Yes."

AJ smiled. He was in the company of the two smartest people he knew and was equally certain the brass they'd be meeting with would discount exactly that. He appreciated the advantage it would give him.

Opening the door to the hallway, AJ started to step out but was cut off by a pair of MPs. While he thought he could likely get past the first pair, he was just as certain the night would go poorly from there.

"All right, kids, maybe give Sergeant Blaise's chain a quick tug. We're ready to get going."

"Mayne, Darby, stand down, I'll take it from here," Blaise called, rolling around the corner. The MPs adjusted such that AJ, Jayne, and Lisa could only move in Blaise's direction, which they did. "I thought you were expecting a group."

"Turns out none of my boys want to meet with a bunch of brass," AJ said. "Go figure."

"That might have been nice to know ten minutes ago."

"If we're talking about things someone might have wanted a bit of warning about, I have things to discuss," Lisa said, taking a quick step toward Blaise.

The man's eyes widened at the perceived threat and raised his hands defensively. "You're right. Not the place."

"Good thinking."

Blaise moved through the hallways like a man possessed, barking orders to clear the way each time anyone ranked less than a general came within range. Finally, they arrived at a pair of double doors flanked not by military police but rugged, combat-ready Marines.

"Mr. Jenkins, it's been a pleasure," Blaise said, stepping out of the way.

"Good luck, Sergeant," AJ said.

A sharp-looking Marine lieutenant in dress uniform stepped forward, carrying a small electronic device. "We'll need a quick scan."

"Fine," AJ said, complying with the man's instructions to raise arms and turn around. After repeating the drill with Lisa and Jayne, one of the doors was opened and the trio were ushered to the threshold where they were stopped.

"Mr. Jenkins, Doctor Jayne, and I believe that's Lisa Jackson. Do I have that right?" a man asked.

The room before them was tall, rectangular, and had large screens covering an entire wall. In the center of the room was a circular arrangement of narrow tables with a dozen occupants. AJ recognized only a handful, specifically Colonel Baird and Toni Calvin, President of the United States.

"And you are?" Lisa asked.

"Tom Richmond, Acting Chief of Staff," he answered quickly. "Thank you for agreeing to meet. It's been a tough couple of days for all of us."

"Hold on, Tom," President Calvin said, standing, which of course caused the entire room full of generals and aides to rise with her. "Mr. Jenkins, Ms. Jackson, and Doctor Jayne, we understand that you've had a harrowing day and Mr. Richmond does not mean to make light of that. On behalf of the United States of America, I express our heartfelt gratitude for courage displayed in combat on our home soil."

"Ma'am," AJ said, interrupting her speech. The action caused a few quickly drawn breaths but Calvin took it in stride.

"Yes, Mr. Jenkins?"

"First, friends call me AJ," he said. "Second, we've all done the 'on behalf of a grateful nation' gig a few times now. I'm not saying we don't appreciate it, but like you said, we've been shot at and blown up a couple times in the last twenty-four so maybe we could get to the meat of the conversation."

"Do you know who you're talking to, son?" a general AJ recognized but couldn't place a name to the face. "This is ..."

"General Hamish, hold on," Calvin said. "Mr... AJ," she continued. "You're right. You and your team have proven themselves time and time again as patriots. I wish I could say I wasn't here to ask for more of the same, but I am. There's just no getting around it."

"Perhaps we could sit," Richmond suggested.

"Will you join us at the table, AJ?" Calvin asked.

"Of course," AJ said. "That's why we're here."

"Great. Everybody, take thirty minutes. I'd like a chance to speak alone with our friends here."

"I'd like to re-register my concern with this operation, ma'am," the same general who'd just come to her defense added. "We have better trained men and women standing by."

"Thank you, General. I value your input," Calvin said. "I'll need the room."

For a few minutes, they waited for the twenty odd people who'd gathered to dismiss themselves. When the door finally closed and they were alone with just Calvin and her Chief of Staff, she continued.

"We screwed up, AJ," she started. "We planned a mission and your name was floated as a possible team lead. Somehow our plans were discovered and handed to our enemy. I apologize."

"I see why you needed to clear the room."

"Hey now," Richmond interrupted. "That's hardly fair."

"No. He's right. I'd never make that apology in front of my security council," she said. "Only a handful of them know the depths of how badly we were compromised."

"Since we're in the dark, do you mind sharing the mission details so we know why they were trying to take us out?"

"I assume you know about Togath and their relationship to the Quarr species?"

"Quarr make Togath in factories and sell them to the highest bidder ... at least sometimes," AJ said. "Togath are brute warriors, genetically engineered to be really good at killing. Is that what you're asking?"

"That's close enough," Calvin said. "We've got a problem."

"One you don't want to commit US forces to."

"That's where you're wrong. I'd be all for committing US forces if I thought we had the technology. No, the problem is, we're outmatched and need help," she said.

"What in the world can we do that the entire US government can't?"

"We know about the suits, Jenkins," Richmond said. "We know you didn't give them back to the Tok. On the record, Commander Cer isn't happy. Off the record, she seems less offended. It's hard to tell for sure. They look like raccoons."

"I'd keep that to yourself," AJ said.

"Not intended to be offensive. It's just hard to read her face."

"You think we have suits. What about it? Surely if we have them, you know where they are."

"We don't. Our best guess is you geo-cached them somewhere out in space. Thing is, we tried to backtrack your last trips and can't find anything."

"That must have taken some work," AJ said. "I'm surprised you didn't ask first."

"Would you have told us?"

"About suits we don't have," AJ said. "No."

"Stop. This isn't productive," Calvin said. "I don't care where you stashed the suits, AJ. I have two hundred men and women who are trying like hell to survive. They're under siege and are barely hanging on. I need to do something. One option has that something being you and your team."

"I see. Is that it?" AJ asked. "The conversation feels short on details."

Calvin nodded her head and gave a quick lift of her eyebrows. "Tom, go ahead and give them the ten-thousand-foot view of Fimil Prime."

"We know about Fimil Prime," AJ said. "We were there a year ago. Surely you know that."

"Indeed you were. And you did a great job of stopping the Lago infestation. Superior work. I mean that," she said. "The problem is, when there's a vacuum of power, it sucks in opportunists."

"The Quarr are making a move on Fimil Prime?"

"No ... we are."

8

SPECIAL PROJECTS
DEKE - EARTH

"So, you're my special project," a gruff voice announced from the entrance to Deke's room. Baird had only been gone for two hours and Deke's primary focus had been given to finishing what seemed a non-stop conveyer belt of liquified food.

"Colonel Corcoran. Sir," Deke answered respectfully. To say she was surprised at the legendary soldier's appearance in her room was an understatement. The man was a legend both in the service and amongst the civilian population.

"Well, are you?"

"A special project, sir. Yes, sir," she answered.

"What if I said I unsuccessfully tried to dump you from Operation Black Turtle? That I'm personally offended you've been given rank of captain when there are thousands of more qualified candidates in line, waiting for a chance to prove their mettle."

"Permission to speak freely?"

"I've read your file, Dekoster. You apparently don't need permission to speak freely. You're special that way."

Deke locked eyes with the man, considering the words – never meet your heroes. He hadn't given her permission and obviously already had a chip on his shoulder. An uncomfortable silence followed as the two waged a silent war of who would speak first.

"Say your piece," he finally growled.

"I didn't ask to be here. I was asked. You got a problem with that, take it up with someone else. I'm doing my part. That's all you can ask. I'm gonna kick some Togath ass and teach my company to do the same thing, because that's who I am. You want someone to kiss your ass, you already have Kersey coming along. You should talk to him."

"You're bordering on insubordination."

"Not at all. I'm just telling you things as I see them. For the record, I kick ass and have no place to store names, only bodies. We both know we're headed into a shitstorm and you're gonna need serious shitkickers. I don't know who you put on my team, but give me two months and I'll give you the best chance at making it through this thing you've ever had. Fuck the odds. I play to win and I do it with guns, knives, and fists if necessary. Do you feel me?"

"God, you really are a hard ass."

"Don't let the blonde hair fool you."

"What makes you think you can lead a whole damn company?"

"Not a damn thing," Deke replied, echoing his tone. "Except my platoon had the highest kill rate and the lowest casualty rate in the entire damn operating theatre. But I bet you already know that, which makes me wonder why you're in here busting my balls. Or did they deny you bringing your dog along to kick?"

"You got a mouth on you."

"Just getting warmed up."

"I've read your sleeve. You certainly read like a shitkicker. You know, I can't afford to have my captains in the field getting their heads caved in, right?"

"Maybe not on the front line," Deke said. "But if I'm gonna figure out how to beat these Togath, I'm going to need some up-close-and-personal time."

"And if you get your head caved in?"

"Then you'll know to stop sending in captains."

This response drew a snort of derision from Corcoran. "You'll report directly to Major Mike Baines but we're going to all be working closely together since we'll be off world, without any f hope of replacements. I don't mind telling you that I wasn't a big fan of bringing you on board."

"Let me guess, I'm a loose cannon," Deke said.

"This is the moment where you keep that smart mouth of yours shut," Corcoran said with steely resolve. "The good news is that I'm all sorts of forgiving for my ass kickers. Are you going to be an ass kicker, Captain Dekoster? Are you going to take the fight to the enemy with extreme prejudice? Are you going to put aside this bullshit, devil-may-care attitude and get serious about keeping the two hundred soldiers who have agreed to place their trust in me alive?"

"Hell, yes I will, Colonel."

"Why didn't you start with that, then? Welcome to the team. Now, Zebra Company is assembling in *Angry Ark's* hold in thirty minutes. I expect you to be there to welcome them aboard."

Deke blinked as she looked at the enigmatic man. Had he been messing with her the entire conversation just to get a rise? He didn't seem the sort. Before she could work it out, he turned on his heel and was gone from the room.

"You like him," Keegs said after a moment.

"He's terrifying," Deke replied. "Have you read any of his past missions? He's the real deal."

"You were intimidated. I have not seen that before."

"Sure. What's next? Get me out of this bed."

"You are not ready."

"And you're not helping. I want you to release the nerve blocks. I can do this," she growled. "I'm not meeting my team on a stretcher, damn it!"

"This is a very bad idea. If you fall, you could break your jaw, or your arms. It would undo much of the work we've spent so much time on."

"Who's my damn staff sergeant?" she growled. "And are we going to have a problem? I'm not asking. I'm telling."

"Sergeant Gera Leisk," he said. "She is standing by."

"What the hell? Get her in here," Deke growled. "Now, dammit."

A few seconds later, a tall, lean, black woman entered the room. "Captain, you requested my presence?" she asked, coming to attention.

"None of that when we're behind closed doors," Deke said. "I'm Deke when we're informal. I need you to keep up and not argue with me, do you copy?"

"Yes ma'am ... er, Deke."

"Good. I need fatigues in my size and with proper rank. I need this in fifteen minutes. Tell me this is something you can do."

"Yes ... Deke," she said. "Are you sure you're ..."

"Keep up. We're doing this. It'll go faster if you don't argue."

"Copy that, Captain," Leisk said and turned on her heels, racing from the room.

"Nerve blocks are removed, Kait," Keegs said.

"Help me sit up," Deke said, struggling to do even a simple sit-up.

"This is going to hurt."

"Make it burn." A moment later her new eyelids flew open and if her cheek muscles worked correctly, she'd have made an extremely pained expression. As it was, her jaw resembled that of a desiccated mummy and her inability to change expressions did not mimic her scream. "Awwww dammit! I didn't mean literally make it burn!"

"I apologize. I will reduce the sensations you are experiencing," Keegs said.

"No. Shit, give me a minute. You're sure this gets me to recover faster?"

"Yes."

Deke closed her eyes and for the first time since awakening felt the tiny sensations of movement that were her eyelids moving across her eyes. A shudder of appreciation at the return of normal sensation momentarily outweighed the raging firestorm at the rest of her body's reawakening.

"I want to sit up," she said. While her jaw moved in response to her command, she became aware that the voice in her ears was not her own. Breath was not moving through her esophagus, and it was clear that the sounds did not emanate from her body. "Wait, who's talking. That's not me."

"I have simulated your predicted vocal resonance chamber and produced an approximation of your future voice," Keegs said.

The reduction of nerve pain throughout her body gave Deke just enough relief to roll her eyes, something for which she was grateful. Recognizing that the next move was hers, she attempted to push her arms down and curl her back in order to sit.

"Ahhh!" she cried out as pain fired throughout her arms where they pressed into the bed. Instead of backing off, however, she kept up the pressure. At no time in her life could she remember being so weak. Even with her greatest effort, she was still unable to sit up in the bed. Instead of giving up, she used her legs to turn her hips until she was on her side and then kicked them off the bed. While not elegant by any means, she managed to pop up to a seated position.

"That was impressive, Deke," Keegs said. "You are quite determined."

"Can it," she growled. "If you're going to be a cheerleader, get a uniform."

Slowly, she opened her eyes. Nausea rolled over her as the combination of visual and aural input assaulted her brain. Her stomach heaved which was enough to knock her off balance and she slid off the side of the bed. Instantly, a red warning light strobed by the only door in the room.

"Aw, hell," she grumbled as she found herself in a disorganized pile of legs, knees, and toothpick-sized arms.

"She's on the floor," a voice announced as the door slammed open. "Ma'am, are you okay?"

Rough hands grabbed at her arms. "Get the hell off me!" she yelled, although *hell* wasn't the word she'd tried to form. The hands beneath her arm faltered but didn't quite let go. "That's an order, dammit!"

Whatever hesitance the man had at releasing her disappeared and she was left to slump forward again. "Ma'am, you can't be down here," he managed, trying to retrieve some manner of control.

"No shit," Deke answered, struggling to push against the floor. "Just help me sit up."

Recognizing she was in charge, the nurse gently moved her body back to a neutral sitting position, while still allowing her to do as much of the work as possible.

"There you go," he added.

"My legs are strong enough to hold me. Keep me steady as I try to stand," she said.

"I don't ..."

Deke turned a steely glare on the nurse and cut him off. The two worked together and finally, Deke found the purchase she was looking for and moved to a kneeling position. After that and with the nurse's help, she rose to her feet.

"That is very impressive, ma'am," the nurse said.

A knock at the half-open door caught Deke's attention and she turned to find that Sergeant Leisk had returned and was holding a folded pile of combat fatigues.

"Come in and close the door, Sergeant," she said.

"Yes, ma'am."

"I want a shower," Deke said, looking at the nurse.

"This unit is not equipped ..."

"I didn't ask that. You know where a shower is, I assume. Take me there."

"That's not my ..."

"Is this really the conversation you want to have, Corporal?"

"No, ma'am."

"Stay close, but I don't want you touching me if I'm not falling over. Good copy?"

"Good copy," he repeated. "We're out the door and to the right. Three doors down."

"See, that wasn't so hard."

Walking through the door, she found herself in a busy hospital ward with dozens of people moving around. That she hadn't heard them before that moment, surprised her, and was something she would speak to Keegs about in the future. In that moment, however, she had an entirely new issue to deal with. The bustling hospital ward suddenly stopped moving, as if everyone was suddenly frozen by some new alien tech.

"What the hell?" she asked, but as she was outside of her room, no actual noise came out of her throat.

A doctor, wearing the designation of major stepped forward and slowly clapped his hands together. Deke wrinkled her forehead as she looked at him. His behavior made no sense. An orderly, with an obvious prosthetic replacement for his right arm also stepped forward and clapped his hands together in time with the major.

"Seriously, Keegs, what's happening?" Deke whispered, which wouldn't have mattered, given her inability to project her voice through her unusable esophagus.

The dam broke in the ward and everyone joined in the clapping. Shouts of hooah resonated around her. For a few uncomfortable minutes, Deke suffered the unexpected celebration with her at the center of the attention.

"You are a hero, Kait Dekoster," Keegs said. "You sacrificed yourself for your team. There is no greater gift to be given, nor any greater moment of heroism. They are acknowledging you."

"What am I supposed to do?" she asked.

"Perhaps you could wave? I have seen videos of such a response," Keegs said.

"Um, sure," she said, raising her skeletal hand to give people a weak wave.

"On behalf of Captain Dekoster, thank you," Sergeant Leisk called over the crowd, stepping in front of Deke. "Please allow her to recover at her own pace and go back about your business. She is grateful for the show of support."

"Oh, I like this woman," Deke said.

Leisk turned her head and looked Deke in the eye. She nodded with a half-smile. "We're Oscar Mike."

"You heard me, didn't you?"

"Yes ma'am. I have ear pods due to your particular injuries. It would not do to have a sergeant who cannot hear her commander. Their feelings are shared by yours truly. It is my honor to serve with you, Captain Dekoster."

"We'll make sure to rub the new off that nickel real quick."

"I could get a female nurse to help you shower," the nurse said as he led Deke into an empty hospital room.

"I don't think this is one of those moments," Deke said.

"Captain Dekoster?" a voice called from behind.

Deke attempted to grit her teeth, which she didn't have and caused pain in her jaw. "What?"

"The captain is unable to speak," Leisk said. "Is that Captain Dekoster's nutrition order?"

"Yes, Sergeant."

"I've got it," Leisk said, taking the tall shake. "Before or after shower?"

"After …" Deke's stomach growled with discontent. "Nope. Now."

"Of course, ma'am."

"Remember, when in private …"

"I understand, ma'am."

Deke raised the ridge of skin over her eyes that was just starting to grow thin eyebrows back. "Oh, it's like that, is it?"

"Indeed, ma'am."

"I'll sit on that chair, and you can turn the water on," Deke said, grasping the shake held out by Leisk.

"Are you sure you have this?" Leisk asked when Deke's hand trembled under the stress of holding the several hundred grams of the tall shake.

"We'll find out," Deke said, slowly settling into the chair set out by the nurse.

She sucked on the shake and nodded at the nurse who busied himself getting the water running. The patter of the water against her skin was soothing as much as it caused pain against her newly growing skeleton and flesh. Not unused to pain, she leaned into both sensations and continued to consume the shake.

"Dang, Keegs, this is amazing," Deke said after the first bits of shake slid down her never-before-used throat.

"I've attuned your body's pleasure response to stimulate on the material you most require," he said. "You would think there to be a more efficient mechanism for onboarding the building blocks I require. The human digestive system is quite efficient."

It didn't take Deke long to empty the shake container and with renewed energy she pulled herself to a standing position. "We need to get this gown off," she said, glancing at the nurse.

"Are you sure?"

"I'm not exactly centerfold material right now."

The nurse shrugged. "People in my line of business see it all. It's just our job to ask."

"Good. Let's skip that from here on out, then."

"Copy that, Captain."

Ten minutes later, Deke had been thoroughly soaked, soaped, and dried. As she'd lost most of her body's fat and much of its muscle, the effort of getting her into fatigues wasn't significant, although it required Leisk to step in a couple of times, which she did without complaint.

"Where to now, ma'am?"

"Where is *Angry Ark*, Sergeant?"

"It's a brisk twenty-minute walk from here," Leisk said. "Colonel Corcoran isn't letting anyone aboard because of the attack in China."

"What attack?"

"The intel I have access to is limited. An interstellar mission was wiped by suspected aliens."

"Define wiped."

"The entire base was destroyed."

"Corcoran thinks that'll happen here?"

"*Angry Ark* is offsite."

"You said twenty minutes."

"There's a ride at the end of that twenty minutes. You'll see. Blow this base and it doesn't get *Angry Ark*. Vice versa is the same."

"Keegs, send a message to my direct, Major Baines. Tell him I'm headed to *Angry Ark*."

"Ma'am, I'll do that if you'll allow," Leisk said.

"Do your thing, Sergeant."

"Do you need me anymore?" the nurse who'd been helping asked.

"No, we're leaving the ward," Leisk said while simultaneously accepting the nutritional shake from an approaching private. "We're changing locations. I'll send an update when we're settled."

Deke wasn't sure who Leisk was speaking to, but the private stiffened. "Yes, Sergeant."

"People are scared of you, aren't they?" Deke asked as they walked down the hallway.

"I don't know, ma'am. I worked hard for my rank. I expect the same attitude from the soldiers around me. Some people have trouble with that. I've accepted it."

"Well, at least we know why you're on my team."

"Oh, no, ma'am. My so-called attitude almost kept me off your team," Leisk said. "Major Baines spoke up for me."

"Tell me more about that."

"Major Baines was my CO back in the day. He's a hard ass. We got along. He heard I wanted to be part of Black Turtle so he got me a spot. Told me I'd have to work with someone who was a bigger pain in the ass than me. I assumed he was making it up."

"He doesn't even know me."

"You have a reputation, ma'am."

"I suppose I do."

A few minutes later, fatigue started to set in, and Deke was forced to slow.

"Ma'am? Perhaps this is a good time to work on this shake?" Leisk asked.

"I suppose." Deke leaned against a nearby wall and accepted the proffered shake.

"That sure is a lot of calories," Leisk said. "Hard to believe you can take more than one of those down."

Deke turned the bottle and found the information Leisk was referring to. According to the bottle, there were eighty-five hundred calories in the bottle. "It's a lot. I have a crazy metabolism."

"And a symbiote," Leisk said. "It's not general knowledge, but given my position, I was read in."

"His name is Keegs. You guys should make friends," Deke said.

"We only have five more minutes until we reach the transport," Leisk said. "Major Baines approved us getting aboard this afternoon. The rest of Zebra Company will be onboarding early tomorrow."

"I thought that was this afternoon."

"We're Army. Orders change."

"Hard to argue with that."

With renewed energy, Deke pushed off the wall and the two continued down the hallway. After a few minutes, they came to several sets of double steel doors all in a row. A pair of guards flanked the one door that stood open. Seeing Deke, they stiffened to attention.

"You're cleared to go through, Captain Dekoster," the soldier on the right offered.

"Welcome to Wonderland," the other said.

9

USS WASP
AJ - EARTH

"What kind of support are you offering?" Lisa's question was simple, but she had just begun negotiations.

"What do you mean?" Calvin asked.

"You're planning other missions. Your general said as much. That means you have budgets and timeframes put together. You're talking to us because you believe we are effective and can move quickly. We're not contractors nor are we mercenaries. We also can't continue funding every wild hair that comes our way."

Calvin raised an eyebrow yet kept her composure as she spoke. "What do you see yourselves as?"

"I'm glad you asked. Now we can have a real conversation," Lisa said. "We're patriots who have offered every part of our lives to the challenge of keeping our fellow Americans safe from the big bad universe. At every turn, however, our own country seems to look for ways to make that harder."

"You don't report to anyone. Do you not understand how concerning that is to all those men and women who just left this room?" Calvin asked. "I'm taking a huge political risk even talking to you."

"So go all in, Madam President," Lisa said. "You say we don't report to anyone, but here we are, sitting at your table, because of your summons. Read the room."

"You're saying I should create a new department? One in which your team freely operates?" Calvin asked.

"Far be it from me to tell you how to organize the world's largest bureaucracy," Lisa said. "What you need to ask is if we'll follow your orders. Will the men who've fought for this country since before you were born stand up one more time and march into battle because they believe in this country? Will they proudly bear the flag on their shoulder and stand for what it represents?"

"I don't know," Calvin said.

"The answer is sitting across the table," Lisa said. "Please understand that he brought me along for the same reason Richmond here gets to ask the nasty questions. Don't go halfway in on this."

Calvin nodded and turned to AJ. "AJ, will you go rescue my team before it's too late?"

Unseen by Calvin and Richmond, Beverly appeared on the table. She wore a white lab coat and projected a black-topped chemistry table with beakers boiling over with bubbling green liquid. In the middle of the table was a holographic projector that shined upward into a smokey pillar. In the middle of this pillar sat a sleek, armored warship, with a large American flag emblazoned on its side.

"This is the top secret, *USS Wasp*," Beverly said. "Built on a Vred spaceframe, it is filled with the best technology humanity has been able to negotiate for. It's capable of holding both *Seahag* and *Bernard*, the second combat dropship you procured, in its hold as well as host a complement of forty. President Calvin is not aware of this vessel as General Bartholomew has carefully hidden its existence."

"Now we're getting somewhere," AJ said.

"Pardon?" Calvin asked.

"I think he's talking to his parasite," Richmond said.

"Symbiote," Jayne corrected. "The relationship between Beltigersk and human is mutually beneficial. It is insulting to suggest otherwise."

"Is this true, AJ? What does our honored guest offer to this conversation? Is there a reason she remains hidden? I believe you address her as female."

"Beverly," AJ acknowledged. "If she wants to be seen, you'll see her. I learned a while back that is not my circus to manage."

"Does she have input for us?"

"What does General Bartholomew have to lose with my team getting involved?"

Calvin shifted uncomfortably in her seat. "What do you know of General Bartholomew?"

"You first," AJ said. "A word of advice. It's better if you don't challenge the exquisitely brilliant, technologically superior sentient who rides with me to a game of name that person. You'll discover things you wish you didn't know. Trust me."

"For the sake of brevity, I'll set that aside," Calvin said. "General Bartholomew has a competing proposal to sending your team. He has a highly trained company of dedicated young men and women who have been gathered to take on this mission."

"Why are you talking to me?"

"This will be General Bartholomew's second team. The first was lost upon contact with the enemy before even entering Fimil Prime's airspace."

"How many were lost?" AJ asked. He would not use the lives of service members to make his point.

"Forty-two," Calvin said. The only tells of emotion on her face were a clenched jaw and a glistening of moisture in her eyes. In that moment, AJ saw how responsibility for the lives of the soldiers weighed heavily on her.

"We'll go," AJ said. "But you'll provide every piece of intel Lisa asks for. If we get a whiff of something being held back, we'll walk. Secondly, you'll tell General Bartholomew to hand over the *USS Wasp*, which is currently being hidden as a Coast Guard Search and Rescue frigate."

"Tom, get every piece of information you can about this *USS Wasp*. If Bartholomew is hiding assets from me, I want to know. Also, ask Colonel Baird to join us," Calvin said, turning to Lisa. "Can I assume you've retained a professional relationship with Ms. Baird and can continue to work with her team?"

"I want to hear your orders to her," Lisa said.

"Fair enough," Calvin said. "What else do you need?"

"We'll need supplies," Lisa said. "I want to work with a quartermaster who can help with organization."

"Will you need support staff?"

"No," AJ said, but was quickly overruled by Jayne.

"Yes," she said. "We need people who can manage supplies and keep a ship running. AJ, we don't need to be dealing with non-essential tasks."

"I agree," Lisa said.

"Fine."

"We'll get to work," Richmond said. "I'm going to need something of my own, though."

"You're getting a team," AJ said.

"Agreed. You will all be hired into Homeland Security under the Special Powers Act of 2027. This act gives me the ability to react without congressional approval for a period of ninety days. I'm not creating a new cabinet position and you'll therefore be under the direct supervision of General Clayton," she said.

"I don't know if that's a good idea."

"It's the only way, AJ," Calvin said. "I need to do this legally. I can't skirt the law. This is going to blow up at some point and your team needs to be protected. Clayton is a good man and understands Washington. If you don't get what you need from him, I'm giving you a phone with direct access to me. You shouldn't need it."

"My boys need benefits. Their families need to be taken care of," AJ said.

"General Clayton will take care of it all," Calvin said. "Do we have an agreement?"

AJ looked to Jayne and then to Lisa to make sure he saw no hesitation. There was none. He then stood and offered his hand. "Congratulations, you've just drafted the oldest combat team in history. We'll be proud to once again represent our country on the field of battle in service to this great country."

"Go get my boys and girls, AJ. They're in danger because of me."

"No, ma'am, they're in danger because they were born to a higher purpose. Hooah!"

"I'D CALL you son if I didn't know you're older than me," General Jack Clayton said. He was a good-looking older man with graying temples, sandy blonde hair and a ruddy red complexion stained by too much sun. "You made quite an impression on the Commander in Chief. Let's skip the posturing and get down to brass tacks. What do you say?"

Three days had passed since AJ's meeting with the president, and he was already tired of being 'part of something bigger.' Between intelligence reviews, planning with the quartermaster, and the training schedule cooked up by Lefty, he found he was running from one meeting to the next without a break.

"I'm definitely not your son," AJ said wearily.

"Non-Terrestrial Security Operations or NTSO," Clayton said, offering his hand. "That's the name of our newest Homeland Security chapter. President Clayton shared with you the articles that allow for the formation of this team. You'll all be brought in at GS14. An HR specialist will give your team the white-glove treatment for onboarding."

"That'd be appreciated," AJ said. "Are we going to knock heads?"

"Remains to be seen," Clayton answered, walking out from behind his desk. "I have something I want to show you."

"You're not much for small talk," AJ said, assessing the man he'd spent less than a minute sizing up.

"Hooah, Sergeant. Life's too short for pissing contests."

"Where were you in 'Nam?"

"Wasn't even a twinkle." Clayton said, waving AJ to follow him through the side door of his office.

The pair entered a hallway AJ hadn't previously been allowed in and he struggled to keep up with the general as they sped down the hallway.

"You're in pretty good shape for a young guy," AJ finally admitted when the general stopped at a tall metal door that was guarded by a single soldier holding a rifle. The soldier had snapped to attention at their approach.

"At ease, Corporal," Clayton said. "We're just through here."

The door opened into a soaring space. A gust of wind indicated that wherever they were entering was open to the outside. He was about to ask where they were headed when saw the flat desert khaki of the eighty-yard-long spacecraft which occupied a good portion of a massive hangar.

Long and narrow, the USS Wasp had a stubbier profile than a similarly long 747, but lacked any sort of airfoils for atmospheric flight. Fully aft were six large engines in a cluster. AJ's eyes skipped over technology he partially recognized and lit on missile tubes and weapon turrets.

"Shit, but she's got an aggressive stance," he breathed. "She's a declaration of war just standing there."

"I wish I could say she's got a chance against anything out there," Clayton said. "Our only advantage is nobody knows exactly how crazy we are and what we might be carrying. Slug-throwing turrets are apparently a no-no, but we can get by with it since we're only semi-sentient, or that's the story I've been given."

"It's one thing to see pictures," AJ said, approaching the vessel. "Another thing entirely to stand next to her."

"Sir, you will stand back!" A soldier warned, lowering his rifle and advancing an AJ, aiming only slightly over his shoulder.

"At ease, soldier," Clayton intervened.

The soldier looked nervously between the brightly painted line AJ had just stepped across and the general, obviously wondering if he was being tested.

"I need a verbal authorization code," the soldier responded.

"Charlie-one-niner-foxtrot-foxtrot," Clayton answered.

"Copy that, sir. You are cleared to approach."

As the pair worked their way around the vessel, AJ became aware of a pair of men wearing spotless coveralls, talking animatedly while they gestured between the vessel and their electronic notebooks.

"Joyce, it's a general," one finally said.

"Ah, right," the second answered. "General Clayton?"

"Brian Joyce, I take it?" Clayton said, extending his hand. "And I assume Marion Tenet. AJ, these are the engineers responsible for most of the important decisions made regarding USS Wasp's myriad technological advances."

The men stopped talking for a moment and both gave AJ a slightly satisfied nod. It was Tenet who was first to fill in the quiet. "Albert Jenkins. I wondered if you were behind swiping our ship. Just exactly how do you think you're going to keep this ship in the air? She's barely seen her first shakedown. Where do you even think you're going with her?"

"Tenet is it?" AJ asked.

"I prefer Marion."

"Marion, then," AJ agreed. "What are your current orders?"

Tenet looked from Joyce to Clayton. "I don't think I can tell you."

"Speak freely, Mr. Tenet," Clayton said. "As of this moment, Mr. Jenkins is in command of the USS Wasp and therefore responsible for all staff assigned to her."

"Great, I need another boss," Tenet said. "My job ... our job, rather, is to get USS Wasp ready for a full combat mission. And what I'm telling you is that's foolishness. This ship has more new systems than if you dropped a modern car into the paleolithic age. Taking her into combat is probably suicide."

"Marion, Jenkins is the guy who made a spaceship in his junkyard and sailed it Xandarj," Joyce offered. "He might have some idea about these things."

"How could he? His ship was a glorified balloon with cobbled together engines. USS Wasp is the most sophisticated piece of technology the United States has ever assembled into one cohesive unit," Tenet continued.

"Marion, would it make you feel better if I told you that Mr. Jenkins has agreed to bring a team of engineers on assignment?" Clayton asked.

"Wait, what? But it's a combat mission," Tenet said. "Why would you bring engineers into combat? We don't know how to fight."

"Can't have it both ways, Marion," AJ said. "*USS Wasp* is heading out in forty-eight hours. I'm sure there are no end of volunteers who want to be part of this mission. It sounds like you've convinced General Clayton that you're the best fit. I personally don't have any skin in that conversation. I haven't found a piece of technology that between Petey, BB and me, we can't fix."

"Petey and BB? I don't recognize those names."

"Beltigersk symbiotes," AJ said. "They've already ingested every piece of documentation available for every subsystem aboard. What that means to you is that if I need to grab a wrench and fine tune things, I'll do just that."

"You're a brute," Marion said. "*Wasp* might be a warship, but she's sensitive. The documentation doesn't tell the entire story."

"Welcome aboard, then," AJ said and turned to Clayton. "I appreciate you bringing me over. I'll take it from here."

"You don't want a tour first?" Clayton asked.

AJ shrugged. "Depends on if you don't have anything better to do."

"I have to admit to some curiosity," Clayton said. "She just got here last night. I haven't had a chance."

"Let's go take a look," AJ said. "BB, drop the starboard ramp, would you?"

"She can't do that, you're not even in the system," Tenet objected and then jumped as a loud clank and the whir of heavy electric motors filled the air. "That's impossible. Our systems are hardened against exactly that kind of intrusion."

"Put on your big boy britches, Mr. Tenet, you're going to be playing catchup for a while," AJ said. "General, if you'll follow me." AJ took off, walking confidently beneath *USS Wasp's* belly.

"I'll admit, I was expecting a little more shock and awe on your part," Clayton said.

"She's a beauty for certain," AJ said. "As to the shock and awe, that's been pretty well ruined by the last few years. Someday over beers, you'll have to ask me about the space liner I leased for salvage. Talk about crazy technology."

Rolling around the side to the ramp that extended to the hangar deck, AJ grabbed the railing and took two stairs at a time, climbing up into the ship. While he was familiar with the layout, it was the top-down floor plan Beverly provided with his current position that gave him the best insight.

"The specifications suggest the max complement is forty," AJ started as he led Clayton forward. "That's a bit aggressive because it requires hot bunking."

"It's doable," Clayton said.

"Agreed, but remember, more than a third of the volume of this vessel is technology, armor, engines and, the like. Take the remainder of that volume and split it one third, two thirds and that's the split between the space given to crew vs. cargo. Travel through space is like living in a submarine. You're gonna get close to your neighbor, there's just no getting around it. No, the practical upper limit is twenty, and that's what I'm going to limit things to."

"You're bringing ten. That only give you room for a support staff of ten," Clayton said.

"We'll need people to wear multiple hats," AJ said.

"Good luck getting Marion Tenet or Brian Joyce to cook dinner."

"I imagine we'll make an exception for that pair," AJ said. "Just so I know, what's their relationship?"

"You read that right," Clayton said. "Generally, the Army doesn't bend for domestic partners. We're happy to make an exception in this case. Is that going to be a problem?"

"You should know, I've got the hots for the good doctor," AJ said. "And, I think Darnell thinks a lot of his wife. I haven't been regular army for forty years. It's just easier to know where things sit."

"I take your point."

"Now, this is how the bridge of a combat ship ought to look," AJ said, grinning as he stepped into the immaculately maintained space.

"I don't understand the need for four chairs up here. Gunnery?" Clayton asked.

"Each workstation is configured by the user," AJ said. "There are six more chairs like these in different parts of the ship. When you log into the chair, it functions based on your profile. Yes, you can have different profiles and switch between them. I could be gunner one minute, pilot the next, and even navigation after that."

"How in the world have you learned all this so quickly?"

"Very little sleep," AJ said. "I'll pay a price for the chemical modifications my symbiote is providing during this learning stage, but once we get into space, things slow down a whole lot."

"Between you and me, I don't suppose you can tell me where you dropped that combat armor I've read so much about," he said.

"Wouldn't tell you if I even knew," AJ said. "Have you figured out who leaked my name, yet?"

"It's probably good you don't trust me," he said. "We have no idea how we've been compromised."

"Back this way there are a few officer cabins," AJ said, leading Clayton from the bridge, aft. "And one of four heads."

"You're not even gonna give me a hint, are you?"

"State of the art galley and mess," AJ said. "Working with your quartermaster, we believe we can set in enough fresh supplies for two weeks at sail. We might decide to take a stopover and resupply. We won't make that decision until we're wheels-up."

"You're a paranoid son-of-a-gun."

"Okay General, cut the crap," AJ said. "What's going on? You're pumping me for information. You're either the devil or something's going down. Which is it?"

"You do know that's a fifty-fifty call on me attacking you, right? You're calling me out. We're alone," Clayton said.

"Trust me when I tell you I would be surprised if you pulled a knife," AJ said. "I've been expecting it. Is that what we're doing?"

"Does your symbiote manage your emotions? You're entirely too calm."

"No, that comes for free with my history," AJ said.

"We're expecting an attack," Clayton confided. "My job, really the job of every man and woman on this base, is to get your team out of here before that happens. We can take care of ourselves, but those men and women on Fimil Prime won't stand a chance if you aren't launched. Forty hours is too long of a window."

"How much time do I have?" AJ asked.

"Our best intelligence says twelve hours."

"Well, as long as intelligence says it, we should be fine," AJ said sarcastically. "General, I want to be in the air in five hours. Can I count on you for that?"

"Hooah, Jenkins. Let's get this old girl into space."

10

WONDERLAND

DEKE - EARTH

"Wonderland?" Deke asked, following Sergeant Leisk through the bank of metal doors into a large hangar.

"I've only read about it," Leisk said. "Wonderland isn't a bad description, though."

"I'm not following," Deke said, following the athletic sergeant across the cement floor with its yellow-painted boundaries, warning against wandering from the path.

"How familiar are you with *Alice in Wonderland*?" Leisk asked.

"Are you going to ask me to eat something so I can shrink?" Deke asked. "Because that's messed up if you are."

"I'm pretty sure we don't change size, but from my reading, it's not going to be obvious one way or another."

"You've got my attention, but I'm going to need more words."

"*Angry Ark* isn't on base," Leisk said. "Not by any reasonable definition at least."

"Where is it?"

"The Toc have hidden it for us."

"Toc is alien, right?"

"Sure is, Deke," Keegs said, popping up a few feet in front of her.

Wearing jeans and a white t-shirt, only his eight-inch height and the wings sticking out of his back, differentiated him from any other person. Deke watched as he bobbed up and down as the beat of his wings countered the pull of gravity.

"What's a Tok" she asked, recognizing that Leisk had stopped walking and was waiting for her to continue.

"We've been warned against the obvious comparisons," Leisk said. "Physically, they look like raccoons but they're uber intelligent, so insulting them is a big deal."

Keegs held out his hand, displaying a device that projected a holographic image. From Leisk's minimal description, Deke had no trouble recognizing the being. "Shit, that's a dead ringer for a coon. No wonder they've got a chip on their shoulder."

"Ma'am?" Leisk asked.

"Sorry, my dude is showing me stuff."

"That will take some getting used to," Leisk said.

"With your permission and additional equipment, you could allow the sergeant visual access with an improved communications device," Keegs said. "*Angry Ark's* manufactories can easily complete this task."

"If the queues are not overloaded, go ahead and get your visual doodad printed. I don't need my right-hand making mistakes because she can't figure out who I'm talking to."

"I will use my best judgment on which conversations to share."

"That's not what I said," Deke said gruffly. "Put her on all of it. We'll figure out later if there's stuff I don't want her hearing. Do you copy?"

"I copy," Keegs said, somewhat cowed.

"Now, don't be doing that either," Deke said. "I need you strong, Keegs. If I'm right, we're about to step in the shit. We got no time to be chasing feelings."

"Ma'am, you can count on my discretion," Leisk said.

"Good. Let's make sure you live up to that so I don't decide to go all lone wolf," Deke said. "Now that we've got that all worked out, does someone want to tell me why raccoons are sending us to Wonderland?"

"Sergeant, would you allow me?" Keegs asked, flitting over so that he sat on her shoulder.

"He's on me, isn't he?" Leisk asked, following Deke's eyes.

"Pretty much."

"It allows Captain Deke to have a single attention focus," Keegs said. "I appear as if I'm resting against your left ear. You will feel nothing."

"Words, Keegs," Deke demanded.

"Right. Some background would be helpful. The Tok are highly evolved, despite their resemblance to the small carnivore on Earth," Keegs said. "And by highly evolved, I am referring to their capacity for cognitive process. There is no known species with a deeper understanding of any branch of physics. Most significant technologies related to space travel were given to the members of the Galactic Empire by Tok. In some cases, these technologies were provided with education that allows capable sentients the ability to understand the underlying physics. In other cases, the technology is shielded so that the devices are usable but mysterious. The so-called Wonderland Device is one of the latter."

"Now we're getting somewhere. What's it do?" Deke asked as she and Leisk approached a rounded hatch that spanned a forty-foot diameter at its widest.

"To the best of our understanding, Tok have discovered a mechanism which creates an interdimensional link across folds of space. Although, it should be noted no current, provable physics support actual folds in space, time," Keegs said.

"That must drive you a little nuts," Deke said.

"I don't love it," Keegs said. "That such could exist invalidates much that has been proven by many revered scientists over a considerable period."

"So Beltigersk, not as smart as you'd like to think. Is that what I'm hearing?" Deke said. "You should keep that in mind while you're silently judging me."

"I don't judge you in the way you suggest," Keegs said. "Each species has a significant range of intelligence. I am not offended that Beltigersk are proven eighty-four percent less than intelligent Tok, on average."

"*On average,*" Deke said. "Let me guess. You're not average."

"Ma'am," Leisk interrupted, her voice slightly elevated.

Deke held up a finger as if suggesting that Keegs should quiet. The move brought a look of surprise to Leisk's face, to which Deke responded with a subtle shake of her head. "No universe has me ignoring my sergeant with that tone. That's how lieutenants find the wrong end of sniper bullets. What's up?"

"There is a limited time in which to enter the transition terminus. Perhaps we could discuss physics once we've passed through."

"A fine suggestion. Lead the way," Deke responded. "Besides, it sounds like we need a Tok to accurately describe the physics."

The painted path they'd followed had led them to the opposite side of the hangar where a single guard stood, casually awaiting their arrival.

"Ma'am, you're cleared for Wonderland access," he said, holding a ruggedized computer tablet in front of him. "Sergeant Leisk, I'll need your DNA scan."

Without hesitation, Leisk stepped forward and placed her palm on the device. A light gray negative of her hand appeared on the screen and then blinked green. It was apparently what the soldier was waiting for because he nodded approval as he tapped on the device.

The sounds of heavy machinery hidden behind the hangar's wall alerted the small group and when a thirty-foot section square of that wall started to move, both Leisk and Deke took an involuntary step back.

"Safe travels, Captain," the soldier said, stepping aside as the door stopped moving, only having opened a few feet.

The hallway was as wide as the large door but only twenty feet deep. On the right was a glass panel that looked into a narrow room that ran half that length. Inside the small room sat a bored looking figure who could have been human if not for the fact that its nose was the shape of a small elephant's trunk which hung almost to its chin.

"That nose. Is that a Fimil?" Deke asked, not bothering to hide her surprise.

"Yes," the Fimil answered before Keegs could. "And it doesn't like to be talked about. There weren't supposed to be any transfers this morning. Let's get this going with as little chatter as possible. Can we do that, please?"

Deke tried to grin, but the motion was largely lost, aside from managing a ghastly grimace. There was something reassuring about a bored alien. "We're on your time schedule," she said.

"Not really," the Fimil answered. "I just need you to get across that white line so I can get back to my breakfast."

Deke followed the Fimil's glance. While she'd been focused on the Fimil, the hallway had somehow, without any sort of fanfare, lengthened. A broad white line that ran from right to left was exposed. Beyond the white line was a fifteen-foot room ending in an oversized reinforced steel door.

"Breakfast?" Deke asked. As she inspected the room where the Fimil sat, she noticed a door on the same wall as the large door from where she'd just entered. Impossibly, the door seemed to open to what looked like a garden space. "Where...?"

"Deke, the Fimil is using the Tok technology we've discussed. He is likely on his home planet and has been given responsibility for managing the Wonderland portal to *Angry Ark*," Keegs explained.

"Oh, shit," Deke said as understanding washed over her. "You're not from around here, are you?"

This earned her a scornful look from the Fimil, who tapped his trunk-shaped nose. "Are you sure you're our best hope of standing up to Quarr on Prime? I have to admit, I'm not seeing it."

"Right. Words of wisdom from Dumbo," Deke said, shaking her head. Confusion washed over the Fimil's face, but Deke had already turned, with Leisk one step behind.

Crossing the line, Deke's ears popped. The temperature dropped enough that the skin on her emaciated arms dimpled with tiny goosebumps.

"Not in Kansas anymore," Leisk whispered to herself.

"Got that right, sister," Deke said, striding to the wall where a security pad awaited. Recognizing the model, she bent so the retinal scanner had direct view. She was rewarded with a flashing red screen.

"One moment," Keegs said. "Your new scans have not been uploaded. I'll make necessary adjustments. Try again."

Deke did and to her surprise, the screen flashed green. "I'm not sure what I'm disturbed by more. Either you just uploaded new retinal scans to a highly secured system, giving me access, or you changed the vascular pattern of my retina. Either way, this system is junk now."

The door slid sideways with a crisp whoosh of air. Despite being ready for unusual situations, Deke drew in a quick breath. The doorway opened onto another hallway that ran to the left and right of where she'd entered. On the wall opposite the doorway, were long windows that ran from about waist height to the eight-foot mark with a ceiling another two feet above that. What had caught Deke's attention, however, is what the windows looked out on.

"*Angry Ark* isn't on Earth," Deke said, awe evident in her voice. "We're already in deep space."

"And we're sailing," Leisk whispered. "Not a fixed point ... that's impossible."

"That is a significant observation," Keegs said, glancing at Leisk. "Very interesting."

Deke couldn't help but cross the industrial carpeted hallway to stand next to the windows, giving her an expansive view of the stars as they moved by. "Where are we? Do you recognize these stars?"

"Yes. We're in the Thamhut Sector of the Galactic Empire. If you're not familiar with this reference, it is the sector shared by Pertaf, Fimil Prime, and Fimil Second, often called Fimil Two. I believe that to be a grammatical error by a translation."

"We're headed for Fimil Second or Prime?" Deke asked, staring out at the stars. "And isn't it dangerous to try to hide our ship so close to a warzone? Why wouldn't we just set up one of those transport thingies right where we want to go?"

"All valid questions," Keegs said, patiently.

"Ma'am, perhaps we could walk and talk?" Leisk urged.

"Do you know where we're going?"

"I do."

"Lead on," Deke said. "Go ahead, Keegs."

"The war to come will be fought on Fimil Prime," he said. "This is where the Fimilent species first evolved. But due to limited, easily accessible natural resources and an unexpected exposure to a somewhat benevolent Xandarj benefactor, the species moved to Fimil Second at an evolutionary stage similar to humankind's bronze age."

"That's quite a jump," Deke said, stopping as Leisk pulled up short. "What's up, Leisk?"

"Your quarters, Ma'am," Leisk said, turning to give Deke access to the entry hatch of a door on the interior wall.

Twisting the handle, Deke unlatched the door and slid it to the side. The space was roomier than she'd expected. To her immediate left, or aft if the direction of the stars travel was consistent with moving forward, was a private head. Entering, she found a round table bolted to the deck. The table was surrounded by four utilitarian chairs and sat next to a small desk built into the aft wall. Finally, a narrow bed sat against the wall furthest to port. At the foot of the bed was a wardrobe.

They'd barely had a chance to inspect the room when a knock at the door drew their attention.

"Yes?" she asked, turning to find a private holding a tall container.

"I was told to bring this to you," the private said, averting his eyes and uncomfortably holding the slurry away from his body.

"I've got it, Captain," Leisk said, taking the vessel from the man and turning him from the room with her other hand. Once he was free of the door, she closed it.

"I guess I'm kind of scary, huh?" Deke asked.

"You have a reputation, Ma'am," Leisk said. "The whole skeletor impersonation is adding to that. Would you consider a short rest?"

"I can keep going," Deke said.

"My briefing said that you are more efficient at absorbing the necessary material from the shakes if you are inactive for at least one hundred twenty minutes," Leisk said. "I will, of course, support you in every endeavor."

Deke attempted a smile, which was once again lost on her nearly featureless jaw. "Very smooth. You're good with people, aren't you? That's why Major Baines assigned you to me, isn't it?"

"I don't like stupid any more than you do," Leisk said. "But you are correct. I am an effective communicator. I worked under Major Baines' command and was successful."

"I'm going to be a pain in your ass. I don't mind pissing people off. You're going to be cleaning up a lot," Deke observed. And despite not wanting to, she allowed Leisk to guide her to the bed. "I suppose a quick nap isn't unreasonable."

"Gera Leisk is correct," Keegs added. "I will be eighty-two percent more efficient in my work if you are not moving."

"The two of you will be my end," Deke said, tipping the bottle to her mouth. At first the substance tasted chalky, but as soon as the thick slurry made it to her stomach, she realized how hungry she'd been. "So, while I'm down, you guys work together to find me a place to work out. I'm not going to keep sitting around."

"Aye, aye, Captain," Leisk said. "I'll give you your privacy. My quarters are forward three doors from your own, but I will know if you are moving and will join you once you do."

"We're going to need to talk about all this," Deke said.

"Of course, Ma'am."

"Don't patronize ...," Deke started but before she could finish, she faded off to sleep.

～

"Ma'am, it's time to wake," Leisk's voice wasn't initially recognizable, but Deke understood that voice had been trying to wake her up for some time.

"How long was I down?" Deke asked, struggling to sit up.

As was usual between rest periods, Deke's body was sore, and she felt little respite from the downtime.

"Three hours fifty-two minutes," Keegs answered, coming to sit on Leisk's shoulder. This time, however, as he did, the sergeant glanced nervously in his direction.

"We agreed on two hours, Sergeant," Deke said, irritation creeping into her voice. "Did we not?"

"Yes," Leisk said. "I was unable to rouse you."

Deke's eyes flitted to Keegs, irritation threatening to turn to anger. "I can't have you overriding my orders," she said, biting each word off as she said it. As her mouth moved, she realized that the pull of the skin was significantly different and further realization hit her. Sound was being produced in her throat.

"Your schedule was clear and there are critical changes to Operation Black Turtle," Keegs said. "I took a calculated risk that the rewards outweighed your likely irritation."

"What in the hell?" she asked, unable to focus on Keegs' response due to significant changes in the feeling of her mouth and cheeks. When her hand touched her cheeks, she was doubly startled. The skin beneath her fingers felt almost natural, if a little thin. Without thinking she sat up and stepped from the bed, making her way to the head. Even the air passing her face felt foreign.

"I feel we made good progress," Keegs said, as Deke inspected her face.

Gone was the thinly covered artificial jaw and exposed mouth. In place was fresh, pink skin that was almost translucent due to how thin it was. Her face, while not a perfect match to what she'd looked like before was recognizable. Opening her mouth, she stuck out her tongue and tipped back her head, peering into the depths.

Almost as a second thought, she noticed the hand she'd reached up with to feel her cheeks had received similar changes. No longer were the bones and ligaments apparent beneath a scant covering, newly developed muscle tissue now fleshed her hands and arms.

"Oh, hell yes," she said, her new voice rough. She coughed, recognizing a buildup of junk in her throat.

"If you were to drink five-hundred milliliters of water, it would be quite helpful at this moment," Keegs said.

"Say that in American," Deke said.

"A glass of water. Two would be better," Keegs said.

"Was that so hard?" she asked.

"Antiquated. Imperial measurements are quite arbitrary," he said. "Why, did you know that a yard is the measurement of one of Earth's old kings?"

"Hmm?" Deke asked, moving her head from one side to the other. "How many more of those drinks am I going to need to start getting some real definition in these bad boys?" To accentuate her question, she flexed her thin arms with little result. "I mean, I like what you've done, but this is pathetic."

"I ran short of necessary material and time to continue rebuilding the muscular fiber," Keegs said. "Even so, significant progress has been made. Your *super* gene is quite unlike anything I've experienced or even read about. No human-Beltigersk combination has ever recorded bone, tissue or nerve growth like you've experienced. It seems that the more that is accomplished, the faster the work moves."

"That'd be helpful. So, what, I need another shake?" she asked.

"Perhaps you should pay attention to other bodily needs as you currently are near a sanitary facility," he said.

The moment the words were out of his mouth, the need struck her. "Damn, where did that come from?" she asked, taking care of business.

"I delayed the signals and have been keeping things in control," Keegs said.

"That was surprisingly non-specific," Deke said, sighing in relief. "Thank you."

"Deke, we need to talk about the changes to Operation Black Turtle," Leisk said.

"Ooh, this must be bad, you're using my first name without me prompting," Deke said.

"Zebra company will arrive in four hours."

"What in the hell? Why does it keep moving up?"

"A large expeditionary force is landing on Fimil Prime's surface," Leisk said. "While they have not discovered the base building materials the Army dropped over the last months, Colonel Corcoran is getting itchy. Or at least that's my read of the change to Zebra's deployment and the order you just received to, and I quote, 'Get your ass to the war room, God damn it.'"

"Help me into my fatigues."

11

SCORCHED EARTH
AJ - EARTH

"Mr. Jenkins, I need your signature on this form!"

The HR specialist had to run to keep up with AJ as he charged between fast-moving forklifts racing up *Wasp's* aft loading ramp.

"Or what, Blanche?" AJ asked. "I don't even know what I'm signing. Trust me, when it comes to the Army, I've learned that's bad approach."

"You won't get paid or have insurance if you don't," the woman explained, exasperated.

"Let's pretend I don't care about those things."

"General Clayton does."

AJ stopped, not because he cared about the general's feelings but because the woman was in the way of the mad press to load supplies. As gently as possible, he guided her to the side and waved the forklift driver on.

"Tell me what this is," AJ said, accepting an electronic notebook.

"The first document is a non-disclosure agreement. You're agreeing not to share mission details or intelligence with anyone not sufficiently cleared," she said.

"Is my entire team cleared?"

The woman looked uncomfortable. "No. Bernard Johnson and James Barnes will not sign our employment agreements. I've talked to the general. We'll need to replace them."

"Gotcha," AJ said, gesturing forward with his head. "Follow me." She followed, he continued. "Did the general have a funny look in his face when you talked?"

"I don't understand."

"What do you know about special forces teams?"

"I exclusively work with special forces team members in transition," she answered.

"Keep up," AJ urged, turning sideways each time he ran into someone in the hallway. "Here's what you're not seeing. A team is like a body. Think of it this way. Lefty is my right arm, James is my right leg. Without them, I can't walk and I can't shoot a weapon. I've trained with these men since before you were born. I will not replace them because the general wants me to sign a piece of paper."

"It's an electronic signature," she offered unhelpfully.

"What else do you have for me to sign?" He turned and continued forward to the cockpit where he found Darnell and Lisa talking with some animation with an airman.

"What's your status, Big D?" AJ interrupted. "Thirty-two minutes. Are you going to make it?"

"We'll be ready," he said, which brought a look of incredulity to the airman's face.

"Captain Jenkins, this man is not ready to fly this craft. *USS Wasp* is an experimental vessel with hundreds, if not thousands of untested systems."

AJ winced at hearing his new rank. He'd always thought of himself as enlisted. Intellectually, he understood why it could be no other way, but it grated on him, nonetheless.

"Airman, do you want to take the chair? Is that what I'm hearing?" AJ asked.

"Of course I do. This is the greatest mission in the history of humanity."

"Ask a dumb question," AJ said, not quite under his breath. "Let me ask a different way. What makes you more expert than my man, Darnell, at flying this beast into combat?"

"I have over four thousand flight hours and have flown every piece of equipment in the Army's repertoire."

"BB, does that check out?" AJ asked.

Beverly appeared on the console wearing one of her favorite outfits, coveralls and a polka dot scarf around her hair so she resembled Rosie the Riveter. "Peter Ignatius Roberts is a highly decorated pilot with considerable combat experience. His reviews show a disdain for authority, which is why he has not progressed rank more quickly. His call sign is Pig."

"I suppose that wasn't a hard call," AJ said.

"Pardon?" Roberts asked.

"Sorry, talking to the voices in my head," AJ said. "Big D, what do you think?"

"Pig's an asshole," he said. "He'd probably survive."

"What? You can't talk about me like that," Roberts objected.

AJ held up his hand. "Quiet. Adults are talking."

"He knows the ship."

"Pig, is it?" AJ asked. The man nodded, although his face was full of confusion. "You have twenty minutes to grab your gear. Just so we're clear, Big D owns this ship. Make this a tussle for control and you'll sit out the mission in a very small bunkroom."

"I ... I'm not ..."

"You said greatest mission," AJ said.

When Roberts didn't move, Lisa took pity. "Peter, you need to move. AJ is leaving with or without you. He won't ask again, so make good choices."

That seemed to do the trick and Roberts jumped from his seat, dropping the clipboard he had on his lap. With a worried glance at the mess he'd created, he turned and ran from the cockpit.

"Lisa, where are we with that intel the general's team has been tracking?" AJ asked.

"I'm sorry, hon," Lisa said, placing a gentle hand on the HR specialist's back to guide her from the cockpit. "You can talk in a minute."

"I'm not sure how to get rid of her," AJ said after closing the door.

"A couple of signatures would do it."

"Can't. Lefty and Rock won't sign. I can't share intel with them if I sign."

"Don't sign, then," Lisa said.

"Right," AJ agreed, long since finished with the conversation. "Intel."

"Baird's team is blind. We all agree that means an attack is imminent," she said. As if her words were prophecy, the ship shook enough that AJ had to grab a bulkhead to steady himself. A moment later, the sounds of explosions filtered into the cockpit.

"Crap," AJ said. "Darnell, get this tub ready to fly. BB, get hold of Roberts and get him to return. We'll have to find him personal effects."

"Aye, aye, Captain," Darnell answered.

"Alpha Two, I need a perimeter." AJ banged open the cockpit door and ran into the poor HR specialist who looked as far out of place as she could be. "Are we missing anyone? This thing is going down, now."

"We heard it, One," Lefty answered. "Rock is out. He's on his way."

"This is for the money, Lefty," AJ said. "If there's a bad egg, this will be the time they make their move. Lethal force is authorized."

"Copy that, One."

AJ disentangled himself from the HR specialist and guided her aft.

"Jayne, where are you?"

"In medical," she answered. "Was that an explosion?"

"Attack on the base has started," AJ said. "Secure your area, this could get bumpy."

"I hear you."

"What's happening," the woman he was guiding asked. "Did you say attack?"

AJ stopped the panicking woman and turned to her, exuding a forceful calm. "Yes. The base is under attack. You've been taught a protocol and you need to follow it now. The most important thing you can do is get as far away from this ship as possible."

"What about signatures?"

"That part of the conversation is over. Right now, our priority is to keep you alive and get my team launched. The best way to do that is to have you exit the ship and follow your protocol. Do you know where you're supposed to go?"

"I ... yes."

"Good," AJ said, grabbing her electronic notebook. "Tell you what. I'll make this easier for you." He tapped and signed the first five prompts that came up and handed it back to her. "That'll have to be enough."

He opened the starboard hatch and verified a ramp was in place. The specialist tentatively stepped out and then turned back to him. "What you're doing is important."

"It's only important if good people like you stay alive," AJ said. "Now, go!"

Gunfire erupted on the tarmac next to the hangar's opening. AJ received a warning in the form of flashing red lights an instant earlier. The lights were provided by Beverly, who indicated the direction of safety as away from the lights. He had already ducked into *Wasp* when 7.62mm rounds peppered the heavily armored fuselage. If not for the warning, he'd have been cut down. The woman he'd been talking to only moments before, was not so lucky.

"Shit!" Lisa's voice filled comms. "Multiple shooters, two o-clock."

The whirring of ship-mounted machine guns filled the air and *Wasp's* venomous response was immediate.

"Dammit!" AJ grumbled. He crawled to the stairs where he grabbed the specialist's shirt and dragged her limp body into *Wasp*. "Jayne, I've got wounded in the starboard hatch."

"Coming!"

"Hang in there, kid," AJ said, pressing his hands against the most accessible wounds. "Help is on the way."

A moment later, Jayne appeared and dropped a bag of supplies. She sank to her knees. "Shit, this is bad, AJ."

"You've got this, Doc."

The pair worked together as they attempted to save the life of the young administrator.

"I need her back in medical," Jayne finally said, yanking a hard board litter from its storage position on the bulkhead.

"Jayne, we're about to dust off," AJ said. "We can't."

"Not your call. She's gonna die if I don't get in there and I'm not doing that on this deck."

That was all he needed to hear.

The medical bay was small, barely large enough for the stainless-steel table centered in the room and cabinets encircling on the walls. With decades of practice, Jayne cut away the woman's clothing and catalogued the wounds. With a clear picture of a course of action she got to work.

"You can go," she said. "I've got this."

"She's probably coming with us."

"Seems like it," Jayne acknowledged.

"Two, what's your sitrep?" AJ asked.

"A small group sitting outside the hangar. They must have air cover. It's currently a stalemate," Lefty answered almost immediately.

"Have Peppers get a bird up."

"We've already lost two. They're using anti-drone tech. We're not even getting a peek."

The news was bad. Pepper's drones weren't Earth technology. Any technology that could eliminate them from the battlespace was sophisticated, even for the highly advanced alien species common to the Galactic Empire.

"Baird, where the hell is the Air Force? We're under attack." AJ wasn't certain his comm would make it to her right away and he raced forward, knowing the cockpit's view would be his best.

"Our on-prem F-35s were compromised. We have an inbound squadron. Three minutes," she said. "Imagery shows a big ship moving in. We're thinking bomber. You need to clear out."

"Blind?"

"Yes."

"Two, get everybody loaded. If it's not onboard in three minutes, it's staying home," AJ said.

"That's a wrap, boys!" Lefty called. "Three, bring 'em in!"

While he'd been talking, AJ had been making his way forward. Without so much as a word, he sat at the workstation next to Lisa and re-familiarized himself with the combat controls. "I'm taking starboard and belly 30mms," he announced, tapping the weapons to assign them to his control surface.

"I'll keep eyebrow and portside," Lisa agreed. "What's the plan?"

"Once we poke our nose out, we shoot anything pointing our way," AJ said. "We have F-35s inbound. We'll have to rely on BB to flag friendlies."

"Good copy, AJ," Lisa answered.

"Two, we're Oscar Mike in thirty," AJ announced. "Big D, I need you to hit that door with as much anger as this thing can muster. They're gonna bring hard rain our way."

"Aye, aye," Darnell answered. "Dropping short runway hooks."

The sound of metallic clamps falling from far aft made it all the way to the cockpit while *Wasp's* powerful engines started spooling.

"What the hell are you doing?" The voice belonged to Pig Roberts. "You can't load up that hard. You'll bend the superstructure!"

"Pig, sit your ass down, shut your mouth, and take the eyebrow mini," AJ growled. "And welcome back."

"Aww, hell," Roberts grumbled. He jumped into the open chair and strapped in.

"One, I'm taking portside mini," Rock announced, obviously having taken control from Fire Control.

"Good copy, Four," AJ said.

USS Wasp shuddered under the contradiction of heavy metal hooks holding its frame in place while powerful engines sought to propel it forward, even while setting fire to the equipment that'd been left behind, aft of the ship.

"Give me a go," Darnell said. "Those hooks aren't going to hold for long."

"Hold on, team. Hit it, Big D," AJ ordered.

Wasp shuddered as the line connected to the hooks released. It was almost as if the vessel disbelieved its freedom. The ship lurched forward, struggling against gravity's grip.

"Contact starboard!" Lisa announced at the same moment her 30mm turret burped deadly fire and *Wasp's* nose slid out from the cover of the hangar.

Chaos erupted as a pair of warships hovering only a thousand yards off the deck pounded deadly payloads into *Wasp's* nose. Emergency lights illuminated forward displays as systems reported damage.

"Too much of a beating starboard. Darnell, can you protect forward starboard?" AJ said.

"Hold onto your lunch," was Darnell's only response. *Wasp* rolled in place as the nose lifted from the tarmac.

It was as if the tone of a locked missile system washed over AJ's subconscious when one of the enemy ships wandered into his sight picture. He bore down on the triggering mechanism, handing out deadly consequences.

"Birds are dropping," Darnell announced, tipping *Wasp* over from the vertical trajectory he'd chosen. His words, while not significant to everyone aboard were chosen to warn his team that bombs had been dropped. "Everybody find something to grab! We won't escape the blast radius."

If there was a single positive to the announcement, it was that the ships pummeling *Wasp* from above had realized their own mortality and cut off the attack to make their own run. "Dammit, Darnell, catch one of those bastards," AJ said.

"Aye, aye, Captain. I like where your head's at," Darnell said, banking slowly as he poured on acceleration.

"I have a clean lock on missile one," Rock announced.

"Go!" AJ agreed.

The missile was no more away than the ground beneath them roiled as if the base had been built atop a steaming pot of oatmeal about to boil over. The shockwaves came next, tossing *Wasp* forward and playing havoc with instrumentation. Finally, an expanding fireball erupted from the impact sites and chased the fleeing ships as if with vendetta.

"We have engine flame-out on one and two," AJ said as calmly as he could manage.

"Good copy," Darnell said. "Engineering, we need restart on engines one and two." If you didn't know better, one might have thought he was asking for a minor adjustment as opposed to saving their craft from falling back to the earth.

"Confirmation on missile strike," Rock added. "Bogey Two is splashed down."

"Bridge, we have engine restart on one," came the calm voice of Brian Joyce. "Two is stubborn. We're working the problem."

"Good copy, engineering," Darnell answered easily. "That should keep us up for the moment. We might grab that bomber if you can get me a working number two."

AJ stared out the window at the bedlam that had erupted around them. Nothing was recognizable and he wondered if any part of the base had survived. Was General Clayton even alive? Had they saved the HR specialist simply because she'd been hit in the opening moments? Or was she dead on Jayne's table?

"Number two is a go, Bridge," Joyce offered. "We're working on starboard control surfaces. Looks like there's been slagging over the ventricle armor. We might be able to free them. Be advised."

"Good copy," Darnell said. "Fire Control, I'm turning on the bomber."

Banking in the smoke, Darnell sent *Wasp* toward the large ship that was beating a hasty retreat from its mission. As the giant mushroom of smoke, ash, and debris lifted, AJ got his first, albeit limited view of where the base had once been. If not for Beverly sketching a wireframe over the ground, he wouldn't have identified the base's location.

"It's gone," Lisa said, her voice still with wonder and regret. "They killed all those people ... just to get to us."

Bright flashing dots showed on AJ's tactical screen. "Fire Control, be advised, I have sensor contact with the Air Force fighter wing. They're coming in at eight-six degrees to starboard and moving at approximately Mach Three. These aircraft are friendly. I repeat, do not fire on the approaching aircraft."

"That's a good copy, Bridge," Rock answered. "Negatory on shooting down the taxi service."

"Oh hell, look at them go," Darnell said as the jets split apart into two pairs of fighters, each taking a target.

The alien craft, while technologically superior in most ways, lacked the dogged simplicity and focus of purpose given to the fighter jets. With flight time limited to minutes instead of days the jets burned fuel at rates no long-range craft could consider. And with airfoils designed to take advantage of Earth's atmosphere without care for travel in the vacuum of space, the jets were perfect for their task.

Missiles streaked from beneath each of the F-35s as they gained positive confirmation of certain hits. Having already been on the tail of the large bomber, the bridge crew of *Wasp* had first row seats to the terrifyingly destructive force of jets.

"There's no hell too hot," Lisa growled under her breath. "I hope they suffered."

AJ sat back in his seat and started reviewing the countless warnings that had popped to his screen but found he couldn't make much sense of them. Like everyone, he had trouble moving past the realization of the base's destruction and the people who'd lived there.

"Engineering, please assess damage and let me know how we're looking for extra-atmospheric operation," AJ called.

"We're working on it, Captain," Joyce answered. "We took considerable damage and are working to bring redundant systems online."

"Understood. Can we pressurize?" AJ asked.

"Wait one," came the reply.

"Darnell, how are flight controls?"

"She seems solid."

"Two, I need a head count and injury report," AJ called.

"No injuries," Lefty answered. "I've got Peppers headed to Medical to check on the doc."

"You can call him off. I'm headed back there," AJ said.

"Good copy."

"What's the call, boss?" Darnell asked.

"Once we verify pressure, we'll proceed to Alpha Point."

"Copy that."

"Fire Control, you have all weapons," AJ said. "I repeat, you have all weapons. Bridge is standing down."

"Aye, aye, Captain," Rock answered. "Weapons transferred to Fire Control."

"What's going on, AJ?" Lisa asked, glassy-eyed.

"Amanda is going to need your help. That HR Assistant got tagged in the opening salvo. Doc's been trying to do surgery in the middle of dog fight. She's going to need help."

"Crap," Lisa said. "I'm coming."

The pair made their way through the hallway, difficult given *Wasp's* current climb. It occurred to AJ halfway there that it didn't need to be quite so difficult.

"Engineering, do we have enough to engage the positive gravity systems?"

"Wait one."

A moment later, AJ struggled to keep standing as the gravity was warped aboard *Wasp*, switching from the angle of the ship relative to Earth to perpendicular to the ship's belly. With solid footing, they continued back toward Medical.

"My apologies, Captain," Joyce said. "That's not a system I'm used to working with."

"You're doing fine, Mr. Joyce. Keep up the good work."

Knocking first, AJ slowly slid open the door. Inside, he found Jayne still working on the woman. "Are we done with all the nonsense?" She was furious. "I'm trying to save a woman's life here."

"We'll be steady for a few hours," AJ said calmly. "How's she doing?"

"Not good, but she's got a chance," Jayne said. "What's going on? You sound like there's trouble. I can't look up. Talk to me."

"They destroyed the base, Jayne," AJ said. "Killed everyone. That woman, I don't even know her name, but if she hadn't been shot, she'd be dead, now. Please say you can save her."

"Dammit. Lisa, scrub up. I need your hands."

"I'm in."

"We've got this AJ," Jayne said. "Do what needs to be done."

12

BLACK TURTLE
DEKE – DEEP SPACE

"Damn Dekoster, you are unrecognizable," Colonel Corcoran said.

With Keegs' ability to display GPS styled arrows atop Deke's vision, she'd had no trouble winding her way through *Angry Ark's* hallways at her top speed, which while significantly improved from even six hours previous, wasn't spectacular.

"Things are improving, sir. Thank you." She looked around the table filled with officers, many junior to herself. When her eyes fell on the captain's bars on Thad Kersey's shoulder, irritation flooded her. That he managed a friendly, almost congenial smile of recognition was a step too far. "What the actual fuck?" she growled.

"Pardon?" Kersey asked.

"Can it, Dekoster," Major Baines said, catching the exchange. "You're late and we're on a schedule, so sit your ass down."

Fortunately, a seat was open between a heavily muscled man and a narrow woman who Deke figured for a runner, given the low body fat evident in her face and exposed forearms.

"Captain," the woman said, acknowledging Deke. She pulled the chair back to make room for her. A floating title appeared over the woman's head reading *Lieutenant Carrole, Zebra Company*.

"Thank you, Lieutenant," Deke said. As she sat, she offered her hand and nodded once, letting Carrole know she was recognized.

"To catch Dekoster up, Black Turtle will commence upon our arrival at Fimil Prime in seventy-two hours." Major Baines said. He waved his hand at the middle of the table.

A smokey, pixilated holographic globe emerged from the center where light shined up into wispy fog. The wispy fog and pixilation disappeared as the image solidified. Without conscious thought, Deke focused on the planet and zoomed in. She discovered an almost unending amount of detail available and almost missed Baines' next statements.

"As of 1130 Zulu, three heavy-lift, intra-stellar craft arrived and took orbital positions around Fimil Prime," Baines explained. "At 13:40 these craft commenced dropping payloads to six locations. This operation was completed at 16:50, two hours ago."

"We need to hit them, now," Deke said, "while they're vulnerable."

"I appreciate your zeal as much as I do the special circumstances as to why you don't know how uninformed your position in this matter is," Baines said. "Simply put, that's not possible."

Deke snapped her jaw closed at the man's words. She'd been put in her place, and it was her own fault. She had no information and deserved the brushback.

"Given *Angry Ark's* estimated payload and engine configuration, it will require seventy-six hours at maximum acceleration to achieve a stable orbit around Fimil Prime," Keegs informed.

"What sort of offensive capabilities do the enemy drop ships appear to have?" Deke asked, using her mouth to form the words but not allowing air to pass her vocal cords. She'd been forced to learn the technique during her recuperation period.

"There is an assumption that the drop ships have cannons, either particle or energy based, although with large vessels it is typically energy based as the weight of batteries is not a significant consideration," Keegs explained.

"How about fighters?"

"A moment, Deke," Keegs said. "Baines is engaging you. He wants to know if you have a training schedule that requires access to the main hold? I suggest that you consider utilizing the time slot from 0500 to 0800 and between 1200 and 1600 each day. That will give you time to meet with your lieutenants between 0800 and 1200."

"I request 0500 to 0800," she said, making eye contact with Baines.

A flicker of surprise crossed his face. He hadn't expected her to know what had been asked.

"0500?" Kersey asked. "Your team will be dead. They're loading two hours before that."

"We're headed to war," she snapped. "Plenty of time to sleep when we're dead. Which is what we'll be if we don't get our teams ready."

"I feel that's reckless."

"Well, as long as we're in touch with our feelings," Deke said. "Is 0500 a problem, Major?"

"Negative, Captain. I'll clear the decks. Connect with Sergeant Haskell if you need a special setup," Baines said. "Deke, do you have information that the rest of us might find useful? I assume you're working with your symbiote to catch up in this meeting."

"I call him Keegs," Deke said. "I'm not sure what is common knowledge at the table. I'm trying to determine what sort of space superiority the drop ships deployed. I didn't get an answer yet."

"That's a good question," Baines said. "Our long-range scans haven't picked up fighter craft. What else are you asking this Keegs?"

"I'm interested in the makeup of our base, its location with respect to the six enemy drop sites, and if we have any sort of information on ground or air-based movement," Deke said. "Basically, I want to know if we're in the shit from the get-go or if we're going to be making house calls. I assume Zebra Company will be tasked with tip-of-the-spear operations."

"Fuck no," Kersey said. "That's my job."

"In a pig's eye," Deke returned.

"Knock it off, dammit," Baines said. "We're a team, and we're going to all live or die based on how effective we operate together. Whatever crap is between you two, figure it out. As to force deployments, our first job will be to secure our base while the Seabees build our new home."

"So will our enemy," Deke said. "We need to test them before they're fully settled. Let me take a small team at a minimum. We can do a drive-by. I guarantee they'll be testing us."

"We have three days," Baines said. "I'm not saying no. Our job is to terminate our enemies with extreme prejudice, so I like where your head is. Bring a plan to our 1800 meeting and I'll look at it."

"Copy that, Major," Deke answered.

"I'll prepare a plan, too," Kersey said.

"Fine," Baines said. "We'll have exactly one chance to make a supply call that could be dropped. The cost of Wonderland is high and the Tok feel exposed. Thad, you've taken lead on *Angry Ark's* loadout. Can you walk us through what we'll have given our updated departure?"

"Of course, Major."

"Can I ignore this idiot?" Deke silently intoned to Keegs.

"Yes," Keegs said.

"Tell me about my lieutenants."

"To your right is Samuel Alan Bing. Born in Brooklyn, New York to a family who immigrated from Honduras. He started working for his father's landscaping company formally when he was fourteen, although I believe I've found evidence that suggests he was engaged in significant manual labor from a much younger age."

"Why are you telling me this?"

"Humans, as most intelligent species with hundred-year life spans, have a formative period at the beginning of their lives. Samuel, or Bing as most call him, is a strong proponent of working hard. He does not expect things to come easily, to use human vernacular. Knowing this should change how you interact with him."

"Seriously?" Deke asked.

"Oh yes. Lieutenant Bing is much more likely to choose a strategy of direct confrontation and protracted battle," Keegs said. "He is less likely to look for extraordinary circumstances from which to take advantage."

"Because he pushed a lawn mower?"

"Could we agree that you will make your own observations and then compare those to the information I provide?" Keegs asked. "This interaction will be more efficient than a full discussion on psychological matters which impact human behaviors."

"That was almost condescending, but in a cool, I'm not gonna tell you you're stupid way," Deke said. "You're walking a fine line. I like it."

"I apologize. I was warned that learning to successfully communicate with my host would require significant effort on both our parts. I am working to come to an understanding," Keegs answered. "Kersey has noticed your inattention and is preparing to ask you a question regarding your troop strengths and requirements for the advanced

M52 heavy assault rifles. I propose that you will need sixty of the one hundred thirty that were loaded. Kersey reported only ninety were loaded but failed to consider the final delivery that will occur when the troops are onboarded."

Deke defocused on her HUD and turned to Kersey just as he was finishing his question. A smug look of satisfaction creased his face as he anticipated her inability to respond. "Any thoughts, Captain?" he asked.

"Without a chance to meet with Lieutenants Bing and Carrole, I believe we'll need sixty of the advanced M52s," Deke started, which caused Kersey to splutter. Deke held up her hand to hold the focus on her. "I imagine you're about to object given the counts you just reported, but I believe Zebra Company will carry forty of these weapons aboard when they load in a few hours. So from the armory, we'll need an additional twenty of these weapons. Does this meet with your expectations?"

"Uh, well, ... forty you say?"

"We'll do a count at 0500. Lieutenant Bing, would you see to reporting actual numbers to the armory at the end of our first training this morning?"

"Copy that, Captain Dekoster."

"What else are you short on, Captain?" Baines asked, his tone having shifted from irritation to business-at-hand.

"I'm not aware of anything at this moment," Kersey said.

"I was talking to Captain Dekoster."

"Major, how about when the door is closed you all refer to me as Deke," Deke said. "This will go a whole lot faster if we can avoid confusion."

"Agreed," Baines said.

"We're short on Strykers," Deke said. "Three for all of Zebra Company is ridiculous, unless you really expect us to go into turtle mode. I can barely move two squads with that and you know those things are in the shop as often as they're active."

"That's a bit of an exaggeration," Baines said.

"Maybe you don't appreciate the logistics of moving material to an entirely different star system," Kersey added, which earned him dirty looks from both Deke and Baines.

"I'll deal with it. You asked a question. I gave an answer."

"Fair enough," Baines agreed. "Sergeant Haskell, it is time to demonstrate the features of *Angry Ark*. While he readies this demonstration, you are all warned that what you're about to see is of utmost secrecy."

"This should be good," Deke said silently.

"*Angry Ark* is more than a heavy lift and delivery vehicle." Colonel Corcoran stood from the corner of the room where he'd observed the meeting without comment or obvious interest. "Each member of the team has been carefully vetted for the psychological impact of what you're about to learn and its implications for each man and woman in our fighting force."

The announcement had the intended impact of riveting the attention of everyone in the room to the slowly sinking globe of Fimil Prime. A red outline around a small patch of land in the foothills on the western slope of a mountain range steadily grew in size. Above the outlined section the words *Fort Indominable* floated. To Deke's eyes it wasn't much of a fort, given it was simply a flat section of land with mountains on one side and plains on the other.

Angry Ark appeared in the hologram and slowed to an orbital position. What she wasn't expecting, and by the gasps, no one else did either, was that *Angry Ark* didn't stop at orbit, but continued to sink into the atmosphere, causing all manner of smoke and flame to roil around the bottom of the vessel.

"That's insane. We're way too heavy to land," Kersey muttered. For the first time in recent history that Deke could remember, she agreed completely with him.

Unable to pull their eyes from the flaming ship, the officers and their support staff watched as *Angry Ark* fell to Fimil Prime's surface.

"Kersey isn't wrong as far as his knowledge allows. But there are things he doesn't know," Corcoran said. "*Angry Ark* is equipped with experimental Vred technology. Its gravity repulsion system is powerful enough to catch us in the final kilometers of descent. I found it easiest to imagine this technology as providing a rather large mattress for us to land on."

"Experimental?" Deke asked. "Or untested?"

"Never one to keep your mouth shut, are you," Corcoran asked. "Untested and experimental. There are many alien vessels capable of landing the mass *Angry Ark* carries, but not with the speed required by potential hostile action. So, to those who are considering that we might just all be red paste in seventy-five hours, give or take, your fears are confirmed. We don't think it'll end that way, but it might."

"Does this mean there's no coming back for *Angry Ark*?" Deke asked.

"We need to work on your timing, Captain Dekoster," Corcoran said. "Since I believe that around this table all questions are fair game, I will not reprimand your abrasive, inquisitive nature. You are correct. You all signed papers that indicated your understanding that Operation Black Turtle could be your final act. This was not just due to the combat situation we are entering, but also because our transportation has been designed as a one-way operation."

Corcoran allowed the group to watch as *Angry Ark* continued its descent. When the elevation gauge displayed above the vessel reached twenty thousand feet, the acceleration numbers dropped even faster than they had been on the initial descent.

At ten thousand feet, airfoils extended from various locations around the ship and small bursts of flame caused attitude and direction changes.

"This is the moment when g-forces are at maximum. Internally, the forces are eighteen to twenty gravities," Baines said. "Enough to scramble most of our brains. All personnel will be loaded into the cargo hold where we have the strongest inertial damping fields and will be able to reduce internal stresses to between three and five gravities. Unpleasant but not troublesome."

The room grew quiet once more as *Angry Ark* adjusted several more times and settled perfectly into place, with a massive cloud of dust rising around it. Features from *Angry Ark's* bulky hull came into sharp focus as thick steel arms attached to massive pins pushed away from its sides. Once fully extended, the arms bent on fat mechanical joints, and spun until legs turned down to the rocky terrain and extended until the ship was perfectly leveled.

"This process is expected to take no more than twenty minutes," Corcoran said. "While we're at our most vulnerable, we will have operational cannons."

"Is there any possibility to disembark Zebra Company after landing? I'd feel a whole lot better knowing we had a heavy platoon taking a defensive position in those hills," Deke said.

"It's not in our plan," Corcoran said thoughtfully. "But work something up. Understand, *Angry Ark's* armor is considerable. Every minute we delay getting Fort Indominable online puts us at risk."

"I understand," Deke said. "We'll come up with a plan that puts us off in five minutes or less."

"That's aggressive," Baines said.

"Let her work, Mike," Corcoran said. "Five minutes is your time budget. Show us what you can accomplish in that time."

"Copy that," Deke said. "Thank you, sir!"

"Do you have anything else, Mike?" Corcoran asked.

"Nothing beyond the recently gathered intelligence regarding Togath fighting tactics. I considered asking everyone to review the report on their own time instead of making it a group effort."

"Sounds like a plan," Corcoran said. "Dismissed."

All eyes turned to Baines, who shrugged and stood. "You heard the Colonel. It's go-time. See you all at 1800. And Dekoster, good job covering up a sloppy start. Do better. You have an entire company depending on you."

"Aye, aye, Sir!" Deke answered.

13

BAD THINGS IN MIND
AJ – DEEP SPACE

"Hey, One, you got a minute?" Peppers asked, approaching AJ where he sat staring out of thick, armored window.

Jayne had been working on the injured woman for six hours without a break. He was having trouble focusing on anything else. With the defeat of the vessels that'd destroyed the Arizona base, they hadn't experienced further pursuit, but it was impossible to know for certain.

"Sure, what's up?" he asked.

"Air Force is tailing us," Peppers said.

"Our Air Force?"

"The same."

AJ nodded. "How do you know?"

Peppers sat and opened a small electronic notepad. "Luck, really." A drone perfectly backdropped by the small blue bubble of a far-away Earth was the image laid out in front of them. "I was getting some readings I couldn't quite jive with and this little gal showed up. If it helps, I don't think they have any idea we've seen them."

"They're trying to find where we dropped the suits, *Seahag* and *Bernard*," AJ said. "Hope they don't mind disappointment."

"Some of the boys are wondering just what you did to stash everything," Peppers said. "Are you ever gonna tell us?"

"It's not much of a secret if I start telling everyone," AJ said. "What kind of solution do you have for our tail?"

"Do we want to go active on it?" Peppers asked. "It's sailing a flat vector. One well-placed 30mm round would take care of things. It's probably a twenty-million-dollar piece of hardware, though."

"Choices and consequences," AJ said. "Take it out if you can."

"Aye, aye," Peppers said. "I'll let you know."

"Appreciate it."

"How's the girl doing?"

"We should know soon. Last I saw, Doc was sewing her up."

"That's good. We need a win after that shitshow."

AJ nodded.

Twenty minutes later, the door to Medical slid open and Lisa stepped out. Her haggard eyes settled on AJ and she managed a tired smile.

"Tell me you have good news," he said.

"She's alive," Lisa said. "Amanda says that's more than we should have expected. Nit had to reprogram the ship's manufactory to build steel inserts to replace missing bone. We need a modern medical facility."

"Is that a message from Jayne?" AJ asked.

"No. That's just how it is."

He nodded. "I understand. Why don't you get a shower and find clean clothing."

"I feel like I could sleep for a week."

AJ stood and walked back to Medical. The door was closed, so he knocked.

"Come in," Jayne answered.

"How's she doing?" he asked, after opening the door. "I talked to Lisa. Sounds like you had a rough time of it."

"That's an understatement. She's a strong woman. She's only alive because she wants to be."

"The guys are struggling. Is there anything I can tell them?"

"The guys? Your team? What's that about?"

"They just watched an entire base get destroyed around them. They had connections. Rock lost a second cousin, or we're assuming that happened," AJ said. "Your patient represents what they're fighting for."

"She's a proxy," Jayne agreed, nodding her head. "Sorry, I'm just tired."

"Whatever that means," AJ said. "But it's gonna be a blow if she doesn't pull through."

"We need access to real medical. We might as well be a MASH unit given how severe her injuries are and the equipment we have to deal with them."

"I hear you."

"You're not convinced."

"It's not that. We have no idea who's tailing us right now," AJ said. "In the last twenty-four hours, someone has made a concerted effort to take us out. We just discovered a US Air Force drone on our tail, completely by luck. How many other ships are following us that we can't see? If we stop moving, will they try their luck at taking us out again? I don't disagree she needs advanced help. I have a larger group to worry about."

Jayne sighed and sagged against the cabinets behind her. "There's never a good answer."

"Let me work on it. I have an idea or two," he said. "I just needed to know how she's doing."

"Holly."

"What's that?"

"Her name," Jayne said. "Holly Blanche."

"I didn't think we had her records."

"She had a credit card in her slacks. I assume it was hers."

"I got this, Jayne," AJ said with resolve.

"I know you do."

"Do you need anything from me?"

"The smooth sailing thing was appreciated," she said, while pulling off bloody gloves.

AJ saw Peppers looking down the hallway at him with some intent. "Understood. If I sent you some help, do you need it?"

"Yes. I'll need to move Holly to the closest bunk. I'll watch her closely for a few hours."

"I'll get Rock and Chach," AJ said.

"Thank you."

"I gotta go."

"I know."

He walked into the hall.

"Sorry, boss," Peppers said. "Stuff's going down."

"Did you get the drone?"

"No."

"Did they see our shot?"

"No. We didn't take it."

"Talk."

"That drone isn't following us."

"Say more."

Peppers handed AJ a notepad. On the screen was a heavily armored spaceship twice the size of *Wasp*, bristling with weaponry.

"Oh, shit," AJ said. "BB, do you recognize this?"

Beverly appeared in midair, wearing her Jetsons-style silver spacesuit complete with jetpack that puttered out smoke rings.

"It is not known to the Galactic Empire databases," Beverly said. "That does not necessarily mean it is related to Quarr."

"Can we get any better scans?" AJ asked. "This is fuzzy."

"No," Peppers said. "The ship has an active blurring tech because a naked telescope doesn't get a better picture."

"They want us to lead them to *Seahag* and the combat suits," AJ said. "If they wanted us dead, they'd have come for us already. They outweigh us by twice."

"Right," Peppers said. "I'm not sure they're as quick, but they're fighting in a different weight class."

"Okay, gather the boys. We're not done earning our supper."

"You're not thinking of taking that guy on, are you?" Peppers asked. "That's suicide."

"Our dance card's full for the day," AJ said, "but our friend back there is complicating what should have been an easy plan."

"Give me ten," Peppers said. "Bald Norm is taking a nap and you know how hard it is to wake him up."

"I'll be in the cockpit," AJ said.

"Copy that, One."

As AJ walked through the ship, the men turned out of the way to give him a clear shot, which made him believe he didn't have the nicest look on his face. It was earned. He was irritated that his team was again under attack in a war he hadn't even known existed forty-eight hours prior.

"Pig, are you up to speed on that ship on our tail?" AJ asked the young flight engineer.

"Aye, aye, Captain."

"What's going on, AJ?" Darnell asked, recognizing that AJ was about to ask him to hand over the helm.

"What's our shortest time getting to Alpha Point?" AJ asked.

"We'd have to talk to Joyce and Tenet," Darnell said. "We've got engine damage."

"Seriously?"

"We keep it under sixty percent and it's fine, but when we get after it, there's an outer flood chamber that got cracked," Darnell said.

"It's cracked?" AJ asked. "I didn't think that was possible."

"It shouldn't be," Brian Joyce said from the entrance to the bridge behind AJ. "It's a crystalline-grown lattice structure that we thought impossible to break due to its resilient properties."

"You do know that made absolutely no sense, right?"

Joyce didn't take the bait and shrugged. "We shouldn't push over sixty percent."

"Or ...?"

"The engine could destroy itself."

"As in explode?"

"No. It would just turn off. Maybe a little extra heat. I'm not entirely sure, but I doubt a fiery explosion."

"Doubt isn't certain. What are our odds?"

"You're not actually considering this, are you?"

"I am, in fact, considering pushing *USS Wasp* to its limits and possibly beyond," AJ said. "We're being chased by a ship twice our size. We won't survive the first sixty seconds inside their gun range."

"There are some things we can do," Joyce said. "Can I have an hour?"

"You have fifteen minutes."

"Dammit."

"I get that a lot," AJ said.

"Pig, don't screw this up," Darnell said, tapping in the coordinates for the mysterious Alpha Point. "Right now you're thinking you need to get those coordinates sent back to HQ. Thing is, that big damn ship back there will intercept your comm and beat us to the punch. Don't give them that kind of advantage. We'll be sitting ducks."

"This is a point in space that wasn't on your original flight plan from two years ago," Pig said.

"Funny how that worked, huh?" AJ said.

"Don't mess this up," Darnell urged, following AJ into the hallway. "I'd feel a lot better if it was me in that chair, AJ."

"I need an experienced pilot out there. We're not going to be able to close the transition window before that ship catches us," AJ said. "We'll need cover while Birdie collects the suits and gets them loaded."

"That's right, so we'll talk to the guys and get this planned out," Darnell said, nodding agreement.

"What's the word, One?" Chach asked when they walked into the crew compartment where the entire team was gathered.

"What about the girl" Bald Norm asked. "Is she going to be okay?"

"Let's get to that, first," AJ said. "Holly Blanche is her name. She's alive but barely. After we're done here, I need you, Baldy, and Rock to help move Ms. Blanche to whatever bunkroom Doc indicates."

Bald Norm started to stand but AJ waved him off. "Hang on, we've got business."

"What's up?"

"Peppers, let 'em see what we're up against," AJ said and waited while Peppers showed them the pad with images of the ship that was following them.

"You gonna tell us about Alpha Point, then?" Peppers asked.

"It's Tok technology," AJ said. "They gave it to us with strict instructions not to tell anyone."

"Seems like we've done a pretty good job with that," Lefty said. "Almost got us killed half a dozen times."

"It's a temporary door," AJ said. "We have a suitcase with tech in it that when it gets to the right place, a tear in the fabric of space can be opened."

"So we geo-cached the suits and stuff, just not where everybody thought," Lefty said. "That's not a bad idea."

"Why don't we just forget Alpha Point and keep going? We could come back," Peppers said,

"Because we're being closed in," AJ said. "As long as we don't have our mech suits and those drop ships, we're sitting ducks."

"Damn straight," Rock grumbled. "I'm tired of taking it in the shorts."

"What are you talking about? You're not thinking about taking on that ship in the Alpha Point, are you?" Darnell asked. "*Wasp* wouldn't stand a chance."

"Maybe we don't use *Wasp*, then. Here's how I see this going down," AJ said and laid out his plan.

∽

KNEELING on the deck of the far aft hold, AJ set the suitcase-sized piece of equipment the Tok Commander, Cer, provided to him. The Tok were known to be the most advanced species in the Galactic Empire and the suitcase more or less proved exactly that point. He opened the device so it lay flat and exposed a few controls.

His men were anxious, all wearing new vacsuits and holding weapons adjusted to work in space and zero-gravity. To a man, they were uncomfortable with the lesser weapons allowing.

"Thirty seconds, One," Lefty announced. "Flight says we have clear sailing."

"Good copy." AJ flipped a pair of levers which locked the operation in place. Nervously, he watched as numbers counted down on his HUD. "Get ready, boys. Ten, nine, ..." He continued the countdown until it reached zero and locked in the final two levers.

The whole thing was anticlimactic. He'd used the device once before when he'd set the equipment into place. Like then, there was no tearing sound as space/time was opened. Lights didn't dim nor even flicker. One moment, they were cruising through space, pursued by a giant spaceship and a tiny drone. The next moment, there was a window in that space a thousand meters in diameter. No fanfare, whatsoever.

"Pig, do you see the planetoid? Set your heading and adjust acceleration per plan," AJ said.

"Aye, aye, Captain."

AJ struggled to keep from rolling his eyes. The title of *captain* still annoyed him. He'd always seen himself as one of the guys, even though he knew that time in his life had ended when he'd accepted leadership responsibilities for his growing team.

"BB, what's our countdown?" he asked.

She appeared wearing a tight black t-shirt, green fatigue pants, and black combat boots. He shook his head at her antics. It was their custom that she try to stump him with outfits matching pop culture and he was to guess who she was mimicking.

"We have ninety-seven seconds," she replied, hanging like a mountain climber from the front of his suit, her heels resting against his chest, a rope attached somewhere over his shoulder. At the last, she lifted her eyebrows in challenge. A countdown timer appeared in six-foot-high numerals against the back hatch.

"Try harder. GI-Jane," AJ said, giving her a small smile as he shook his head.

"Captain, our pursuer has given up all pretense of stealth and is at full-burn," Pig called.

"Keep to the plan," AJ said, resolve edging his voice.

"Roger, wilco."

With ten seconds on the clock, AJ pointed at Lefty, who was watching for his signal. The exchange resulted in Lefty operating a plunger stick that released the aft hatch's primary seals and caused the hold's already thin atmosphere to be exhausted in a controlled manner.

"Alpha Two, Alpha Six, go, go, go!" AJ urged with measured excitement. While the well-seasoned operators wouldn't over-react, it was good practice to add the right amount of energy to the moment. He'd split the ten-person team into teams of five and four. Lefty, or Alpha Two, would lead the team of five and AJ would pick up the remaining four.

He slapped his weapon's magazine out and fell in behind his line of commandos, with Alpha Six or Frenchy, in the lead. While often the numbering of unit members speaks to seniority, that was not the case with Frenchy. Having served with Frenchy on several tours in 'Nam, the man was held in AJ's highest regard, his number selected to keep him at the head of AJ's smaller team so AJ could focus on managing the mission but not stay back in a more conventional officer's role.

Like ants on their way to a party, the two lines of commandos exfiltrated *Wasp* using their positive gravity boosters to control the final five-hundred meter fall to the unnamed planetoid in a galaxy completely unrecognizable by AJ or even Beverly.

As each man touched down, small plumes of dust erupted at their feet, causing them to sink into the upper strata before finding solid ground. Having practiced and lived through combat jumps in a multitude of environments, none of the commandos so much as stumbled.

"I have positive response from *Seahag*," Darnell announced a moment later. "I'm instructing her to execute an emergency start."

"We have affirmative response from *Bernard*," Birdy chirped.

"AJ, the enemy vessel is nineteen minutes from arrival," Beverly said. "There is not sufficient time to load all equipment and gain sufficient escape vector."

"Good copy, BB," AJ said. "You heard her, boys. Nothing changes. Get those damn suits. We're going to war!"

"Hooah!" came a unified reply. No one desired to engage in the hostilities that were to follow, but that didn't mean they shied from battle.

"I have a ping-back on the first suit. We're two point five clicks out," Lefty announced. "Time to pick up the pace, boys. Double time this. You can rest when you're dead! Hooah!"

AJ smiled at his number two. "Hooah!" he answered with the rest of the team as they increased pace, sending rooster tails of dust as they half-jogged, half-jumped across the planetoid's barren scape.

"AJ, I've contacted our suit," Beverly said. "I've given instructions for emergency startup and diagnostic."

"Good call," he answered.

His team turned, orienting on the signals they each received from the mechanized suits. His heart thudded in his chest as he gained sight of the majestic killing machine simply referred to as his mech suit. The suits, outlawed by the Galactic Empire, had been given to AJ's team by Commander Cer of the Tok Supremacy. The 'gift' had been provided so AJ and his team could rebuff an alien invasion on the very same planet that was their current destination.

In that first mission, AJ had learned about the devastating capacity of the ten-foot-tall monstrosity. With hundreds of hours wrapped in a shell made of nearly impervious metals that were both flexible while moving and unforgiving when tested, he became nearly indestructible. The biggest risk was impacts that scrambled his insides. But even that possibility was offset by the original engineer's thoughtful inclusion of inertial damping systems powerful enough for small ships.

In addition to their rugged, nearly impossible-to-destroy nature, the mech suits had no lack of offensive weaponry and manufactured varying rounds and energy payloads on demand. The projectile ordnance production system was probably the least reliable of the suit's systems as it required replacement supplies depending on how heavy the demands were. Energy, however, was not a problem, as like the inertial systems, the power plants produced the equivalent to that of vessels twenty times the suit's mass.

"What's she telling you, BB?" AJ asked, his heart thumping hard as he tore across ground that had shifted from layers of dust to the now recognizable rock formations.

"All systems report full capacities and one hundred percent repair status. As expected," BB said. "Bald Norm's suit has reported auxiliary servo failure in the latissimus dorsi. This will need attention post engagement and can safely be isolated."

AJ felt almost a twinge of jealousy as his forward team members reached their suits and slid into the awaiting cocoons. His delay, however, ended soon enough as his foot found the familiar toehold just below the articulated knee joint. With practiced ease, he twisted and slipped his left foot through the thigh opening. Each subsequent twist and turn further seated him into his suit until it completely enclosed him and the environmental systems took over the task of life support.

"Big D, tell me you've made it to *Seahag*," AJ said, confidence coursing through his body so much so that he punched his elongated, gloved fist into the stone wall next to him creating a shower of rocks.

"Oh, but I've missed this old girl," Darnell said. "Daddy's got some bad things in mind. Tell me we're gonna play."

"It's time to teach some lessons," AJ said flexing the responsive musculature of his suit. "BB, get me a position on our target."

14

NO PLAN SURVIVES CONTACT
DEKE – PLANET FIMIL PRIME

"We're taking heavy fire!"

Deke could do nothing about that. To plan, they'd arrived at Fimil Prime and entered orbit. *Angry Ark* had entered the atmosphere with a significant fanfare of smoke, flames, and even some lightning.

"Fuck, I hate being right," Deke muttered when a small swarm of enemy fighter craft harassed the heavily armored vessel as it fell toward its new home. "Why couldn't we figure out they'd have air support? Every damn fight since World War I."

"We can't deploy troops without air cover," Lieutenant Bing said. "*Angry Ark's* cannons can't keep up with those little fighters. We'll be sitting ducks."

"Assume we're going to plan. Figure out what you'd change. You have four minutes," Deke said. It was an unfair ask, but battle was all about plans going to shit.

"Aye," Bing replied tersely.

"Carrole, talk to me," Deke said.

"Thank you, ma'am," she answered. "If we can get it freed, I have one Stryker with an anti-aircraft mount. We'd need six minutes of cover to get that installed once we were free of the hold."

"Major Baines, I need a word," Deke called into comms.

"Little busy here, Deke," he answered.

Over the prior three days, *Angry Ark's* team had gelled into a more cohesive team. Now that bullets were flying, communication was reduced to its most efficient forms.

"I'm aware," Deke answered. "Zebra is going to get our butts kicked if we disembark without anti-aircraft cover."

"We don't have any way to get those fast cannons going until we're stable," Baines said, repeating much-discussed information.

"Understood," she answered. "I need you to order the cargo crew to free one of my Strykers and put it first on the ramp. We have an aircraft weapon that will take us five minutes to assemble once we're off."

"Five minutes is going to be an eternity," Baines said. "What's your plan to keep it whole in the process?"

"Asking Bing to cover my Stryker," Deke said.

"That's a tall order, Deke. Are you sure you're up for that? What about the shoulder mounted missile system?"

"It won't work. Those fighters are faster than our missiles," Deke said, regurgitating the information provided by Baines' own intelligence. "Bing will use those to give Carrole's team breathing room."

"Shit, this is completely FUBAR," Baines said. "I'll give the order."

"Thank you, sir," Deke answered.

Carrole hadn't moved, aside from tapping away at virtual controls on her HUD. "Did we get our cargo move?"

"Yes, Baines gave the order. Make it work," Deke said. "Bing, I need you."

"I'm getting there," Bing said, sliding in next to Deke.

"New information."

"Thank God. Tell me you have something."

"I'm not sure it's a thank God thing," Deke said. "Carrole has anti-aircraft capability on one of her Strykers. She's working with the load master to shift things around. She'll roll out first, but needs five unmolested minutes in the open."

"Fuck."

"Right."

"I can't give that order," he said. "It's suicide to stand out there."

"Ask for volunteers," Deke said. "Tell them I'll be right there holding a missile tube."

"You can't do that, ma'am."

"Watch me," Deke said. "I've already died once. It doesn't suck as bad as you'd think."

"Damn it."

"I don't disagree," Deke said. "Leisk, get me armor and a tube. I'll be first off."

"Yes, ma'am. You do know that Major Baines won't be happy with this choice. He'll see you as taking an unnecessary risk. He'll say it isn't your job," Leisk said.

"That's the good thing about being dead. You don't have to listen as much."

"No, I'm thinking you'll make it," Leisk said. "Then you'll wish you're dead."

"Acceptable. I need that armor. We'll be on the ground in one hundred twenty seconds."

"It's here," Leisk said, opening a kit she'd pulled over shortly after the fighters had started attacking *Angry Ark*.

"You need a raise," Deke said, slipping her arms through and into the chest armor.

"I'm not sure the dollar has the same value on Fimil Prime as it does back home," Leisk said. "And since we're not going home anytime soon …"

"That's reasonable," Deke said, clipping the final pieces of armor together, then called out, "Carrole, what's your status?"

"Almost there, Deke. We might have a thirty second delay, but it'll be close."

"Bing, talk to me." Deke ran through the assembled soldiers who looked hopefully at her as she passed. Over the prior three days, Zebra company had drilled together. During that time, Deke's physical appearance had continued to change as her hair and fingernails grew and her musculature filled in.

"What's going on, Captain?" a faceless soldier asked.

"We're in the shit, soldier," she snapped back. "Back home we just call this Friday. Strap in boys and girls. Today we get to earn our paychecks. Hooah!"

"Hooah!" came the immediate response.

"Hooah!" Deke cried out as loudly as she could manage.

"Hooah!" came the even more enthusiastic response.

"Deke, I've a squad assembling by the back hatch. Carrole's got her Stryker in place. There's no reason for you to get in this," Bing said, answering her unanswered question.

"Bing, get your ass off that line," Deke said. "If Carrole and I go down, I need you to take Zebra."

"Don't do this to me, ma'am. This is my team. I can't ask them to go without me," he said.

"And today, you're going to have to figure out how to do exactly that. Zebra needs one of us, and my aim with a shoulder mount is unparalleled in our fighting force."

"What are you talking about? That's not in your jacket," he fired back.

"Neither is the fact that I have an alien living in my head," she responded. "Doesn't change the fact. The mission is scratch if we can't get those damn fighters off us. They'll peel off our legs if we can't keep them back. Will you follow my orders?"

"Shit ... shit!" he said, struggling.

"It's the right thing, Bing," Carrole said. "Don't leave my team under Kersey."

"Shit. Fine, dammit!"

Over the last three days, Deke's strength and agility had grown faster than she could have imagined. Between that and her highly enhanced eyesight, she was able to race through the ship by leaping off crates and occasionally swinging between skeletal girders with the grace of a monkey.

"Give me that tube," she demanded, landing squarely next to Bing.

"You need the rocks first," he said, setting the launch tube against *Angry Ark's* bulkhead. With an easy motion, he swung the overloaded pack from his shoulder and held it in place for Deke to slide into. "Tell me you know how to launch this thing."

"Even if I didn't, which I do, I would," she said, tapping her temple.

"That's messed up," he said. "When were you going to say something?"

"When it was important."

Twenty seconds to touchdown. Current estimated impact exceeds safety standards. Please engage crash positions.

"Of course," Deke grumbled. "Crash landings when I'm carrying a backpack of high explosives. Sounds glorious."

Watching the display on her HUD, Deke stepped back from the Stryker and bent her knees, not wanting a bounce to cause the vehicle to inadvertently land on her.

The first thing to contact *Angry Ark's* belly were tall, scraggly trees. Between the vessel's mass and thick armor plating, the trees were quickly snapped off. The trees, however, made significant noise as they were broken, while also deflecting the ship's trajectory.

"No, no, no," Deke said, watching a third-person view generated by Keegs. Fort Indominable's initial site wasn't large and had been chosen for the natural protection created by the mountain range to the east. What Deke was seeing, however was that while *Angry Ark* would land close to the right place, it would be rotated almost ninety degrees. Exiting the craft would be on the downhill side, possibly without touching the ground.

Brace. Brace. Brace.

The landing was even more violent than she anticipated. So much so that she was barely able to keep from falling over, which was better than the rest of the two squads queued to roll out the door.

A flicker of movement was her only warning when straps on the stack of supplies next to her snapped. Drawing on her strength, she twisted and leapt, even though loaded with an additional hundred pounds of gear.

"Get that damn door open," she cried, churning her legs forward when she recognized no one stood by the hatch controls.

"Move, dammit," she ordered. Arriving at the hatch controls, she found the problem. The crew who'd been given the singular job of opening up was on the deck, either dead or unconscious. "Keegs, can you get that door open?"

"You have access. Place your palm on the pad," Keegs answered.

Ripping the glove from her hand, Deke placed her hand on the security pad as she straddled the downed crewman. Groans of pain echoed as soldiers attempted to regain lost footing and push off gear that had fallen around them.

"Carrole, report!" she demanded.

"Up, ma'am. We had protection inside the Stryker."

"I'm shooting you a view from outside. It'll be tricky navigation. We're on a slope," Deke said.

"It's coming in now. How did you get that?"

"Generated video, but you'll find it's accurate."

The groan of steel under stress sounded as the back hatch slowly lowered. Deke hadn't considered the additional time of the slow ramp and kicked herself. In most hot combat situations, there were ways to override slow machinery. "Can you make this go faster, Keegs?"

"Negative."

"I hear you," she answered, jumping against the near vertical ramp and using her fingers to lock into small channels where steel tracks were separated. It was a calculated race to the top and when she arrived, she discovered that the ramp would, in fact, be suspended over the ravine next to the fort's intended build site. It would be up to the engineers to figure out how to fix things. Her only job was to get to a place where she could see enough of the sky to defend Carrole's squad.

A handhold above her was just out of reach. "Keegs, I need extra juice. I need to grab that handhold," she said.

"I'll give you what I can," he agreed.

Deke's stomach soured and her hand visibly jittered as adrenaline poured into her system. Suddenly filled with angst and confidence, she crouched against the lowering ramp and leapt with abandon. Instead of falling short, she jumped too hard and had to adjust so she didn't bounce away. Fortunately, her fantastic reaction time allowed her hands to slip around the metal structure. Even with the extra hundred pounds of equipment, holding on was easy. Swinging her legs back and forth, she gave herself enough lift to jump to a second handhold and then a third. By this time, she was well outside the ship, where she found significantly easier grips.

"I'm almost on top, Carrole," she said. "What's it look like down there?"

"We'll drop almost fifteen feet, but a group of small trees should break our fall without turning us over," Carrole answered.

"Tell me that sounded as crazy to you as it did to me," Deke said.

"It's crazy. Do you want me to call it off? I don't see another plan aside from hoping you get some lucky hits," Carrole said.

"Bing, get your boys on the ground," Deke grunted, pulling herself over the final ledge. She stood. If not for a buzzing sound flying at her from behind that caused her to drop to her knees, she might have been struck by an incoming spray of energy bolts just before a fighter zipped overhead. "What in the hell? How did I dodge that?" she asked, rolling back to her feet.

"I simulated a warning," Keegs said.

"Give me a target." She pulled the tube onto her shoulder. "Fast is slow, slow is smooth, and smooth is fast."

A throbbing red light drew her attention to the ship's starboard side. Instinctively, her new eyes zoomed into the distance until she saw the fighter, which was banking to come back around. "There are four other ships on similar headings. None of the others are directly targeting you."

"I want to get this guy when he can't adjust in time. Can you give me that?" she asked.

"That is not advised. You will be in weapon's range for six seconds if you want the most efficient strike," Keegs said.

"Find me cover," she demanded, not taking her eye off the approaching fighter.

"Move to your left fourteen paces, there are numerous trip hazards, I'll warn you. Step up!"

Deke stumbled but kept her feet while maintaining sight of the fast-approaching fighter.

"I see it," she said when she came next to a tall, armored structure. She wasn't sure what would happen if it was hit by a missile but felt certain it could absorb rapid fire bullets. Or at least that was in her head when she stepped behind it as the fusillade started. Fortunately, either she or Keegs was right because by ducking back, she was spared.

"In three seconds, pop out to the left. Don't fire right away. Use the extra second to find your target. I'll use ship sensors to provide reticle."

"Make this work, Keegs. This mission is depending on us," she said, staring at the back of the bulwark that provided cover. Remaining in her vision, projected onto her HUD was the fighter still bearing down on her position. The staccato thuds of deadly energy-laced tiny projectiles plowing into the armor was a constant reminder of the fate that awaited if she didn't perfectly time her actions.

"Raise your weapon," Keegs said.

A steady calm pervaded her senses as she stepped back and raised the tube onto her shoulder. Instantly, the weapon's controls claimed their rightful position on her HUD. Gone was the frenetic energy of adrenaline. In its place was clear thinking and a sense of purpose. Only two things existed in the universe – her missile and the fighter that needed to find its destiny.

"Step left," Keegs said calmly.

She found his voice soothing and did as he bade. Time seemed to slow. The fighter's stream of bullets were relentless in their assault of *Angry Ark's* topside, but it might as well have been gnats on an elephant for the damage caused.

With the tube already aimed, it took only the second Keegs had requested to acquire weapon's lock. With her enhanced vision, Deke zoomed in on the fighter's cockpit. The gray-skinned being behind the glass with its broad shoulders was larger than she'd expected. She'd encountered Togath on Earth but had never been close enough to see them in person.

"Why are you not firing?" Keegs asked.

"I don't want him to have time to react," Deke said, inspecting the Togath's face. In that moment she saw a flicker of understanding cross its face. For a moment, they were locked together in synchronized understanding as Deke launched her missile. With flared nostrils and slightly widened eyes, the Togath pulled away from the missile that hadn't even yet launched.

With frustrating deliberateness, the missile gained separation between itself and Deke, the designers of the weapon understanding that to use all possible thrust would likely have blowback on the soldier holding the tube. At ten yards, a flare of the second stage blasted the missile forward as it anticipated the Togath's flight path.

"It knows," Deke said, watching the Togath as it closed its eyes and tapped its forehead with two thick fingers. With surreal clarity, she watched the missile streak forward and slam into the fighter, exploding on contact.

"Target acquired, three thousand feet, sixty-three degrees to right," Keegs said. "Place tube on the hull, I'll engage its magnetic stabilization. You will withdraw a missile from the rack you carry on your back. Use your right hand to grasp just below the fins and pull up and over your shoulders. This is the orientation necessary for loading into the tube."

Ordinarily, Deke would have been frustrated by Keegs' over-explanation, but in the heat of combat, his words were simple reminders of the steps she knew were necessary. What's more, she understood that an over-tasked brain could miss details.

"Fast is slow, slow is smooth," she repeated as one might a mantra. As expected, the missile pulled free from its mount and slid easily into the tube.

"Right fifty-three degrees," Keegs said quietly, reinforcing his instruction with a slowly throbbing red indicator to the right in her vision.

Targeting lock sounded in Deke's ear and the fighter slipped into center view. She released the missile and only watched for a moment as it slipped forward and ignited second stage propellant.

With familiarity born from repeated behavior, she ignored the missile's flight and dropped the tube's end onto the armor plating at her feet and pulled a third missile from her back.

"The fighter has adjusted flight and is running," Keegs said. "A second missile could potentially create a conflict in escape vectors."

"How much burn time does the missile have?" Deke asked, tipping the tube onto her shoulder.

"Ninety seconds on average," Keegs said.

"Give me a new target. Maximize keeping them from Carrole's team," she said.

"Ten seconds to target acquisition."

"Carrole, check in," Deke ordered.

"It's getting hot down here," she said. "Bing's squad is taking a lot of heat. We're down four."

"Shit," Deke cursed under her breath.

"What do you need?"

"Just keep blowing those bastards up," Carrole answered. "We're getting picked apart."

"ETA on gun?"

"We had a setback. The drop from *Angry Ark* jammed the Stryker's front right suspension and we got hung up in a tree. Long story, we're just about free and can start setting the turret."

"Understood, Deke out."

Deke inspected the approaching fighter's vector and traced a path along *Angry Ark*'s spine that would give her a longer window of visibility on the fighter as it harassed her team. The sounds of M52 rounds and the contrails of spent missiles filled the valley below, where the Stryker and Bing's team were fighting for their lives.

"You are at maximum weapon's range," Keegs said, just as a pair of missiles jumped up from the valley and streaked toward her target.

Deke withheld fire, knowing a third missile would have little impact. Whatever evasive moves the Togath took for the pair of already fired missiles would just as easily evade whatever she threw out.

"Carrole, get your ground crew to flush that fighter up the hill toward me," Deke said. "Intentionally aim to vessel's port side."

"Good copy, Captain," Carrole answered.

Holding her fire was perhaps one of the hardest exercises of her life. She held hope that her position wasn't known by the attacking craft. Even more painful was to watch as the approaching craft fired its deadly ordnance on her team's position. Lives hung in the balance, but to strike too soon would have no impact and even more lives could be lost. It was a devil's choice, but she remained steady and waited for Carrole's team to drive the quarry.

"Give me Carrole's team status on the HUD," Deke said.

"That's not wise," Keegs said. "You need to focus."

"That's an order, dammit!"

Deke's heart sank when the team status appeared on her HUD. Of the eight team members from Carrole and Bing's platoons, five remained, two of whom were injured, including Carrole. The price of minutes in the warzone had been high.

A pair of missiles streaked into the air from the valley below, causing the fighter to jump predictably away from their launch points. Even as the missiles gained speed, though, a fourth team member was hit, her life snuffed by enemy fire. Deke's stomach boiled with rage, and she watched the fighter bank toward her position.

"I want the perfect shot, Keegs," she growled.

"There's a ..."

"Shut it. Focus." In the back of her mind, she knew there would be a price to pay for silencing Keegs, but it didn't matter.

A countdown timer showed next to the icon of an emptying thermometer. She stood resolute in the oddly quiet moment between. A soldier, one of her own, had sacrificed her own life to drive the enemy to her. She would honor that sacrifice with excellence.

"Die, fucker," she spat, releasing the missile. In that moment she realized just how successfully Carrole's team had directed the fighter. In moments a ball of fire would splash against *Angry Ark* armored radio masts directly above.

"Ah, hell," she groaned, releasing the tube. Deke took two quick steps and flung herself over the side. In the first moments of freefall, she assessed just what trouble she'd gotten herself into. There were trees below. Whatever happened next would hurt beyond anything she could imagine. At least that was on her mind as she twisted, trying to direct her fall. She had little luck.

"Oophf," was all she could manage as the first branch struck her armored chest sending her cartwheeling through the treetops. Each new strike spun her in a new direction. She was little more than a ragdoll and lost consciousness on the third strike to her helmeted head.

15

WITHOUT MERCY
AJ – DEEP SPACE

A THROBBING AMBER light on AJ's HUD warned of missiles in flight. Close impact, but targeting wasn't directed at him. With his suit closed, ordinary ship-to-ship missiles were trouble but even direct hits weren't necessarily fatal. Much depended on if the explosive impact could be deflected and if the suit were caught against a solid surface.

This amber light warned him that one of his team was targeted. With a flick of his eyes, AJ found the targeted team member. Rock Island hadn't made it to his suit and was caught in the open. AJ gritted his teeth. His long-time friend wouldn't survive the next seconds and there was nothing he could do.

"Alpha Two, I need a toss," AJ called, running at Lefty with every dram of force his overpowered suit could manage. "BB, make the calcs and get me on that damn ship!"

"Good copy, One," Lefty answered. He spun forty-five degrees and planted his armored boots against the planetoid's rocky soil.

As he ran, AJ couldn't help but watch the missile's progress. Impacting a few yards in front of Rock Island, his friend was instantly vaporized by the explosive blast. "God damn it!" he growled. Rage bloomed in his chest. War was a ridiculous waste. Greed drove the universe and that greed killed good men and women without concern for the cost.

"Stay on target, One!" Lefty shouted, knowing the impact Rock Island's death would have. "Don't fuck this up."

"Put me on that god-damned ship!" AJ planted a foot, and leapt just next to Lefty. In response, Lefty grabbed AJ in the middle of his launch from the low-gravity planetoid and added his suit's power to AJ's leap. The effect was to fling AJ on a collision course that only a pair of Beltigersk could calculate on the fly.

"I'm taking control of attitude jets," Beverly said calmly, appearing in front of AJ in her Jetson's foil suit.

"Do it, BB. Just get me there!"

"Right behind you, One!" Peppers said.

"Ten seconds back, One!" Chach added.

AJ grimaced in fury as the fat warship grew in his field of view. There would be no missing the large ship. Whoever was sailing the ship had no idea of the shitstorm they'd invited. And with Rock's death, AJ wasn't about to stop before he had his pound of flesh.

"Two, take the rest of the team and converge on *Seahag*. Pig, get *Wasp* on the ground in defensive position. This asshole is coming for you! Big D, protect *Wasp* at all costs. Do you copy?"

With Beverly's help, AJ didn't need to listen to the answers. If anyone disagreed, she'd point it out. The ability to free up his thinking time was crucial for making decisions.

Still in flight, AJ's suit turned as Beverly used the small attitude jets located at strategic points. While nothing like a spaceship, boarding ships was one of many primary functions the suits were well designed for. The ability to orient was a critical function for successful zero-g operations.

Slowly, and in perfect timing with his arrival at the warship's hull, Beverly rotated AJ so he landed feet first and was able to use the powerful legs of his suit to absorb the impact and bleed off his inertia instead of bouncing off like a billiard ball. Heavy magnetic clamps engaged as his soles touched armor and AJ bent as he jammed open claws into the ship like an eagle reaching into the water and grabbing its dinner.

Even with inertial dampers at full, the impact jarred him enough to cause a momentary stun. Shaking his head, he forced the fog away even as Beverly lightly tapped his adrenal system.

"Go easy on that stuff," AJ growled. As much as he loved the adrenaline hits, he hated the aftereffects even more.

His HUD showed a green dot that grew to the size of a penny and then diminished to the size of a pea. Peppers had arrived and made a successful landing.

"I'm down," Peppers announced.

"We're on Six, Peppers," AJ answered. "On the double."

"Good copy," Peppers agreed.

Beverly shone a path across the ship's hull that would have him arrive at Chach's projected landing site. Attitude jets pushed him against the hull and AJ bounded forward as if the ship had its own gravity.

Shortly before he and Peppers arrived, Chach landed in a classic superhero stance, driving his fist down as he crouched to absorb impact.

"Missiles are off! Dammit, you gotta do something about that, One!" Darnell called over the radio.

"BB, I need missile tube locations."

"They're using two forward tubes," Beverly answered, highlighting the locations on the hull.

"Five, Six, take the highlighted tube." AJ said. "I've got the other."

"We're on it," Peppers answered, reaching for and steadying Chach, who hadn't landed quite as cleanly.

"Boss, we've got company," Chach called.

AJ's HUD lit up with a pair of new targets.

"Shit, that was fast," Peppers said. "They had to know we'd be coming."

"No mercy," AJ growled.

"Not a damn inch," Chach agreed. "This one is for Rock!"

With a sense of wonder, AJ faced a pair of Togath between him and the missile tube he was racing toward. The hulking humanoids wore no spacesuits and wore only small masks over their gray-skinned faces. They could exist in vacuum for periods of time and there'd been speculation that oxygen supply would limit their ability to move with any speed or power. The masks seemed to confirm this speculation.

The two Togath stopped and calmly lowered to their knees while at the same time orienting their heavy weapons on AJ. He wasn't about to stop.

One option was to shift his weapon to an energy weapon, which would have no recoil. He dismissed that. Togath would certainly be counting on this, but with their natural defenses against energy weapons, they'd likely survive. His next option was to shift to slug throwing. In zero-g, the idea was even worse than the energy bolts his suit was capable of discharging.

AJ chuckled darkly as he pulled a two-foot-long knife from where it was strapped to its leg. "We'll do this all up close and personal. Too bad nobody told you boys about the twenty-one-foot rule," he chided, not caring the aliens couldn't hear him, nor that he was well over twenty-one feet away.

A pair of energy bolts flashed and streamed toward AJ. His own reflexes too slow to respond, he had to rely on Beverly. As it was far from their first battle together, he wasn't particularly surprised when his suit twisted in a *Matrix*-styled configuration and he bent around the bolts, one which passed harmlessly, the other deflecting without damage against his armored chest plate.

Regaining control of his suit, AJ twisted back into line and powered the knife in a sweeping arc at waist level of the right-most Togath. Even heavily armored, the Togath's carapace was no match for the suit's power, much less the added inertia of his pell-mell charge. Even before his blade completely passed through, AJ jammed his free hand into the ship's armor and used both the impact of the blade and his arm to arrest his momentum.

With a small boost from Beverly, AJ became aware that the second Togath's tracked his position. To the Togath's credit, it continued to move fluidly and without overreaction as it released its own long-barreled weapon and grasped a bladed weapon.

AJ grinned with satisfaction. There was no such thing as a fair fight where the mechanized suits were concerned and if was to be a knife fight, it would end quickly. AJ knew the purpose of the Togath was to delay his team's assault. He had no choice but to deal with it, and allowed the knife to rotate in his hand so the blade ran along his forearm in time to block the Togath's slashing strike. AJ lashed out with his gloved fist and smashed the Togath's jaw, sending the massive alien spinning up and away from the ship's hull.

"Lock me down, BB!" AJ demanded, taking a knee so he was locked in against the ship.

"Magnetics on full," Beverly answered.

AJ dialed in his slug-throwing ammo and stretched his right hand forward, having dropped his blade in favor of the barrel on the back of his glove. The stream of armor piercing rounds drove AJ back against the ship's armor. Without the ability to maneuver in zero-g, the Togath was a sitting duck and was torn apart by AJ's assault.

"We're moving!" AJ growled, pushing against the magnetics still in place. Beverly released his legs, allowing him to lunge away from his locked down position.

"*Wasp* is taking fire!" Darnell called over comms.

AJ had lost track of the larger battle, although he knew the attacker would want to take *Wasp* out of the action now that they'd discovered AJ's cache of mechanized armor. The mechanized suits were overpowered and could turn the tide in any conflict. Those thoughts galvanized his actions as he closed on the missile tube just as a slim silver torpedo shaped weapon slid away into the inky night.

"Take it, AJ!" Beverly exclaimed in an unusual display of excitement.

He swung his arm and searched for the targeting reticle he knew would show as soon as he was close. Without a firm lockdown, he'd pay for what would come next, but preventing a missile's flight was worth a lot, especially if it was locked in on *Wasp*.

The audible tone AJ associated with successful targeting sounded in his ears and he loosed a stream of the same armor piercing slugs he'd just used to tear apart the alien Togath.

He was driven back and then cartwheeled as the weapon's kickback found only small resistance from his boot magnetics. Instead of fighting the roll, AJ arched his back and allowed the suit's armor and inertial dampers to absorb the impact. Beverly took control of attitude jets and AJ lashed out with clawed hands to grab onto any surface, unfortunately with little success.

"Grappling line!" he demanded. Instantly, his gloved weapon hand shifted modes. Using a similar firing movement, AJ was surprised that the grappling line didn't immediately release. A moment later, however, the delay's necessity became obvious as his backwards flight exposed a tall radio tower and was quickly wrapped up by the grappling line.

"We're going to hit hard," Beverly warned. "Going armadillo."

Her warning was shorthand that described one of the suit's many defensive modes. In this case, the suit's back arched and the flexible armor hardened into a semi-circle.

"Ugh," AJ said as breath was driven from his chest. The impact was minor and he pulled at the grappling line, which oriented him on the radio tower and reversed his momentum. "What the hell happened? Why'd we get thrown so hard?"

"You hit the missile. You got blowback."

"Oh, that tracks," he answered almost sheepishly.

AJ drove his thighs into the suit's leg activators and raced forward. A new pair of Togath appeared on the horizon of the ship's surface. Calculating distance, AJ grinned. They were on the wrong side of the missile tube to stop him. They'd get a lick or two in, but he'd make that tube his bitch in the process.

"Explosive charges at the ready," he ordered. In response, the mini armory in his suit's backpack assembled a small package of the good stuff – Blastorium. Having played baseball in high school and been invited to play college ball, he prided himself on his natural throwing ability. "Set to explode on impact."

"You're a go!" Beverly answered.

AJ plucked the explosive package from the armory's exit port and planted his left foot, following through with a well-practiced throw. Just as the ball of doom left his hand, AJ saw a silver missile appear in the tube.

"Oh, shit!" he yelled. It was too late to do anything about the trouble he'd started, the only choice left was to minimize the impact. He curled into armadillo mode and was batted away from the ship like it was named Hank Aaron.

For a moment, his vision darkened, the g-force of his explosive lift almost too much to overcome. With nothing between him and space, he was carried along by the blast wave, which was partially absorbed by the ship's armor.

"Well, hell," he said, when focus returned. "Get me back in this thing. Five, Six, sitrep!"

"Charges set," Peppers answered. "This ship is lousy with damn Togath, though."

"Blow it!" AJ ordered as Beverly spritzed small doses of propellant to stop his tumble through space. "Shit, I'm gonna toss my breakfast, BB."

"Got it," she answered.

His nausea started to pass even as his eyes stopped jittering back and forth from the spin-induced sickness. "Line me up, I'm going kinetic."

While not part of the original design of the suit, AJ had discovered a benefit of the rapidly expelled bullets while attempting another high-risk boarding maneuver. The move was only made possible by the ability of his symbiote's unparalleled understanding of math and physics. It was as simple as firing different massed bullets into space as a means for arresting and reversing inertia. While not particularly efficient, it worked.

"Are you done lying around yet, One?" Peppers teased. "We're setting breaching charges."

"I'm coming already," AJ answered, his flight reversing as he fired bullets in time with Beverly's instructions.

"Leave it to the grunts to get the real work done," Chach added. "Fire in the hole."

AJ turned his attention to a small spot on the warship's hull where a gout of flame erupted. A moment later a long vaporous stream followed as atmosphere expelled violently from the ship. Instead of attempting entry, Peppers and Chach peeled explosive rounds from their own armories and tossed them through once the spout settled. Their efforts were rewarded by a second round of atmospheric decompression and bought AJ time to join them.

"Five, you've got point and go left. Six, you take right, I'll go forward," he instructed.

While it was generally a good idea to keep a boarding team together, that was not the case with the mechanized suits. Almost impossible to penetrate with ship-board weapons, the fight would turn quickly south for the crew aboard, regardless of how many Togath were employed.

Right out of the box, the trio were met by a solid wall of Togath who filled the decompressed hallway. Energy weapons pinned AJ's team against the bulkheads as they entered. It was a short-term advantage, however as Peppers rolled forward an explosive charge into the group.

AJ felt a certain remorse for the instant death faced by the Togath. With their superior tactical minds, not one of the powerful alien warriors would have entered the hallway with any expectation of survival. It was their job to protect, and they stoically accepted that responsibility.

"Move!" he ordered, bulling his way forward.

The battle had shifted from the first moments when the armored warship had arrived. Allowing a breach had been a colossal mistake and AJ wasn't about to take his foot off the gas. With shipboard gravity in place, the kinetic weapons were balanced as long as magnetic clamps were engaged on his boots.

AJ's gun turned into a hammer and every problem became a nail. If a door needed opening, he blew it off its hinges with automatic fire. If an opponent stepped in his way, it received the same treatment. There might once have been the possibility of lenience, but that had flown out the window when they'd killed his Rock.

AJ did what he and his team did best as he pushed his way toward the bridge.

"Five, Six, status," AJ ordered.

"Heavy resistance in engineering," Peppers grunted. "They're making a decent stand. Tough going but I've got it."

"Same shit over here," Chach said. "I'm about through it though. I've run into a couple of Cheel and a goofy looking dude."

"Tell me about goofy," AJ said.

"I've got plenty of video. Dude moves fast. Well, moved fast is probably a better description. He almost mag-locked a grenade on me. Feels like that might have been a deal killer. Be careful," Chach said.

"Interesting," AJ said. "Make sure you have the polarization controls handy. Your rider can reverse magnetic fields."

"Shit, I didn't know."

Just then AJ came face to face with his own *goofy-looking-dude*. Slim, and five and a half foot tall, the humanoid had tattoos all over its body. With hands that boasted eight fingers each and odd growths on its body, the being moved with unnatural grace caused by too many joints in its limbs. With a feral cry, it launched itself at AJ.

Taken off guard by the flesh and bone something charging his mechanized suit, AJ was momentarily short of ideas. Chach's description of speed turned out to be wholly accurate and AJ found the being locked on in a weird sort of wrestling hold.

He struggled to grasp the alien's body as its oddly jointed body thrashed around and started twisting at the different connective points of the mech suit.

"AJ, it's looking for a weakness," Beverly said. "Your suit is not well defended against this sort of attack. You need to do something quickly."

He chuckled darkly and dropped a grenade on the deck. The explosion launched him into the ceiling and filled the room with fire. He landed on the deck below and glanced around, finding charred remains scattered around him.

"Let me guess, that was a Quarr," AJ said.

"It certainly fits all descriptions," Beverly said. "This encounter will significantly increase what's known about the species in Galactic Empire records."

"Glad we could contribute," AJ said.

"There will be many who share that sentiment."

He rolled his eyes and approached the door that had been guarded by the Quarr. "Five, Six, status. I'm about to enter the bridge."

"Engineering is locked down," Peppers answered.

"Comms are locked down," Chach added.

"Blow comms," AJ ordered, placing breaching charges around the door.

"In five, four, three ...," Chach answered.

A shiver rippled through the heavily armored vessel but nothing else. AJ rammed a shoulder against an adjacent door hoping to gain cover. Once inside the room, he ignited the bridge door charges. Even behind cover, debris and flames licked around the corner. Without significant atmosphere, the flames were quickly doused.

Knowing that initiative was often the difference between success and failure, AJ raced around the corner and through, into the bridge. The chatter of alien radio communications filled his ears as threats, negotiations, and pleas simultaneously assaulted every channel. With a single glance, AJ muted the incoming comms.

Dispassionately, he cleared the bridge of all sentient life.

16
NO GOOD DEED
DEKE – PLANET FIMIL PRIME

"Captain Dekoster?" a voice asked quietly as an annoyingly bright light burned into her eyes.

"Get that damn thing outta my eyes," she growled.

"She's over here!" Deke heard someone cry out.

The smell of pine sap filled her nose as the light returned. She slapped the hand away and blinked furiously. When she tried to move, however, pain coursed through her body.

"What in the hell?" she struggled to say.

"Ma'am, you need to lie still. I'm a medic with training specifically designed to assist your symbiote," the man said. "I'm unable to reach your symbiote and as a result, I'm taking minimal steps to stabilize your condition."

"What happened?" Deke asked, not completely sure how she'd ended up in a forest.

"You're on planet Fimil Prime on the mission Operation Black Turtle," he said. "Our ship *Angry Ark* is under attack from enemy aircraft."

The man's words were interrupted by the nearby sounds of 20mm rounds filling the air. The experimental weapon on the new Strykers had an extreme rate of fire, so much so that there was no obvious pause between individual rounds. The whole thing sounded like a waterfall more than bullets being fired.

"Carrole, talk to me," Deke mumbled.

"We're moving to high ground." Lieutenant Carrole's speech was labored as she struggled against the vehicle's movement over rough terrain. "They don't like the anti-aircraft fire. I don't know how effective, though."

Deke shoved concerned hands from her chest and struggled to sit up. Crying out in anguish, she allowed the medic to push her back to the ground. "What the hell is wrong with me?" she growled.

"Ma'am, you've broken your back," the medic said, gravely. "You shouldn't even be alive."

"Bing, tell me you have reinforcements ready to take position," she said.

"Aye, aye, Captain," he said. "I have an entire platoon ready to lay down serious hurt. Say the word."

"Lieutenant Carrole, you need to make the call," Deke said. "I don't think I'm ..."

She was unable to complete the conversation, passing out from the pain cause by grave injury.

"Captain? Are you with us?"

It was a new voice.

"Still kicking," she whispered.

"We're about to move you onto a stretcher. We have immobilized your neck and spine. This will hurt, though," the man said.

"I had not anticipated you would leap from the vessel," Keegs said, his voice sounding tired.

"What happened to you? Did you fall out on the way down?" she asked, silently speaking only to Keegs.

"I am uninjured. The extent of your internal damage was problematic, and I needed to adjust how I am integrated into your body."

"If I had a dollar for every time I heard that."

"You would have precisely one dollar."

"That's a joke."

"I see," Keegs said, clearly unimpressed. "You fractured the only original spinal material in your back. Your arms have dislocated from your shoulders on both left and right sides. You are fortunate that your jaw and skull were reinforced. In short, you have no reason to have lived from your foolish, impulsive behavior."

"You're angry," she said, with surprise. "I didn't know you did angry."

"Of course I'm angry. You cannot take such risks. To die on the first encounter is not why we traveled across the galaxy," he said.

"Oh man, that's some serious tone you have going there," she said. "You do realize that if those fighters had kept us pinned down, we'd have been sitting ducks for whatever came next, right? With no ability to extend our stabilizing arms, *Angry Ark* would have been a giant deer tick sitting on the side of the mountain, waiting to be popped."

"You are no longer the lead of a small squad," he snapped back. "Others should have taken the risks. You are too valuable to be placed in such a position. You could have died. I'd have had to find a new host."

"You're really upset, Keegs."

"Yes! We are a team, Kait Dekoster."

"I had no idea you felt like this," she said, her voice softening.

"Do you think Beltigersk have no feelings?"

"I hadn't given it much thought. We've been on the run since I awoke," she said. "I guess I should say I'm sorry."

"But you are not."

"I am sorry for the stress I caused you. I can't say I'd do it differently if I had it to do again. Our teamwork saved the expedition. Sometimes an individual needs to be sacrificed for the benefit of the team. It's a tough lesson but necessary, nonetheless."

"Apology accepted," Keegs answered after a moment's pause.

"Are we good?" Deke asked.

"Yes."

"So, how do we get me fixed up?"

"I'll instruct the medics on how to seat your arms into your shoulders," he said.

~

"What in the hell were you thinking?" Baines asked. "You're a god-dammed captain with responsibility for eighty-three troops. Sixty percent casualties on your half-baked mission returned and I'll be god dammed if I can figure out how you're alive. Do you care to explain?"

"Major?" Lieutenant Carrole spoke quietly. Like Deke, Carrole had barely survived the attack. Her body was covered with bandages, her face a quilt of steri-strips, bruises, and bandages. That her breathing was labored implied other serious injuries.

For as angry as Baines was, his face softened when considering the heroic lieutenant. She'd volunteered for the wildly dangerous duty and seen it through to the end without complaint.

"What is it, Carrole?" he asked, struggling to keep irritation from his voice.

"We'd have been screwed if Deke hadn't knocked out those two fighters. They had us dead nuts. I'm alive because of Captain Dekoster's extraordinary skills."

"The plan had a million holes in it," Kersey said angrily. "It was irresponsible and like always, put this ship and everyone aboard at increased risk. Those soldier's deaths are on you, Dekoster. They died because you sent them into harm's way."

"That's bullshit," Bing interjected. "We had five minutes to come up with a plan. Deke looked at the available resources and weighed the risks. Those men and women were from my platoon. I grieve their deaths, but don't you dare badmouth a plan made in the heat of battle, Lieutenant Kersey. You were in the same hold everyone else was. Without Zebra team on the ground, we'd still be pinned inside with no way to defend ourselves. What do you think would have happened if the enemy figured out we were pinned? That's right, they'd have rolled in something big enough to crack us open."

"We could have taken a few minutes to construct a plan. Dekoster is a loose cannon and has no business as a leader. Flinging herself off *Angry Ark* should have been enough evidence of that. She has a death wish and she's going to take her entire company with her," Kersey spat.

"What was the plan you had?" Dekoster asked calmly. "Remember, you had five minutes before a squadron of fighter planes arrived and established air superiority."

"I ... well ..."

"That's enough," Corcoran said. "I'd like a word with Captain Dekoster and Major Baines. Lieutenant Carrole, that was a damn fine job out there. Your bravery under fire is truly an inspiration to us all."

The room quieted. Corcoran was not known for any sort of praise. To lavish two entire sentences on anyone was unheard of.

"Thank you, sir!" Carrole said, struggling to stand to attention. "Just doing my job."

"Get healed, Lieutenant. Our war has just begun. Dismissed."

Kersey made no attempt to leave when the lieutenants and support staff stood to leave the conference room. It looked like he'd get away with it as Baines allowed the room to clear.

His self-satisfied look was interrupted, though. "Thad, we'll need the room," Baines said.

"Oh." Kersey stood and dismissed himself.

Fully expecting a new raking over the coals, Deke readied herself. She looked to blunt the issue by speaking as soon as the door closed.

"Look, Colonel Corcoran, Major Baines, I think either Lieutenant Carrole or Bing would make good replacements for me," she said. "You can bust me back to lieutenant and give either a field promotion. My personal pick would be Carrole, but Bing would be just as good a choice."

"Did you know you would survive that jump into the forest?" Corcoran asked.

"I didn't really think about it that deeply," she answered. "What I knew for certain was that I wouldn't survive what was coming my way. I remembered the pine below and hoped it would be enough."

"That fall would have killed any normal human," Corcoran said. "I've watched the video several times. There is no rational reason you are alive. I know all about your skeletal upgrades. It still makes no sense."

"I was just trying to give myself the best possible chance at survival."

"Is that what you think you were doing by rolling that squad with no air cover?" Baines asked.

"Yes, and I stand by my actions. Maybe I don't have the finest strategic mind, but one thing that was clear to me was that if we'd let those fighters roll up on us, we'd have been in for a world of hurt. Maybe we could have come up with something, but in my mind, we'd have lost more than half a squad after the fact."

"And you're okay with your losses?" Corcoran asked.

"That's a shitty thing to ask," Deke said. "No, I'm not okay with my losses. I haven't really dealt with it yet. I've lost soldiers in combat before. Even worse, I've lost them because I didn't think through every facet of a problem. I carry that guilt. Those soldiers died today defending the brave men and women aboard *Angry Ark*. I'll carry the question of what I could have done to keep them alive with me forever, but that's as far as I can go."

"I'm inclined to agree with you, Dekoster," Baines said.

Deke gave the man a double take. "What? But ... you said."

"I said what I had to. I can't have my leaders jumping into combat at the drop of a hat. Discipline would break down and we'd be screwed. I happen to believe you did exactly what was required and there's no one else that could have knocked down one, much less two of those fighters. You used your assets to your best ability and sacrificed a few to save hundreds. That's real leadership, Deke."

"And next time you pull that shit, I'll have you cooling your heels in the brig," Corcoran said. "Don't test me on this."

Corcoran's words were interrupted by the sounds of *Angry Ark's* anti-aircraft guns firing and rocking thud of missiles impacting the vessel. "They're testing our armor," Baines said.

"And paying a hellova price," Corcoran said. "They're looking at this as a war of attrition. I'd wager they have a supply line set up."

"You need to let me take this fight to them," Deke said. "We can't sit back and wait while they chip away at our armor. If they're worried about us attacking, they'll be less interested in sending their fighters out. I'd like to test the southern base. We take all three of our Strykers, one of them carrying the anti-aircraft cannon."

"And do what?" Baines asked.

"Quick hit," Deke said. "Test their strength with a limited engagement. Ten minutes of contact and we pull back. Send some real hurt their way."

"We could launch Tomahawks," Corcoran said. "We have no idea how effective they'll be since we've never gone against their armor."

"What's the team composition?"

"Carrole's team is the light infantry with the Strykers," Deke said. "They're set up for attacking infrastructure. Bing's platoon would be much better against troops. I'd like to go along to see what we're up against."

"Have you heard nothing I've said?" Corcoran asked. "You can't go. That's the whole point."

"We need intelligence more than we need anything," Deke said. "What if there's a target of opportunity? Do we really want to pass on it? Like it or not, I'm the sharpest stick in your quiver. You need me on this mission."

"You've misread the room, Captain," Baines said. "While we're very impressed by your combat instincts, you're in limited supply. Imagine you're everything you think you are. How is it any sort of strategy to send you out against an unknown enemy? What if they roll over the team we send?"

"What if I could make the difference?" she asked quietly, knowing it was the wrong question.

"That kind of thinking will get you killed. We're here for the duration," Corcoran said. "There is time for taking calculated risks. This isn't one of them. We have no idea what we're up against."

"I recommend we go in hard," Deke said. "If you're committing Tomahawks, we send them first and soften the target. We need to know what it's going to take to breach."

"We should misdirect and send Tomahawks at several bases at once," Baines said. "We've already deployed high-altitude surveillance drones. We need to understand how coordinated their efforts are. With the radio chatter we're picking up, it would seem they're in constant communication."

"How soon do we roll?" Deke asked.

"You don't. I'm giving the mission to Kersey."

"You can't do that. You've got to let me lead this mission," Deke argued.

"Stand down, Captain," Baines said. "You're barely standing and your light infantry lead is in even worse shape. You've already done quite enough for *Black Turtle* this day. Fix your perspective. This isn't an in-and-out mission. We're going to be here for months, possibly years."

"What's between you and Kersey?" Corcoran asked. "Did he pour salt in your Wheaties or something?"

"His report on the attack at Normanville paints a very different picture than what I saw," Deke said. "When my squad came over the hill, he had his team hiding at the bottom of a ravine. He said they were pinned down, but we couldn't even see the enemy. He was scared shitless and if I hadn't knocked down that grenade, his entire squad and half of mine would have been dead."

"You're not wrong," Baines said.

"I know."

"What I mean is that his report reads differently."

"I know that, too. I can't believe there's no helmet video available. My account can't be that hard to verify."

"You suffered a traumatic brain injury. Your memory of those events is hardly reliable," Baines said.

"Is that why he's here? Because you can't rely on my memory and his report showed him some sort of hero?"

"Kersey is part of the team. The sooner you come to grips with that, the better we'll all be. I want you to support his mission with everything you have. I'm also ordering you to take sixteen hours down. You are not to command troops, exercise rigorously, or whatever else you're planning."

"Can I at least get a feed of the op?"

"That's fine," Corcoran said. "And when it goes to plan, you'll give Kersey the professional courtesy he deserves. No one says you need to be friends, but we can't be working against each other. Do you hear me, Captain?"

"Yes, Colonel," Deke answered in her most conciliatory tone. "Zebra Company will support Lieutenant Kersey in every possible way. I will always prioritize the good of the mission before my personal concerns."

"That's good to hear," Corcoran said. "Now get out of here."

Deke stood, drawing to attention.

"You're dismissed, Captain," Baines said.

Outside of the conference room, Deke was met by Bing and Carrole. "How bad is it?" Carrole asked.

"Bad enough."

"Looks like you still have your bars," Bing said. "That's something."

"Probably wouldn't have gone that way if you'd missed those trees on the way down," Carrole said.

"We need to do ..." Deke stopped and turned as Carrole's words caught up with her. "Because I'd be dead. Is that right?"

"Don't make me smile," Carrole said. "It hurts too much."

"You're on your own with that one, sister. I was playing this straight, but you just had to go and start something."

"The video of you jumping off *Angry Ark* is going around the crew like wildfire," Bing said. "That's why people are staring at you."

"I figured it was something like that," Deke said. "Not my first time getting videoed doing something dumb. At least this time, I'm not headed for the brig."

"Did you really kill your CO's dog?"

Deke sighed, shaking her head. "No," she said weakly. "Rehomed."

"There you are," Kersey said, catching up from behind the trio.

Deke failed to keep the wince from her face as she stopped. "You could have contacted me on comms if you were looking for me."

"I assume you got the word from Baines."

"I had a lot of words with Major Baines," Deke said. "Which one were you interested in?"

"The one where the mission to the southern base is mine and you're being benched," Kersey said with satisfaction. He turned to Carrole and continued. "I'm going to need your vehicles."

"Boss?" Carrole asked, looking at Deke.

"We'll supply drivers and support," Deke said. "We have one anti-aircraft that you'll need for sure."

"Negative, Ghost Rider," Kersey said, surprising everyone with his vernacular. "I have enough infantry guys with certifications in combat vehicles. We just need someone to check us out."

"No way," Carrole said. "Those vehicles are my responsibility and I'll be the one responsible for getting them back to spec once they come back."

"What's the big deal, Captain?" Deke said. "Zebra Company will follow chain of command. Don't you want the best drivers you can get? This is, after all, an alien planet."

"Fine, but if I get a single whiff of attitude, I'll leave 'em by the side of the road," Kersey said.

"Is that an official statement?" Deke asked. "I wonder what Major Baines would think about all that."

"Clearly, he thinks I've got the goods for your mission," Kersey said.

"Lieutenant Carrole, please work with Captain Kersey or his representative to make necessary arrangements," Deke said. "And let's be clear, Kersey. If those vehicles come back busted up because of some dumb strategy you come up with at the last minute, we're gonna have trouble, you and me."

"It's kind of ironic that we barely get here and already the major is giving me your equipment. What's next?"

"You're a pompous asshat." Deke took a menacing step toward the man, who stepped back and flinched as he expected a punch to fly.

"Take your best shot, Dekoster," he said. "You're so easy to bait. I'll have you sitting in the brig by the end of the week."

"You little fucker." This time she raised her arm with full intent to follow through. Fortunately, Bing saw it coming and stepped between the two, using his significant bulk to slow her. If not for her wounds, she might have worked her way around him. As it was, the contact brought on fresh waves of pain, and she groaned painfully.

Kersey sneered. "Better luck next time. Make sure you get some popcorn. This mission is going to be epic."

17

DEFEAT IN VICTORY
AJ – DEEP SPACE

"You didn't need to kill them all," Beverly said, flopping her legs over the console where AJ was staring at alien symbols and a weird sort of video screen that caused written language and general shapes to become raised.

"Some of these guys must not have such good eyesight," he observed, running his armored glove across the screen. For as resilient as the armor was, the glove was designed to transmit tactile sensations. "These screens would cost a fortune to manufacture."

"You changed the subject," Beverly said, staring up at him with concern in her face.

"How many was the right number to kill?" he asked impassively.

"You do not need to be angry with me."

AJ shrugged. "Maybe you don't understand, then. If I kill one, I might as well finish the job. They're either deserving or not. I either worry about them killing my team or I don't. We're in enemy territory and I'm not about to start taking prisoners I don't know how to hold. Are any of these Quarr? I suspect not, given how normal they look. But what happens if I stop when I enter the bridge. What if there are two Quarr and they get on my suit and breach?"

"It could be trouble, I see that," Beverly said. "I could let you know when there are no Quarr in the room, though."

"That could be interesting," AJ said. "Or maybe you let me do what's been keeping us alive and not rock the boat. Imagine what happens when I start questioning my decisions every time I get ready to pull the trigger. What happens then? How many milliseconds is it okay for me to delay to wait for your warning?"

"I'm upsetting you."

"Damn straight you are. Nobody likes the sharp end of the stick. Everybody wants to be considered nice or loving or whatever it is people who don't kill things are. Me, I know what I am. My team knows who we are. There's no ambiguity."

"I am sorry."

"For?"

"Acting insensitively. You have been asked to push aside emotions related to your actions so that you are an effective warrior. I am causing doubt. That is not helpful."

"It was a conversation you've been hinting at for a while. We were bound to get to it eventually," he said. "Maybe you could hold those conversations until we're not deep in an enemy's vessel and I need my concentration."

"That is sensible."

"Now, the captain is obviously stowed away somewhere. Will you help me find it?" AJ asked.

"Are you going to kill it?" Beverly asked.

"Are you asking if I intend to dispatch an enemy who tried to kill my entire crew?"

"Yes."

"It's a reasonable question. I'm not sure. Where is he?"

"I am not sure of the captain's gender."

"And I don't much care. I'll be honest, though, if it has a bunch of arms and legs and jumps at me, it'll end up a pile of goo like the last one. That I *can* promise."

"That's reasonable."

"Where?"

"There is a vault," she answered. "It may be difficult to open as it is heavily armored."

"Yeah, that'll stop me." AJ turned toward the bright, throbbing blue light that outlined a bulkhead on the port side of the bridge. "Are you in communication with this captain?"

"I believe it is possible. I have not made any overtures, however. I believe we are still in a tactical situation and that is in your purview."

"That's reassuring," AJ said dryly. "Go ahead and tell the captain to come out or I'll come in after it."

"Transmitting now."

Pulling a solid metal allow bar that had a flat end from where it was seated into the suit's thigh, AJ approached the captain's vault. Almost casually, he tapped the virtual HUD projected ahead of him and started a one-minute timer.

"You might suggest it hurry and unlock. I'm going to be agitated if I dig it out of there."

"I will communicate this."

"You're starting to slip back into the *too-many-words* thing again," AJ said.

"I will be more concise."

"Any answer?"

"There is negotiation. The captain does not believe your prybar is capable of breaching his vault."

"We have a gender. That's progress. Do we know species?" AJ asked.

"Cheell."

"I could have guessed. Those guys really are anything for a buck," AJ said, rearing back with the prybar. "You might let the captain know that this bar is probably worth half as much as his ship given how rare the material is."

"Why is the value significant?"

"Because shit that works gets expensive," AJ said. "If it costs more, it probably does more."

"That is not always the case."

"Yup. Feel free to argue that," he said, focusing on the outlined door's edges.

With his suit's magnification, he found a tiny seam that was invisible at normal magnification. Making small adjustments to his suit's controls to allow a precise strike, he rammed the prybar's edge into the hidden seam.

In that the bar only sank in an inch, AJ found that it pulled away easily. Undeterred by the limited progress, he repeated the strike with similar results.

"You should compliment him on his vault construction. This stuff is hard," AJ said. "It's gonna take me a minute to get through."

"Are you taunting him?"

"Maybe a little." AJ rammed the bar home again with continued if not minor success. "As an engineer, I can admit this is good stuff."

"I'll pass that along."

"Good," AJ said, grunting as he drove the bar home again. This time, the end of the bar sank more deeply, to the point it became stuck. "Oh, I might have spoken too soon. This doesn't look good."

"I don't understand. The bar is stuck," Beverly said, appearing on a rope line and looking at the end of the bar.

"I hit something soft. I think their armor wasn't as thick as advertised. Might be a good time to mention that to our guy," AJ said. "This could get messy. I'd hate to have collateral damage."

"You are not as concerned as you are communicating. I will make sure to communicate that as well."

"That sounds reasonable." AJ used the powerful suit actuators to help lift the end of the bar hoping to dislodge it.

"The captain asks for an accord."

"He's our prisoner. Food, water, and lodging for as long as I think he's giving us good information," AJ said. "Otherwise, he walks the plank."

"You're not a pirate."

"Some people used to see me that way."

"Jarnok has agreed to your terms and will exit the vault."

"Good," AJ said. "Tell him we're short on O2 out here and he'll want to put on a mask."

With a final heave, AJ pulled his prybar free and seated it back into the thigh armor. Stepping back, he waited for the vault's door to open. Even with the damage he'd caused, it opened a moment later.

"Chach, Peppers, I need a status," AJ called. Technically, he was supposed to use unit numbers while communicating over comms, but it didn't seem to fit his mood in that moment.

"Comms are fully locked down with zero resistance," Chach answered.

"Same in engineering," Peppers answered.

"I need you boys to exfil to the surface," AJ said.

Jornak gingerly stepped from within the vault where he'd been hiding. AJ shook his head in disgust when he caught the outline of a multi-jointed being's hand or whatever it was, wrapped around the Cheell's shoulder. The simple deception might have worked if not for AJ's prior experience with the multi-jointed Quarr. Without hesitation, AJ flicked a golf-ball-sized explosive charge into the vault while at the same time, he pushed the Cheell backwards. With nowhere for the explosive charge to go, the result was devastating to the non-armored Quarr as well as the captain.

"Someone really needs to tell these boys about how this armor works," AJ said. "They're having a really bad week."

"You are being flippant again. Should I be concerned?" Beverly asked.

"Defense mechanism. Read about it in your psychology magazines," AJ said. "Before you do that, though, help me figure out how to steer this thing."

"Where to?" Beverly asked. "I do not have access to most of the ship's functions."

"Steerage?"

"Yes, at a limited level."

"Put us into that planetoid," AJ said. "We should go as fast as we can as long as we're nowhere near our team or *Wasp*."

"Do you find no value in this vessel?"

"If we can't use it, we don't want to leave it behind for our enemy," AJ said. "And we can't use it."

"I have set a decaying orbit that will result in the destruction of this vessel in forty-five minutes," Beverly said. "Is that timely enough for your purposes?"

"Yup." AJ turned to the bridge entrance and retraced his steps. "When's the closest point for me to jump if I want Darnell to grab me with *Seahag*?"

"We are traveling away. You will want to disembark as quickly as possible."

"Copy that," AJ said, orienting himself on the vessel and pushing off toward the planetoid. "Big D, any chance I could get you to come over and grab me? I find I'm suddenly without transportation."

"On my way, One," Darnell answered. "Fifteen minutes out."

"I'll make my way your direction," AJ said, flipping over so his suit would catch his return to the planetoid's surface feet first. With little gravity and only the force provided by his jump, AJ landed easily on the surface, throwing up a large cloud of dust. Not one to sit around, he jogged across the alien surface toward *Seahag*.

Fifteen minutes later, *Seahag* dipped down with grappling hook deployed. Both men had executed the difficult retrieval sequence dozens if not hundreds of times, and AJ was plucked from the surface on the first attempt.

"Nice move, big man," he said.

"I need to tell you, you're walking into a shit-show back at *Wasp*."

"Did they drop troop?" AJ asked. "Why wasn't I notified."

"Wasn't that.

"What was it?"

"*Wasp* took a missile."

"Aww crap. Who's hurt?"

"That gal we picked up at the base, Holly."

A pit formed in AJ's stomach. The woman's death, while not critical to the mission, would be hard on team morale as she represented the survival of what many thought had been left behind.

"How?"

"Wrong place at the wrong time," Darnell said. "It was really just a fluke. Thing is, Doc is pissed."

"What the hell? What's she pissed about?" AJ asked defensively.

"I suspect you'll have a chance to find out," Darnell said. "Lisa said it's bad."

"Well, hell," AJ said to himself. "Lefty, can you take care of getting the equipment loaded onto *Wasp*? Looks like I've got a bit of a situation."

"Roger that, One," Left answered. "Good luck, sounds like you've got trouble brewing."

AJ sighed. Apparently, everyone knew he was in trouble but himself. "You know what, belay that order. We've got a job to do."

"Your funeral," Lefty answered.

"Pig, do we have any personnel still planet-side?" AJ called.

"There are three dirt-side, One," Pig answered.

"Get them loaded and bring *Wasp* to the initial site where we had the suits stored," AJ said. "We'll meet you there."

"Good copy, One," Pig answered. "We'll roll in once I have confirmed all personnel loaded."

"Perfect," AJ answered. "Big D, reroute to Alpha."

"Are you sure this is how you want to play it?" Darnell asked.

"I am," AJ said.

Landing at the Alpha site a few minutes later, AJ took stock of the remaining equipment. While there had been missile strikes when they'd arrived, there was little damage to most of the equipment aside from the loss of Rock Island. Uninterested in dealing with that pain, AJ stuffed away the feelings.

"Clear the LZ," Pig called over comms. "Alpha Three, you're danger-close and I don't want my bird damaged by the giant dome on your head."

"I happen to like the size of my head," Birdie answered. "But I copy and am clearing out."

"Two, let's get a team on those generators," AJ called. "Birdie, I want all those ammo warehouses loaded. Chach, you and Bald Norm help Three load."

It took a few minutes to organize the team, but soon, everyone had switched stances from combat to logistics. When they were nearly done, a distant explosion registered on AJ's HUD.

"The Quarr vessel has impacted this planetoid," Beverly said. "The damage was catastrophic."

With the team working efficiently, AJ moved into *Wasp's* hold and stepped into the specially designed bay created to stow a mechanized suit. Pushing booted toes beneath a lip of steel, he grasped an overhead bar, effectively locking the suit in place. With the suit taken care of, AJ opened the chest cavity and worked his way clear.

"Tenet, talk to me about damage," AJ said, locating one of the two engineers.

"It could have been worse," Tenet said, not bothering to stop his work to answer. "We got lucky most of those missiles didn't make it in."

"That wasn't luck," AJ growled. "I'm looking for an answer about damage."

"Right. There are some things we can't manufacture. Critical things. Do you want me to give you part numbers?"

"Don't be a smart ass. How is our capability impacted?"

"Somehow, the alien ship found a weakness in our armor," Tenet said, unperturbed. "We're running scans to see how prevalent. I'd like a month at a shipyard if you want to know the truth."

"That won't happen."

"Something needs to." Tenet stopped working and turned to AJ. "You're not hearing me. They knew about a weakness and hit it. Intercepting those missiles saved everyone aboard. If that information is out there, we might not be so lucky next time."

"Shit. That bad."

"That bad."

"Okay."

"Okay, what?"

"Okay, we'll deal with it. For now, get us ready. I want to be space-side in an hour.

"That's not much time."

"I agree."

AJ exited the engineering bay and was taken off guard when he caught the look on Jayne's face as she approached. He could see she was mad, but for the life of him, he had no idea why.

"What's going on?" he asked, imagining one of the crew had stepped over a line.

"I'm done, AJ. This is too much," she said, tugging at her hand.

"What do you mean, too much? We were attacked and we figured it out."

"No, we didn't. James Barnes is dead. Did you know he has a great grandchild he plays t-ball with? Or that he's been married for forty-five years? Did you know this? Or how about Holly Blanche. I found an engagement ring in her pocket. I imagine she was engaged to someone who was killed on the base. Did you know that?"

"What's going on, Jayne? Of course I knew Rock Island had great grandkids."

"One. He had one great grandkid. Cody. Six years old."

AJ and Jayne moved aside as a crew member passed forward. "Can we have this conversation later? I've got to deal with getting us off this rock."

"You can deal with whatever you want," Jayne said. "But know this. I'm done with this life. I can't keep sewing people up only to have them back in combat. I can't watch you die, AJ, even though that's what you seem hellbent on doing."

"That's not fair," AJ said, reaching for her.

In response she put up her arms and batted his hands away. "No! I've said what I'm going to. It's time for you to make a decision. I'm getting off this vessel at the first stop we make. I'll make my way to Dralli Station and start back with the university. If you want there to be an us, you'll join me."

"You know I can't do that," AJ said. "We have troops depending on us. There are people who will die if we don't go."

"And if you do go, how do you know it'll be enough, that you'll be enough."

"It just will," AJ said.

"What, because you're the great Albert Jenkins? What happens when you're not? What happens when there are a million Togath and they run over the top of whatever stupid piece of land we've decided to protect at all costs. Those costs are human lives. People who shouldn't die. People who could be leading productive lives. Why is Alpha Prime worth all this?"

"I don't know," he said softly, reaching again for her. This time, he managed to get a hand on her arm. "We can't leave people behind."

"I know, AJ," she whispered between tears. "I know you have an unending sense of what's right to do. I don't have that. I want it to be over. I can't live every day with the worry that you might die tomorrow. It's too much."

"What are you saying, Jayne?"

"It's simple."

"No it's not," he said. "None of this is simple."

"Give up this life. I'll go anywhere you want as long as you stop all this. We can build a life together on an alien planet. We can learn to be new people. The Galactic Empire is full of exotic locations where there's been peace for centuries. Why can't we just have that?"

"You know the answer."

"What? Because there are soldiers in trouble? There are always soldiers in trouble. There's always the next fight. That's the nature of life. Why do we always have to answer the call? Why can't enough be enough?"

"Can we compromise?"

Jayne's eyes drooped at the sides as sadness filled them. "No, AJ. How can we do that? I can't."

"Hear me out," AJ said. Jayne nodded her head as tears ran down her face. "I'll drop you at Dralli Station when we get repairs for *Wasp*. You take a position at the university and do your thing. We'll finish the mission. When we're done. I'll come back to you. We'll do what you say. I'll put down my weapon and we'll grow turnips on an exotic, alien planet. We'll look at having a family and settling down. Maybe I can even get a junkyard going."

Jayne shook her head slowly. "No, AJ," she said, softly, bumping her fists into his chest. "I can't wait for you. You're asking too much."

"I don't understand what you think I can do? I have an entire team depending on me to lead this mission. There are over a hundred combat infantry holed up and under fire with exactly one hope."

"That you'll come and save them," Jayne whispered, defeated.

18

LILY PADS

DEKE – PLANET FIMIL PRIME

"Are you ready for this?" Kersey asked as Deke, Bing, and Carrole joined the remainder of command in the mission room.

On the wall were five video feeds of fast-passing terrain. From the back of a cruise missile was a view Deke was plenty familiar with as she'd watched plenty of similar. She wasn't sure if she should be surprised by the fact that the terrain felt very Earth-like, at least from a thousand feet up.

"Have a seat," Baines said. "We're about to see how much trouble we're in for."

A flash on screen number two caught his attention.

"What in the hell?" Kersey asked.

Suddenly, the video feed was cut off.

"What happened?" Kersey demanded.

"Our plan has met with the enemy," Corcoran said through gritted teeth. "Did we get a data package?"

"What kind of package?" Kersey asked.

"Hold on a second, Lieutenant," Baines said, tapping his tablet with fervor. "No, Tubs, nothing."

"Comms are completely out?"

"That's right. I have engineering trying to reestablish."

"We're closing on Base Four," Baines' sergeant announced. "And we have eyes in the sky. I'll replace video number two with the overhead view."

"There it is," Kersey said excitedly.

The screen showed a base that looked like it had been in place for a couple of years rather than the reality of only a few days. On the far edge of the screen a black missile flew so low it raised a rooster tail of dust in its wake.

"What's our payload? Tactical nuke?" Deke asked.

"We went conventional," Baines said. "If they're not throwing nukes, I didn't want to start. It could push them over the top."

"So much for going home early," Kersey said with disappointment evident in his voice.

"How far out is your strike team?" Deke asked.

In the several hours since her last contact with the man, vehicles had been rolling. Having been forced into rest, she'd taken full advantage and downed three shakes, while even allowing Keegs to put her to sleep. As a result, she'd awakened recharged and stronger than before.

"We're ninety minutes out," Kersey said.

Deke nodded. She'd have liked the time between the team arriving and the missiles striking to be tighter, but she understood the desire to separate the actions.

A bright light flashed on the overhead view at the same time the missile's data feed stopped. This time the missile found its target.

"Confirmation of direct hit," Haskell announced triumphantly from where he sat next to a communication terminal.

"Thank God," Corcoran said with a sigh of relief.

One problem when assessing post-blast damage was the resultant dust cloud, which generally obscured video for several minutes. The room remained quiet as the team tried to make out what was left behind. As the scene started to clear, a grim truth set in. The base was completely intact.

"Mr. Haskell, are you certain the missile impacted?" Corcoran asked.

"We have coordinate verification fifty milliseconds prior to blast," Haskell answered. "It couldn't have been more than ten meters from the targeted coordinates. One moment. We have video of the blast."

"Show it," Corcoran said quietly.

With only a few milliseconds of unobscured video, the drone's feed, showed the payload exploding. The predictable force wave preceded the ball of escaping gasses and flames. When the blast reached the base, the roof responded as if it was a loose sheet of material, the wave pushing but not breaking it.

"That's remarkable tech," Baines said.

"You need to turn your team around," Deke said.

"No way," Kersey answered.

"You're not getting it," Deke said. "We just dropped a Tomahawk missile and didn't make a dent. What exactly is your team carrying that will penetrate better than that missile? We need to re-tool with new information."

"We prepared for this eventuality," Kersey said. "We'll look for a way in. This is an opportunity we can't afford to miss."

"You have a fast reaction team, not heavy infantry," Deke argued. "If they get stuck trying to breach and don't get in, they'll be sitting ducks."

"Why don't you worry about your own team," Kersey said.

She was about to respond when she caught Baines' warning glance. "Are you certain your plan holds up after a strike?"

"My engineers believe a shaped charge is more effective than a large, widespread kinetic blast like what a Tomahawk generates. They believe the Togath have an impact absorption field or similar technology, so large scale explosives are ineffective."

"How in the world do they believe this?" Corcoran asked, on the edge of anger. "What evidence do they present?"

"Apparently, we've run into Togath technology back on Earth. It's a working theory, but do we really have a choice to turn around?"

"I can't believe this is happening," Deke said to herself.

"We're about to lose number three," Haskell announced, which brought all eyes back to the screens. Sure enough, a few moments later, the screen went blank as the video feed was lost. "And there goes number five."

"I'm sorry, Captain Kersey, but Deke brings up a good point. If we can't get our Tomahawk past their front gate, we have no business sending in light infantry units. You need to turn your team around," Baines said.

"That's a mistake, Major Baines," Kersey said. "Let them do their job. We need the intel."

"They'll be slaughtered," Deke said. "Togath know we're coming and we're blind."

"Haskell, where in the hell is our drone view?" Baines asked, irritated.

"We've lost contact with all our drones," Haskell said. "It looks like some sort of software problem."

"We'll lose our ability for fast transport if all three of our Strykers are taken out," Deke said. "I'm not saying they're more important than the mission, but it'd be a real setback."

"Turn them around, Kersey," Baines said. "We're not ready."

"No can do," Kersey said.

"What do you mean by that?"

"They're running quiet. No radio traffic to keep them from being tracked."

"You're not serious. That's ridiculously irresponsible. No one can track an incoming radio transmission and we're transmitting from a known, fixed point," Baines said. "This is basic, Kersey. You know this."

"I've got video from our observer drone," Haskell said. "It's already at Base Six. There looks to be a lot of activity."

"That's interesting. Tell me you're recording this."

"It's recorded as it's captured," Haskell said. "We're storing the streams in *Angry Ark's* data vault for later analysis."

"Good."

"What if we take that drone out to the Strykers? We could get their attention and send them home."

"How? Fly in front of them?" Kersey asked.

"Haskell, retask that drone. Turn that team around."

"Aye, aye, sir!"

Tension further filled the room as the command team watched the video feed from the descending drone.

"Did you see that?" Deke asked. "There were flashes on the horizon. Keegs, replay from five seconds back."

"See what?" Baines asked. Deke had used subaudible communications to address Keegs and had simply posed a question.

"I thought I saw something on the horizon. I'm reviewing," she answered.

"Evasive, Haskell," Baines said. Without hesitation, the drone jumped to the side. "Make random course changes every thirty seconds or so."

"What are you getting all jumpy about, Deke?" Kersey asked.

"Soldier's instinct," Baines said. "Doesn't matter if she did or did not see something."

"There's a sniper at twelve miles," Deke said, focusing on the grainy image Keegs captured from the drone's feed. "Haskell, you should have a data packet with approximate location and the image."

"Copy that, Captain Dekoster."

"That's impossible," Kersey said.

"Stop, Captain Kersey," Baines said. "If you don't have something useful to contribute to the conversation, do not speak. We are engaging with aliens who have as of yet unknown capabilities. We all understand that with our technology our best sniper would find a twelve-mile shot on a moving target impossible."

"Haskell, you need to try to raise that team," Corcoran said. "I don't care if you have to ring their cell phones. Get them turned around. This is no surprise attack. It just became a trap and our soldiers are in the open."

"Cell phones ...," Kersey started.

"Not another word!" Baines snapped, his voice rising in an uncharacteristic shout. And just then, the drone's data stream ended.

"Dammit!" He slammed his fist onto the table. "Haskell, tell me someone on that team is receiving."

"Negative, Sir," Haskell said. "I'll keep trying."

"What other ground transportation do we have?" Corcoran asked.

"Aside from loaders and digging equipment, we have a general-purpose truck, probably better equipped for moving equipment than troops," Haskell answered quickly.

"One of those old Oshkosh six wheelers? I seem to remember seeing it on the list. I didn't recall if it made the trip."

"It is confirmed," Haskell said.

"What are you thinking, Tubs?" Baines asked.

"Nothing yet," Corcoran answered. "We need more drones in the area. For some reason they let us fly at fifteen thousand feet but knock it down when we got too low. What can you put in place, Mike?"

"I have three more deployed to bases to check on the impact of the Tomahawks. Do you want me to pull one?" Baines asked.

"Pull all three. If we get through this, we'll send something back for an after-action look," Corcoran said. "What's your timeframe for getting over our team?"

"We won't make it in time," Baines said. "About an hour past contact and that's assuming the Strykers make it all the way to the base. With snipers sitting out at twelve miles, I don't think that's a certainty."

"If I was the Togath, I'd let us come," Deke said. "Otherwise, why haven't they sniped those Strykers?"

"What do you mean?"

"They don't want those Strykers stopped. They want to see what we bring to the party, so they're letting us approach," Deke said. "This is their way of learning our capabilities. Or that's my read on it."

"Oh. Come. On," Kersey said. "You were just busting to get a run at one of these bases. Now you're suddenly concerned?"

"I still want a run at them, but not if they know we're coming," Deke said. "I wouldn't run three Strykers at Fort Indominable, even while under construction, if it wasn't a surprise. Our goal was to gather intel and we did. We know that they can see our drones once they're in the lower atmosphere. We also know their bases are extraordinarily resistant to explosive damage, at least from elevation."

"Sergeant, when will we have eyes again?" Baines asked.

"Right at dusk, which is 1940," Haskell answered.

"We'll reconvene at 1915," Baines said. "Deke, I want you and your team to stick around. Everyone else is dismissed."

Deke watched Kersey and his team file out and then sat straight.

"You do realize that if you hadn't been injured, it would be your team feeling the breeze on their asses, right?" Baines asked, once the door closed behind Kersey.

"I'm aware of that, Major," Deke said. "And I'd have expected to react to the news of the Tomahawk's effectiveness to gauge go or no-go for the strike team."

"And you said you'd still want to follow through," he said.

"That's not wrong," Deke said.

"But you want to pull Kersey's team."

"I do."

"Do you want to explain that?"

"My goal in attacking Base Six is to gain intelligence on weaknesses," Deke said. "Knowing they are aware of our approach puts us at a disadvantage for gaining that intelligence. I'd have turned around with this new information."

"I'm tracking now," Baines said. "Tell me, Captain, how do we get out of the situation we find ourselves in?"

"I can only see one possibility," Deke said. "But it's a whopper."

"This should be good," Corcoran said.

"Shoot," Baines said.

"Move *Angry Ark*. Set it down right on top of Base SIx. Use the rock drillers we have for stabilization and break that fucker open like the overripe coconut it is," Deke said.

"That's ridiculous," Baines said. "That's risking the entire mission on information we don't have. We don't even know if our drills could penetrate Base Six's armor."

"If it doesn't, set down next to it and use the ship's cannons. It's not like we're going to miss at point-blank. You wouldn't need stabilization at all," Deke said.

"No ... you're nuts ..." Baines stared across the table and stopped talking but continued to shake his head at the audacity of her proposal.

"Haskell, show me relative size between *Angry Ark* and Base Six. Project drill points," Corcoran said quietly after a few minutes of silence.

"Tubs, you're not seriously considering," Baines said quietly.

"It's a hellova risk," Corcoran agreed. "If we can't crack those bases, what are we doing here?"

"On the screen," Haskell said.

"What about all of the equipment on the ground?" Baines asked. "Do we just leave it?"

"Let's work the problem, Mike," Corcoran said. "Figure out what we'll lose if we do this, what we can load before we take off, all that."

"And what happens if they attack while we're in transition?"

"They haven't been extremely effective, yet. We've knocked down seven of their fighters. How many more are they willing to give to the cause? We, on the other hand, will be severely damaged if we lose our fast attack vehicles. This is an audacious plan. We have to at least entertain it," Corcoran said. "I'm not saying we're going to execute."

"I read you, Mike," Baines said. "Okay, Haskell, get us a list of everything that would be lost if we pulled up stakes right now. Assume anything inside is gone."

"Aye, aye," Haskell said. Two minutes later, a long list of items showed on a projection on the wall.

"There's some important equipment in that list," Baines said. "I'm not sure we're moving that generator anytime soon."

"It'd be a loss," Corcoran agreed.

"All of this," Baines said, standing next to the projected list, "could be brought in while we're pulling up stakes."

"Make an order, Mike," Corcoran said. "Load equipment that can easily be brought aboard. Even if we're not going forward, it's preventative."

"Aye, aye," Baines answer, nodding at Haskell in turn.

"Operation Lily Pad could be brilliant or the last thing we ever do," Corcoran said.

"You sound sold on it," Baines said.

"Work it through with me. Assume that our dwindling supply of Tomahawks never penetrate and that our fire-pisser Dekoster can't bust through a wall with whatever angry bullshit she throws at 'em. What's next? How do we conduct war? There are no cities to attack, nor are there encampments out in the open. On the other hand, our enemy seems content to simply probe our defenses without putting much on the line. One strategy would be to outlast us."

"Or wait for us to expose weakness and bring in material specifically designed to combat exactly that," Baines agreed. "That assumes our enemy has a supply chain and they understand we don't."

"Always assume the worst because that's likely the best case," Deke said, nodding grimly.

"Well put," Corcoran said, smiling for the first time that afternoon. "Where'd you hear that?"

"I believe it's your quote," Deke said.

"So it is," Corcoran said. "Haskell, can we get estimates on how soon we could lift off if we started the process right now?"

"Eighty-seven minutes," Haskell said. "With a direct path, we'd beat the Kersey's squad by seven minutes."

"What would get left behind?" Corcoran asked, knowing full well the sergeant had been prioritizing gear and planning to execute base extraction since it was first proposed.

"Here's my best list," Haskell said. "Everything in green is for sure. Items in yellow are in danger. Anything in red is not possible."

"This isn't so bad," Corcoran said. "Mike, any word back from our engineers about landing *Angry Ark* on the roof of Base Six?"

"Yes and no. We have no idea of the structure beneath Base Six's roof, assuming it's a roof at all. For all we know it's a big tablecloth."

"With excellent resistance to Tomahawks," Corcoran said. "If that's the case, I'd like a bolt of that fabric."

"There is plenty of opportunity for landing," Baines said. "According to the pilots, it'll be a significantly easier landing than our last. They were excited about flat surfaces and no mountains in the way. I suggested this was more of an out-of-the-frying-pan-into-the-fire kind of thing."

"I haven't heard a reason to not go," Corcoran said. "Dekoster, talk to me about what we do first thing we land."

"We put Bing's platoon through the back door first and have them lay down as much heavy fire as forty soldiers can muster. We don't stop until everything on the inside looks like everything on the outside," Deke said.

"Shit, I like that description. That's some serious soldiering right there," Corcoran said.

"What if we can't crack that egg, Dekoster?" Baines asked.

"We set down next door, roll Zebra Company out and attack that base with maximum avarice," Deke said. "We try to dig under. We try to break through. We punch, we prod, we apply shaped charges, we go at this like it got handsy with our little sister."

Baines couldn't resist laughing but managed to stifle a bark of laughter. "Let me guess, you want to lead that attack."

"From behind," Deke said. "I can learn my lesson. But I would like to be in armor and follow the Company out the back door. I think it gives our boys and girls the right idea about our commitment to the mission."

"Dekoster, are you sold on this mission? Would you commit the lives of everyone aboard *Angry Ark* to its success?" Corcoran asked.

"That's a big ask," Deke said. "I have no idea of our chance of success. What I do know is that if we sit back, our enemy will eventually figure out a way to hurt us for real. The loss of those Strykers and the team will hurt us in the long run. Like you said, we don't have a supply run. We should take risks when we're strong enough to recover, not when we're on the ropes."

"I see. Okay. Mike, what's your take?"

"I'm on the fence, which is movement," Baines said. "At first, I thought the idea was ridiculous. Now, I'm starting to see the merits of a bold move. Unless Togath are genius level, they'll never see it coming. It's that audacious. Based on that and the fact that Kersey's team has no chance of survival if we don't go, I'd say I'm in. How about you, Tubs?"

"We're calling it Operation Lily Pad," Corcoran said. "If this works, we won't stop at Base Six. We'll run these bastards off planet and go home early."

"Hooah!" Deke said.

"Hooah!" the room replied.

"Get Zebra Company ready, Dekoster. We have no idea what we'll run into at Base Six, so I need you to be ready for anything."

"We'll make plans for both scenarios. First, that we bust through the top," she said. "Second, that we have to play broadsides with it while we set our anchors."

"Okay, people, Operation Lily Pad is a go. Meet back here in thirty minutes, Dekoster. I want to hear a more detailed plan for Zebra Company than you'll get angry and shoot things."

"Yes, sir!"

19

ENDINGS
AJ – DEEP SPACE

"Where to, boss?" Pig asked as AJ appeared on the bridge. The change in the young captain's attitude gave AJ hesitation. Up to that point, the man had comported himself as an equal. Something had changed and AJ imagined it had to do with the humbling experience of the man's first exposure to combat where victory was not assured by superior equipment.

"Once everyone is aboard, we'll head to the transition point and cross over if it's still open," AJ said.

"That's a negatory," Pig said. "Closed about twenty minutes ago. I hope you can get us another ride. The computer says it's a bit of a hike from here."

Despite the heavy conversation with Jayne, AJ snorted a laugh at the man's understatement. "I suppose that's right, but what's a couple of galaxies between friends, eh?"

"Really? Galaxies?"

"I think the headline there is don't get into a fight with the Tok," AJ said. "We're not sure how to get between solar systems and they have suitcases that jump galaxies."

"Whoa. Where will we jump to when we re-open?"

"The device is keyed to a pair of locations," AJ explained. "We'll be right back where we came out behind the moon."

"Be a lot of people interested in that device," Pig said. "You're smart to keep it quiet."

"A lot of good it would do them," AJ said. "Commander Cer specifically keyed that location because it's so far away from everything that it's of no practical use other than to stash things."

"Makes you wonder what else they've stashed," Pig said.

"I'd file that under the heading of things that can get your memory wiped."

"What's that?" Pig asked with a momentarily blank look on his face. For a moment, AJ thought he was sincere but then the young captain smiled, giving away his joke.

"Once we're through, we'll take the transition point to Xandarj," AJ said.

"Why Xandarj? Will you contact Blue Tork to resupply or arrange for repairs?" Pig asked. Surprised to hear the name of his Xandarj friend's name coming from Pig, AJ raised an eyebrow. Pig nodded understanding at his surprise and filled in. "Everyone near this project had to take an intensive study on everything Army Intel has documented on your trips to alien worlds. Blue Tork gets a lot of ink."

AJ sighed, not thrilled to have his life under a microscope. "That makes sense. Mads Bazer can connect us with a ship engineer for repairs. The rate of exchange on precious metals is pretty good on Xandarj since their home planet has been tapped out and their asteroids aren't overly rich."

"What are you boys working on?" Darnell asked, entering the bridge.

Instead of answering, AJ turned the conversation around. "How's loading going?"

"*Seahag* and *Bernard* are last to load in the hold," Darnell said. "It was a tight fit, but we're all in."

"Thank you," AJ said. "Pig, put out an all-hands to meet at the bottom of the cargo ramp. We're going to honor an old friend before we set off."

"That's the right thing to do," Darnell said. "There wasn't much of Rock Island left, so some of the boys filled a jar of sand to bring back with us."

AJ nodded, unable to speak. He'd pushed off mourning the loss of his friend long enough and it was time to allow grief its due. Somberly, the trio walked from the bridge and through the ship, picking up a tail of followers as they did until they'd made it out where the ground had been packed by all traffic.

"I feel bad that I'm not real good with words," AJ started, feeling the eyes of the entire crew on him. "Rock deserved better than this, but he knew the score. A good friend and a better warrior no man nor country could ask for. James Barnes served his country and his teammates with honor, never once backing down from a fight and never once failing to stand in the gap when his country called. It's men like Rock Island who give me hope. That there are men and women who will always answer the call of their country, knowing that to turn away opens the door for evil."

AJ turned his face to Jayne, who was looking at him with tears in her eyes. When their eyes met, her chest shuddered, knowing in that moment what his answer would be to her demand. "In Rock's memory, I ask every man and woman to commit themselves to this mission and to our great country. That Rock's sacrifice would be honored and that future generations find prosperity and peace in a universe filled with danger in small part because we did not falter when the call came. Rock, I'll miss you, brother."

"Hooaah," LeBeau said, with weak bravado.

"Hooaah!" the remainder of the team answered.

"Thank you, AJ," Lefty said after a few minutes of silence. "That was good. Rock deserved to be respected."

AJ nodded. When he finally found his voice, it easier to lean into the mission and avoid the emotions that threatened to overcome him. "Okay, folks. Let's get loaded up and we'll head to Xandarj where we'll contract for repairs. Joyce and Teton, stay back a minute, I'd like to talk about where we're at with those."

"I'm glad you're taking this seriously," Tenet said. "We'd be sitting ducks if we didn't fix this problem."

"How is it we missed the flaw?" AJ asked. "Were we sabotaged?"

"Maybe," Joyce said. "But that would have had to happen when *Wasp* was in engineering."

"I thought that was all handled by you guys," AJ said.

"We led teams of people," Tenet said. "The flaw is subtle. Without highly advanced weaponry, it would have never been found."

"How sure are you that Quarr knew about the flaw?" AJ asked. "Could they have discovered it by scans?"

"Anything is possible," Joyce said. "I'd say that finding this flaw with any kind of scan we're aware of is impossible."

"But alien technology might as well be magic for as much as we understand it. Sure, there are common building blocks, like the equivalent of wheels and levers, but maybe Quarr have some way to find problems."

"Like how they attacked your mechanized infantry suit," Joyce said. "Who would have thought they'd jump on you."

"That made sense," Tenet said. "Nothing made of flesh and bone could stand in front of a mechanized suit. Jumping on the suit made perfect sense."

"But then it knew it had to start attacking the joints. It even knew how to attack," Joyce argued.

"Guys, stop," AJ said. "Too much ambiguity. I need to know if we have an information leak or if we're outmatched by technology."

"I'd say you have both," Joyce said.

"He's right," Tenet agreed. "Not one of our engineers would have left a hole like this in our armor plan. It's unconscionable. Right, Brian?"

Joyce nodded his head in agreement.

"And you can fix it if we get access to a manufactory that can make armor?"

"Shouldn't be a problem," Tenet agreed. "We'll need at least five days, though."

"Skip sleep and make it two. It's a long haul out to Fimil Prime," AJ said. "You can rest while we drive."

"Get us the parts, we'll do our best. We just don't have enough able hands and we can't trust aliens to help us. We'd be right back in the same mess we're in now," Joyce said.

"Almost true," AJ said. "You do know I was the lead engineer for my company, right? And, I have friends on Dralli Station. One of them is a very talented shipwright. The other is handy. He'd just need a little direction."

"Three warm bodies with wrench skills would go a long way," Tenet said. "Maybe bring us down to three days if we don't sleep much. It only works if they can hit our specs. There's no way they can get the armor manufactured. That would take us six months back home."

"Money talks," AJ said. "Get me designs in the next twenty-four hours and I'll reach out to my contacts on Dralli."

"Maybe we won't die after all," Tenet said, turning to Joyce.

"Oh, we're totally gonna take it in the shorts," Joyce said, walking up the ramp next to his friend. "If they introduced one flaw into our design, there's probably another."

"Maybe we need to work this back the other way," Tenet said. "Think like a saboteur. What's the easiest way …"

AJ smiled as he watched the two men disappear into the ship. Sighing, he let the events of the day settle over him. It felt like his team had been under fire for days, which to some degree they had. Add to that the death of his friend and then the breakdown of his relationship with Jayne, it was a lot to handle, and he felt stuck.

"Are you coming in?" Lisa asked, appearing at the top of the ramp. "Or do you need a minute?"

"I don't mind admitting I'm struggling," AJ said. "Today's been a lot."

Lisa nodded and walked down the ramp to join him. "That was a nice ceremony for James," she said. "People need permission to grieve."

"He was a good man."

"You're a good man, too, AJ," Lisa said, which caused his eyebrows to rise. Lisa smiled at his response. "Nobody can hear me. If you bring it, I'll deny I ever said it."

"That, I believe," he said.

"I was talking to Amanda," she said. "Sounds like you guys are going through a rough patch. Want to talk about it?"

"I'm not sure what's left to say. She wants something I can't give."

"Nobody will blame you if you decide that's your path," Lisa said. "You've done more than enough for your country. You don't owe anyone anything."

"I know that," AJ said. "How do you walk away from those men and women on Fimil Prime, though?"

"Don't get too full of yourself. There are plenty of men and women on this ship who would continue the mission," she said. "I'm just sayin' it doesn't always have to be you. I've got some of the same concerns Amanda has. One of these days, one of us might be on that butcher's bill. How's that going to feel?"

"Like shit," AJ said. "That's how I feel about losing Rock."

"That's right," Lisa said. "You're going to lose something more now. If you go on to Fimil Prime, do you think Amanda will wait for you?"

"I can't control what she does."

"No, but you can control what you do."

"I can't turn my back on those soldiers."

"You can," Lisa said. "What you mean is you won't."

"True."

"And you're willing to lose Amanda over that."

"I have no choice," AJ said. "You know I was once a prisoner of war. I remember being held in a pit, hoping someone would come for me. I remember when Lefty and his boys showed up like it happened yesterday. I can't walk away from that."

"That's not an answer. Are you willing to lose Amanda over it?"

AJ swallowed hard and his voice was quiet when he finally answered. "Yes. I'd never be able to look at myself in the mirror again if I stayed behind."

Lisa stepped forward and pulled AJ into a hug. Not one to cry, he felt shame when tears rolled down his cheeks and wicked onto her shoulder. She didn't let go but held him as he allowed emotions to roll over the top of him. For an unmeasurable time, the grief was almost too much to bear.

She held firm, unflinching at his uncharacteristic display, knowing full well how hard the losses were to her friend. When the grief abated to a point where it was manageable, AJ pulled back.

"Shit, I'm sorry, Lisa. I'm a mess," he apologized, embarrassed by the look of empathy in her face. He rubbed calloused hands across his cheeks, not wanting the tears to be evident.

"Don't do that, AJ," she said softly. "A man isn't an island. I may give you the business from time to time, but we've been friends for a long time. You kept my Darnell safe in 'Nam. When you're hurting, so am I. It's not weakness to lean on a friend when life is kicking your ass. We've got you, Albert Jenkins. Don't you ever question that."

"I didn't think that was where my head was at," he said, blowing out a hot breath.

Lisa gave him a warm smile. "Maybe Amanda will change her thinking. You should talk to her."

"Do you think it would help?"

"If you're asking if she'll change her mind about being okay with you going to Fimil Prime, I don't know," Lisa said. "But you started out as friends. Maybe you can salvage that. That'd be worth something, right?"

"I don't want to lose her."

"So don't," Lisa said. "Be her friend if she can't be the other."

AJ nodded, his thinking clouded with the heavy emotions. "That'll be hard."

"And worth working for."

"When did you get so smart?"

Lisa's smile broadened. "Finally. I've been waiting thirty years for you to finally acknowledge that."

AJ chuckled. "I'll deny ever saying it."

20

CASUALTIES

DEKE – PLANET FIMIL PRIME

"We have no idea what we're going to find inside Base Six," Deke said, looking out over Zebra Company. "We haven't seen more than a few Togath since we've landed. Our goal is to take this base. We will not stop until we have."

"Hooah!" Leisk shouted to which eighty voices responded in kind.

"The base is covered in some sort of advanced fabric. We hope the weight of *Angry Ark* will cause it to settle. If it resists our ship's weight, we'll use the articulating anchors to drill in. If that doesn't break through, we'll lift off and set down for a good, old fashioned broadsides war. *Angry Ark* is shit for space combat maneuverability because of her ridiculous armor. I like our chances in a straight up slugfest, though."

"Hooah!" Leisk called out again.

"We have exactly one message we want to deliver today," Deke said, straightening. "That the US Army is in the business of winning. And we'll do that by any means possible."

"Captain, we're on final approach." The voice on Deke's comm belonged to Baines, who she knew to be on the bridge, coordinating the various teams. "We've detected energy signatures that are likely ground-to-air batteries. Things might get a little rough from here on out."

"We're ready, Major," Deke answered. "Let's get this done!"

"Bring me a victory, Deke," Baines said.

"You can count on Zebra Company, Major!"

Brace, brace, brace, missile impact imminent.

Deke grasped *Angry Ark's* exposed super structure to hold herself steady. Her grab was just in time as the massive ship jumped to the side under the stress of a massive explosion. Barely able to keep her feet, she watched as Zebra Company was brought to its knees. Everything in the ship's hold that wasn't tied down leapt into the air and became a deadly menace.

"Norvell, secure those crates!" Bing shouted. "Bostitch, get a medic over here."

Deke wanted to jump into the fray as her company struggled to right itself after the ground was knocked out from beneath them. As she looked for some way she could be helpful, she realized her team was working their long hours of training and reorganizing back into the elite fighting force it was. With a swell of pride, she looked on as chaos quickly turned to order.

"How many more of those do we have coming, Major?" she asked.

"More," Baines said, his voice grim.

Seeing a soldier pinned beneath a crate, she jumped from her elevated position and sliced through the crowd. She could have ordered a team to help, but time would work against the man's survival given how it lay across his body.

"Move!" she ordered as a single soldier struggled to lift against the only viable handhold.

"We need a jack," the soldier answered.

Deke muscled her way into position. "We'll see."

Crouching, she locked her fingers beneath the crate's edge. The soldier looked on as if she'd lost her mind, then stepped awkwardly in next to her, trying to find a grip of his own. He wouldn't be able to help much, but it was the right thing to do.

"Lift!" she growled as the weight of the crate settled against her fingers. Chords of muscle bunched along her arms and shoulders as she pushed against the weight. "Holy, shit, what's in this thing?"

A groan from the deck spurred her on. She was relieving pressure from the trapped soldier's abdomen.

Brace, brace, brace, missile impact imminent.

"Get something under the crate, she's going to lose it!" someone yelled from behind.

An explosion rocked *Angry Ark*. At first, Deke held fast, the weight of the crate holding her to the deck. Unfortunately, that security was lost when everything on the deck became weightless as a second missile struck high on *Angry Ark's* armor.

"Oh, hell no," she cried out as the oversized crate floated toward her. The weightlessness ended as quickly as it had begun when *Angry Ark's* deck reached up for its momentarily lost contents, crushing the trapped soldier in a final embrace.

"Fuck!" she yelled in fury, lashing out to repeatedly kick the side of the crate.

"Boss, stop. There's nothing you could have done." Leisk's voice cut through the fog. "We need you here. We're just about to make contact."

Those words snapped Deke from her rage. "Keegs, give me an external view," she ordered. "Leisk, get a team on this. This soldier deserved better than to die like this."

"Yes, ma'am," Leisk answered. "We'll take care of him."

On her HUD, Keegs displayed one of several drone's views of *Angry Ark's* approach. Base Six's roof looked as impenetrable as always, however, weapon's fire from the base was both constant and withering from a dozen once hidden turrets mounted high on its outer walls. Deke shook her head at the prospect of a Stryker team maneuvering through the sort of fire the mounted guns were pouring onto *Angry Ark.*

For no reason she could understand, Baines had chosen not to return fire, but instead allowed the onslaught to go unanswered. That *Angry Ark's* armor was holding fast was some consolation, but she couldn't imagine why he'd hold back while at point blank range.

"*All hands, prepare for impact,*" Baines' voice floated over the public address. "*We're going to set down hard and crack this base open like an egg.*"

Deke dropped to a knee and placed a hand on the deck for further stability. "Here we go."

A moment later, it felt as if the world had dropped out from beneath her as *Angry Ark's* pilots cut off the artificial means that the massive ship used against Fimil Prime's gravitational pull. Like a stone, it dropped from fifty meters in the sky, which was the maximum impact the ship's alien-supplied inertial dampers could absorb without causing excessive injury to the humans aboard.

The calculation for excessive injury had looked good on the computer screen. In practice, the jarring impact inside the vessel, while survivable, snapped bones, stretched ligaments, and generally wreaked havoc to all aboard. Stunned to silence, Deke blinked as she pushed herself to standing.

She'd been told to expect ten percent casualties from the hard landing. The injuries would trim her fighting force but not permanently. It was a calculated risk borne of necessity. Even as she straightened, her mind cleared from the pain.

"Keegs, give me that external view back!" she growled, noticing the drone video was no longer available.

"The drones were dispatched on impact."

"What's that mean? What's happened? Did we break through?"

"This is not clear," he answered.

"Command, what's our status?" she called into comms.

"We lost power on the bridge," Baines answered. "We're not sure what they hit us with. Secondary power is sixty seconds from live."

"Did we break through?"

"We don't know."

"Do we know anything? Are we go?"

"Hold tight, we're blind right now."

"We can't afford to let them organize," Deke said. "Give me the order. The time is now!"

"I can't give that order," Baines said. "We have no idea if we've breached."

"Deke, this is Colonel Corcoran, you're clear for external operation. Take this fight to the ground. Get me this base!"

"Hooah!" Deke cried out. "Zebra Company, pick your asses up. We're going hot and heavy by the numbers! If you're too wounded to roll out, step to the side."

While there were grumbles and groans, the majority of Zebra Company was back to standing. Looks of confusion were replaced by grim resolve. Every man and woman on the deck had long combat histories and knew what awaited them on the other side of *Angry Ark's* loading ramp. Each with their own mechanism for coping with impending combat, the hold bristled with anticipation.

"Lieutenant Bing, are our heavy hitters ready to lay down some fire?" Deke called over general comms so all could hear.

"Zebra Company brings the hurt!" Bing answered. "Give me something to shoot!"

"Deck crew, open that door before we blow it off its hinges!" Deke ordered.

Puffs of explosive charges set against thick pins released the back hatch, allowing it to fall unencumbered by machinery designed to keep from damaging the massive door or more likely anything that might be lined up beneath it on the outside.

Deke blinked as bright sunlight flooded *Angry Ark's* hold. A roar of excitement arose from Bing's heavies as they surged onto the ramp and out from the safety of the ship's armor. Weapon's fire splattered into their midst and soldiers were cut down. Instead of scattering for cover, Bing's platoon returned fire. Working furiously, he handed out target assignments, organizing squads to keep them from doubling up.

"Talk to me, Bing," Deke said, watching as her soldiers bravely stood and returned fire, causing the enemy to take cover against their overwhelming, well-organized response.

"We're behind the walls. They weren't expecting us to make it in," he said.

"I'm sending light infantry," Deke said. "Make a hole."

"Copy that," Bing grunted between bursts of automatic rifle fire. "We're advancing into a courtyard so we can take covered positions.

There are two levels, we're entering at ground. We need someone to get up on that second level and clear it. They're sniping on us."

"We've got two stairways leading up," Carrole joined in. "I'll send two squads on either side."

"Good coordination," Deke said. "Move out!"

Slowly but surely, *Angry Ark's* hold cleared as Zebra Company filed out into Base Six's main courtyard. Deke followed slowly. She hated that she wasn't on the front line, battling it out. As if to answer her unspoken desire, a pair of Togath jumped onto the deck and raced into *Angry Ark's* hold, clearly intent on using the opportunity to their favor.

Bringing the rifle to her shoulder, she fired. The commotion caught the attention of *Carrole's* rear squad.

"Intruder!" the squad's sergeant called out. "Fire at will and watch for friendlies!"

Deke raced to the side, knowing she was just as likely to get shot by a well-intentioned but combat blind soldier. The Togath were quick to respond and jumped in behind haphazardly fallen crates still littering the deck.

Even as fast as they were, Deke was certain her rifle's bullets had found their home a few times.

"Kersey, we have intruders in the hold," Deke called. "Sergeant Ferrell, we've got this, I need you back in the fight!"

"Aye, aye, Captain," Ferrell answered. "I hate leaving you open, though."

"I have them pinned down. We've got this. Kersey has a team incoming," Deke said, not completely sure she was right. Kersey's petty behavior could cause trouble if he was slow to respond.

"You need to wait for backup," Keegs said as she sprinted across the deck, taking cover behind a heavy crate. A handful of soldiers were still recovering from *Angry Ark's* hard landing and when green energy bolts flew from the invading Togath's position, she jumped atop the crate and loosed a heavy stream of automatic fire.

"I'll wait in hell!" she growled. "They're firing at my team."

The green energy bolts tore into one of the fallen soldiers sitting against the hold's outer wall. He slumped forward. Dead. Deke mentally kicked herself for sending Carrole's squad out, even though she knew that one wounded soldier's life was not as important as securing the base.

Leaping from one crate to another, Deke peppered the Togath pair's position, knowing that to fire while taking fire was difficult for anyone, regardless of if you were genetically bred for war.

Her efforts were rewarded as green energy bolts soon started flying her way. With a quick dodge, she jumped off a crate, and while in mid-flight captured the Togath's position. One Togath was sitting, the other standing next to it. She'd heard that Togath fight as mated couples. What she didn't know was if they would defend each other. It appeared that was the case.

Pulling a grenade from her belt, she lobbed it with a lazy arc over top. Having been an elite athlete, her aim was impeccable, and she heard shuffling as a Togath scrambled to change its position. An explosion followed, sending crate shrapnel upward and then to rain down. She wondered what piece of expensive equipment she'd just ruined or how many days rations she'd destroyed. It wasn't terribly important. She would take the fight to her enemy with unyielding violence until it stopped moving.

Jogging up and rounding the corner, she found one of the two Togath lying prone, a victim to her grenade. "Rest in pieces, asshole," she growled.

A flicker of movement caught her attention and likely saved her life as a giant Togath bull rushed her from its hidden position. Twisting just in time, she brought her rifle across her chest and blocked, realizing in that moment she couldn't possibly withstand the beast's charge.

Never having experienced a Togath closer than the length of a grenade's toss, she analyzed the alien even as she bent her knees to accept its charge. Likely out massing her by twice, she was on unequal footing in hand-to-hand combat. Impassively, she watched the Togath's face as they fell to the deck in perfect synchronicity. She found intelligent eyes and discovered very human looking anger etched across its face. In one hand, the Togath held a fat knife, that in her hands would be more of a short sword, presuming she could even wrap her hands around its hilt.

"Now, now, getting stabby won't bring back the missus," she said, using all her considerable strength to block the Togath's arm as she rolled the two of them onto the deck. At the last minute, the Togath seemed to understand that she was not simply falling beneath his onslaught but was guiding them. His adjustment came too late and when, at the last second, she kicked off, leaving her rifle behind, she separated with the Togath flat on the deck and her on the balls of her feet.

The Togath's face filled with rage. It apparently thought humans to be lower on the pecking order. That one had killed its mate and then evaded it, further provoked the gray-skinned alien. It roared angrily and spoke in a language not instantly translated.

"No Togath, Keegs?" Deke grunted, pulling her sidearm from her waist. Like all officers, her standard uniform included a pistol. Unlike others, she preferred the maximum stopping power of her Desert Eagle over standard issue sidearms, even though it was heavy to be carrying on her hip.

"That is no language understood by Galactic Empire," he answered. "I'm recording and will work on recognizing phonemes for a future translator."

Deke fired at the Togath, who moved more quickly than expected for its mass. Even so, the Desert Eagle barked angrily as she punched its chest with armor piercing full metal jackets and hollow point bullets, both of which she loaded into each magazine.

With a howl of pain, bright blue blood welled up on the Togath's chest as it gained its feet. As bullets punched against the alien, its body jerked backwards, but for no reason she could imagine, it was able to keep its feet.

"Well, shit," Deke said, her magazine running dry. "Now, what?"

"Your hollow point ammunition is not penetrating," Keegs explained. "You are fortunate to have alternatively loaded full metal jackets which appear to be piercing the natural armor, but with much less damage than you would hope for."

"Now you tell me," Deke said, springing to the side, barely avoiding the Togath's lunge. Even as she dodged, she tracked the large alien's movement. It was faster than any opponent with whom she'd sparred. Similarly, however, she was also moving faster than ever before. "Am I running on massive adrenaline?" Deke kicked off the Togath's knee, hoping to cause it to trip. It was to no avail, but having planned for things to go poorly, she didn't mind using the immovable appendage to allow her to gain distance.

The Togath lunged and slashed wildly. Ordinarily, Deke appreciated an angry opponent that was making wild moves. The problem with the Togath, however, was that its reach was almost twice that of any opponent she'd faced. And that realization came too late when the Togath's thick blade found her midsection and sliced through the Kevlar chest armor and into her abdomen with little resistance.

"Holy shit!" she cried out, moving to the side as she could back no further without running into supply crates. It was then that she discovered a key weakness of Togath. The Togath attempted to side-step to find her and stumbled slightly over its own feet. Not willing to ignore the possibility that its foible was momentary, she pulled a magazine from her belt and slapped it home, reseating the slide and brought fresh ammunition to the chamber. "Oh, you shouldn't have allowed for that, big fella," she taunted.

The Togath roared, catching itself and turning on her. Ordinarily a center-of-mass shooter, she had to adjust if she were to survive the combat. Taking aim at the Togath's head, she fired repeated shots. For some reason, bullets skipped off the alien's bony structure, tearing skin back and leaving bloody trails but the damage was minor. The Togath barked out a noise that seemed to be a laugh.

"Well, aren't you just all arrogant," she shot back when the Togath shook off the final round she fired.

"Hey, jackass, over here!"

The sounds of rifle fire filled the air. Instead of looking to the source of the noise, the Togath leapt past Deke and took cover behind crates. While it left itself open to Deke, it shielded itself from the much larger danger.

She jumped at the opportunity. Or more accurately, the passing Togath. Not considering the possible danger that would come from failure, she kicked off a crate and looped an arm around the Togath's thick neck. In mid jump, she dropped her Desert Eagle and found her k-bar knife at her side. In a single, fluid movement, she brought the knife around and buried it in the Togath's eye. She felt the moment the knife hit home. Like a light switch had been flipped, the Togath froze up and toppled over.

"Sonnofabitch," she panted, struggling to free her arm, trapped beneath the Togath's mass.

"Do you need help, Captain?" a soldier from Kersey's team asked.

"Yeah, find my pistol, would you? Hate to lose it after all that," she said, wrenching her arm free.

"What about your knife?" another soldier asked. "Sorry about announcing ourselves. We needed to get some separation so we could shoot it."

"Let's leave the knife for a minute," she said. "I'd hate for that thing to wake back up."

"It can do that?" the first soldier asked, handing Deke her pistol.

"I have no earthly idea," Deke said. "I wouldn't have thought it could take two dozen .50 AE bullets, either, but it did. Let's assume we don't know what it's capable of."

"Yes, ma'am!"

"Bing, talk to me," Deke said.

"Captain, are you up? I got word you were fighting boarders."

"I'm up," Deke said. "What's the word out there?"

"It's grim, ma'am. We're making progress," Bing said.

"Do we control the base?"

"Not yet," he said. "We've only run across a dozen Togath so far, but that's enough. We're taking heavy casualties. I had a report there was a breakthrough pair that made it into *Angry Ark*. What's the damage?"

A pull from the side reminded Deke that a medic had started working on her abdomen. "We handled them," Deke said. "Have you secured a temporary command post?"

"Yes, but I'd request you stay back. Secure is a tenuous condition," Bing said.

"Understood. I'm coming forward."

21

HERO'S DESTINY
AJ – DEEP SPACE

"We're going to Dralli Station for repairs," AJ said to Jayne. She was in the medical bay, treating Birdie, who'd somehow broken a finger when exiting his suit.

"Heya, Boss," Birdie said.

"Are you going to be okay?"

"Oh, hell yeah," Birdie said. "I just need Doc to set it straight, so my buddy here can get me all fixed up."

"This is going to pinch a little," Jayne said, grinning at Birdie.

Birdie shook his head. "Why is it every time ..." Not giving him a moment to consider what was to come, she yanked on his finger, pulling it straight and setting it in a single movement. "Holy shit, damn, that hurts."

"Pain fades," Jayne said. "You'll need to grab a shake. You're running low on calcium and other basic minerals. You should pay more attention to what you're eating. Your levels are generally too low."

"I know, Doc, but those shakes taste like chalk," he complained.

"They should."

"You'll be fine," AJ said. "Do you mind if I have a word with Doc?"

Birdie jumped off the table. "Oh, sure. Sorry."

"Don't take that splint off for at least four hours," Doc said. "And bring it back. I can reuse it."

"Sure."

"I take it you've been thinking," Jayne said, looking at AJ evenly.

"I have."

Jayne nodded her head. "What did you come up with?"

"I don't like the position you've put me in. You're asking me to choose between you and my life's work," he said.

"That's a tough position," she said. "You're asking me to put my life on hold while you chase around the universe on one crazy mission after another. I'm a researcher, AJ. I'm a surgeon. Running from one battle to the next doesn't let me have a life either."

"Do you want to get off at Dralli and go back to the university?" AJ asked.

"Yes. But where does that leave us?"

"I guess I don't know," he said. "Why is it this hard? I thought we were supposed to fall in love and live happily after."

"It probably works that way for a lot of people," Jayne said. "I do love you, AJ. If you were willing to stay on one planet for more than a month at a time, we could make this work, but running from one combat zone to the next is no way to live. Especially for someone who's dedicated their life to healing."

"I can't believe I'm saying this," AJ said. "I think we need to take a break."

"I think so too."

AJ paused, her words hurting more than he could ever have expected, even though he'd brought up the conversation. "I was hoping you wouldn't agree."

"I was hoping I wouldn't either. I just can't do this anymore."

"Shit," he said, hanging his head.

Jayne reached for him and placed her hand on his cheek. Her palm caught a single tear that had escaped. "It's okay, AJ. We can still be great friends. Didn't that Star Trek captain have a girl in every port?"

"You're funny," he said. "Like that'd work."

"You never know," she said, lifting an eyebrow and smiling.

"I'll move my things from the cabin so you can have your privacy," he said.

"Thank you," she said, lowering her hand to take his. "You're a good man, Albert Jenkins, and I'm glad for the time we've had together."

The lump in his throat made swallowing difficult and all he could manage was a wan smile as she pulled him into a warm embrace. "I'm going to miss you, Amanda," he whispered. "I'm sorry we couldn't make this work."

"Me too."

In the small ship, there weren't many options for gaining separation and AJ found himself going forward to the bridge, where he found Darnell and Lisa quietly talking. When they saw him enter, they paused, their attention directed to him.

"What's going on, buddy? You're looking kind of rough," Darnell said.

AJ swallowed hard, trying to find his voice, which he discovered wasn't possible without doing something he never did, which was to cry. "Oh, AJ." Lisa jumped up and pulled him into a hug, which didn't help his current state. He allowed tears to silently slide down his cheeks. "That's okay, baby, I've got you."

"What's going on? Did you break it off with Jayne?" Darnell asked.

"Would you just hush, Darnell?" Lisa said and then lowered her voice. "Talk to me, AJ. What's happening?"

"We're done," he said, his voice shuddering as he tried to breathe. "... friends."

"Good for you. You'll appreciate being able to have her as a friend later, when the hurt fades," Lisa said. "You've got friends. We'll be with you."

"I just ... I didn't see ... coming."

"You did the right thing," Lisa said, again.

And she held him in place as he struggled to find his footing.

"I hate to be this guy, but we're about to enter transition," Darnell said. "We'll be in Xandarj in four hours. It might be a good time to take a nap so you're fresh when we get to Dralli Station. You don't want to deal with Mads Bazer in this shape."

"I need to move out," AJ said.

"Nah, we've got you." Lisa placed a guiding hand on AJ's back and pushed him toward the hallway exiting the bridge. Instead of stopping at his quarters, she turned toward the small berth she shared with Darnell.

"I can't take your room," AJ said. "I'm okay, Lisa. Seriously, I've got this."

"I know you do. But sometimes letting a friend help is okay, too," she said, guiding him to the neatly made bed. It occurred to him the reason she was re-directing him was that his own berth would smell of Jayne.

"Thank you," he said, feeling uncomfortable accepting his friend's help.

"Just lean into the help for a minute. This gets easier," Lisa said, gently pushing him back onto the bed as he tried to get up. "When you wake up, you'll need to eat something."

"This isn't that bad," AJ said. "I'll be fine."

"You certainly will," she agreed. "Beverly, make sure he doesn't get up for a few hours. We don't need him and he's not going to be any help to anyone."

"I have an agreement that I won't change his chemistry to manipulate his emotional state without permission," Beverly said, appearing on the edge of the bed, her doll-length legs hanging over the side. She'd chosen to wear a yellow flower print sun dress.

"It's fine, BB," AJ said. "I could use the sleep."

"Well then, sleep you'll get."

The transition back to normal space woke AJ from a deep slumber as much as his growling stomach did. The smells around him were both unfamiliar and familiar in the same moment. It didn't take him long to realize where he was.

"So that was all real, huh," he said. "Are we in the Xandarj system?"

"Good morning, AJ," Beverly said, appearing next to him in her Jetson's silver space suit complete with a jet pack that shot perfect exhaust rings from a tiny port. "We have successfully transitioned to normal space. If by *that* you are referring to the discussion you had with Doctor Jayne regarding your relationship status, yes, that was not imagined during your REM cycle of sleep. Do you want to talk about how you feel?"

"Where did Lisa and Darnell sleep last night?"

"Only four hours have transpired since you arrived in their cabin," Beverly said. "They are enjoying a light breakfast in the bridge. I recommend that you engage in self-care and utilize the head to wash your body."

"I don't have time."

"That is an untruth, AJ. Lisa will mention this to you as I overheard her discussing this specifically with Darnell."

"That I stink?"

"No, that you will be distracted and will likely avoid paying attention to your basic needs."

"Why is everyone up in my business?"

"It is natural that your friends are concerned for your wellbeing during an emotional trauma."

"I think that's overstating things a bit, don't you?"

"Perhaps. Also, the best way to avoid further conversation is to demonstrate you will take care of yourself," Beverly said.

"Ooh, that's good," AJ said. "I really like the way you turned that around on me. I'm helping myself by doing what you want."

A broad grin spread across Beverly's small face. "I thought you'd like that."

"Okay, shower then," AJ said. "Tell me how much time until we arrive at Dralli Station."

"Darnell has contacted the station and registered *USS Wasp* as a US-flagged war vessel with peaceful intent," Beverly said.

"Tell Joyce and Tenet I want a meeting in fifteen minutes. I'll come to them," AJ said, stepping into the shower and turning the water to as hot as it would go.

"You have a meeting in fifteen minutes in the engineering bay," Beverly said.

"Perfect," AJ said, allowing the water to run over his body. "You know, I can't help but think if that woman hadn't died under Amanda's care, she wouldn't be doing this."

"I see. Perhaps it had been on her mind for a while prior to Holly Blanche's death," Beverly said.

"It was. You're right," AJ said sighing. "I just ... I suppose I was trying to see if there was a chance."

"I understand," Beverly said.

AJ looked in the mirror and checked his beard growth. It was scraggly but he couldn't bring himself to care, so he grabbed a towel and dried off. Without access to the room he shared with Amanda, he was forced into the clothing he'd been wearing. It wasn't his preference.

Instead of joining Darnell and Lisa on the bridge, AJ walked back to the galley where several were working on breakfast.

"Cup of joe, One?" LeBeau asked.

"Uh, yeah, that'd be great," AJ said.

LeBeau handed a cup to AJ and gave him a sympathetic look. "There you go."

The sympathetic tone was a flag. "Shit, Frenchy, how do you know already?"

"One of the boys said he overheard a private conversation."

"So the whole crew knows."

"Definitely everyone who drives a suit," Frenchy said. "We've got you, brother."

AJ nodded. The fraternity of his brothers was something he almost always cherished. Right now, he felt more vulnerable than supported and did his best not to lash out.

"Let's keep things on the down-low, could we? I'm still working this through."

"Copy that, One," LeBeau said. "We'll let you drive."

"Much appreciated. If anyone is asking, I'm back in engineering."

"Yup. Got you."

He shook his head as he walked aft.

"AJ, look up," Beverly said, appearing in his field of vision, which was focused on the deck.

Too late, he looked up and stopped so quickly that coffee sloshed from the cup he carried. Worse yet, the person he'd almost run into was none other than Jayne.

"Sorry," he mumbled, stepping around her as he tried to ignore the pain of hot coffee dripping from his hand.

"AJ," she called quietly to his back.

"I can't right now, Amanda," he answered, not knowing what else he could say, but he knew for certain he was in no position to talk to her.

He expected her to demand he stop walking and when she didn't, he released the breath he'd been holding. Pushing through the hatch to engineering, he held up, allowing it to close behind him.

"What's happening to me?" he questioned. Normally confident and always in charge, he felt lost and anything but confident.

"Anxiety," Beverly answered. "It will pass, but you will need time to adjust to your new life's pattern."

"Well, good, at least it's something they make pills for," he quipped.

"You do not need chemicals to overcome a relationship breakup. Also, I am proud of you for not engaging with Doctor Jayne. She is feeling guilty for the changes you are both experiencing and wishes to provide comfort. I propose that you should not gain comfort from her at the risk of prolonging your uncertainty."

"Oh, AJ, I thought I heard someone over here," Marion Tenet said, coming around the corner. "Brian is using the head and will join us shortly."

"Sounds good," AJ said. "I'd like to review the repairs to be done on Dralli Station. I need to have a good list so I can know what I'm negotiating."

"That is perfectly sensible," Tenet said, bringing an electronic notepad to a comfortable writing position. "I've broken the repairs into four categories. The first is large-scale armor reconstruction of a critical nature. The second is armor repairs that are less critical but still important. Third on the list is the structural repairs critical to *Wasp's* success entering an atmosphere. Finally, the fourth item is more along the lines of functional but not critical. I have not prioritized cosmetic changes."

"Okay, let's walk through those lists," AJ said.

"Did I miss anything?" Joyce asked, joining the pair.

"No, we're just getting started."

After twenty minutes, AJ felt like he better understood the scope of the work requested as well as the priorities given. While he might have organized it differently, he didn't mind using the two men's structure.

"So, I understand you and Doctor Jayne are calling it quits," Joyce said when there was a lull in the conversation.

"Brian, a little sensitivity, please," Tenet said.

"What? I was only curious."

"Do you mind?" AJ asked, placing his hand on the tablet.

"Sorry, AJ," Tenet said, handing the tablet to AJ. "Brian does not have much experience with interpersonal relationships."

"BB, can you transfer this data, please?"

"I've got it, AJ," Beverly answered.

"Really, I can't ask a simple question?" Joyce asked.

AJ gave the man a sympathetic look. "You can. It's a little sensitive," he said. "You're right. Doctor Jayne and I will be parting ways at Dralli Station."

"That's right, she was part of the university here," Joyce said. "That is very convenient for you both, especially since you're feeling sad about it."

AJ closed his eyes and shook his head, trying desperately not to lash out at the man. When he opened his eyes, he handed the tablet back to Tenet and turned on his heels, leaving the pair behind.

"That was very rude, Brian," Tenet explained as AJ exited engineering. "Do you remember when you asked me to tell you when you were being rude?"

"That was rude? I was showing care for his emotional situation."

"Sometimes it's ..." AJ was saved from the remainder of the conversation by the close of the hatch behind him.

He made his way back to the hold where *Seahag* and the mechanized suits were stored. The smell of the oils and solvents used in suit and ship maintenance filled his nose. Looking around, he found he was alone.

Working his way back to where *Seahag* sat, he leaned against the versatile and deadly craft. There was something reassuring about the machine which allowed him to push away some of the building anxiety.

Several minutes later, he was just starting to calm when a chirp told him of an incoming comms request. "This is AJ, go ahead," he said.

"Heya buddy, where are you at?" Darnell asked.

"In the main hold."

"Everything okay?"

"Maybe best if we didn't keep asking that question."

"Copy that. We're forty minutes from Dralli. I was thinking you might like to get a contract rolling so we can figure out which shipyard we're going to aim for," Darnell said.

"Good call," AJ said. "I'm on it."

"I'm on the bridge by myself, if you want to join me. I might even have half a burrito left over from this morning," Darnell said.

"I'll come up," AJ said. "BB, can you see about raising Mads Bazer?"

"I'm initiating a communications request," Beverly said. "It is 1000 on Dralli Station, for your reference."

Instead of going directly to the bridge, AJ stopped in one of the storage bays and pulled a glass bottle filled with a twenty-year aged single-malt Scotch.

"Albert Jenkins, why is it that you are irritating Mads Bazer in the early hours of this ordinary day." The thickly built, permanently scowling, four-foot-six tall Xandarj with blue highlights in her gray fur appeared in front of AJ as if she was hovering just above *Wasp's* deck a few feet in front of him.

"Well, darn nice to see you again, too, Mads Bazer," AJ said. "Are we done with pleasantries, then? It sounds like I might have caught you at a bad time." As he talked, he lifted the beautiful cut-glass bottle of Scotch so she couldn't miss it.

"What are you holding, Albert Jenkins?" she asked, her pudgy pink tongue slipping over her teeth as she talked.

"It was something I'd considered sharing with an old friend," he said. "Perhaps I've over-valued that friendship given the lack of interest I seem to have discovered."

"Oh, you are toying with my emotions," she said. "I do not like this. What is this that you hold? Please tell me."

"A twenty-year Scotch straight from the Isle of the Scots," he said. "I personally haven't had a chance to taste this vintage, but I understand it is a particularly good year."

"You are such a manipulative human," Mads said. "I am not interested. No, wait. What is it you want from Mads?"

"You act as if I do not bring good deals to the table, Mads," AJ said, arriving at the bridge and settling into the navigator's seat next to Darnell. "I believe you've benefited greatly from every opportunity I've brought your way. And yet, you treat me with such disdain."

"This is indeed better treatment than most receive," she said, allowing a familiar twinkle to enter her eyes. "You do so complain."

"It's in my nature. So, am I drinking this and the eleven other bottles it accompanied all the way from Earth by myself?" AJ asked.

"Twelve bottles of Scotch from the Isle of the Scots? Tell me, is this the highest quality that Earthmen produce?" Mads asked.

"This is in fact some of the highest quality Scotch Whiskey produced on Earth," AJ said. "I know many aboard who would have broken into the case had they known of its existence."

"Bring it to me," she growled, stepping forward quickly as if she were physically present.

"Now, now," AJ said. "Business first."

"Oh, I so hate you," she said. "What is it you need?"

"We're sailing a warship – USS *Wasp*," AJ said. "We ran into a little trouble and need a quick turnaround armor job. We brought precious metals for payment. We need someone who can broker a deal so we won't be taken advantage of."

"What makes you think I will not become your broker and make this price high so that I benefit more?"

"I will ask for your word that you will not do exactly that," AJ said. "If there is one thing for which I'm confident, it is that Mads Bazer is no liar and will fulfill a contract."

"And this Scotch. What price do you ask for it?"

"First bottle is free," AJ said. "We'll negotiate once you've cracked the seal."

"That is not a good position for me," she said.

"I could directly contact the shipyards. Perhaps I would find someone interested in a bit of extra Earth gold," AJ said. "Or even a few cases of a fine wine we brought from France."

"What is wine?"

"A grape is a fruit on Earth. Fermented grapes are used to make wine," AJ said. "It's been an evolving discipline for thousands of Earth years."

"This grape is very good?"

"Similar to ahunga fruit from Xandarj," AJ said. "A little sweeter if red, a little tarter if white."

"And you would trade this wine for a fair contract with a reputable shipyard?"

"Fair and speedy," AJ said. "We're in a military action in another system and need to keep a schedule."

"You would leave quickly?"

"As soon as the work is complete," AJ said smiling. "But you're giving me a complex. It's like you don't like it when I'm around even though I bring you this Scotch."

"You have a deal, Albert Jenkins. Bring me a case of this wine from France and that bottle you hold of Scotch from the Isle of Scots and I will broker a fair and speedy deal with a reputable shipyard on Dralli Station. You will make me a deal for the remainder of your so-called Scotch, though. Send me the specifications of work that must be completed."

"A deal will be brokered and fair. Also, the specs are being transmitted," AJ said. "I'll have Beverly send a contract over for your services."

"Yes," she said, ending the transmission.

"That sounded like it went well," Darnell said.

"I can't figure if the grumpy old lady thing is an act or if she's really that hard to deal with," AJ said.

"Without that Scotch, I think you'd have been kicked to the curb," Darnell said.

"Did you watch the whole thing?" AJ asked.

"Yes, Petey tied me in."

In the distance, the white spec of Dralli Station that had seemed so small for so long suddenly started to grow. And with it, so did the traffic of local space. Having registered *USS Wasp* as a warship ensured that a Dralli patrol would accompany them to the station. As he looked out at the approaching station, he located the patrol ship already inbound.

"*USS Wasp* this is *Dralli Fourteen*, please respond," came a high-pitched voice that AJ instantly recognized.

"*Dralli Fourteen*, this is *USS Wasp*," AJ answered.

"You are cleared to dock on your current heading," the high-pitched voice answered.

"Hello there, Blue Tork," AJ said. "Fancy running into you out this way."

"My good friend, Albert Jenkins, I did not know we were to expect such a pleasant surprise. How is your mate, Amanda Jayne?"

It was as if someone had hit him in the stomach and he even coughed. "Well, uh, she's good," AJ said. "She's even going to stay behind this time and go back to the university."

"Ah, that is wise. She is highly revered," Blue Tork said. "I would not like being parted from my mate for so long, but I understand the necessity of things such as this."

"Since we're talking about it. Jayne and I aren't really considered mates anymore," AJ said. "We're going different ways with our careers."

"I do not understand. Why would you do this? You are both delightful to be around and I am certain you find each other's company restful," Blue Tork said.

"Um, well, it's complicated. Maybe we talk about it over dinner? Do you have time later today to get together?"

"How long will you be at Dralli Station? I have heard that you are looking for repairs."

"How did you hear that already?"

"Mads Bazer placed an inquiry onto the station-wide work board for ship repair. It is wise to utilize her. She is shrewd in the way she approaches her contracts," Blue Tork said. "And yes, Red Fairs and I would enjoy greeting you and not Amanda Jayne?"

"That's right. We're not visiting the same places at the same times at least for now," AJ said.

"I will let Red Fairs know to have our staff prepare a meal. I am very glad you have visited Xandarj again, Albert Jenkins."

"I'm looking forward to seeing you, too," AJ said, closing the comms.

"Uh, AJ," Darnell said, raising his eyebrows at the hatch.

When AJ turned, he found Jayne standing in the doorway. Her eyes were puffy she'd clearly been crying. He entertained the idea that she'd changed her mind and would stay with him. The idea had no more crossed his mind that he knew that wouldn't be the case. She was gone and was just starting to grieve.

"Hey, Amanda," he said quietly, standing.

"We're getting close to Dralli," she said. "I wanted to say goodbye. This all came so quickly but I … tell me we can be friends … you know, after we do some healing."

The lump in AJ's throat was the size of an apple as he approached the woman he'd expected to spend the rest of his life with.

"You'll always be one of my best friends, Amanda," he said. "I wish there was another way through this. I just don't see it."

"Neither do I," she said. "I can't watch you throw your life away. I worry so much for you when you're out. I'm losing me in all of this."

"I know," he said, allowing her to embrace him. "I want you to have your best life, Amanda. I hate that's not with me, but I'll come to understand it."

"Thank you, AJ," she said. "You could have made this a lot harder. In some ways, it is even that much harder because you know me so well that you know this is what I need. I'm babbling. I'm sorry."

"Jayne, you need to build your life," AJ said. "Go represent humanity. Show the Galactic Empire what we bring to the table."

"I'll do my best, AJ," she said. "And you go save the world again. I know your mission is terribly important and that hundreds depend on you. Go be a hero. It is certainly your destiny."

22

FAILURE OF INTUITION
DEKE – PLANET FIMIL PRIME

An entire squad of medics jogged past Deke as she finished her conversation with Bing. The stretcher poles strapped to their backs wasn't a good sign.

"You need to be done," she said, pushing at the hand of the medic who'd been tending her wounded abdomen.

"But, ma'am, this is deep. You shouldn't even be standing."

"And yet, here I am," Deke growled. "Cut it off and tie your final suture. I need to move."

"Aye, aye," the medic said, resigned.

"I need an engineer, Keegs," Deke said.

"What's up, boss?" he asked.

She walked back to where the Togath's knife still lay on the deck. Picking it up, she found the grip uncomfortably large and the weight of the blade on the heavy side, but not unwieldy.

"I want this grip reduced to fit my hand," she said. "Can you coordinate that for me?"

"Well within the scope of my agreement with the US Army," he said. "Hand it to Corporal Whitehead, who has received an order to deliver this weapon to the ship's primary manufactory."

Deke turned and searched for anyone walking in her direction. With a visual clue in the form of a blinking arrow overlaid on her vision, she found Corporal Whitehead beelining to her.

"Ma'am, I've been given orders to deliver this shake?" he said, seeming to question the reasonableness of a food delivery in the middle of combat.

Deke took the shake and handed him the long Togath knife in exchange. "You should have new orders regarding this weapon. Take care that it arrives at its destination. Do you copy?"

"Aye, aye, Captain Dekoster," the man replied. "It'll get delivered."

"You're dismissed." She strode toward the open aft hatch.

"Dekoster, report," Baines demanded.

"One minute," Deke said, finishing the shake before tossing aside the empty container.

At the end of the ramp, she found remnants of the battle. Dead soldiers had been pulled to the side and covered respectfully. She'd seen plenty of death in her time in special forces, but having been the one to give the order, she felt more responsible for the line of bodies.

"Tell me you're not fighting forward with your troops," Corcoran said.

"Negative, Colonel," Deke said. "Zebra Company has established a forward command post. I'm making my way there. We've had heavy casualties, but I don't have a solid count just yet."

"Estimate," Corcoran said.

"First contact at the end of *Angry Ark's* loading ramp looks like a loss of eight with that many injured enough to be removed from the field of battle," Deke answered, picking a heavy rifle up from the deck as she moved around the medics.

"What of the boarders?" Baines asked.

"Two Togath dispatched with extreme prejudice," Deke said. "I'm approaching the forward command post. There's fighting ahead. I'll report back once we're clear."

"You look like shit, Captain," Bing said as Deke approached a hastily constructed temporary armored blockade made for urban warfare.

"Just a flesh wound," Deke said. "Talk to me about casualties. Where are we making progress? Where are we outmatched?"

"We're struggling with the light infantry weapons," Carrole said. "Togath have armor that absorbs just about anything we throw at them."

"Switch to armor piercing. You'll need more bullets, but you'll get through that armor."

"We don't have much of that in our current kits," Carrole said.

"Switch out for the M-52s when they become available," Deke said.

"That's what we're doing."

"Casualties?"

"We're down fourteen with another eight wounded to the point of being unable to stay in the fight," Bing said. "I've given my platoon the order to be cautious when approaching anything more than a single."

"That's reasonable," Deke said. "Keegs, show me a base map. Update with known casualties and enemy deaths. Share that with command once you have it."

"Yes, Deke," Keegs answered. "One moment."

A three-dimensional overlay showed a top-down view of Base Six, complete with *Angry Ark's* aft tipped slightly downward. Like a large, cotton sheet, the roof material sat beneath the ship and lay on the ground. Their gambit that *Angry Ark* would overwhelm the Togath base's roof structure had paid off. That payoff, however had resulted in high casualties against an enemy with inferior numbers.

"Colorize the captured sections in blue and the unknown in orange," Deke ordered. Without hesitation two-thirds of the base turned light blue, the remaining light red. "Show current conflict zones in red."

The floating base updated instantly.

"Are you seeing this, Major?" Deke asked.

"We see it, Captain," Baines answered. "We need to keep pushing. Don't worry about damage to the structure. Use explosives at will."

"Good copy, Major," Deke said, swallowing hard. The casualty numbers were too high. By all accounts, the operation would be considered a raging failure. That she had soldiers still in harm's way meant she still had a job to do and would focus on labels later.

"What's command got to say?" Bing asked, pinning his mic on mute after instructing a squad to move forward. "Any suggestions?"

"Negative," Deke said. "There's not much we can do other than gut it out and try to learn a better approach."

"These are expensive lessons. We need heavier weaponry. It's like we're fighting armor, except they're ridiculously mobile," Bing said.

"Let's treat them exactly like that," Deke said.

"What are you saying?" Bing asked.

"If these were armored personnel carriers, what would you do differently? Carrole, what's your biggest fear when in a Stryker?"

"IEDs and shoulder mounted RPGs," Carrole said.

"We don't have time to get clever with IEDs or mines," Bing said.

"Nothing is stopping us from RPGs, though," Deke added.

"These are close spaces," Bing argued. "We'd get blowback. RPGs are danger-close."

"Couldn't you soften the positions by blind firing them?" Carrole asked. "Maybe not the most cost-effective, but if we kept up the pressure with RPGs, it would stop them from rushing our line."

"I ... sure," Bing said, struggling with the concept. "Worth a try."

"Sergeant Tern, change of plans," Bing said. "I'm sending a squad with RPGs. We're going to switch to scorched earth."

"That's damn fantastic!" came the immediate reply. "Let's light these gray bastards up!"

The pace of the battle changed as Zebra Company shifted from attempting to overrun positions with overwhelming automatic fire to the use of grenades and even heavier explosives. The time required to deploy the explosives, however, was offset by a quickly dwindling rate of casualties.

Ninety minutes later the final section of Base Six turned from red to green status and victory was announced.

∾

"That was a disaster," Kersey said, taking an early swipe.

"A twenty percent casualty rate is abominable by modern combat mission standards. Especially for an entire company. That is certainly true," Major Baines said thoughtfully.

"I knew it would be hard. I had no idea how tough those Togath are," Deke said. "They don't make mistakes when they fight. They have no wasted energy to their movements. It appears they feel no fear, although I discovered they do experience anger."

"Genetically manufactured with the singular purpose of war," Corcoran added. "It is interesting Quarr did not find it possible to remove anger."

"Or social bonds," Baines said. "I observed, as has been previously reported, that each soldier had a mate. I believe the anger Deke observed was when she killed one of the two that boarded *Angry Ark* through the ramp. That second, mated Togath showed significant anger and its actions were not as precise as others we observed."

"Is there an advantage in this?" Corcoran asked. "Target mates and try to catch them on tilt?"

"I can tell you, that second Togath was no pushover, grief or otherwise," Deke said, setting the Togath's modified blade on the table in front of herself.

"Taking souvenirs already?" Kersey asked with a sneer.

"No, and do you want to talk to me about why not a single member of Xray Company managed to make it to the hold until after I had both Togath killed?"

"Are you accusing me of something?" Kersey asked. "I think you'll find the orders were given and executed in a timely manner."

"You do know that when one company gets weaker, we all get weaker," Deke said.

"Would you two stop it? This competitive bickering is expected back on Earth. We will die if we fight amongst ourselves here. We have no backup plan," Baines said. "Captain Dekoster, exactly how many boots can Zebra Company put on the ground at this very moment?"

"Fifty-eight," Deke answered. "Sixty-two within two weeks, optimistically."

"What did we learn?" Corcoran asked.

"We need better cover to begin with," Dekoster said. "We lost too many good soldiers on the ramp, just trying to disembark."

"That's on my list, too," Baines said. "What else?"

"Switch to explosives earlier," Bing offered. "It creates distance."

"Have team members ready to handle hand-to-hand. We had three situations where Togath felt it would have better luck jumping into the middle of one of my squads. That was a real problem as we're not used to fighting hand-to-hand, despite our training. And we're certainly not on par with Togath. When they got in the middle of us, it was tough and we took losses," Carrole said.

"Deke, there's a rumor that you single-handedly dispatched a mated pair," Baines said. "Further, that you dismissed a Zebra Company squad that would have provided you aid at stopping this incursion into *Angry Ark*."

"Close but not quite there. Let me clean that up," Deke said. "The squad injured one of the pair and drove both to cover. At that moment, our troops were taking heavy fire, trying to clear the insertion zone within Base Six. The unknowns of what the rest of Zebra Company was up against versus two lone Togath soldiers, one of which was injured, prompted my decision to send that squad forward to the true front line. I had hoped there would be support from Xray Company available within the hold, which is why I've expressed my irritation at my perception of a slow response."

"And you killed two Togath?" Corcoran asked.

"One was already near death," Deke said. "I sent a grenade into their cover. It was effective."

"And the other? Was it also wounded?" Baines asked.

"Not to my knowledge," Deke said. "Even worse, I was holding a rifle when it came at me. I had no ability to raise my weapon for self-defense and had to resort to street brawling. I also used my Desert

Eagle, both full metal jacket armor piercing and hollow point loads. As Carrole has already reported, small arms have limited effectiveness against Togath armor. I even shot it in the head within a few feet and my bullets ricocheted off the skull plates. Togath are fighting machines."

"But you somehow managed to kill not one, but two. How tough can they really be?" Kersey asked.

"You're an idiot," Carrole said.

"Careful, Lieutenant," Baines warned.

"I'm sorry, Major, but I lost friends today. Warriors who've seen combat and made a difference. Those friends were torn apart by these Togath. It's insulting to their memory to have Captain Kersey suggest they just weren't good enough," Carrole said.

"I understand," Baines said. "Today is a tough day, which is why I'm not pushing you on the insubordination. Keep that temper locked down. We're going to be here for a while."

"There's one piece of good news," Corcoran added. His statement quieted the room. "Glad that got your attention. The three Xray Company squads have returned with the Strykers intact."

"We spent sixteen lives to save fourteen," Kersey said darkly.

"Is that how you see it?" Corcoran asked. "Do you think your father can pull strings all the way out here, Thad? Do you think I give one rat's ass about Senator Kersey's legacy? Despite heavy losses, we had our first victory. If not for dropping in on Base Six, we'd still be sitting back at our original location, trying to figure out what we could possibly do next. So, do I like that we lost sixteen of our brethren? No, of course not. Don't you ever presume to lecture me, Captain Kersey, or I'll bust you down to second lieutenant and get you to earn that star on your lapel."

Kersey refused to look up. The Colonel's speech had been delivered with cold anger. He'd clearly been holding it in for some time.

"Tubs, we need to keep moving," Baines said. "Togath are smart, and they'll come up with a counter to our attack. We need to strike while there's some possibility we've maintained an advantage."

"It's going to be bloody, Mike," Corcoran said. "We've learned about our enemy, but I'll bet they've learned just as much about us."

"We need to set explosives around this structure and make it unusable. What if that dropship is headed home to grab more troops?" Deke asked.

"That's a reasonable precaution," Corcoran said. "Figure out which base we'll attack next and why. Meet back here in thirty minutes. And Dekoster, two things ..."

"Colonel?"

"First, that was a damn fine job fighting off that Togath. I'd like to know why you kept that blade, but I'm afraid to ask," he said.

"I plan to add it to my kit. I'd have loved to have this blade when I was fighting that gray bastard," Deke said, spinning the blade over her hand and grasping the newly modified grip. "What's the second thing?

"You're bleeding through your uniform."

Deke looked down and found her fatigues were starting to saturate with her own blood. "I'll get that taken care of, sir. Can I ask who's got point on this next base?"

"Kersey and Xray Company are up," Corcoran said. "But don't get complacent. Zebra Company needs to be ready to go in sixteen hours, give or take. Get your people some grub and some down time, because we're officially in the zone of suck."

"Hooah!" Deke answered. "Let's finish this now!"

"Damn straight."

⁓

"Four bases in five days," Deke said, tossing her blade wearily onto the table next to her bed. "I don't know how we consider this any sort of victory."

Keegs sat on the table, legs hanging off the side. "I discovered a secret communication that likely explains Colonel Corcoran's obsession with these bases."

"You spied on the US Army?" Deke asked, not managing to sound surprised. The stress and fatigue of constant combat and mounting losses had worn her down.

"That is an accurate statement," Keegs said. "Do you wish to hear what I've discovered?"

"Doesn't that make me an accessory after the fact?"

"I am not certain how US Law pertains to a symbiote's host when the symbiote acts without the knowledge of its host," Keegs said. "I believe that without case law, there is no precedence."

"So fifty/fifty I'm going to jail even if you don't tell me?"

"I would not expect the odds to be quite so high," Keegs said. "Beltigersk-Human relations are still quite new and there is considerable benefit to humankind to stay within the favor of Beltigersk."

"Got us by the short and curlies, huh?"

"If I understand the vernacular, I believe that is correct. Fortunately, Beltigersk finds significant advantage to its relationship with humanity. I do not believe punishment is likely."

"You're doing it again and I'm too tired to stop you," Deke said.

"Too many words, not enough cartoons?"

Deke chuckled. "That's a new one. You're getting better with your insults. And yes, blah, blah, blah. Just tell me what you found."

"There is a provision for re-equipping this mission."

"There's always been that. We just need to make it another eleven months and twenty-six days," Deke said. "We're losing too many people a day to make that work, though. Check my math. I think I'm right."

"I do not understand how humans are equally terrified of dying and so casual in referencing it," Keegs said. "Starting with a fighting force of one hundred sixty, Operation Black Turtle has been reduced to ninety-two active soldiers. There is hope that eight of those who are currently under doctor's care could be returned to duty within a few days to a few weeks. That there remain two bases, suggests we could be as low as sixty soldiers if the trendline continues."

"Right, but you're saying we might have a resupply faster than a year? I thought it was too expensive," Deke said. "That's the whole point of calling the ship an ark."

"If Colonel Corcoran is able to clear Fimil Prime of enemy forces, a second mission will be launched, bringing an even bigger occupational force," Keegs said.

"How big?"

"Fifteen hundred people," Keegs said. "An entire small city, complete with civilian contractors doing regular civilian type duties."

"Mowing lawns and eating hotdogs?"

"That wasn't specifically mentioned. I believe trade was the expected focus of civilian duties," Keegs said.

"Sure," Deke said, lying back on her bed. "How much downtime do I have? I'm exhausted."

"Six hours," Keegs said. "Do you have anything you would do aside from sleep?"

"Negative. Wake me with thirty minutes to spare, okay? My shoulder is sore. I'd like to get it stretched out."

"I will repair the tear while you sleep. I will also honor your request. Good night, Deke."

"It's freaky when you do that, I don't get any semblance of having gone asleep," Deke said, sitting up, feeling significantly more refreshed than when she'd entered her quarters. Checking her watch, she found she had almost an hour before the next incursion and that she'd been down for five hours thirty minutes on the nose.

"I was looking to maximize your REM sleep."

"Always thinking," Deke said. "You know, I've got a bad feeling about this next mission. I'm not sure where it came from, but I do."

"Humans are notorious for valuing their instincts or intuition," Keegs said. "Most higher order sentients do not believe human intuition is a real phenomenon."

"That's kind of a relief," Deke said. "Because I feel like something is about to go super wrong. I'd like that to be just a dumb feeling."

"Words like wrong, dumb, and stupid present difficulty for clear communication," Keegs said. "Perhaps you could explain why you feel like something will go wrong on this next mission?"

"That's the tricky thing about intuition," Deke said, stepping into the shower. "If I knew why I thought things were going to shit, I wouldn't have to call it intuition. I'd just say what the problem was."

"Perhaps explain how you think a problem will arise," Keegs said.

"Logically, the Togath are getting smarter with each mission. So are we, but I can't help but think they're learning faster than we are. We're not changing up our approach between bases. We're becoming predictable. That's dangerous. You don't need intuition to tell you that."

"I see. Place yourself in the position of the Togath. You know a ship is coming and the vessel will land in the middle of your base and overrun your defenses. What would you do to prevent this?"

"Geez, at a minimum, I'd take all the soldiers from one base and put them at the other. We've been struggling to take down the small force at each base. If it was doubled, that would create a real problem."

"I've considered this," Keegs said. "The real problem the Togath have is that their bases make the basic assumption that their barriers to entry prevent penetration. The interior of their bases provide virtually no defense against intruders."

"They've come up with something," Deke said. "I don't know how I know this."

23

CATASTROPHE

DEKE – PLANET FIMIL PRIME

"Boss, we're getting our asses kicked out there," Bing said, his weary eyes staring at her across Deke's small table. "Morale is at an all-time low."

"We all knew this was a one-way trip," she replied. Even as she said it, she understood she wasn't giving Bing the support he needed.

"You need to talk to Zebra Company," Carrole said. "Nobody signed up for fifty percent casualties."

"I know. I'm sorry," Deke said, shaking her head. Without the benefit of a super gene and a symbiote to aid in healing, her lieutenants looked considerably worse for wear. "This mission is tougher than any of us could have imagined."

"You're not telling us something," Carrole said, peering intently at Deke. "We're past secrets, right?"

"It's not a secret. More of an intuition thing," Deke said. "I have no information."

"And?" Bing asked.

"The Togath will have an answer on these last two bases," she said. "They're not going to let us wipe them from the planet."

"I know you said no knowledge, but do you have any guesses?" Carrole asked.

"What would stop an incursion?"

"Putting a roof over the base that's as strong as its walls." Bing answered immediately.

"That's good. What if they can't get access to building materials?"

"They should rush the loading ramp with everything they've got. Letting us disembark eventually is their failure," Bing said.

"They don't need to rush it," Carrole said. "They know how we're attacking. Make it a trap. Let us land and drop the ramp. Set off explosives or launch missiles right into the hold. We have plenty of weaknesses."

"Why haven't they done either yet?" Deke asked.

"We've moved fast," Bing said. "They might not have the right material in the right place."

"What if they don't have any more explosives? They did drop six bases and it's not like we've found a large cache of ordnance left behind. The weapons they're fighting with are energy-based, which is efficient for long space journeys. We're lucky we had data from a previous mission that gave us the location of mineral deposits and could mine what we needed that first night."

"If they don't have explosives, we should expect an all-out assault through the back door," Bing said. "Kersey is first through the door this time. We need to have Zebra Company in place to repel a boarding party."

"That's a solid idea, Bing," Deke said. "I'll inform the major that we'll be loaded heavy for the next landing."

"Do we have a countdown yet?" Carrole asked.

"Thirty-eight minutes," Deke answered.

"I'll get my platoon ready." Bing sighed. "I'll be combining squads that have been hit hardest."

"We only have two more bases to go," Deke said. "If there was ever a time for us to kick ass, that time is now."

"We'll be ready," Carrole said.

"You two come up with a plan for where we'll place our squads. We need to consider firing lanes because any invader's backs will be to Kersey's company. Given we can't use explosives inside our own ships, we need as many M52s as possible."

"Damn, I forgot about the explosives problem," Bing said. "That's a big deal. We're not nearly as effective, even with the heavier rounds. Worse yet, we'll be using armor piercing and that'll be tough on *Angry Ark*."

"If it comes to fighting off boarders, we'll have to deal with the damage," Deke said. "Togath are very good at what they do. They'll be going for command and control if they can get past our teams. It would only take one loose Togath to take out most of the crew."

"Should we inform the crew in that case?" Carrole asked. "We could at least make available the lighter rifles. It'd be something."

"I'll talk to Baines. Go get your platoons organized. We're down to thirty minutes," Deke said.

"Aye, aye," the pair responded in unison and exited without a formal dismissal.

Deke made her way forward, knowing she'd find Baines and Corcoran in the mission room, working through last minute details, and preparing to watch the action as it unfolded.

"Captain, I'd expect you to be getting ready to provide backup just in case we run into a larger force on this base," Baines said.

"My platoon leaders are on it, sir. I have something I'd like to discuss if you're up for an open conversation," Deke said.

"Shoot," Corcoran said. As a whole, the conversations over the previous seventy-two hours had become more and more informal as even command struggled with fatigue.

"Just thinking," Deke said.

"Here we go, again," Kersey said.

"Jam it, Kersey."

"Everyone is tired. Let's give it a rest already," Baines said. "What's on your mind, Deke?"

"With your permission, Zebra Company is going to set up with the expectation that Togath will try to board when we drop the ramp," Deke said. "While it's not the only strategic move available, it feels like something we should be ready for."

"We were ready for it at the last four bases," Kersey said, dryly.

Deke didn't spare him even a glance and kept her focus on Corcoran and Baines. Corcoran was the first to talk. "That's a good decision. Get Baines to bring a couple of M52s up to command."

"Do you want us to post a squad up here?" Deke asked.

"Negative. If the fighting gets up here, we've got bigger problems and I'm certain we wouldn't want Zebra Company to be a squad down," Corcoran said. "I can handle an M52 just fine."

"Never had a doubt, Colonel," Deke said. "I have two M52s leaning against the bulkhead just outside. Let's hope you don't need them."

"Why should we think we'll need them?" Kersey asked. "We've hit four in a row and the Togath are taking it straight to the face. They're on the run and they know it."

"It's one thing to be cocky, Thad," Baines said. "We need to make sure we're looking at every angle."

"I don't like wasting energy on the ridiculous," Kersey said.

"God, I hope you're right," Deke said and turned to Baines "Am I good to go?"

"You're dismissed, Captain."

"Your blood pressure is up," Keegs said as Deke exited the mission room. "I don't understand why you're so convinced this incursion will be different."

"I just have a feeling. What's our countdown?"

"Eight minutes to touchdown. You should make your way to wherever you want to be when we land," Keegs said.

"Okay" She turned sideways as she passed crew rushing through the hall on their way to whatever last-minute preparations required their attention. Technically, as captain, they were to yield right-of-way to her, but much of that was lost in these final moments.

She entered the final hallway that led to where Bing and Carrole had set up Zebra Company's temporary armored command post.

"Twenty seconds, Deke," Keegs said.

"Copy," Deke said, sliding over to where one of *Angry Ark's* exposed structural beams ran up an interior wall. Bending her knees, she waited for the impact which came a moment later. As always, *Angry Ark* grumbled and groaned at the insult.

Shouts and clambering of almost fifty troops rushing toward a loading ramp that would fall at the last moment began. Despite it being the fifth time for the Black Turtle mission team, Deke's heart raced. The lead squad would likely come under withering fire. Her throat constricted as she considered the bravery and sacrifice of that lead team, many of whom would not make it back.

Watching from cameras high in the hold, she observed the troop movements. This time, however, there was no response from base. Not a single energy bolt or flash of a long Togath knife. There was no attempt to board any more than there was an attempt to defend the base.

"Captain Kersey, we have zero contact," was the report from the lead squad's lieutenant. "I will execute to plan and we'll clear this base. I'm formally requesting approval to move temporary command off ship."

"Copy that, Lieutenant Parker. You are approved to advance to position one," Kersey answered.

"Kersey, belay that," Deke called over private comms. "This doesn't feel right. Don't put your officers in the field."

"Get off this channel, Deke," Kersey said. "I told you we had them on the ropes. Watch us ..."

Kersey's retort was followed by a massive explosion that started beneath *Angry Ark's* belly and filtered out into the base's courtyard, sending a concussive wave into the confined space where his company was trapped. Mercifully, they died in a split second as the explosion took them.

Sitting atop the blast reflective tarp that made up the base's roof, *Angry Ark* was suddenly wrapped like a burrito as explosive gasses sought escape. Deke fell to her knees when the force of the explosion lifted *Angry Ark*. The design of the base created an almost perfect rifle barrel holding the massive ship as its sole bullet.

"Oh, shit," she breathed when the ship's deck twisted beneath her in a moment of free fall.

"*Angry Ark* has turned over," Keegs said, tweaking the signals to Deke's brain that were causing her disorientation. "Six Togath are approaching *Angry Ark*. It appears they intend to board while there is confusion from the explosion."

Angry Ark slammed into the ground, only this time, since the ship's experimental inertial dampers were installed in the deck and not in the ceilings, there was no cushioning of the inglorious landing.

"Fuck!" Deke said, absorbing the heavy impact.

In the moments that followed, she knew very well that Operation Black Turtle was in crisis. Zebra Company had been tossed around within *Angry Ark* like so many kernels of popcorn in a hot pan.

She had to decide if she would give aid to those in the worst shape, those that she thought might be able to find their feet in the minutes to come, or if she would take the fight directly to the Togath who looked to board and eradicate the humans aboard. She knew the answer as soon as the options presented themselves to her. She was really good at exactly one thing, killing, and kill, she planned to do.

"Track those bastards," she growled at Keegs as she grabbed the M52 partially buried by Zebra Company's temporary command center, which had fallen from the deck above.

Racing forward, she hooked an arm through a backpack full of ammunition, not slowing as she nimbly raced over the ceiling now turned floor. With the chaos of the crates that were secured to the ship's deck periodically falling as the straps failed, she focused on the four lead Togath.

She had little chance to stand against half a dozen Togath. Her resolve was spurred, however, when she heard quadruple shots of energy and on her HUD saw a Togath dispassionately killing stunned soldiers who were trying to make sense of the events.

"BACK OFF!" she yelled, nonsensically, steadying her arm against a crate. She lined her first shot on the Togath's eye socket. Firing five single shots, one after the other, she zoomed in with her enhanced vision and watched with satisfaction as three of her bullets entered her enemy's skull and did not exit.

A keening cry of rage filled the chaos of the hold as its mate sought out Deke. "Want some!?" she taunted loudly as she shifted fire to the angered mate. As expected, Deke's bullets both entered and skittered off the angry alien that moved with unexpected speed.

"Blag floshk snar foshink!"

"Would you like me to attempt to translate?" Keegs asked. "Also, I've activated your adrenaline."

"No, I know what she's thinking," Deke said, as the M52's magazine clicked empty. Instead of grabbing a fresh magazine, time she didn't have, she dropped the rifle and pulled the pistol to hand and fired in one smooth movement. The bullets were having an impact, but the Togath would reach her before she'd finish the job.

"Cawk fsnar cawk!" the Togath cried out as it leapt across open space. It chewed up the distance like an angry gorilla, only in this case, a gorilla brandishing a glinting dagger.

Dropping her pistol, Deke jumped to its side, having discovered in a previous fight that Togath were less effective at sideways movement than they were at racing forward. Her timing wasn't perfect and the warmth of a blade opening a line across her back was a warning of a too tight maneuver.

With blood running down her back, she tracked the Togath as it tried to follow her around with the grace of a toddler. Kicking against a bulkhead, she pushed into the alien's back and dragged the blade low along its back. And while she caused damage with a Togath blade, her understanding of its anatomy made the strike less effective.

"Gootk Gootk!"

The alien words were close but did not emanate from the avenging mate. Deke's heart sank. She barely had a chance against a single Togath. To add another would spell her end. She dove away from the sound, knowing she'd reacted too late and had no idea why there'd been no contact.

"Focus on the single Togath," Keegs offered.

"What?" Deke asked, dodging beneath an angry strike, this time avoiding the blow.

"Three of the others have gathered but are not attacking."

"Oh, shit," Deke said, rolling on her shoulder in a slick move that allowed her to arc her blade along the back of the Togath's heel. "Does this thing have an Achilles?"

"You did not strike deeply enough to catch its tendon. Try again, that was a valid attack."

"Sure, that was easy," Deke sniped. Reacting just a moment too slowly, the Togath's blade once again struck home, this time on her right arm, causing her to drop the blade from her hand. "Shit!"

Hoots of encouragement from the gathered Togath suggested they awaited their compatriot's quick vengeance. From the corner of her eye, Deke spied where she'd dropped her Desert Eagle. It was a lot of gun for single-handed but it packed an incredible punch close up.

She managed to avoid a finishing blow as she dove and landed such that her hand wrapped around the pistol's barrel. Her movement was erratic enough that the Togath struggled to follow her path, giving her enough time to reorient the weapon in her left hand. When she aimed, she fired at the wound she'd started on the creature's ankle, sending the magazine's remaining half dozen bullets point blank into the bleeding crease.

The sound of a band snapping rang out in the small space and the Togath screamed in agony and fell to its side. With no ability to reload, Deke didn't waste time watching the damaged alien fall but dropped the weapon while searching for her Togath knife. With Keegs' help, she found it.

With no mercy, Deke spun and drove the blade beneath the agonized Togath's neck, driving all fourteen inches up into the soft tissues of its head. The alien's body rattled in death as its nervous system sent out random signals.

Like a cat caught in a dog yard, Deke stayed low and extracted the blade, searching out the faces of the quartet of gathered Togath. The five were locked in quiet contemplation.

"I'm totally screwed here, aren't I?" Deke asked.

"I do not like the danger we are in," Keegs said. "There is a slight gap to aft. Perhaps you could race between them. I do not like your odds, but I will amp your muscles with adrenaline. It is our best chance."

"It's been a good run, Keegs. We almost had 'em," Deke said. "Shit, I hate being right."

"You were not right. You did not anticipate a bomb flipping *Angry Ark* like an earth tortoise."

"No, but I knew they'd come up with something."

Thap, thap, thap

The air filled with the sounds of automatic fire.

"You must keep low, Deke," Keegs warned.

"Right," Deke said. She crawled over the dead Togath and hunkered next to it as the sounds of more automated fire joined that of the first, and the four remaining Togath came under heavy fire.

"Captain, I don't know how you got up there, but you need to stay in place. You are in direct line of fire," Bing said.

"I'm not going anywhere," Deke said, pulling at the dead Togath's arm to further cover her.

Through her HUD, Deke watched Zebra Company establish lines of fire and advance on the knot of Togath who'd stopped their mindless killing to watch the vengeance duel of one of their own. With thirty heavy weapons focusing fire, the Togath armor was steadily chipped off and finally one and then another died until all three were on the ground.

"Bing, we're missing a Togath," Deke called, picking herself out of the pile when gunfire finally stopped. Even then she raised her hands to show she was no threat to jittery soldiers who'd been firing automatic weapons with abandon.

"It got past us," he said. "We couldn't stop it."

"Shit," Deke said. "Carrole you've got cleanup. Bing, I need a squad of heavies on me!"

"Good copy. Barnhardt, on the Captain!" Bing called immediately.

"Roger that, Lieutenant!" came the instant answer.

"Barnhardt, we're going to command. Try to keep up, I'm going to be moving fast," Deke raced along *Angry Ark's* ceiling, managing changes in decks as gracefully as she could, given the stairwells were hardly built for navigation while upside down.

Her heart sank as she saw the door to the mission room wide open and Kersey's body draped over the door's opening. "Shit, shit, shit. Baines, tell me you're up!"

"About time you got here," he answered a few seconds later.

"I'm coming in. Don't shoot me," Deke said.

"Nope, got no bullets, no shooting," Baines said. For a man always in control, Baines' slurred words were the warning Deke didn't want to hear.

"We need medical to the mission room!" Deke called into her comms as she stepped over Kersey's body. As soon as she made it into the room, however, she knew her request was needless.

"I'm afraid we've got a bit of a situation," Baines said, with a goofy grin.

"Did you hit a med pack?" she asked.

"Nothing wrong with a few Valium," Baines said. "I should probably avoid driving for a minute."

"Dammit, Baines, what happened?" Deke asked, not really needing the information. A Togath lay across his body. Someone had utilized a grenade, killing the Togath. The bad news was that the alien had been dangerously close to Baines at the time and the man's wounds were grievous.

"Whose grenade?" Deke asked, certain she knew the answer.

"Mine," Baines said. "Hey, you should know, Kersey didn't run. He actually met that dude at the door. Well, shoot, now that I think about it, maybe he was trying to get out of the door. Dang, I hope that wasn't it. I was so impressed. That's messed up."

Deke laughed despite the circumstances. Baines was blathering on as if he had no other cares in the world.

"How can I help, sir?"

"I sent word that we were in trouble. Do whatever you have to do to let them know we survived. Close up the ship and go into full turtle mode. They won't crack us if you can get turned over. There's a whole protocol called Big Neck."

"You're making that up."

"I'm really not."

"Survive, Deke. Hunker down. Help will come."

24

WHO'S IN CHARGE
AJ – XANDARJ SYSTEM

As much fun as it was to visit with his Xandarjian friends, AJ's heart wasn't in the social event. It was as if a black hole occupied his center and anything not essential was being sucked into it. So, instead of hanging out and catching up with his friends, he stayed aboard *Wasp*, moving from his quarters to entirely different quarters.

Darnell knocked on the hatch to AJ's berth. "Still treading water?"

"I know I'm a mess," AJ offered. "It makes me feel so mentally weak. Like I could have done something different."

"You could stay behind," Darnell said. "That's a choice you could make."

"*Wasp* will be ready to sail in eight hours, give or take," AJ said. "I don't know what Mads Bazer did to get them so motivated, but they're flying across this vessel. I've been checking their work, too. It is first class workmanship."

"At least that keeps you busy," Darnell said. "I thought you'd want to know. Lisa checked in with Amanda. They had dinner last night."

"How's she doing?" AJ asked, though he wasn't sure he wanted to know.

"She's sad," Darnell said. "Like you."

AJ nodded. "This is tough."

"Yup."

"You should know, her symbiote, Nit, has requested a move," Darnell said.

"That's odd," AJ said. "Jayne will do important things at the university."

"That's actually the problem," Darnell said. "The university doesn't want a Beltigersk influencing a human scholar. They believe a Beltigersk will skew Jayne's perspective."

"I doubt that," AJ said. "Jayne has her own mind."

"Feel like playing a game of ping pong? The boys have a table set up in the galley but they're all on station, having a good time," Darnell said, looking to change subjects.

"I haven't played in years."

"No time like the present, don't you think?"

"Sure."

~

"What do you think we're getting into here," Lefty asked. He scowled. "And you need to pick up your clothing. This is embarrassing."

AJ looked around the room. He didn't think things had gotten that bad. Sure, there were undies that hadn't quite made it to his hamper and maybe a few shirts unfolded on a chair. Of course, in the small area allowed a spacer aboard *Wasp*, it didn't take much to seem untidy.

"Nah, the shirts are clean, I just need to fold and put 'em away."

"Let me guess, Doc did that for you." The mention of her name set AJ spinning but he caught himself when Lefty tapped his knee. "I get it, brother. I ran through this about a year ago. Breaking up sucks. First time since losing your wife?"

"That's right," AJ said. "Really messes with my head."

"It's gonna be part of things for a while. Don't fight it," Lefty said.

"That's not encouraging."

"I'm your number two, not your fairy godmother. You need the truth. I'm telling you straight up. Now, do we have anything at all to work with from the intel boys?"

"Actually, yes." AJ sat straighter in his chair. "I got a report straight from a dude called Deke on Fimil Prime. Apparently, they've really been run through the shit."

"Oh? And they just now figured all this out? We've been at it for a few weeks. I sincerely doubt it's new news. What gives?"

"That's the thing. This is the first contact they've had since getting us rolling."

"We were told there were almost two hundred soldiers holed up and stranded on Fimil Prime and if they tried to move, a big bad was going to put them down," Lefty said. "That might be paraphrased, but I think I have the details."

"If you read between the lines, they knew Operation Black Turtle was doomed shortly after it launched," AJ said. "Once they got whatever this new intel was, they expected total mission failure."

"Why send us, then? We're hardly an occupation force. That's the goal, right? A second world for humanity," Lefty said. "And who is they?"

"Best I can tell, POTUS got involved shortly after they knew the mission was in trouble. She decided to send us in, in case there were survivors," AJ said.

"We don't know if there are survivors? Who's this Deke? I'm so confused."

"Deke is a soldier. The report is he's in command of what remains of the Black Turtle mission team."

"AJ, Deke is a woman," Beverly said, appearing on the table which separated the two men. She wore a fuzzy old white robe that looked like it'd been used to dust the floor and her hair was held in place by a red scarf. From her lips a half-smoked cigarette hung, the ash on the end perpetually flaking off.

"Is he really that bad, BB?" Lefty asked.

"Not sure what you're talking about," Beverly said, rolling her head lazily in Lefty's direction. "Everything is just fine."

"Oh, knock it off already," AJ said chuckling. "I'm not that bad."

"You left your underwear stripe side up," Lefty said, nodding at the deck.

AJ's head spun to the source of where Lefty was indicating. In truth, while there was underwear on the floor, it was mostly covered by a shirt. The stripe to which Lefty was referring was non-existent.

"You're both assholes," AJ said looking first to Lefty and then cutting his eyes to Beverly. "What makes you think this Deke is a man?"

"Kait Dekoster," Beverly said. "She has a rider."

"Can you talk to her? Can't she see a communications tower of some sort?"

"No. Something is blocking radio traffic. It was a fluke that her last communication made it out at all."

"Okay, so what, they're hunkered down, and the enemy can't figure out how to finish them off? Is that about it?"

"The vessel *Angry Ark* was built as a fortress class planet squatter," Beverly said.

"Is that an actual designation?" Lefty asked.

"Classification and yes," Beverly answered, taking the cigarette from her mouth and tapping it in midair to cause ash to fall. "The United States Congress approved a program for building spacecraft with offensive capabilities. Prior to a few years ago, those were illegal. In this program, there are classifications for a wide range of craft, including fortress and planet squatter."

"Planet squatter feels rather mission specific," Lefty said.

"It's certainly descriptive, though," AJ said, picking up the few articles of loose clothing that he hadn't put away. "Are you guys happy now?"

Lefty looked at Beverly and shrugged. "Yeah, sure."

The pile of clothing that had been put away appeared back on the floor. When AJ looked over at Beverly with raised eyebrow, she stood and flicked her cigarette in a practiced manner toward the pile. The ember at the end of the cigarette glowed as it arced through the air toward the virtual clothing. When it finally landed, the entire pile burst into flame and disappeared.

"Works for me," Beverly said casually, her housecoat and slippers replaced by Army fatigues.

"What kind of shape is this fortress class, planet squatter in?" AJ asked.

"According to Captain Dekoster, or Deke as she prefers to be called," Beverly said, "*Angry Ark* was unsuccessful in executing the Big Neck protocol, which since you're going to ask, was a procedure designed to flip *Angry Ark* off its back and onto its stomach."

"The ship is lying on its back and they're still alive?" Lefty asked incredulously.

"Yes. Captain Dekoster successfully deployed two high speed projectile turrets," Beverly said. "Before *Angry Ark* was flipped over, it successfully took out five of six bases. According to Captain Dekoster, they have run into a limited number of Togath on Fimil Prime. Analyzing her description, I surmise that whoever deployed the bases expected they'd be unchallenged."

"And that was enough to nearly destroy an expeditionary force full of highly trained soldiers with the best equipment we could send," AJ said.

"That's not exactly true," Beverly said. "The equipment provided by the US Army was general purpose and limited by weight constraints."

"Weight? That doesn't make sense. Lift isn't a big issue," AJ said.

"The fortress class vessel has extreme armor," Beverly said. "Also, the commanders had no idea what they'd run into and chose equipment with a bias to defense over incursion."

"But they were taking out enemy bases. I don't get it. That's not defense," Lefty said.

"Changing priorities," AJ said. "I bet they didn't expect those bases to be there any more than whoever sent those Togath expected the US Army to have an expeditionary force on the ground."

"And before any of this was resolved, someone brought us in on the action," AJ said. "Someone who had enough information to know the US mission would be in big trouble but might have survivors."

"It sounds like you have an idea who that might be," Lefty said.

"It's not even a question. This has Commander Cer's little fingers all over it," AJ said. "She's been yanking my chain ever since she let me grab those mechanized infantry suits."

"What are you going to do about it?" Lefty asked. "I don't like having my chain yanked around."

"Right now, I'm not going to do anything," AJ said. "Just because we don't like how we got in this thing, it sounds like this Deke is Army and she needs our help. Jayne said it right – I'm not walking away from a fight, especially if someone's got a gun aimed at their head."

"I suppose it's not a lot different than Intel back in 'Nam," Lefty said. "Grunts never knew why we were doing anything. It was just our job to die."

"Hooah!" AJ said. "Let's get into this. This ship or fortress is upside down but functional enough to be defended."

"That is what Deke is reporting," Beverly said. "The Togath have tested their defenses with ground forces but nothing more. The weapons put in place under Deke's command have been sufficient to hold these Togath off, but the team is also held in place by Togath forces, who sit just outside of the range of the base's weapons. And for clarity, they'd declared the name of the fortress to be *Indominable*."

"Sounds right," AJ agreed. "Our job is what, then? Help them get turned over? I don't think *Wasp* probably has the kind of lift that would be required to accomplish that sort of thing."

"Maybe not," Beverly said. "It's possible the Big Neck protocol that failed might be fixable, or more answers will present themselves."

"There's more going on here," AJ said. "This doesn't add up. I'm all about rescuing a few dozen soldiers, but we're not set up for personnel extraction. We're a pointy-end-of-the-spear team."

"Yeah, I'm ready to see what these Togath have to offer in a fight," Lefty said. "If there's only a handful of them mixing it up, they could have just sent reinforcements. We're missing something."

"A bigger fight is coming," AJ said. "That's what we're missing. What if Commander Cer's end game was all about getting us on Fimil Prime with her mechanized infantry suits."

"Are you suggesting she duped the US Army into putting the lives of two hundred soldiers at risk just so we'd go fight some war for her?" Lefty asked.

"Yeah, I guess I am."

∼

"Talk to me, Pig," AJ said, looking over to the young navigator focused on *Wasp's* sensors.

"There are two large vessels in orbit over Fimil Prime," Pig answered.

"Do they see us yet?" AJ asked.

"Not sure. They haven't broken orbit if that's your question. Also, I don't see any smaller vessels coming in our direction."

"Can you tell what they're doing?"

"Orbiting?"

"Right, my bad. Let me be more clear," AJ said sarcastically. "Can you discern if they're using orbital weapons against Fort Indominable?"

"Oh, no, nothing ... well, there is an energy signature that I can't quite make out," Pig said.

"Darnell, could you come to the bridge?" AJ asked.

"Be right there. What's up?" Darnell answered.

"Pig has an energy signature from the ships in orbit over Fimil Prime. Can you have Petey take a look?"

"Pig's been sending the data, we're already looking," Darnell said.

"Perfect. Let me know," AJ said. "BB, I assume you have access to all this. Define fairly large."

"Fifteen thousand tons," she answered almost immediately. "Big enough to deliver a thousand troops and equipment enough to support them."

"Bad news on the energy signature," Darnell said, his voice dualling on the comms and in person. "That's a weapon they're directing at the surface. It could be clearing land, but our best estimate of location lines up with Fort Indominable."

"Can't say we didn't know what we were getting into," AJ said. "Now, the real question is if they were expecting those bases to be there or if they already knew that this Captain Deke spoiled the fun for them."

"Petey has run the numbers, it's iffy if the fort can withstand a constant bombardment. Those ships have access to a lot of energy," Darnell said.

"Someone on that ship believes Indominable is still operational," AJ said. "They wouldn't be firing, otherwise."

"I'll take that," Darnell agreed.

"If those ships are still in orbit when we get there, we'll send squads over and scuttle them," AJ said. "Until then, let's see what kind of data we can get about Fimil Prime. Pig, you need to work on getting a message to Captain Dekoster. She'll be listening, I guarantee it. Get creative. If you run out of ideas, ask questions. Soldiers are at their most dangerous when they have hope. Give her something to be hopeful about."

"Aye, aye, sir!" Pig answered.

"AJ, you need to get in here," Darnell called.

Still fifteen hours from Fimil Prime, *USS Wasp* had executed the maneuver to turn so the ship's acceleration focused on bleeding off the ship's velocity toward the planet.

AJ rolled to a sitting position with legs hanging off the side of the bed. He gave himself a moment to gather his thoughts and then pulled on pants and shoes he'd left next to the bed.

"What's going on?" he asked, after making the short walk to the bridge.

"They sent a message," Darnell said.

"Did they now?"

"You'll like it."

AJ raised his eyebrows questioningly as he read the short message.

Human.

You endanger your species by your presence in system Quarr-19410227.

Cease all activities and withdraw or humankind will be subject to eradication.

Quarr Command.

"Short and to the point," AJ said. "BB, would you send that message back to Colonel Baird? Let her know that we're pushing forward with the mission as there are US citizens in need of assistance."

"The interstellar bridge is receiving but not transmitting," Beverly said. "The Quarr are actively blocking outgoing transmissions. I've loaded the message. If we're able to break the Quarr's hold on the bridge, the messages will move."

"We'll get to that when we can," AJ said. "It's not like we need armchair quarterbacking from a hundred light-years away."

"You're not worried about Quarr following through?" Pig asked.

"Explain how a threat of extinction works differently if we don't piss them off? They wait a few more years before stepping on our heads? Or how about we apologize and sneak out with tails between our legs. When they come to Earth, do we just hand them the keys to the White House? Or maybe we give these guys a little taste of what it's like to tangle with a species only a couple thousand years from running around with clubs and loin cloths. I know what I'd do."

"Up until this moment, we didn't know we were directly fighting Quarr. This information is critical. It's more important than those forty-five lives on Fimil Prime," Pig argued back. "You need to turn this ship around and get back to a neutral system so we can let command know what's going on."

"Is that an order, Pig?" AJ stood and glared at the young intelligence officer who'd done a decent job of integrating with his team, but was still considered an outsider. "And I'd be real careful with your next words."

Pig clamped his jaw closed and glared back at AJ. For a moment, neither man spoke.

"I asked you a question, Pig. Are you part of this crew or are you running your own show? I strongly believe that if I have to explain to you that I'm in command that maybe I'm not. And if I'm not in command, that makes me real itchy. That's not a good place for me to be. Especially in my current mood."

"Captain Albert Jenkins, by the power vested in me by US Army Command, I, Peter Ignatius Roberts, officially relieve you of command and require to you to remove yourself from the bridge of *USS Wasp* and place yourself under house arrest within your quarters."

Pig stood and straightened so that he stared directly at AJ.

"Oh, hell," Darnell said quietly, looking at the two men who'd squared off behind him. "That's some shit right there."

AJ managed a grim smile, his face hardening at the same time as he locked eyes with Pig. "That had to feel good getting off your chest," he said flatly. "How do you want to play this? We scuffle a bit and I take you back to the brig or maybe you just walk yourself back all gentlemanly like?"

"I've entered override codes into *USS Wasp's* main core," Pig said. "This vessel will not continue without my approval."

"Sure," AJ said. "I need an answer on the scuffle thing, though."

Pig blinked at AJ a few times and finally answered. "I also have a Beltigersk rider. I will not be easily subdued."

"AJ, he is right. I've just received contact from 842823348-6-A. This is not a friendly Beltigersk faction. I am sorry, I did not detect its presence. There were signs I should have picked up on but didn't," Beverly said, hanging her head and not looking directly at AJ.

"So, it's the hard way then?" AJ asked, stepping back to balance his weight.

"You're not getting it," Pig said. "I'm in charge. You're not in control of this vessel. I have authorization to take over this mission."

Done with the conversation, AJ's arm snapped forward, his fist clenched. Pig's response was preternaturally fast, and he blocked AJ's attack with an arm. Bringing his knee up and stepping into AJ, Pig drove his weight forward, catching AJ in the chest. It was a bold move that caught AJ off guard, and he stumbled, his shoulders ramming into the bulkhead.

The crackling sound of electrical discharge sounded. AJ felt hundreds of thousands of volts of electricity surge through him, and his body seized. Slowly, he crumpled beneath Pig and fell to the deck.

25

LIMPING INTO COMBAT
AJ – FIMIL PRIME SYSTEM

"What in the blazing hell?" AJ asked, rubbing his head. The cold steel of a bulkhead at his back indicated he was sitting on *Wasp's* deck, but he had no idea how he'd gotten there.

"Are you with me, One?" Lefty said, slowly coming into focus.

"I feel like I got hit by a Mac truck."

"Sorry about that. I had to take Pig down and you guys were connected," Lefty said. "You were on the wrong side of a grounded discharge."

"You Tazed me?"

"That's one way to look at it," Lefty agreed. "But it's probably not the headline here. We've got new trouble."

"Pig?"

"Yeah, that sonnovagun did something to *Wasp's* central computer," Lefty said. "Darnell is working with Tenet and Joyce to see if they can regain control."

"What sort of control? Atmospheric? Navigational? Fire Control?"

"All of the above. The central computer is one hundred percent FUBAR."

"How FUBAR?"

"You know how silicon is basically melted sand?"

"Sure."

"Imagine we're working on figuring out what melted silicon makes."

"You're kidding, right?"

"Not kidding. There was a failsafe put in by Army Intelligence, according to Tenet," Lefty said.

"What's our status?"

"We're drifting and will pass Fimil Prime like it's a gnat on a freeway if we can't get those engines back online. We have enough O2 and we can manually dump and mix it for now."

AJ looked around. He hadn't been moved from the bridge. "Where's Pig?"

"Locked in quarters," Lefty said. "I have Bald Norm looking after him."

"Wait. You hit me with the Tazer? But you weren't even on the bridge," AJ said. "I'm so confused."

"Let's just say I was playing a hunch," Lefty said. "I wish I'd played it earlier. Pig's Beltigersk melted the computer right when you went after him. I hit you guys with the volts because it disrupts Beltigersk signals."

"How'd you know Pig was making trouble?"

"Rebel had a hunch," Lefty said as his generally reserved Beltigersk showed up on his shoulder wearing her normal cutoff jean shorts and sleeveless white t-shirt. She gave AJ a cheery smile.

"BB's not going to feel like herself for another six hundred thousand milliseconds give or take," Rebel said. "Sorry about the hit you took. We were hoping Peter Robert's guest hadn't sent that kill signal."

"How could we not know about something that would melt our central computer?" AJ asked.

"Tenet knew," Lefty said, helping AJ to his feet.

"Seriously?" AJ asked, holding up a finger to let Lefty know he was about to make a comms request. "Big D, what's the word on the computer? ... Big D? ... Darnell? ... BB?"

AJ looked across at Rebel who was shaking her head.

"She was disabled," Rebel said. "You'll need to use a comm set for the next hour. Sorry about the milliseconds reference. I forget that humans don't easily translate mathematical quantities."

"Let's go," AJ said, motioning for Lefty to follow.

While staying out of the way, the crew watched with interest as AJ and Lefty raced aft to engineering. As professional soldiers, they knew better than to ask for updates on a rapidly evolving situation. Raised voices echoed in the hallway before they were even twenty feet from the entrance.

The shouting stopped when AJ and Lefty entered the smaller engineering space. "What do you have so far, Darnell?" AJ asked.

"We were just discussing how we weren't informed of that computer kill device," Darnell said.

"Water under the bridge," AJ said, earning Darnell's raised eyebrow. "Tenet, Joyce, what's our real option right now to get *Wasp* back under our control?"

"Not possible," Tenet said. "The kill switch was designed to take out a piece of the core that has no replacements."

"Could we take something from one of the suits or Seahag?" AJ asked.

"That's not a horrible idea. I've already thought about that," Joyce said. "The problem is the technology doesn't interface well. We'd spend days trying to figure out how to make stuff communicate. Running a ship takes a lot of different kinds of connections."

"You're thinking too grand," AJ said. "We need to control one thing right now, acceleration."

"I don't get it," Joyce said. "So you can slow down. We'll still die. Those ships will kill us if we get into local space with them. We're defenseless."

"We're not defenseless," AJ said. "We're far from it. Can you get the acceleration thing figured out? I don't care if you give Darnell a pair of joysticks from Chach's PlayStation."

"Chach might not like that," Lefty said.

"He'll take one for the team if he needs," AJ said.

"We don't need a gaming machine's joysticks," Joyce said. "Give us an hour and we can have rudimentary control of acceleration with some sort of pseudo manual control."

"You have thirty minutes," AJ said. "Those ships don't know we're sailing dead-stick. As far as they know, we're coming to get them, because that's exactly what we're doing."

"That's suicide," Tenet said. "We've detected laser turrets. Once we're in range, and especially if we don't have steerage, they'll have no trouble hitting us."

"That's why it'd be helpful to solve problems more quickly."

"If we don't solve life support, we won't live beyond the next twelve hours," Joyce said. "We won't need them to shoot at us. We'll all be popsicle sticks."

"See, now that's good information," AJ said. "I bet we can come up with manual controls on the heat panels, too. Rebel, what's your knowledge of *Wasp's* heating system?"

"Extensive," Rebel answered.

"Lefty, do you think you guys could do some good old-fashioned redneck engineering and keep us nice and toasty?" AJ asked.

"I can get into it," Lefty said. "I'll grab Bob Travis; he owned an HVAC business before we picked him up to come play intergalactic soldier."

"I'll leave that to you." AJ turned to his friend. "Darnell, what am I missing?"

"Tenet isn't wrong. We'll be sitting ducks to their turrets," Darnell said. "We'll have no way of dodging anything and our active energy armor isn't powered."

"That's crazy," AJ said. "Lefty, where did you say Bald Norm was keeping Pig?"

"Three down from my quarters," Lefty said. "There's a couple of boys hanging out, making sure things stay copacetic. You can't miss 'em."

"Tenet, Joyce, I'll be back," AJ said. "Let's see what we can cobble together so we don't turn *USS Wasp* into a floating museum."

"We're working on it," Tenet said, his irritation showing.

AJ shrugged and took off at a jog back through the center of *Wasp*. Taking a slight jig to starboard, he stepped into the hallway where most of the team's quarters were located. A knot of men clogged the hallway, and it took a moment before they recognized that it was AJ.

"Make a path," he said.

Slowly the men moved aside. AJ wondered if Roberts had been mistreated, such was the mood of those he passed.

"That guy is driving me nuts," Bald Norm announced when he recognized AJ at the narrow entrance.

"What's he saying?"

"Oh, just going on about how we need to let him go and how he's going to prosecute every one of us," Bald Norm said.

AJ stepped around Bald Norm. "I suppose it's time for a good-old-fashioned reality check."

"Door open or closed?" Bald Norm asked.

"Open is fine. I think the boys have every right to know what's going on," AJ said.

"You're all going to jail when we get back," Roberts said, spitting in frustration.

"Most of us would happily accept that," AJ said.

"That's a dumb thing to say. Nobody wants to be in prison for the rest of their lives."

"Couldn't agree more, but alive in prison is a whole lot nicer than dying of hypoxia or hypothermia," AJ said.

"Instruct the computer to take us back through the transition point. You point this ship home and it'll go right there," Roberts said.

"For a smart guy, you're universally stupid," AJ said. "What is it you think your symbiote did to *Wasp*?"

"Locked everyone out."

"Try ... set off a series of micro explosive devices that rendered USS *Wasp* derelict," AJ said. "Not one system is operating right now. We have a couple hours of O2 available, and we'll freeze in less than twelve hours. You might want to ask him about that when he wakes up."

"That wasn't the deal," he said. "The switch was to take the central computer's firewall offline while he installed our own firewall. You're just not seeing it right."

"You're completely clueless. Good luck with your life," AJ said, turning from the confused man. "Norm, get the Beltigersk antidote before his symbiote wakes. I want it taken into custody. We'll deal with Roberts after we figure all this out."

"You can't just leave me here," Roberts said angrily. "We'll get this ship going. It's just a firewall!"

AJ couldn't help but turn back. "You allowed an alien force to subvert our mission," he said angrily. "Tell me how that doesn't make you my enemy."

"I'm an officer in the United States Army ..."

AJ cut him off. "Who has sabotaged the transport and delivery of critical men and materials to an active war zone. You *hope* you'll make it to your court martial."

"We'll take care of him, One," Bald Norm said as AJ stalked from the room.

"Not a scratch, Norm," AJ said.

"Not even a scrape," Bald Norm agreed.

"AJ?" Beverly's voice was weak. "I'm feeling poor. I believe there was a powerful electrical surge. Are you well?"

"Good to hear your voice, BB," AJ said. "I'm up. That was friendly fire. Rebel had us popped with a couple hundred thousand volts to take down Pig's Belti. It wasn't a perfect time to be filling our dance card."

"Hmm, yes, that is a reasonable explanation," she said. "I sense several ship's systems are inactive. The ambient temperature is abnormally cool and is continuing to drop. What has happened?"

"Back to that Belti," AJ said. "There was a kill switch installed in the central computer. Your buddy inside Pig set it off when he knew the jig was up."

"What kind of kill switch?"

"Petey has details."

"I see," she said, pausing while she contacted Petey. When she came back she continued, "Your planning is reasonable so far."

"You haven't heard the half of it yet," he said. "Lefty, how are we coming on the heat?"

"Need about an hour. It's gonna get a bit cool in here, but we'll get it," he said.

"Big D, any word on thrust control?"

"Five minutes, max," Darnell said. "Joyce came up with a way to patch around part of the burn out."

"Good copy," AJ said. "BB, when will we be within those Quarr ship's firing range?"

"Six hours forty-two minutes," she answered immediately.

"Well, that's good," he answered. "We need to figure out how to get that energy reactive armor back online in six hours forty-two minutes or we're gonna get crisped."

"The armor has its own controllers," she answered. "The central computer primarily provides an on/off type of function so as to save energy while in non-hostile environments."

"So we need to install some sort of switch, then," AJ said. "Seems like I saw some spare parts back in engineering. What kind of specs are we talking about? Can we get before the relay so we don't have to take the entire load of the armor?"

"Yes, it is not a difficult matter. It will require extra vehicular activity," she said.

"Show me where to get the parts and let's get building," AJ said. "Darnell, we're going to need to shut down your engines in about thirty minutes. Are you cool with that?"

"Changes the acceleration vectors we're working on, but it's manageable. What's shakin'?"

"BB has a plan for getting the armor back online," AJ said. "We need an EVA to make it work."

"Let me know when."

"Good copy," AJ said.

Thirty minutes turned into ninety as AJ scrounged and scrapped for the parts and equipment necessary to accomplish the task Beverly outlined. That she projected a virtual representation of *Wasp's* hull so he could visualize the task at hand made things go more smoothly. On the flip side, it required repurposing common items to locate the parts and tools required.

"Hey, Big D, we're finally ready," AJ said, his teeth chattering from the forty degrees ambient temperature of *Wasp's* interior his body had been subjected to while stripping down.

"Does that EVA suit have a heater in it?" Darnell asked.

"Sure does," AJ said, feeling the first moments of heat warming his limbs. Lefty and Rebel had been successful in manually starting many of the ship's heating panels. While it wasn't comfortable, they'd managed to avoid the dangerous cold.

"I'm about to put on my vac-suit so I can warm up my toes," Darnell said.

"Why don't you?"

"Because most of the boys don't have a suit they can easily wear," he said. "I don't want them to feel badly."

"Aww, you're such a softy," AJ said, closing up his helmet. "For the record, this thing is toasty warm."

"You're an asshole."

"That's not news," AJ said. "Cut engines?"

"I need forty more seconds."

"I'm entering the airlock now."

Forty seconds later, the ship's engines shut down and USS *Wasp* quieted as she continued to slip through space at a constant velocity.

"You're clear for EVA," Darnell announced.

AJ opened the exterior hatch and spritzed the propulsion jets to push outside. Like Darnell, he owned a Vred made vac-suit that fit like a loose pair of jeans and comfy t-shirt. That there were small thrusters built into the suit and he had significant experience utilizing them meant he had little fear of operating outside of the ship, as long as it wasn't accelerating away from him.

"I'm outside," he said, tapping the thrusters to take him to the first of several points where he would install improvised switches.

"Be careful on this first," Beverly warned. "The highlighted conduit carries significant amperage at two thousand volts."

"Nicely done," AJ said.

"I prefer that we do not repeat the experience from the bridge," Beverly said, virtually flitting along beside him in her silver vac suit and cartoonish rocket pack.

"You took a pretty good wallop," AJ said. "Let's be clear, I only survived because of the low amps on those volts. I'm pretty sure I'm a cloud of pink mist if I touch two thousand volts with all those amps. BTW, the compliment was that you rounded the volts from two thousand one hundred fifty-three and just said two thousand. I was kind of impressed by that."

"I'm trying to be more flexible, AJ," Beverly said.

AJ nodded as he settled onto *Wasp's* hull and got to work. An hour later, he was working on the final task when he received a concerned communication.

"Bubba, are you about done out there?" Darnell asked.

"Just about," AJ answered. "Sorry, but I got hung up on the starboard side. There was some sort of buildup."

"We're coming in pretty hot to Fimil Prime," Darnell said. "I'd sure like to get those engines back on. How much longer do you think?"

"Six minutes and I'll be inside."

"That'd be much appreciated. I'll leave you alone," Darnell said, closing the communication channel.

"We'd better get this done. He's not one to hover," AJ said, struggling to seat the final fitting that would power a large portion of the ship's belly armor. "Man, this thing is not sitting in there. We must have more of that buildup. How bad is it if we take another thirty minutes? Are you talking with Petey about Darnell's concerns?"

"We do not have thirty minutes," Beverly answered. "Your six-minute timeframe is what we need to work within."

"Fair enough. Duct tape it is."

Working quickly, AJ shook his head at a job not perfectly done. Zipping back to the airlock, he called Darnell even before he closed the hatch.

"I'm in, Bubba. Fire it up." AJ slapped the button to lock himself inside the ship.

The engines lit up and he experienced an uncomfortable moment when he was tossed into the aft bulkhead and started sliding toward the still-closing hatch. For no reason in particular, he found himself laughing at the absurdity of the moment.

"AJ, you are cutting things very close," Beverly said. "I would like you to slow your actions in consideration of personal safety."

"I was just thinking that very thing."

It was a short distance through the main hold, filled with mechanized infantry suits and the pair of drop vessels, forward to engineering. Unlike his previous visit, he heard no arguing on his approach and when he entered, he found only Darnell seated at a workstation which had his sole focus.

"That you, AJ?" he asked.

"In the flesh," AJ said. "Is it warmer in here or is it just me?"

"You're wearing a vac-suit," Darnell said. "It's definitely just you."

"Just doing my part."

"You're definitely not."

"We might need another EVA. I want to be ready to go."

"We will not need you to EVA. We'll overshoot Fimil Prime if you do."

"Never say never and if I need to stay warm to be ready, I'll take one for the team."

"I have no words."

"AJ, there is a new communication from the Quarr," Beverly said.

"Put them through."

"This is *USS Wasp*," AJ said.

"You have not altered your course. We consider these actions to be consistent with hostile intent. We are at war with humanity."

"Please clear from Fimil Prime," AJ responded. "We intend to support the vessel *Angry Ark* which you are currently attacking. If you thought that wasn't an act of war, you're quite confused. You have seventy-two minutes to clear orbit. We will not negotiate when we arrive. You will experience devastating loss."

"Humanity does not possess technology to deliver a threat of this magnitude. Your confidence is unwarranted."

"Won't that be fun to explore, then," AJ said. "While you're thinking about it, I'll transmit a video of the battle cruiser you sent to trail us. I have a fun homophone for you as our last word on this. You can leave in peace, or we'll send you away in pieces. *USS Wasp* out."

He closed the comms with the Quarr.

"Is it wise to announce your plans?" Beverly asked. "We will struggle against these vessels if they vigorously attack us."

"Construct a video of that battle cruiser we tore apart," AJ said. "I don't want any video that shows our mechanized infantry suits, though. Just show them chasing us and then cut over to them dead-sticking into the planetoid. Make sure there's video of the wreckage we made on the back of their hull."

"Do you believe they will respond emotionally to seeing their compatriot's failure?"

"That warship we took down was a whole lot better equipped to fight than those two massive drop ships," AJ said. "Every time they contact us, they're trying to stop us from coming. If they think they've got us, why keep calling? It's easy to look at a fight and believe your enemy knows what you know. That's not the case here. I think Quarr are an advanced civilization and they knew we were being followed. Further, I'd bet they suspect we had something to do with losing contact with that warship. Our video will just prove it."

"And you think they'll just run?"

"I think there's a chance they'll run," AJ said. "Doubt is a powerful ally in combat."

26

HOUSE CALLS
AJ – NEAR PLANET FIMIL PRIME

"Two, talk to me," AJ called.

"Your squad is loaded, hold is depressurized," Lefty answered. "We're ready to rock and roll."

"Six minutes to contact," AJ said.

They'd decided to load the soldiers who operated the mechanized infantry suits prior to battle. The primary idea was that if *Wasp* had any sort of breach, the suits would provide significant added protection. Of course, if the ship were destroyed, that survival might mean a long, lonely, eventually very hungry trip toward the nearby stars until oxygen was depleted.

The second reason for loading into the suits was specific to the squad AJ would lead when they attempted to force themselves aboard if any Quarr vessel decided to let Darnell get up close and personal.

"Looks like they're sticking with sending that big boy our way," Darnell said.

"If I was looking to check out the competition, that's the one I'd send," AJ said. "They want to know what kind of pain we can take and if we've got any punch."

"They're calling your bluff."

"I would have," AJ said.

"AJ, the enemy vessel is charging laser batteries," Beverly warned. "It is time to load into your suit."

"You've got this, Big D," AJ said. "Remember, you just need to get close enough to let us drop in and board that thing. It's big enough, even you can find a dry spot to land."

"Seriously? You're bringing that up now?" Darnell asked. The reference to dry land was an old dig from back in 'Nam when Darnell had misjudged the width of a finger of land next to a marsh and nearly stuck his helicopter. As it was, AJ and his team had to jump into thigh deep water while Darnell struggled to keep his bird upright.

"Just keeping it real," AJ said on the way out of engineering.

He was climbing into his mechanized suit when the first laser bolts impacted *Wasp's* energized armor. The impact sounded like that of thunder from nearby lightning strikes. At first, AJ worried the armor he'd repaired hadn't worked at all.

"BB, that sounded big. Did we get holed?"

"Negative. The armor absorbed the energy as designed."

"Boy, I'd hate to hear what it sounds like without that armor," he said, tugging on a panel which caused the chest cavity of the mechanized suit to retract and seat firmly. Originally designed for much larger operators, the suits had been modified for human form by use of mesh fabrics that held them firmly but comfortably in place.

"Their weapons would cause a hole in *Wasp's* armor in a single shot without the armor supplied by the Galactic Empire," Beverly said.

"Your point being that puny humans don't stand much of a chance against Quarr?" AJ asked, tapping on the controls that brought his suit to life.

"Perhaps," she said. "Although I am concerned that the Tok, having involved Galactic Empire equipment, have poked the bear and our long, unspoken truce with Quarr is threatened."

"I think you're looking at it wrong," AJ said. "Fimil Prime is clearly in Galactic Empire space. Quarr is the invading force. We're defending what's ours and humanity has the added incentive that we'll be allowed to settle on a second planet. One, might I add, that we didn't discover due to some stellar scientific breakthrough."

"I dislike this arrangement. It feels manipulative. Human lives are being used to fight a war that is not yours," Beverly said. "If the Galactic Empire wishes to stand in front of Quarr, we should place troops of appropriate training and tenure on Fimil Prime."

"Are you nervous, BB?" AJ asked. "You've had a nice long while to think about all this and it's only coming up now, right before we get into this."

"I do not think so," she answered, but as she spoke her voice became softer. "Is this what fear feels like?"

"I'm not sure. Describe what you're thinking. Feeling words are best if you have them," AJ said.

"I find that we've been placed into an unfair position. Tok have calculated that the objective for defending Fimil Prime is more valuable than our lives. I am angered at this calculus," she said. "I question the validity of using sentient lives for geopolitical gain."

"You're officially a soldier, BB," AJ said. "This is where faith in something larger than yourself comes in handy. For me, that's the good old red, white, and blue. I'm a sucker for the stars and stripes. I'm all about defending my country against all threats and I don't mind takin' the pain right to the enemy. If we die trying to make a place for seven billion of my fellow humans, I say it's a good way to go out. Added to that, those boys and girls already on the ground? Why, I'm all in. It doesn't mean I'm not afraid. It's just part of the game. Embrace it and then let it go."

"You surprise me, Albert Jenkins."

Their conversation was cut short when the lights in the hold blinked and then turned off. A hull breach klaxon rang, and heavy hatch doors slammed shut, closing the hold off from the rest of the ship.

"That can't be good," AJ said. "Darnell, talk to me."

"We just took a big hit from below when I was taking a turn," he said. "They ripped into us pretty good on our belly. It's like we don't have any of that armor left."

"Aww, dammit. How big of a hole?" AJ asked.

"Not overwhelming, but those Quarr gunners are good. They're trying to force me to roll again. I'm trying not to show them my soft underside. They're going to lay down the hurt and I'm pushing to get us close enough to get you guys aboard."

"I know what the problem is," AJ said. "There's a coupling that wasn't a hundred percent. We didn't have time to make it right. I need to get out on the hull and fix it."

"You can't do that," Darnell said. "I'm accelerating all over the place. I'd throw you clean off."

"There are handholds and I'm in a mech suit. I've got this."

"That's crazy talk."

"Well now, we're just singing from the same hymnal," AJ said. "Open that damn hatch, Two. I'm going EVA."

"Roger that, One," Lefty answered crisply.

"If I don't make it back, you've got the team, One," AJ said, passing his old friend on the way out.

"Been bailing your sorry ass out since before you started shaving. I don't suppose that's gonna change any today," Lefty answered.

"Okay, Big D, I'm headed out," AJ said, using the powerful claws of his suit to grasp the wide armor plates on *Wasp's* hull and pull himself out.

"Hold firm, now!" Beverly said with more volume than usual. Her shout struck AJ just right and he held tight as *Wasp* slung starboard at a hard angle.

"AJ, shit, are you okay?" Darnell called.

AJ's legs flew away from the ship as he held on for dear life. Fortunately, the powerful claws didn't move. "Yeah, I'm still here," he said. "Try harder next time."

"Hold on, there's a ..."

AJ's visor blackened and his suit controls flickered. He found himself slammed into the mesh of his suit, his face against his visor.

"AJ, pay attention to my rendering and grab the handle."

His vision was taken over by a simplistic cartoon space. A handle that looked very much like the end of a garden shovel appeared in front of him. In the way of his reach were several two-by-fours haphazardly stacked. It was a significant change from what he'd been looking at before, but its simplicity made the task easy enough to process, so he reached for the handle and grabbed it.

"What's that about?" AJ asked, holding on as his body floated over the top of the shovel's handle.

"There was too much visual clutter for me to show you exactly what I needed. We were about to be separated from *Wasp*."

"Good call," AJ said as the scene melded back to reality. "I'm good, Darnell."

"Thank God," Darnell breathed. "They forced me onto my side. I tried to dodge. It's damn near impossible with these controls."

"You're doing fine," AJ said, keeping his voice level. "I'm just about to the broken armor. Let's clear the channel for a minute."

"Good copy," Darnell answered.

"Your heartbeat does not match the calm projected in your speaking," Beverly noted.

"Right," AJ said. "That's our job while under fire. We keep things calm so the next guy doesn't panic. Panicky people make mistakes."

"Can I presume you are going to bridge the power coupling with that steel bar you brought along?" Beverly asked.

"I assumed you'd figured that out," AJ said. "It'll be hard on the batteries, but we can figure that out once we're through the big moments of this battle."

"Yes," Beverly answered.

"Feels like we've had something of a breakthrough in our relationship," AJ said as he grasped armor panels to move himself carefully across the ship's hull.

"This is what you wish to talk about?" Beverly asked.

"Why not?" AJ asked. He pulled up next to the broken power coupling where his make-shift switch was nowhere to be found. "I figure I just bend the tips to get a sort of U-shape and then I'll hammer each end home. Do you have a better idea?"

"I'll admit, I would appreciate a more elegant solution, but I admire the raw simplicity of your approach."

"Why, that's almost fawning, Ms. Beverly," AJ said, adopting a southern belle quality to his voice. With a quick shove, he seated the steel bar into place and then regripped his stabilizing hand. Withdrawing his multipurpose tool, he held it so the flat, butt-end was even with the bottom of his fist, forming a sort of crude hammer. With several quick strikes, the seated steel was driven home like a massive staple. "And that should do it. Darnell, are you getting any sort of reading on the armor?"

"Negative, but that's par for the course. We're not getting readings on anything."

"Fair enough," AJ said. "I've done what I can. We might just have to tough it out."

"Get back to the hold, AJ. I think I know how to get us close in. I sure hope you got that armor online, though. Otherwise, we might be walking home," Darnell said.

"More solid than when it rolled out of the factory," AJ said.

"Why don't I believe you?"

The trip back was almost as harrowing as the trip out had been. Fortunately, Beverly's ability to predict strikes had improved to the degree that AJ was able to brace himself with both hands and feet and keep from being blown off the hull.

"Do you understand that a direct hit will likely burn through the suit's armor and we will not live?" Beverly asked after one particularly close hit.

"Right," AJ agreed. "I figured that. Good thing there's no way they're good enough to target a man-sized target on a ship moving at a few thousand feet per second on an oblique angle."

"That is not comforting."

"No, but this should be," AJ said, curling his body around and landing inside the open hold.

"Good to see you back," Lefty said, grasping AJ's arm with his own. "Did you get that armor repaired?"

"We'll find out when Big D rolls over," AJ said. "We need to get ready to jump. He's going to make a bombing run."

"That sounds interesting ... and painful," Lefty said.

"It's not going to be like that," Darnell said, joining the channel. "But you will likely hit with some force. You might want to use those magnetic clamps to lock you in. I'd hate to bounce anyone off."

"Peppers, mag clamps and cables," Lefty ordered. "We've practiced this. Tell your suits we might have excessive g-force upcoming."

AJ initiated a ready-check which forced the members of the squad to acknowledge the change in orders. The simple protocol allowed him to add importance to an idea. Handily, if an operator didn't catch the change, they could replay the information before acknowledging it. Thirty seconds later he had acknowledgements from the entire squad.

Three loud strikes in a row had Lefty and AJ exchanging curious looks. AJ was the first to speak. "Feels like Big D is closing in."

Lefty didn't have a chance to respond because it was Darnell, over tactical comms, whose voice was heard next. "Insertion team, prepare to disembark in thirty seconds, that's three-zero seconds,... mark!"

"You heard him boys, let's line it up," Lefty said.

The team shuffled forward with heavy magnetic clamps connected to braided steel cable hanging from their armored gloves. When the countdown reached zero, they ran and leapt blindly forward.

A flash of light nearly blinded AJ but didn't prevent him from following through. Searching his squad bio monitor, he was pleased to discover no serious injuries.

"I got that," AJ said tersely. "Stay focused."

"I will," Beverly answered.

The Quarr's vessel raced toward AJ, and he loosened his grip on the magnetic anchor. His landing was imperfect, which caused him to fall to the side and then slide. Fortunately, the anchor held, and he steadied himself easily.

"Let's get to work, boys," AJ said, pulling his multipurpose tool to his hand and wedging it beneath a fish-scale like metal piece. The scale-like material popped off and AJ repeated the process until he'd exposed a sizeable area.

He was about to start hammering away at the substrate when Peppers called out, "Fire in the hole!"

AJ checked proximity. He wasn't close enough to be impacted by Peppers's explosive, but he was close enough to take advantage of an opening if it was successful.

"I've got atmo!" Peppers announced. AJ watched the gout of atmosphere shoot out from the alien vessel like a whale's blowhole.

"Damn, those boys need to put some hatches in," Frenchy said. "That's a whole lotta O2 finding a new home."

AJ switched mental gears and grabbed a medium grenade. Pulling the pin, he extruded a small amount of sticky and placed it on the substrate he'd exposed.

"Fire in the hole," he added, moving away from his explosive.

"Get 'em, One!" Birdie called. "Dropping my own sparkler. Fire in the hole."

A few moments later, two more vents were added.

AJ grinned a moment later when his vent hole was suddenly stoppered from within. The material placed against the hole was a flexible fabric, likely designed for that purpose. He waited to see if anything else was coming and when the fabric bulged as pressure built up behind it, he pulled out his multipurpose tool, extended the long blade and sliced it open, causing a catastrophic failure. To make matters even more interesting, a long, multi-jointed arm slipped through the opening. AJ grabbed the arm as he braced his legs against the ship and pulled.

The figure that came into view was as misshapen as a humanoid could be and for a moment, its oddly shaped head swiveled to look at AJ, its expression equal parts anger and horror. When a third limb attempted to explore the collar where AJ's helmet connected to the suit, AJ felt a surge of fear.

"Oh hell, no!" he exclaimed as he swept his knife arm around and cut cleanly through biological material next to a lumpy shoulder. It wasn't a fair fight between flesh and mechanized armor. Separated from anything that held it to the ship, the Quarr spun off into space, leaving a spray of critical fluid in its wake.

AJ pushed away the image and turned back to the entry from where he'd pulled the Quarr. Atmosphere no longer blew out from the hole, which meant someone was actively working to seal the opening, likely by closing a hatch further within the vessel.

"Two, enter on my breach," AJ said.

"Hold tight, One. We're on our way," Lefty called back.

"Copy that." AJ hated being required to not charge in first, but as mission leader, he was already over the line by demanding to be part of the breaching team.

"Good job, One," Lefty said, slapping AJ's back plate on the way past.

"Nice hole, boss," Frenchy added, following closely on Lefty's tail.

"Show off," Peppers said, turning sideways as he slipped in behind Frenchy.

AJ drew the line at three and jumped forward, nearly colliding with Birdie, who was about to enter. Once inside, he became aware of the staccato flashing of automatic gunfire. Instinctively, he reached for the rifle attachment and seated it in place. Targeting badges started showing on his HUD and he tried to find a clear firing lane but was unable.

"One, you go starboard and head aft. Three, port side and aft," Lefty ordered. "I'll take Five and Six forward."

The five men, including AJ, toggled their acknowledgement of orders. Though AJ was in charge of the mission, Lefty had tactical control while on the ship. AJ did exactly as he was told and kicked down the first hatch he ran into. It took three strong kicks to break the seal of the hatch and he discovered, after it broke free and ricocheted off him, that he'd found a pressurized section of the ship.

He found no joy in moving through the ship and killing the dozen inhabitants he ran into. A few times, they employed clever tricks that set him back, tripped, and even blinded him. The problem was that the material of the mechanized suits was virtually impervious and also flexible enough not to be physically trapped.

Finally, he found himself in the large vessel's engine room where a pair of less muscular Quarr looked at him with surprise.

"If you've got escape pods, you might consider utilizing them," AJ said, certain Beverly would translate to the common language they'd used over comms. He wasn't particularly concerned with their answers and started chucking unpinned, sticky grenades at important looking controls.

At first, one of the Quarr started quacking. It started toward him, and he thought he'd be forced to deal with the angry alien. At the last minute, the Quarr's companion pulled it away. AJ stepped away and around a corner into a hallway, timing his escape with the grenade's countdown. Kneeling and with his back to the blast behind the wall, he waited.

The explosion came hard, the force multiplied by a reaction with the engine's fuel supply. Fire filled the hallways and AJ wondered if he'd made a critical mistake. Just as quickly as the explosion ripped through the ship, the fueled fire was sucked into space through a new hull breach.

"Well, hell, that was a lot," AJ said. "Two, I'm making progress in engineering."

"What the hell, One?" Lefty said. "Was that your explosion?"

"Yeah, that was me. And if you're worried, I'm still up."

"I'm pissed. You threw my team across the ship and knocked us all over like a bunch of rookies," Lefty answered. "Maybe a little communication on the big explosions?"

"It was only a pair of grenades," AJ said defensively. "For the record, Quarr crap their pants when you're about to do something crazy."

"Literally?" Lefty asked, barking a laugh.

"Didn't check," AJ said. "I'm gonna run over and help Birdie with the other engines. How's your progress?"

"We've only run into a handful of those twisty bastards," Lefty said. "They don't run when they should. We're about to breach what we're figuring to be the bridge. Go ahead and help Birdie, but for the love of God, let us know when you're going to knock us about again."

"Good copy, Two," AJ said.

27

BELLY UP
DEKE – PLANET FIMIL PRIME

DEKE STARED AT CORPORAL HARMEN, the sole surviving combat engineer as he finished welding *Angry Ark's* aft hatch closed. It had taken the efforts of a dozen soldiers to hold the hatch in place after the ship was dropped on its back.

"That should do it, Captain," Harmen said, casting a tired look at her. "We'll have a crap time moving supplies in and out, but no damn Togath is gonna bust through that. Hell, they'd have better luck coming through the sidewall. What's next?"

Deke felt empathy for his exhaustion and appreciated that he understood there was no time for personal comfort if they were to survive what was to come.

"Talk to me about Big Neck protocol," she said, accepting the welding torch as Harmen climbed down from the precariously constructed scaffolding.

"I heard you talking to Lieutenant Bing," Harmen said. "Honestly, I've never heard of it. Over my pay grade. It sounds like something Sergeant Jakes might have been in charge of."

"Well, son, today's your lucky day," Deke said, trying to adopt the swagger she'd experienced so often from COs in the past. "You're receiving a field promotion to Chief Engineer. All this is now your domain." She swept her arms broadly to indicate the entire ship.

"Well, shoot, that's certainly not how I wanted that to happen," Harmen said humbly.

"Keegs, can we get Harmen the access he needs?" Deke asked.

"Yes. Commander Baines placed you in charge shortly before he lost consciousness the last time," Keegs said. "I'll make the requisite entries in the mission log. There are rank emblems available in Commander Baines' office, although they will be disturbed due to *Angry Ark's* current anti-vertical orientation."

"Sure, being upside down sucks," Deke agreed. "We'll take a swing through and see if I can find 'em. Harmen's going to be up to his ass in alligators, be good to keep him motivated."

"Ma'am?" Harmen said, staring intently at her. "Are you saying something?"

Deke shook her head. "How long will it take for you to research Big Neck protocol?"

"I've got a problem with gray and black water systems that I really need to look at. Being upside down is messing with our septic flows," he said. "We're not set up for long-term upside down."

"But we can deal with it in the short run?"

"Technically yes, but the system just shut down," he said. "I don't know how many butts we've got to count, but they're all gonna need a working system if we're not going outside for a while."

"Good point. We don't have a butt count, much less a head count," Deke said. "Lieutenant Bing, are you available?"

"Go ahead, Captain," Bing answered over comms.

"Timed at your discretion, would you get me a good head count?"

"Aye, can do, Captain. We're dealing with a nasty spill, it might be a few."

"Copy that," she answered, closing comms. "Sergeant, talk to me about how we get septic working. I'm beginning to think this might be a stich-in-time sort of solution."

"Waste is historically a problem for armies," Harmen said thoughtfully. "We don't need the trouble that comes from that."

"How many bodies do you need? Right now, you get the pick of the litter," Deke said.

"Four," he said. "I know two I'd like to recruit. I don't know about others."

"I'm putting you directly under Lieutenant Carrole," Deke said, tapping approval of the reassignment on a command interface presented on her HUD.

∼

"Have you slept?" Carrole's question startled Deke from semi-wakefulness.

She'd only leaned against the bulkhead for a minute. She couldn't recall how she'd arrived at the particular location, but she did remember the relief she'd felt when she'd allowed her eyes to close for just a moment.

"I think I just was," Deke answered. "I need to get back to the hold. They're having trouble ..."

"Stop," Carrole said. "We all get it. You're super woman and only need to sleep one night in five, but seriously, Captain, you've been going for seventy-two hours. I bet your tag-a-long ... Keegs, right? I bet he says that's not okay."

"We need to get flipped over," Deke said. "We can't afford to stay on our back like this."

"That's why I came to find you," Carrole said. "Sergeant Harmen is ready to give Big Neck a try, but we've got a problem."

"There's always a problem," Deke said wearily. "What is it now?"

"Twenty Togath setting up. Port side, aft," she said. "We think they're targeting the loading ramp, since they know it comes off."

"How confident is Harmen in his welds?" Deke asked as she followed Carrole through the ship.

"He has a welding team securing I-beams every eighteen inches," she said. "He won't admit that he's concerned his initial welds won't hold, but suggested that since we had the I-beam stock it'd be silly to leave it sitting on the floor."

Deke managed a slight smile. Harmen was a hard worker and liked to be thought of as an expert.

"Ah, Captain, thank you for coming," Harmen said, stiffening but not coming to attention as she entered the engineering space.

"Sergeant," Carrole prompted with raised eyebrow.

"Oh, right," he said, pulling to attention.

"As you were," Deke said, returning the salute. "Talk to me about this protocol."

"Basically, we spin all eight leveling pylons one-hundred-eighty degrees. That takes roughly forty minutes, and we need crew and equipment moved outside to make it work," he said.

"How much crew?"

"Two or three per pylon," he said. "We can probably only do two ... maybe four at a time. So, max of twelve outside."

"Not counting tactical support," Deke added. "We have enemies setting up on us."

"Seriously?" Harmen asked. "How many?"

"More than we can defend against," Deke said. "What will it take to deploy ship turrets? We're upside down, I get that, but what kind of access do we have to fire control?"

"Damn, if we have to put turrets out, we can't extend the pylons," he said.

"We could have had them out already?"

"It's not difficult. We'll need people outside if there are obstructions on the turrets," he said. "They fire just fine upside down. Basically, that's because in space there's really no up or down."

Deke bit back angry words. They'd had days unchallenged by Togath. Plenty of time to extend *Angry Ark's* turrets. Instead, they'd left them retracted because she'd asked to get to the Big Neck protocol as soon as possible. She felt a flash of irritation at her own inadequacy to ask the right questions while they solved the ever-changing list of critical problems.

"Sergeant, you should watch your tone just now," Deke growled. "Forty-six soldiers are currently at dire risk because you and I have not communicated well. Very carefully explain to me how we will extend our turrets so the enemy at our door will not overwhelm our defenses."

"The turrets aren't completely unusable," Harmen said.

Simmering with irritation, she resisted striking the man. She had believed *Angry Ark's* weapons were usable in the current configuration, and then had also believed Harmen when he'd suggested the opposite only moments before.

"You're not making this better," Deke said. "I need clear communication. For some reason your conversations are shifting sand."

"Ma'am," Lieutenant Carrole said, interrupting Sergeant Harmen. "I apologize for the confusion. That's my fault. The turrets in their current configuration have only a few degrees of freedom. Keeping them retracted is appropriate as we can protect the workers deploying the pylons under this configuration. I should have explained the options and why I decided not to make changes."

Deke considered her lieutenant's words. "I feel like I'm further behind than when I started. You're saying the turrets are usable now, but just not as much as they could be if we extended ..."

"In fortress mode," Harmen filled in, unprompted, which earned him glares from both women. "Sorry."

"That Togath are amassing is problematic, but they'll pay heavily if they attack our ground team while we're attempting the Big Neck protocol," Carrole explained.

"And you're ready to execute Big Neck, now?" Deke asked.

"That's right," Carrole said. "Lieutenant Bing has a squad ready to go. We have to be careful with those Togath nearby, but we think we've got it."

"And I'm not in the loop on this because I'm falling asleep in the hallway ..."

"You're not in the loop because so far we've only been planning. Now that we're prepared to actually do something, we were ready to bring it to your attention," Carrole said, turning a hard look in Harmen's direction. "We're learning hard lessons about chain of command."

"Walk me through slowly," Deke said. "Show me firing lanes and how we'll keep our ground team safe. I also want to see a plan for what happens when those twenty Togath rush the ship."

"We have all that," Bing answered, joining the group. "Here's what we have."

Projected on the bulkhead, an overhead view of *Angry Ark* in its upside-down state appeared. Translucent blue cones on the rocky soil bobbing back and forth showed individual soldier firing lanes as they disembarked from the ship. Longer and wider, orange cones appeared at regular intervals next to the ship, showing the reach of the ship's turrets. There were obvious holes in the protection, but there were also many zones of safety. When the pylons were highlighted, the execution of Big Neck protocol became obvious.

"That's good work, lieutenants," Deke said, after several simulations ran to completion.

"Our worst projection has casualties," Carrole said. "I believe the risk is justified, though."

"What are your thoughts, Mr. Bing?"

"I'm with Lieutenant Carrole," he said. "I volunteer to be in the crew that works the pylons."

Deke wanted to deny the man's request but paused before speaking. Bing's platoon had been savaged by the Togath more so than any other platoon. While she didn't want him acting in a self-destructive manner, she also understood more than most that he couldn't look at himself in the mirror if he didn't face his demons.

"You'll lead the team," Deke agreed. "Keep your head up and out of the actual work. Your battlefield instincts are to be top priority. I don't care if someone asks you to hold a screwdriver to save the mission. You're a soldier first. Do you copy?"

A grim look of satisfaction spread over Bing's fact as he accepted the unexpected turn of events. "It'll be as you say, Captain," he agreed. "Everybody comes back."

"That's right," Deke said. "Let's do this. No surprises."

"We're ready, ma'am," he said. "You're making the right choice. We're stronger if we can get on our belly."

"Actually," Harmen said. "*Angry Ark's* construction has a bias toward an armored belly. We're not as defendable with our turrets, especially if they're not fully deployed, but we're a harder target when upside down. It has to do with the expectation that we might have to land on ground that could be mined."

"You're making things up," Deke said. "I've read our armor specs. Top and bottom are the same thickness. Our biggest problem is the interior systems in need of specific gravity."

"The super structure has more connectiveness beneath the decking," Harmen said. "I'm not messing around about this."

"Does this change anything?" Deke asked, looking at her lieutenants.

"No way," Carrole said. "Right side up gets us better firing lanes. I want to take it straight to these assholes. We can also hop around if necessary."

Deke smiled at the woman's embrace of curse words.

"I agree," Bing said. "Give us fifteen minutes and we'll be ready to launch, provided you give the order."

"So ordered."

Bing snapped off a quick salute which Deke immediately returned. "Aye, aye!"

"Go get 'em, Lieutenant!"

Deke's heart hammered in her chest as she stood at the top of the semi-permanent platform installed near one of the airlocks in the hold. In her arms, she held a heavy M52 rifle. Strapped to her back was the Togath blade she'd captured. She'd decided to back Bing's team with a squad of her own if the Togath decided to make a move. She'd rationalized leading it herself due to the cost of losing so many at such a critical moment being worse than losing her leadership, especially with Carrole backing her up.

"Captain, we have two squads of Togath working down the eastern rockface," Carrole informed. "You better get out there and provide fire support."

"We're Oscar Mike," Deke said, nodding at a wounded soldier who'd volunteered to man the airlock. "Go, go, go!"

Sleep-deprived, the adrenaline pumped into her system by Keegs was a sour taste in the back of her throat. That she was moving pushed away much of the fatigue, but she'd have to be at the top of her game if she was to meet what was coming.

"Set up on position Alpha," she commanded.

Having simulated many of the Togath responses to their EVA, she'd chosen the most successful position in which to set up. Alpha position gave solid cover for her soldiers while allowing them to cut off any approach by the Togath that would lead them closer to the team deploying the pylons.

"We're at twelve minutes for the first pylon," Keegs announced, forcing a countdown timer to appear on her HUD. In her mind, she acknowledged the absurdity of keeping a superior enemy at bay for an hour.

"This is gonna suck," Deke said subvocally, so only Keegs could hear.

"I'll add the overlay *Angry Ark's* firing lane to your visual field," he said. "This is doable."

"Doable?" she asked, chuckling as she loosed several short bursts of fire at a Togath who'd crossed into range. A small twitch on the Togath's chest was the only indication of her bullets' strikes. That the mostly flesh and blood alien could take such a hit in the field was still something of a wonder to her.

"You've asked for concise language," Keegs explained. "I find no flaws in the lieutenants' strategy. We worked many simulations to finetune it."

"I didn't know you were helping them."

"My ability to convert conversation to simulation was quite handy. Also, I have some understanding of the utilization of weapons and how Togath perceive threats," he said. "This knowledge was acquired under difficult circumstances. Utilizing this learning is my way of honoring the dead."

"That's touching, Keegs," Deke said, tapping her trigger again. "Carrole, send the second squad to Beta position. The Togath are spreading out."

"I'm watching it," Carrole responded. "The squad is coming through the hatch now."

Deke watched an hour float by as the crew of *Angry Ark* adjusted to Togath movements. It was like a grim game of checkers that every few moves ended in bloodshed for one side or the other.

"Pylons are deployed," Carrole announced after the ninety-minute mark had barely passed. "We're bringing back the engineering team and Squad One. Squad Two, you need to hold that line, our engineers barely have armor."

"Good copy," Deke answered as she'd taken lead of the second squad.

There was no better motivation for moving quickly than that of energy bolts splashing off every nearby solid surface. Squad One joined Squad Two as the engineering team flowed up the stairwell. A cry of pain warned Deke that one of the engineers hadn't made it unscathed. She knew better than to divert her attention, and focused on her section of the battlefield, trusting the other squads to do their jobs.

"Squad Two, you're next," Bing called over tactical comms. "Go now!"

"Shit." Deke cursed under her breath. She'd given tactical control to Bing and he'd forced her retreat ahead of his own. Her curse was acknowledgement that to argue would place them both in greater danger. "Squad Two, move out!"

The Togath, recognizing the retreat, pressed forward, taking advantage of the dwindling fire support. But as the airlock was strategically covered by one of the turrets, the enemy had difficulty getting close enough for much beyond long shots from behind cover.

"Doggone it," Deke said, jumping over smears of blood on the ceiling-turned-deck. She shook her head ruefully as she jogged through the ship to engineering, where they'd set up a temporary command post.

"One dead, three wounded," Keegs reported quietly.

"How badly wounded?" she asked.

"Full recovery is possible. I'd like to advise the medical technicians, though. They lack access to some of *Angry Ark's* medical equipment due to our orientation," he announced.

"Make contact and let me know if you receive resistance so I can deal with it."

"I understand," Keegs said.

"Talk to me, Lieutenant," she said, coming up next to Carrole.

"Squad One is inside. We're all aboard," she said. "I was about to have Sergeant Harmen begin Big Neck phase two."

"All hands, this is Captain Deke. Big Neck phase one was successful and we're moving to phase two. Please move to a designated location to avoid falling equipment. This isn't a well-rehearsed protocol, so be about your wits."

"How much time do you want to give them?" Carrole asked.

"Go ahead and start," Deke said. "If I recall correctly, it'll take a couple of minutes before we actually try to roll over."

"Forty-seven seconds," Harmen answered.

"Do it," Deke growled.

A projection on the bulkhead showed a sideview of *Angry Ark* as pylons pushed downward from thick support beams that extended from the ship. Almost immediately, the floor beneath their feet shifted and caused everyone aboard to bend their knees, grab for support, and pucker.

"That's progress," Harmen said, urging the ship's movements as the hydraulic jacks slowly filled. "Oh, crap."

"What?" Carrole asked.

He jumped from his chair and stabbed his finger into the projection. "Look at that outcropping."

"What about it? We're not close enough to contact it," Carrole pushed back.

"We will be in about twenty seconds," Harmen said. "There's a rock shelf beneath the forward pylons. It's slanted at twenty degrees and is going to push us into that hill. Shit, shit, shit."

"Are you certain?" Deke asked.

"Not certain, but it'd be a hell of a time to start being wrong."

"We can't afford to be stuck on that hill," Bing said, out of breath from running back from the hold.

"Hold operation!" Deke demanded.

"Aye, we're holding," Harmen answered quickly.

"Talk to me, Bing."

"That will take out two of our turrets," Bing said. "I asked you about that shelf, Harmen."

"And I told you I wouldn't know until we started moving."

"This isn't the time to argue," Deke said. "Are we or are we not going to hit that shelf?"

"We've moved twenty feet starboard already," Bing said.

"Keegs, I need you to look at this," Deke said.

"Lieutenant Bing is right," Keegs said. "There's no way to know if we'll continue to slide, but that we've moved this far already suggests we will."

"Shut it down and level us out," Deke said. "If we get stuck on that outcropping, Togath will have a substantial tactical advantage. We're just going to have to deal with being turtled and make the best of it."

"That's ridiculous," Harmen said. "We'd have to re-seat every piece of equipment on the ship to get back to full function. What happens when we do get rolled over?"

"You act like we've got somewhere else to go," Deke said. "We're all going to have to face the facts. We're here for a minute. We'd better get comfortable."

"I want to get those turrets deployed," Carrole said. "There are twenty Togath out there right now. What happens when more show up?"

"They've had plenty of time to amass everyone on planet," Harmen said.

Deke held her hand up as Carrole prepared to shut the recalcitrant sergeant down. "How much time before we're leveled again?"

"How level?" Harmen asked.

"Best effort. We need a stable base."

"Three hours, give or take."

"Call me when it's done," Deke said. "I'll be in my quarters."

"Aye, aye!"

28

WRAPPED IN THE FLAG
AJ – NEAR PLANET FIMIL PRIME

"Hmm, I guess they're not extra stupid, after all," Birdie ruminated. He floated away from the Quarr ship which was now in a decaying orbit over Fimil Prime.

After having witnessed the destruction of their ship's propulsion, the few remaining Quarr had jettisoned in life pods and were headed for the planet's surface, albeit in a more controlled manner than the ship. The second vessel, which had stayed back to observe the encounter between the now derelict vessel and *USS Wasp*, was in full retreat.

"Letting us get all up-close and personal was a pretty big mistake," Peppers said. "Of course, if they hadn't, we'd have just headed to the surface to make our own brand of trouble down there."

"Boys, we need to keep the chatter to a minimum," AJ reminded. "Encrypted comms aren't considered secure when we're combatting more advanced species. Assume everything we say is being heard."

"Copy that, One," Birdie answered quickly. "Still feels good to take care of things."

"I couldn't agree more," AJ added. "Job well done, team. Now, don't get cocky. They dropped a whole crap ton of trouble on our boys and girls down on the surface. We need to get our game faces on. All we did was run off the troop transports. Hardly a victory worth excessive celebrating."

"Aw, One, you could suck the joy out of a milkshake," Bald Norm complained.

"Big D, talk to me, man," AJ called over comms, ignoring the good-natured complaints of his team.

"What's shakin', AJ?" Darnell asked. "Gotta say, I'm pleased to see those ships pull off. *Wasp*'s taken quite a beating. I don't know how we're ever gonna hold atmosphere again for all the new holes."

"That feels like a problem for the wonder twins," AJ said.

"Wonder twins, that's rich," Darnell said.

"What's the chance we can do an orbital entry with *Seahag* and *Bernard*?"

"With or without half a dozen rangers hanging underneath like teats on a milk cow's udder?" Darnell asked.

"You've been holding that line for a minute, haven't you?" AJ asked.

"About a year, yeah."

"Does the udder thing matter?"

"Not a bit. Those dropships are strictly in-atmosphere. If we try to drop them through the atmosphere, we'd come in way too hot," Darnell said. "I've been thinking. Maybe there's another way. You're not gonna like it, but it could work."

"I don't like it when you get ideas," AJ said. "I assume *Wasp* is too messed up to make an orbital entry."

"That's mostly true," Darnell said. "Get aboard and I'll tell you what I'm thinking."

"This should be good."

Ten minutes later, AJ slipped from his mechanized infantry suit into *Wasp's* cold, airless hold. Jogging forward, he was met by Lisa before he could exit the hold to join Darnell in engineering.

"Uh oh," he said, reading the concerned look on her face. "What's going on?"

"You need to talk him out of this," she said. "It's suicide."

"I don't even know what we're talking about," AJ said. "He has some plan he wants to throw by me."

"It's a bad plan." Lisa kept up with AJ as he moved forward. "He wants to take *Wasp* into the atmosphere until it breaks up and then unload *Seahag* and *Bernard* once we're going slow enough to survive."

"Hey, no fair," Darnell said, catching the tail end of the conversation. "And that's not the whole thing."

"Oh, really?" Lisa said, dryly. "Which part of you riding a dead ship to the surface after we jump free is wrong?"

Darnell paused, looking back and forth between his best friend and his wife. "Well, that part isn't specifically wrong."

"I'm going to need more," AJ said. "It doesn't seem like much of a plan, especially since you're our best dropship operator. With a thousand Togath on that planet, we'll need to be nimble. I don't like being hamstrung before we even get in the fight."

"I see the quandary," Darnell said. "My approach puts our teams on the ground with minimal casualties."

"One casualty. You," Lisa said. "And he won't talk to Phillip."

"Pig is unstable," AJ said. "There's no reason to talk to him."

"Have you?"

"I've been busy," AJ said. "No reason to get into things with him. He made his choice."

"Did you know his Beltigersk symbiote was acting more like a parasite? It simulated communications from home. Presenting him with false reports and data. It was fully gaslighting him."

"You talked to Pig?" AJ asked.

"We'd become friends," Lisa said. "We were pulling late shifts because Seamus thought some things might be off."

"And you think he'd want to ride *Wasp* down as some sort of last, heroic act," AJ said. "How could we ever trust him?"

"We extracted his Beltigersk," Lisa said. "He's broken up by it all. At least give him a chance to say no."

AJ glanced at Darnell, trying to read the man's face.

"We already had this conversation," Darnell said. "I think it's a bad idea. We can't trust the entire mission to a man who's had his brains cooked by an alien."

"Three, bring Pig to engineering," AJ said. "He and I need to chat."

"You can't be serious," Darnell said.

"I need to look in his face and understand what we're up against," AJ said. "We're all out of good options. It's time to look more seriously at shitty options."

"I don't like it," Darnell said.

"You're such a jerk some days," Lisa said, slugging her husband in the shoulder as hard as she could before storming out.

"What?" Darnell asked, standing. "Wait, Lisa. Don't be like this. Don't let her do this, AJ. I'm our best bet here."

"Explain to me how you'll get us to where we launch the dropships," AJ said. "I need to understand what we're up against. Is it something Pig could do without a Beltigersk along to make calculations?"

"Technically, the work isn't hard," Darnell said. "We have enough of *Wasp's* computer back online. It's a matter of paying attention to gauges and keeping us level. The thing is …"

"Hold on," AJ said as Peppers brought Pig into the engineering bay.

Unlike the last time they'd met, Pig had no more angry words and remorse filled his face. "I have no right," Pig said, "but please, let me say something. I know you have no reason to trust me."

"You mean because you sabotaged this vessel to the degree that it almost killed everyone aboard and endangered the forty-five soldiers trapped on the planet below?" Darnell asked angrily. "That reason?"

Pig nodded, accepting Darnell's ire. "You're right. I did that," he said. "I accept responsibility for my actions and agree that you have every justification to lock me in a cell and allow me to burn up in the atmosphere when you attempt to land on Fimil Prime."

"There's no landing *USS Wasp* anywhere," Darnell said. "You've seen to that."

Confusion crossed Pig's face. "Then, what? You try to do an atmospheric entry with the dropships? It won't work. You'd have to drop the mechanized troops too high if you were to have any chance. They won't survive. At a minimum, they'd be too spread out."

"That's not the plan," AJ said.

Pig blinked in confusion and then stepped back as realization struck. "You're going to sacrifice *Wasp*. It's a suicide mission. That's why you're talking to me," he said, looking at Lisa.

Guilt clouded her face as she was thought through what they were asking.

"Don't look at her," Darnell snapped. "You haven't earned that right."

"That's true," Pig agreed. "But don't act like this doesn't change things."

"It doesn't," Darnell said. "I can make sure this mission has every advantage. I'm the best pilot on this ship. I do this and my wife, my best friend, and my whole team gets a chance to live. How do I give that responsibility to a man who caused it all in the first place?"

"You give that responsibility to a man who believes his actions are that of a true patriot," Pig said.

"That's not a winning argument," Darnell said. "People wrap themselves in the flag all the time to justify their actions. It doesn't mean they're right."

"I'm all about following orders, sir!" Pig said. "Do you have any idea why I joined the service?"

"How is this helpful?"

"It's helpful because you need to know about the man you're speaking to," he said. "I'm fifth generation US Army. There have been twenty-three service members in my family. I would never do anything to harm the reputation of the army, much less the country I serve. And I never believed I was. I was duped by a hostile alien force. I know my life is forfeit. Let me do one last thing to try to set things right."

"You have a lot of never," Darnell said. "Go screw yourself."

"Darnell," AJ said softly.

"You can't be serious," Darnell said, looking at AJ like he'd grown a second head.

"We need you to fly *Seahag* on Fimil Prime," AJ said. "We're going up against an entire division of Togath. There are only fifteen operators. We need every advantage."

"If you don't make it to the surface, where's the advantage in that?"

"I believe him," AJ said. "There was a time when Beverly decided to try to push me around. She didn't even go with the telling-me-lies things. If our symbiotes decide to act against us, we have few defenses."

"And you're willing to risk everyone ... Lisa, me, everyone on this feeling?" Darnell asked.

"No, what I'm saying is that if you're not flying *Seahag*, our odds of survival on the surface go down substantially," AJ said. "Add to that my belief that Pig was duped and needs a way to make things right, I think this is the best way forward."

"I hate it."

"Not like I love it. I just want to give us the best chance of surviving," AJ said. "Winning is off the table, but there are soldiers on the ground for whom we're their best hope of survival. I know what that hope felt like and I know what it felt like when Lefty and his boys showed up and rescued me. This whole thing is FUBAR. It's our turn to make a difference. Are you with me?"

"I hate it when you do that."

"Do what?"

"Make sense."

29

TROUBLE FROM THE SKY
DEKE – PLANET FIMIL PRIME

"That's our last drone," Lieutenant Bing reported miserably as the command team watched the figures beyond direct line of sight of *Angry Ark's* video capture freeze at their last observed positions.

"We need to look at relocating that manufactory again," Deke said. "If we're going to survive, we need to do better than turtling up and hoping someone will come for us. I don't think Army Intel even knows we've got trouble since our outgoing comms are blocked."

"There is a possibility for a single message," Keegs said, appearing on the table.

"We're nearly forty days into being poked and prodded like a goat at a petting zoo and just now you have an idea on how we can get a comm out?" Deke asked. She was too tired of it all to only manage mild annoyance.

"That is not a productive question," Keegs said. "I am not sure my method will work although I am certain it will work only once."

"Do I want to know how?" Deke asked.

"I can explain. The Fimil Prime stratosphere has interesting properties given the low saturation of..."

"Stop," Deke said. "You're saying we need to compose a message and that it's not certain it will transmit but there's a better than nil chance it will. Is there a limit to the length of this message?"

Loud banging on the door to the conference room interrupted the conversation.

"I've got it." Bing stood and manually opened the hatch which had been reconfigured to be accessible in the upside-down environment. "Sergeant?" he asked, looking at a disheveled soldier, clearly upset by the news she held.

"They're coming. Dozens. Maybe hundreds," she said, breathlessly.

Just then the low-pitched, rapid thup, thup, thup of turret fire stilled the conversation. "Roger that, Sergeant. Go back to your post. It's go-time. We knew it was coming and now it's here. Let's make sure we show these bastards how much they don't want to mess with the US Army."

The sergeant straightened and tipped her head back defiantly. "Damn right, Lieutenant. Hooah!"

"Hooah!"

"Keegs what can we see?" Deke asked.

"The Togath have reinforcements," Keegs said. "We should decide what message we would like to attempt to send. This might become more difficult."

"Propose appropriate language and I will review it, Keegs." Deke stared at the projection on the table in front of her, unable to see what had the sergeant was concerned. "The turret has stopped firing. What's going on?"

"There is an orbital dropship," Keegs said. "One of the loads floated through the targeting range of *Angry Ark's* turrets. The load was destroyed but landed outside our visual range. You can see the debris field on the hill."

"That tracks," Deke said. "First, they drop their gear because they know we can't attack without exposing ourselves. After that, they'll drop troops. How did Sergeant Collins get to dozens, maybe hundreds?"

"I'm not sure," Bing said.

"Sergeant Collins is not incorrect," Keegs said. "She was, however, premature. We are tracking two-hundred thirty individual payloads that have been dropped. I estimate three hundred tons of material has been delivered. We don't know how Togath travel, but this is a significant escalation."

"*Angry Ark* won't hold together forever," Deke said.

"It might," Keegs said. "If they know there are no reinforcements coming, there is no advantage for them to expend resources to attack *Angry Ark*."

"They'll starve us out," Deke filled in.

"That's right," Keegs said.

"I won't go down without swinging," Deke said. "That's just not going to be how this works."

"We need to send the message," Keegs said.

"You keep going back to that," Deke said. "I haven't pushed you on why, but I think you know something you're not sharing. Now would be a good time to come clean, Keegs."

"I do have something going on," Keegs said. "but I just don't know if it will turn out. Can we leave it at that? I do not wish to spread false hope."

Deke bit the inside of her cheek. No soldier under her command could ask her the same question and expect to come out unscathed. Holding back information from command was a cardinal sin. Keegs knew it.

"How much of a long shot are we talking?" she asked.

"I am trusting a cryptic message from someone I have not spoken to for over two-hundred years," he said. "I have a proposed message ready for US Army Intelligence."

Deke scanned the communication Keegs proposed to send. The message was short and described their current predicament in few words, causing her to wonder if message length was important. "The message is fine," she said. "We're going to prepare to make a last stand and/or a final assault. We're going down with a fight. That's the only way."

"Hooah," Carrole said, prompting Bing to respond in kind.

30

OUTNUMBERED

AJ – FIMIL PRIME ORBIT

AJ HELD FAST to the side of *Seahag* as *Wasp* shook so violently that its hold soon became littered with flying debris as the ship tore itself apart.

"Ninety-thousand feet." Pig's voice was calm, though shaking as he spoke. "We've lost thrust control on one. Thirty seconds to go-time."

AJ attempted to focus on his HUD, but the shaking was so extreme that even with Beverly's adjustments, he couldn't make sense of it. Idly, he wondered how the engineers and regular crew were making out aboard the two dropships. They'd signed up for service aboard USS *Wasp* and while they knew the mission was dangerous, had no idea they'd have front-row seats.

"Peter," AJ said. "You've lived up to your end."

"That's kind of you to say," Pig answered. "I know what I did."

"And today you're making it right," AJ said. "If I live through this, I'll talk to your family. I'll make it right with them."

"You don't ...," Even through the madness, AJ heard the emotion clogging Pig's throat. "Shit! All engines are offline. We're going to tumble. Go, go, go!"

"Godspeed, Peter Ignatius Roberts," AJ said. He dug his feet into the deck and pushed forward as he and the other mechanized infantry in his squad manually slid *Seahag* out the aft hatch.

"Holy crap!" Bald Norm said excitedly. *Seahag* reacted to the freefall by pointing straight down due to *Wasp's* accelerating tumble. "I lost grip!"

"I have you, *mon ami*," Frenchy said, calmly grabbing Bald Norm's armored wrist before the man entered his own freefall trajectory.

"Holy moly, Frenchy, you just saved my life," Bald Norm said.

"Tell me you're wearing your adult diaper," Birdie quipped. "Nobody wants to be cleaning all that up."

"That's enough, boys," Lefty chimed in before anyone could retort. "Focus on the task."

When AJ's feet cleared *Wasp*, he found himself, *Seahag*, and seven of buddies dealing with the fact that they were upside down and still slowly rotating high over Fimil Prime.

"Squad One, I need a ready-check on travel position," Darnell said calmly. "I'd appreciate you getting to that right away, so I don't turn you all into pink goo when we make it downstairs."

The environment shifted from violent shaking to being buffeted by the constant wind of the atmosphere rushing past his suit. "I'm struggling, BB," AJ warned. "I can't see my handholds."

"Close your eyes," Beverly said.

He complied and was presented with what looked like the rungs of a ladder floating over a gray background. When he reached forward, it was his unarmored hand that appeared in his vision and once again, with a simplified problem, he had no difficulty executing.

"I'm a go," he said when he was finally seated in *Seahag's* drop harness. Moments later Birdie chimed in with acknowledgement.

"Way to add drama, boys," Darnell said over comms while igniting *Seahags* powerful engines. "One, are you getting any sort of read on the battlefield yet? We're going to need instructions on exactly what we're doing."

"AJ, *Wasp* is making final entry forty degrees starboard," Beverly said somberly.

Following her directions, AJ saw the large flash of a massive explosion. "What happened? Was he attacked?"

"No," Beverly said. "That appears to be some sort of overload condition."

"He's trying to attract attention away from us."

"The Quarr are capable of tracking much smaller objects than a mechanized infantry suit," Beverly said. "I understand a desire to take matters into one's own hands."

The pull on AJ's harness continued to increase until finally, his suit was oriented with the planet's gravity.

"Lisa, I need sensors pointed at the area around *Angry Ark*," AJ said. "We need to know if they survived that orbital bombardment."

"I'm working on it," Lisa answered. "We're seven hundred kilometers from ground-zero. I'm sending data your way."

"Good copy," AJ said as Beverly prepared the data for his consumption.

"Lefty, are you seeing this?" AJ asked.

"I am."

"Eight hundred, that's an entire division," AJ said. "This is gonna be a long ass day."

"AJ, we're tough, but eight hundred Togath is more than two squads can deal with," Lefty said. "I didn't want to believe they'd pile them all up in one place. We need to admit we're out-matched. This is suicide."

"As opposed to riding a derelict ship down," AJ said. "Bubba, this is far from a suicide mission. We're going to insert on that northwest corner and make our way to the Togath base next to *Angry Ark*. This is asymmetric warfare at its finest. We're small, fast, and deadly. They're big and unwieldy. Do you copy?"

"Northwest, you say?" Lefty asked. "Oh, you're going to follow that ridgeline down, then? It should give us some break from the main force."

"That's right," AJ said. "We keep the dropships back and low so they don't get picked off by anti-aircraft."

"And you think when we get to that base, we can take it over?"

"No idea," AJ said. "But that's my best plan so far. BB, any luck raising the crew on *Angry Ark*? A little support from a stationary position would go a long way, here."

"Nothing yet," Beverly answered. "Togath are actively blocking all comm attempts. Once we're within stable line-of-sight, they might pick up a tight-beam comm."

"What happens if there's nobody home?" Lefty asked. "What's our bug-out plan?"

"We focus on that base," AJ said. "There's no bugging out. Only surviving. You know that."

"I was hoping I didn't know that," Lefty said. "Let's do this."

"Hooah!"

"We have birds in the air," Darnell called. "I'm taking us to four hundred feet. Could you boys do something more than chat and see if someone gets a prize for knocking down one of those birds?"

While shooting at missiles tied into the belly of a dropship was a low percentage operation, it gave the squad an enemy to focus on. Instead, the real hope came from *Seahag* and *Bernard's* gunners, both of whom had extensive combat experience.

"Who hoo!" Lisa cried out over tactical comms. "One down!"

Having flown several missions as gunner aboard *Seahag,* she had by far the most experience of any of the crew, even though her only training had been to be thrown into the deep end of the swimming pool with a suggestion that survival probably involved swimming.

"My God," Birdie said, awe filling his voice as the team got their first view of the horde of Togath warriors amassed below. As if in direct response, hundreds of bolts of energy streamed at the pair of dropships.

"Hold on, kids," Darnell said, accelerating while banking away from his predictable flight path.

While not pleasant and predictably eliciting complaints from the attached soldiers, *Seahag and Bernard's* harnesses did exactly as they were designed to do, which was to keep them securely in place.

"Tell me again why we don't have barf bags?" Bald Norm asked shakily.

"Not again. I thought your old lady had you fixed up on this," Chach added. "You know better than to eat eggs before a fight."

"Eeeww, eggs?" Frenchy asked. "Again?"

While somewhat irritated by the unprofessional conversation, AJ knew better than to interrupt as the men blew off steam in preparation for the fight ahead. Some soldiers preferred to be deadly quiet as they prepared for battle. Others wanted to talk like it was any other day, seemingly oblivious to the battle in front of them. He'd long ago learned that if at all possible, he should just stay out of it. His team would get to business when it was time and not a second before.

"They have a big gun up there. Are you tracking that, AJ?" Darnell called.

AJ had just seen a pulsating red glow on the horizon. The glow was a cooperation between AJ's infantry suit, *Seahag's* combat computer, and the Beltigersk symbiotes in each team member, to provide real-time information on the battle.

"I've got it," AJ said. "You're going to have to drop us early. Boys, we're going hot in twenty seconds. There's going to be a big group on the other side of this ridge."

While they didn't have direct eyes on the ground, AJ was referring to an aerial survey they'd gathered on the way down that showed a concentration of enemy where they were about to come out. The heavy gun high on the ridge reinforced the intel.

"Give me something to shoot," Bald Norm said.

"Clean it up, boys," AJ said. "We'll go in by twos. Keep your partner close. Togath aren't your average soldiers. Check your kills. Big D, after we're dropped, take that gun out. We don't need that thing picking us apart once we make some room down there."

"Good copy," Darnell said. "Thirty seconds to an inclined ramp drop. Mark."

The ramp drop was a technique they'd perfected the last time they'd fought on Fimil Prime. It wasn't sophisticated, but had the advantage of keeping cover for the squad up until the last moment. By flying low up the side of a hill and pulling the stick back so the dropship went vertical when reaching the hill's summit, the squad maintained the forward momentum of the approach and would appear in the middle of whatever lay on the other side of the hill.

AJ's stomach lurched as weightlessness grabbed him when he was released from *Seahag's* harness. Shouts of exultation were held in check as fifteen mechanized soldiers became airborne and used well-honed skills to pick out landing spots, even as they opened fire.

Gritting his teeth, AJ forced himself to leave behind strategy and long-range thinking. For an infantry soldier, war is a personal, in-your-face type of event. There was no thinking beyond the next target or an enemy that's taken a personal interest. AJ found his first target and thumbed a different loadout into position just before opening fire.

"These old boys can take a punch," Bald Norm said. "Almost better to cut 'em down with the multi-tool when they're all up close and personal."

"Give me some biology lessons, teach," Chach added.

"Yeah, what you got?" Birdie added.

"Back of knees, under the pecs," Bald Norm said. "Looks like armor in layers, so don't go stabby. Think sliding it up and in."

"Stop," Chach said. "You'll make me blush."

"You're such a pervert, Chach," Birdie shot back.

"I can't help it," Chach added. "Armpit works too."

"I see what you're saying about checking kills," Frenchie said. "I just had one stand back up. Boy, was he pissed. Not sure what that was all about."

"You *were* trying to kill him," Chach said. "Most folk get a touch irritated about that."

AJ shook his head as his squads worked along the hillside. After only a few minutes of battle, the counter on his HUD showed over forty Togath kills.

"Bubba, you've attracted attention," Darnell said over comms. "We're about to drop this gun, but you might want to clear that valley or get hunkered down. I'm getting an itchy feeling."

"Team One, Team Two. Ground hog, ground hog, ground hog," AJ ordered.

With hand-to-hand combat having slowed due to lack of available combatants, the pairs had naturally spread out. With AJ's order, each pair changed their approach, with one soldier taking a defensive position and the other switching from an active weapon to their multiuse tool in shovel form.

For almost five minutes, excavation of the ground occurred at a startling rate even as one team member of each pair held off a surging enemy.

"Incoming!" Darnell called over comms, but the announcement was unnecessary. Without any obvious signal, the Togath withdrew at high speed.

"To ground!" AJ ordered.

In the short time they'd had, the pairs had dug in so deeply that both were able to jump into the foxholes.

Moments later, a massive explosion sent a shockwave through the valley. Following the shockwave came flames and debris moving at just below the speed of sound.

"Squads, check in," AJ called a full thirty seconds after the initial blast.

"We've got a cave-in," Frenchy said. "But we're digging out."

"What the hell was that?" Bald Norm asked. "They glassed off the side of that hill."

"Holy shit, that was hot," Birdie added as he pulled himself out of the hole.

"We took down that bomber," Darnell said. "They dropped some big old payloads and took out a whole bunch of their own. Glad you boys are all up. Looks like you have a good run south."

AJ reviewed the current updates to the battle on his HUD. The devastation caused by the bombs was widespread. He saw corpses of Togath unable to clear the blast radius along the edges. "I guess that answers the value they place on their troops," he said.

"Or the value they place on our heads," Lefty added.

"We move south to that fortress next to *Angry Ark*," AJ said. "The Togath army is likely to fold in behind in our wake, so we need to move with speed, but make sure we're clearing as we go."

"Bet they thought they burned us down. We need to lay down some hurt!" Chach growled with fervor.

"Let's roll!" Lefty added. "We're Oscar Mike. Keep your lines straight. I don't want anyone getting too far forward or too far behind. You all know the drill."

"Conserve ammo," AJ added. "And use multitool when close in. We've got a lot of baddies to roll through."

"How far are we from that bunker or fort ... whatever it was," Birdie asked. As the information was available to his Beltigersk symbiote, it was immediately reported. "So, I'm thinking, what if we blitzkrieg it? It's like TL said. They're just going to fold in behind us. Might be nice to have a wall at our back."

"You're not wrong, Birdie," AJ said. "What we need is to get over the rise I'm highlighting on your map. Once we make that rise, we'll have line of sight on *Angry Ark*. I'm going to want us to make a solid effort at raising our troops. They might be saving a Hail Mary pass for just this sort of event."

"You want that hill, One, we'll get you that hill," Birdie called out, doubling down on his efforts as if he alone would end a battle where they were still outnumbered nearly fifty to one. "Come on, boys. Time to get our slog on!"

The team increased the pace of battle as they pushed forward with a clear objective. Knowing the team couldn't possibly continue at the rate they were operating for the long run, AJ considered calling them to slow. As outnumbered indicated they should conserve energy to stay in the battle. But contacting the besieged craft still on its back was too tantalizing to call them off.

The team cut a brutal, bloody swath through an enemy that constantly adapted to their strategies but couldn't overcome a flaw they seemed unable to grasp. The Togath were not the most fearsome warriors on the field, not even by half. The juxtaposition must have been too great for them to fathom because they continued to throw themselves at the mechanized warriors with increased fury and frenzy.

By the time Birdie led them to the top of the rise that would give them line-of-sight to *Angry Ark*, the numbers of Togath had dwindled substantially, if only because it took time for reinforcements to fall into place.

"Hold this hill, boys," AJ said. He raised his arm and switched his equipment package to point-to-point communications. "*Angry Ark*, this is Captain Albert Jenkins, over."

He swung his multitool which was in a long-bladed configuration as a Togath reached his position and attempted to engage with its own knife. Although the Togath were faster with natural armor, they were weaker by almost an order of magnitude. Adding to that, the mechanized armor was made of a material the Tok refused to share with any other species due to its unmatched hardness and resilience. As a result, the strike on AJ's breastplate, which would have killed any other sentient species left not a single scratch to mark its passing.

"Bad choice, pal," AJ said, backhanding the Togath. It was dead before it hit the ground.

"Captain Jenkins, this is *Angry Ark* actual, please transmit security handshake."

AJ recognized the woman's voice as the one he'd heard before on the intercepted plea for help. "What was her name, BB?"

"Captain DeKoster," Beverly said. "On a subchannel, I got a message from a symbiote she's calling Keegs. I know him. He's on the right side. Would you like me to transmit the security handshake?"

"Yup," AJ agreed subvocally and then responded on the tight beam. "So, we were just in the neighborhood and wondered where a handful of infantry grunts could get a decent burger, maybe a beer or two."

"Oh shit, you have no idea how good it is to hear your voice, Captain Jenkins. How many did you bring? We're not picking up much of a force where this signal is originating," she said.

"Call me AJ. We're fifteen plus a couple of dropships," AJ said. "We're mechanized infantry that you'll have to forget about later."

"Fifteen? There are a thousand Togath out there," she said. "I'm sorry, Captain, but you're about to be overrun."

"That's possible," AJ said. "Talk to me about that fort next to your ship. Is that a place we could set up shop?"

"You'll never make it, Captain Jenkins," she said. "I don't know how you're alive even now. I'm sorry. Shit, I thought we had a chance."

"Need the intel, Captain DeKoster."

"Call me Deke. This whole captain thing wasn't my idea."

"Same. Call me AJ, and I'm serious. How loaded is that fort?"

"We've kept it mostly clear. We're running low on just about everything aside from energy for our weapons and armor," she said. "Was it you who got that bombardment to end? That was messed up."

"We might have had something to do with that. We're clear to grab that fort, then?"

"I tell you what, you get within a click and I'll roll out a welcoming committee," she said.

"Step that back, Deke," AJ said. "It's gonna get ugly between now and then. We don't need any of you fine folk getting caught in the middle. We've already taken an incendiary that glassed the sand down to five inches for half a mile."

"That's one of their go-to moves," Deke said. "Melted a couple of antennae, *Angry Ark* wasn't overly impressed. She's a tough old gal."

"Okay boys, move out, we've got word that fort is just waiting for us," AJ said. "Two, take the lead."

"Copy that," Lefty said.

31

LAST MAN STANDING

"How many more could they possibly have?" Birdie asked, leaning against the wall of the Quarr base. The Togath had managed to retake the base and fighting had been particularly intense.

"We're putting that number at around four-hundred twenty-three," AJ said, reporting the number Beverly presented.

"What dumb-fuckery takes sixty percent casualties and keeps coming? It makes no sense," Birdie said.

"Really? Because we have two suits damaged to the point of not working and we're running at eight percent ammo reserves," AJ said. "You have to know what's coming next, Birdie."

"They have reinforcements," Birdie said with a sigh, giving words to the fear every team member had.

"Deke, talk to me," AJ said as he leaned against the wall, looking out over the battlefield. For whatever reason the Togath had pulled back. Throughout the day, they'd seen similar pullbacks. The established pattern suggested they'd be back between fifteen minutes to an hour.

"I never believed you'd make that fort," she said. "You want to make entry to *Angry Ark*? She can take quite a punch."

"Not yet, we need to keep our mobility," AJ said. "We figure the Quarr have reinforcements coming. It's the only logical explanation as to why they're throwing themselves at us in such numbers. They don't care about the troops as much as they want to figure out what it takes to put us down."

"What army doesn't care about its soldiers, right?"

"It's that whole grown in vats thing," AJ said. "They're nothing more than a journal entry in an accountant's ledger."

"I think those are two different things," Deke said. "But I get your point."

"I have crew that I need to move over to your care, though. We lost the ship we came in," AJ said.

"What kind of crew?"

"Engineers, medical, that sort of thing," AJ said.

"You have engineers? Are they any good?"

"They sure think so."

"That sounds like every engineer, ever," Deke agreed. "We can take them off your hands. If we could get rolled over, we might be able to get in this fight."

"We're strong, but not that strong," AJ said. "There's no way fifteen of us can lift a ship the size of *Angry Ark*."

"Keegs, send his Belti our problem," she said.

"AJ, they can't roll the ship because of a rock shelf," Beverly reported.

"If that shelf is gone, you could get off your back?"

"It's not quite as simple as that. We've been moving equipment around. Lots of it is on the ceiling now."

"If you fixed it once you could do it again," AJ said. "Right?"

"And then what? If they bring another thousand or hell, four thousand, we can't possibly stand up to all that," she said.

"One thing at a time," AJ said. "Beverly, figure out how much of that shelf we need to take down. Deke, how about we work on getting you on your belly?"

"Sounds like every bad date I've ever been on," Deke said.

AJ barked out a laugh. "Well put. Give us ten minutes and we'll put one of our dropships wherever you tell us so we can offload crew."

"Topside above the port turret is reasonably clear. They've brought in sharpshooters, but if we go dark at night and put up a screen, we move in and out without too much trouble."

"We'll get to work and wait for word that you're ready for a transfer."

"Good copy."

～

"FIRE IN THE HOLE!"

Three waves of fifty Togath suggested the Quarr understood that breaking off the rock shelf would dramatically turn the battle to the human's advantage. To make matters worse for the Togath, *Angry Ark's* turrets were in play due to the ship's proximity. Even so, night had passed with dawn just starting to break when the explosives were set and ready.

"Blow it!" AJ said unceremoniously.

Puffs of sand spit high in the air at twenty newly-drilled locations. At first it seemed the efforts were for naught, but then the hillside shook as a huge chunk of rock broke loose and slid to the bottom of the hill, not far from where *Angry Ark* lay upside down.

"That's a beautiful thing," Deke called over comms. "Can I count on your team for EVA support?"

"If by EVA you mean stand out here in the sand and shoot at Togath, then sure."

"I like your attitude," Deke said. "You might not be quite the asshole I first thought you were."

"Aww, you're gonna make me blush already."

"I have a team coming to hatch. We need to keep 'em alive. My only combat engineer will be exposed," she said.

"HVT, got it. We'll keep the squishies up. How long will they be outside?" AJ asked.

"Forty-five minutes, give or take. We'll have to pull the turrets in. We can do that in phases if it would be helpful," she answered. "How can we support your team?"

"We estimate two hundred seventy-five Togath remaining," AJ said. "We're low on just about every supply and I have two units running at twenty percent efficiency due to mechanical issues."

"The Quarr are still blocking communications."

"We see that," AJ said. "My team is running pretty low on sleep, too."

"If we get this old girl upright, it'll take an hour to open the back hatch and you can pull everyone inside," she said. "We don't have a ton of extra supplies, but we'll share what we have. How'd you get out here without supplies? Also, my EVA team is at the door."

AJ stood atop the nearby hill and looked out over the barren landscape. "We're in position, send them out."

He couldn't help but wonder why the Togath would throw themselves at a superior force with such abandon. His interaction with Togath made him think they were reasonable, thinking beings. He'd seen fear, concern, anger, and even compassion for a wounded teammate. They were not without a depth of feelings.

Perhaps it was his own experience of being in a war where men from thousands of miles away sent boys to die on missions that often seemed pointless. Or possibly it was just the calloused waste. What was crystal clear, though, was that the Togath had little say in the matter. That bothered AJ a great deal.

"Bubba, there's movement twenty clicks out," Darnell called over comms.

"Good copy," AJ said, wishing for another few moments of quiet while Fimil Prime's sun broke the horizon.

"Looks like they're bringing the kitchen sink."

"That makes sense," AJ said. "Deke, you need to get your EVA team inside. They're bringing a last run our way."

"We need twelve minutes," Deke answered. "Give me that and we'll have twice the range on our turrets and four times the ground coverage."

"We can't hold back what's coming," AJ said. "We can advance and try to move the battle space, but if they get around us, there's not much we can do."

"Eleven minutes and we're coming out."

"That's a terrible idea," AJ said. "You don't have armor."

"I wasn't asking."

"Don't do this. We need time to deal with this wave."

"Your team is running on fumes, you said it yourself," she said. "My soldiers have been cooped up for almost two months, going mad. We need to be part of this."

"Your soldiers are going to die."

"And what happens when you run out of ammo? Or those two units that are at twenty percent fully fail? We've been fighting these assholes for a long time; we'll use their base as cover. That'll draw the fight away from *Angry Ark*."

"How do you know they'll come for you?"

"It's in their programming. Every last one of us is bait to them. It's like they're programmed to seek us out."

"I've seen that," AJ said. "BB, how big of a force?"

"Optic sensors aren't well-focused. We estimate one hundred, give or take twenty," she said.

"I'm proud of you being okay with a generalization. Could you hit me with a bit more adrenaline? I'm about to nod off here."

"It will not have the desired effect. Your adrenoceptors have reached their limits," she said. "You are pushing your body hard. It has limits."

"I need two hours, BB," AJ said.

"There will be a price in downtime later," Beverly said. "I will do everything possible to keep you alert."

"Jenkins? Are you still there? You're not answering," Deke called over comms.

"Sorry, I guess I was ... I'm not sure ... What's the question?"

"Not a question," Deke said. "I'm putting three heavy squads into the fort. We'll do our best to stay out of your way. I'd like to link you into our combat data channel."

"We'll play it your way."

"One, we have four fast-moving vehicles sixty seconds out," Birdie reported on comms. "I estimate sixteen hostiles attempting a shake-n-bake."

"Good copy," AJ said. "Lefty, what in the heck are they doing? Flanking us won't help."

"They're intercepting comms," Lefty said with certainty. "They want to grab Deke's soldiers. They're fighting like they have infinite resources and are trying to rub us out, no matter the cost to their army."

"They're going to pay dearly," AJ said. "Squad Two, split up and stop those vehicles. I want zero casualties for Zebra Company, but play it smart."

"Good copy, One," Lefty answered.

AJ watched as seven mechanized infantry units loped off across the dry ground kicking up dusty rooster tails.

"Squad One, we'll make our stand in the gap between *Angry Ark* and the fort. Anything gets beyond us will get heavy fire. We have to hold that line against the main force," AJ said.

"Let's do this!" Bald Norm said with more enthusiasm than AJ felt he could personally manage.

AJ's squad had barely found their position when the sounds of combat renewed again. At first, there was nothing as Squad Two intercepted the racing vehicles and dealt with the inhabitants.

"Captain Jenkins, we're ready to try to flip *Angry Ark*," Deke called over comms. "You should clear the area between the ship and the hill where we knocked off the ledge. *Angry Ark* will slide that way once we drive those pylons down.

"We'll be on the lookout," AJ said. While he didn't want any of his men trapped beneath an eighty thousand ton flying fortress, he felt they were all capable of keeping clear of danger, especially with Beltigersk symbiotes providing them real-time information.

The first wave of Togath warriors crashed onto the scene and the team was again lost in an insane ballet of man-driven machine fighting genetically engineered flesh and blood.

"I have full system failure," Birdie announced. "I'm totally locked up."

"Squad, move to Three's position immediately," AJ ordered, locating his friend on the map.

The tenor of the pitched battle changed as six titans, fighting against a sea of aliens, turned to their fallen comrade.

"Big D, we need air support, now!" AJ called as he recognized a shift in the Togath's strategy. No longer were they fighting to destroy the mechanized infantry, but were working to draw them away from Birdie's position.

"Shit, they've got me," Birdie complained, his voice annoyed more than upset. "They're trying to drag me south ... and now they're carrying me. What in the hell?"

AJ surveyed the battle scene. There were still more than eighty Togath, which meant they'd been reinforced as the battle progressed. While the local Togath focused on taking Birdie, as a whole, they were even more focused on breaching the abandoned base where Deke's soldiers were fighting.

"Squad One, move back and hold our line. If we abandon our base these Togath will overrun it. We'll lose the people we came to rescue," AJ said.

"Those regular army should've stayed home," Bald Norm growled angrily.

"Knock that crap off," AJ barked immediately. "We're on the same team and I'm the one who was happy to take the help."

"But they've got Birdie."

"Grousing about water under the bridge isn't helping," AJ said. "Big D, can you find Birdie?"

"We've lost his signal," Darnell said. "They must have put something over his suit to mask the RF."

"Dammit! Keep looking!"

"We're tearing it up," Darnell said. "We'll have to be careful to approach their base. They have anti-aircraft that will knock us out of the air."

"Only way to Birdie is through," AJ said.

"Fine, let's get medieval on their asses," Bald Norm said. "I'm ready to party. They harm one hair on his head and I'll burn down the fucking world."

"They're pulling back!" Chach called over comms. "Don't let up."

The shift was almost immediate and suddenly the Togath were no longer surging toward the base, but away. It was a horrible position for the warriors on the front line as they were cut down by enraged mechanized infantrymen. But Togath numbers were so great that even with the mass casualties, it was impossible for the group to fully destroy the entire invasion.

For nearly an hour, the two squads raced after the retreating army, chewing up the slow and wounded, only to find more ahead. When the chamber on AJ's weapon finally dry-fired from lack of any material for ammunition manufacture, he made a hard decision.

"Squad One, Squad Two, I'm calling a halt to our pursuit," he announced over comms.

"You can't be serious," Bald Norm immediately objected.

"Bald Norm, you haven't had ammo for the last twenty minutes and your right ankle and left shoulder are frozen," AJ said. "I'm telling you, we're done for the minute. Birdie's as much my friend as he is yours, and he wouldn't want me risking the entire squad."

"He could still be alive," Bald Norm said, pressing his luck.

"I'm counting on it," AJ said. "But for now, we're pulling back. Stand down, Bald Norm."

"Dammit," Bald Norm said, but his forward progress stopped.

"Take us back to *Angry Ark,* Two," AJ said.

32

FORCING VICTORY

"Form up on me, platoon," Lefty said, taking over tactical command. "Run diagnostics and figure out what's wrong with your suits on the way back. Once you have that, get into that inventory list Rebel downloaded from *Angry Ark* and figure out how you're going to fix your rig. There aren't any mechanics, so it's up to you all. I'm not putting broken gear back in the field. If you want to be on the team that goes after Birdie, you'll get your rig right."

While they'd been chasing the fleeing enemy, Deke's engineering team had set *Angry Ark* upright.

"*Angry Ark*, don't shoot, we're coming back," AJ called over comms.

"We're tracking you," Deke was quick to answer. "Did you find your teammate?"

"Negative."

"I'm sorry, AJ."

"Same," he responded. "What's it look like back there?"

"Hard to feel too good about things," Deke said. "You're looking at a mission team with seventy-five percent casualties."

"Should have been one hundred, Deke," AJ said. "You know that. How you all survived will be taught at every war college on Earth for the next two hundred years."

"Why'd they leave once they got your man?" Deke asked, changing the subject.

"I can only come up with one reason," AJ said.

"Me too," Deke said. "And I don't like it."

"Nope."

"What's your plan, now that we're upright?"

"The plan was a rescue," AJ said. "Only we don't have a ship to take you home."

"You were an evac mission? I was told this was a one-way ticket," Deke said.

"I guess things weren't overly specific," AJ said. "We might be using equipment not exactly sanctioned by the Galactic Empire. Tok were pretty specific about us not showing off our mechanized armor."

"I get it," Deke said. "Never seen something that can take quite that much damage."

"Above my paygrade, too," AJ said. "We could really use some rack space and access to whatever tools you have. Our rigs are in tough shape."

"Mi casa, Captain," Deke said. "Things are jumbled about since we flipped over again, but we'll have that back hatch operational in forty minutes, give or take. We'll make space for everything, including your dropships."

"How are comms?"

"Still blocked."

"We'll work on that after some downtime," AJ said. "We're getting into dangerous territory on the sleep front."

"I don't want to abandon our mission," Deke said. "Maybe some crew want to go home, and I'll honor their wishes, but we've lost too much blood here. I'm not going to let that be for nothing."

"I hear you, sister," AJ said. "I fought that war, and it was hard to get on that plane home."

"You're really him, huh?" Deke asked.

AJ considered playing it coy but was too tired for pretense. "You're thinking Korgul invasion? Yeah, that's us."

"Tell your boys I've got our chef working on a big meal as way of saying thanks. Just make sure no one asks what kind of meat we're having in the spaghetti," Deke said.

AJ blinked several times as her words filtered into his sleep-deprived brain. "You wouldn't."

"I wish I could have seen your face," she said. "No, we have plenty of food stores. We were supplied for two hundred and we're counting forty-five ... low seventies with your crew."

"We're outside now," AJ said. "Let me know when you can open up."

"Why don't you come up for a confab," Deke said. "I have an idea about your man."

"You have my interest," AJ said. "Lefty, I'm going to need someone to look after my rig. I'm taking a meeting with the local commander."

"We've got it, One," Lefty answered.

Wearily, AJ climbed out of his mechanized infantry suit and shielded his face from the sudden downdraft caused by *Seahag's* arrival. He walked to the ramp that extended from the dropship's man-sized hatch on the port side and waited for his exhausted friends, Darnell and Lisa, to disembark.

"You look like crap, brother," Darnell said, embracing his old friend.

"You smell like a latrine," AJ replied, returning the embrace. "Crap, but I'm tired."

"I think that goes for all," Darnell said. "Why doesn't it feel like a win to get this old girl upright?"

"We lost Birdie," AJ said. "You know that. There aren't any winners in war. Especially not among the enlisted." Darnell nodded his head in agreement. "That was gnarly combat, Lisa. How are you coping?"

"Careful, AJ, your crusty exterior is slipping," Lisa said, hugging him. "It almost sounds like you care."

"I do, Lisa."

"You are tired."

"I am. Do you want to meet this new commander, Deke?" AJ asked.

"She's the one everyone's in such an uproar about?"

"I suppose so."

"Hey, Old Guy, you need to look at this," Deke said, stepping out from *Angry Ark* with a provocative look on her face.

"You must be DeKoster."

"And you're Jenkins. Are we done with the small talk? Because we've got something cooking that needs your attention."

"You have it."

"Maybe get your pilot back in his bird. We need to take a drive." Deke gestured over her shoulder with a wave. From a side-hatch, a six-wheeled truck with an open canopied cargo bed rolled out.

"A drive? This isn't exactly the safest territory," AJ said.

"We're operating under a white flag," Deke said.

"Seriously?"

"Got a call from the Quarr commander on the other side of this mess," she said. "He's wants a confab. Has a trade for us."

"Color me interested," AJ said, clambering into the back of the truck after Deke.

"What's the play here, AJ," Darnell asked.

"If you're amenable, I'd like your birds to follow us at half-a-mile offset. I've agreed to cease hostilities, but we have no idea if Quarr keep their word or not," Deke said. "It could be a trap."

"What's the upside?"

"They want to trade for prisoners," she said. "We didn't know they had any. Your man is among them."

"That fast," AJ said. "What's their play? Did they say what they wanted to bargain for?"

"Negative."

"Can't exactly ignore it," AJ said. "Let's go."

"I figured that'd be your play," Deke said. "Just so you know, I'll take down the lot of 'em if things go south. Just keep your head down, since you won't be wearing your fancy suit."

"That's big talk," AJ said. "These Togath are tough."

Deke pulled the long bladed Togath knife from between her shoulder blades and placed it on the seat between them. "I took that from a pair of Togath," she said. "They weren't happy with the exchange."

"Bare-handed?"

"Are you kidding? I used an M52, my Desert Eagle, and a grenade," she said. "The third one I put down with this knife, though."

"You'll have to give me the whole story at some point," AJ said as the truck rolled across the barren landscape.

In addition to the pair of dropships close behind, AJ's entire platoon followed, allowing only enough space to appease the conditions of the momentary truce. That violence would be met with even more violence was a message well-delivered.

"You may stop." The mechanical voice grated on AJ's nerves.

"There was an attempt at neural interface," Beverly said.

"What's that mean?" AJ asked sub vocally.

"They were trying to hack your brain, AJ," she answered.

"And you stopped it?"

"Yes, it was not a sophisticated attempt given the medium of radio waves," she said. "It was provocative, at least."

"Tell them to knock off the crap, or we're going to mix it up right here and right now," he said, furious.

"Apologies," came the single word reply. "Negotiation."

"What are you offering?" Deke asked, beating AJ to the punch. For a moment, he was irritated that she was taking first chair, but she'd been on the rock a whole lot longer and probably had more invested, even though he badly wanted Birdie back.

"Twelve human lives. No pursuit," the voice added. "Vacate for twenty rotations around star."

"Something feels off," Deke said. "I'm going for a walk. Join me?"

"I've done stupider things," AJ said. He jumped out of the back of the truck and followed the narrow woman across the sandy landscape to where a small collection of roughly humanoid forms stood.

"Where are our people?" Deke asked, closing until she was within ten feet.

"Careful, Deke," AJ warned. "Quarr have unusual capabilities. They modify their bodies and can move fast."

"You are not wise, human."

It was as if AJ's words came to life as the humanoid's arms untangled and became a roiling mass of octopus style arms. As if not to be outdone, another Quarr shifted so that its limbs became significantly more angular, almost cutting surfaces.

"We've got a double cross!" AJ warned, although he knew his team would be too late to save either of them. The Quarr he'd run into were fast and extremely dangerous. He'd known better than to trust an enemy alien to honor a truce and he mentally chastised himself for not listening to his own instincts.

"Not wise," Deke said. "But then, again, not entirely human."

AJ's eyes widened as the lithe woman became a whirling dervish of frenetic movements. He struggled to follow the strikes of the Quarr almost as much as he struggled to keep up with Deke's own acrobatics.

"Team, give this a second to resolve itself," AJ said, hearing the rumble of his platoon's hasty arrival.

"Son of a gun, she's wrecking those bastards!" Bald Norm said. "What is she?"

"She's badass," Chach said. "And she's on our side!"

"We got a runner," Lefty said. "Bald Norm, Chach, since you're all chatty, why don't you take care of that."

And in the space of a minute, the short-lived fight was over.

"I guess we all have our secrets, eh?" AJ asked, approaching Deke as she cleaned off her hard-earned Togath knife.

"Oh, those guys are way easier than a pair of Togath. They think they're all that and a bag of chips because they go all crazy-arm," she said. "A little speed and a knife in the right place is pretty hard on all that."

"Didn't think you had it in you," AJ said.

"Yeah, you thought we were toast, huh?"

"Pretty much."

"Think that was their command team? I say we see about paying homebase a quick visit. What do you say?"

A heavy vibration filled the air and AJ couldn't help but turn to see what was coming up behind them. Unexpectedly, *Angry Ark* floated through the air at a thousand feet like a giant balloon in the Macy's Day Parade.

"You had this in mind already?" he asked. "I didn't know your ship was mobile."

"Wasn't until we got right-side-up," she said. "We were going to talk about it when you got inside. Quarr just pre-empted us."

"One, could I get you two squishies to move inside a ship where there's some armor? I know we're all bad-asses, but there are at least fifty Togath still floating around, if you catch my meaning," Lefty said.

Seahag landed nearby, Darnell having anticipated the need. The pair of captains climbed aboard.

"Lieutenant Bing, explain to the good mechanized infantry people how we take down a Togath base, would you?" Deke asked. "Maybe they'd like to give us a hand on this one."

"It would be my pleasure."

EPILOGUE

"That's something you don't expect to see," Bald Norm quipped as *Angry Ark* passed overhead and was lit up from below by a trio of energy belching turrets. The ship's thick armor, which prevented any chance of orbital escape, glowed white hot to mark each impact, but then, almost as quickly turned back to cherry red as heat was dissipated.

"Squad One, southwest turret," AJ ordered. "Squad Two, northeast. *Seahag, Bernard,* stay clear until all three turrets are down. They're not messing around."

AJ watched his HUD as his team leaders checked in, acknowledging his orders. Whether because he was exhausted or due to the sheer spectacle of an eighty-thousand-ton flying fortress passing overhead, he found it difficult to focus. *Angry Ark* was a miracle of army engineering, although he had no illusions that substantial alien technology had been shared for the good of the mission and ultimately that of the Galactic Empire.

"*Angry Ark*, there's a small interstellar craft launching under cover of that central turret," Lefty announced over the command channel shared by him, AJ and Deke's officers. "I'm painting it up with a targeting laser."

"Ground, we've picked up your target," came an answer almost immediately. "Please clear immediate vicinity."

"You're clear to fire," Lefty answered.

"Say again, we're showing four units, danger close."

"*Angry Ark,* you're clear for danger-close operation. Ground will take appropriate precautions," Lefty replied.

Three turrets on *Angry Ark* turned in synchronicity and fired. The small, well-armored vessel's pilot must have realized its peril as it scooted away at ground level, trying to maximize cover from recently erected buildings.

"Squad Two, target craft with whatever you've got left," Lefty called out with uncharacteristic excitement. "Do not let that thing escape!"

"There's no chasing it at this point," Deke announced over comms as the craft slipped away, arcing into the sky. "We need to get those turrets down. Our armor is taking a beating."

"Did someone call for a cleanup batter?" Darnell's voice cut into the command channel just before a stream of trace-laden fire stitched a fine line across the back of the escaping vessel that had just turned vertical for escape.

"Hooah!" AJ barked, pride filling his chest as his old friend appeared at just the right place and the right moment.

"Yee haw!" Darnell responded when fire poured from the vessel's aft engine compartment.

"We're gonna put a bookmark in 'yee haw,' Big D," AJ said, backhanding a Togath that had jumped at him from shadows. Out of ammunition, he was operating with only his multi-tool and the impossibly hard knuckles of his armored glove. Against flesh and bone, it wasn't close to a fair fight, even against the Quarr's genetically designed warrior caste.

"Let's get this!" Bald Norm cried out with excitement while swiping his own armored glove across the skin of the turret's base, exposing a morass of cabling and bundles of wiring. Like a kid opening a sea of Christmas presents, he pulled at everything that looked important and whooped with delighted glee as massive arcs of electricity jumped around him, grounding out on everything within twenty yards, including a few unlucky Togath. It came as no surprise when the turret stopped belching out its deadly payload.

"Hey, I think you got that," Chach said a full minute later when Bald Norm continued to work his way into the machine he'd turned to scrap.

"You never know," Bald Norm said. "Maybe it's like Cracker Jacks. There could be a prize inside."

"You're such a dumbass," Chach said.

"Figure once a guy understands his place in life, it's just easier for everyone," Bald Norm said.

"Okay squad, I think we're okay on the turret," AJ said. "What say we get that central turret before Lefty and his boys take all the fun?"

"Oh, hell yes!" Bald Norm said, turning away from his prize search. "I'm on it."

"Bet I get there first," Chach said.

"Get 'em, boys," AJ said, stepping atop a nearby building as *Angry Ark* lowered itself over the prefabricated Togath base identical to the one they'd occupied earlier.

"You might want to watch this," Deke said.

"What's that?" AJ asked, still focused on the fortress class vessel. Suddenly, it was as if someone had pulled a chair out from under the ship. Dropping unceremoniously onto the base's roof, *Angry Ark* disappeared behind its walls, blowing a cloud of dust high into the air.

"Well, that's one way to go," Chach said.

Ignoring the few remaining Togath engaging his platoon, AJ raced forward and at the last moment, leapt, firing the small boosters in his suit to gain elevation. He almost didn't make his destination but managed to lock his outstretched gloves on top of the base's wall. With a quick pull, he cleared the wall.

"BB, do we have a map of this? What's my best shot at finding prisoners?"

"I have them loaded from Black Turtle mission archives," Beverly said. "Follow the smoke trail."

AJ extended the blade on his multi-tool and followed the virtual breadcrumbs his companion created. While resistance was light, he fought off the few still-loyal warriors that stepped in his way.

With his heart in his throat, and like an enraged elephant, he broke open door after door searching for his friend. Having been held for a time as a POW in Vietnam, old feelings washed over him and, in his panic, he started spiraling.

"Hey."

Birdie's quiet voice cut through the fog of AJ's growing disfunction.

"Shit," AJ muttered, having already turned from the room, no longer in control. He blew out a hot breath and filled the doorway, looking in at his friend.

"Um, I feel like you're doing the rescuing, but are you doing okay?" Birdie asked.

"Old stuff," AJ said. To just about anyone else in the world, the explanation wouldn't have been meaningful.

"Yeah, that sucks," Birdie said. "Can you get it under control? I'm a bit messed up, so we're going to need to take it easy. Do you copy?"

"Words are working. I'm gonna hold this position. You good with that?"

"That's right, brother," Birdie said. "I got you. You got me. That's all we need."

"I activated a virtual flare," Beverly said softly. "The platoon knows you have Birdie. They're closing in."

A tear rolled down AJ's cheek as he released the knot of worry in his stomach for his missing brother-in-arms.

First on the scene was Lefty who slowed to a stop twenty yards from AJ's position, picking up on AJ's struggle. "Friendly," Lefty said. "You squared away, Jenkins?"

"Friendly," AJ answered, lowering the bladed multitool he'd been holding defensively.

"We're going to hang here for a few more minutes while the team clears the rest of the building," Lefty said. "You'll be interested to know that we found eight more of Deke's crew. They were in tough shape, but they'll pull through."

"That's damn good news," AJ said, his voice thick with emotion.

"You're doing good, AJ," Lefty said. "This was a big damn win. We found their comms jammer and it's about to get pulled offline."

"I'm back, Lefty," AJ said, finally releasing the last bits of tension.

"You kind of went to a dark place there, AJ," Lefty said. "Visit any place I know?"

"Yeah, you were there," AJ said, referencing the pit cage Lefty's team had found AJ in after he'd been captured.

"I figured. Some stuff leaves a mark."

"Sure does."

"Hey, Boss? I've kind of got a stupid question," Bald Norm called over comms.

Lefty exchanged quizzical looks with AJ and both men stifled laughs. "Bald Norm, go for One," AJ answered.

"I kind of pinned this little bugger down and he's squirming around like some sort of starfish-squid-monkey-badger mix and I'm kind of afraid to let him up without takin' his head off. But now I kind of feel like that's hardly the right answer since we're not exactly fighting anymore."

"Ground team, are you saying you captured a Quarr?" Deke cut in on comms.

"Well, it sure ain't no Togath, if that's what you're asking. Ask me, not one of these little freaks looks like another so far as I'm concerned this could be something entirely different," Bald Norm said. "My Belti says it probably is, though, and he thinks maybe we should keep it around for anal probes and such."

"Anal probes …" Chach chimed in, cackling.

"Keep it professional, boys, you're not talking on a team channel," AJ chastised. "Hold steady. We'll probably want to build some sort of containment. I'd be willing to bet you just secured us a ride home with your new buddy."

"Now, that's just damn fantastic," Bald Norm said.

"No probing, Bald Norm," AJ said.

"Oh, come on, it was just a joke."

∼

AJ LEANED against the cold steel bulkhead of the Army's transport and stared out the tiny window as Fimil Prime grew smaller and smaller. It had been only a month since they'd successfully kicked the Quarr army of Togath off-planet and captured one of the elusive, genetically engineered beings.

"What are you thinking about?" Deke asked, plopping into a chair next to the window.

"Forty years is a long time to hold that planet," he said. "Think we have a chance? We get kicked off, all those lives lost ... it's hard to take."

"Those lives put us in the game," Deke said. "Humanity is trying to climb out from the bottom of the barrel. I'd do it again."

"That's a good attitude."

"That's not what you're really thinking about, though. What gives?"

AJ chuffed out a laugh. "Damn. Well played. I was thinking about something my ex-girlfriend said."

"See, now we're getting somewhere," Deke said. "What was that?"

"That I was a sucker for anything that made me feel like a patriot. Those weren't her words, but it was the general idea," he said, sighing.

"Feeling sorry for yourself, then?"

AJ smiled. Soldiers who'd shared combat had a way of cutting straight through the crap to the heart of things.

"Pretty great woman," AJ said wistfully. "She was the first surgeon who sewed me up back in 'Nam."

"Looker was she?" Deke asked.

"Oh, hell, you have no idea," AJ said. "And then put her in an environment where there were ten thousand men to every woman. I wasn't the only one with stars in my eyes back then."

"Right, I have no idea what you're talking about," Deke said.

"You're on the wrong side to understand," AJ said. "I thought we had a future. She did, too, but she couldn't deal with all this."

"You made a choice, AJ. That's called putting on your big-boy pants and owning your life," Deke said.

"I was surprised to see you on the return trip," AJ said. "I thought you'd stay behind and command the fort. Word was, they offered you fast track promotions."

Deke rolled her eyes. "Peter principal doesn't much suit me. I'm more of a doer than a talker. I imagine you can understand that. Besides, have you heard about that kerfuffle on Kanderi? Sounds like US Army has a contract to step in."

"I've heard of the place. What's our interest?"

"Would you believe they're having trouble with a Togath mercenary army? The Kanderi heard about our success on Fimil Prime. Suddenly we're the hot ticket. I've got some room on my team if you're interested."

"You do know that the Tok seized our infantry suits," AJ said. "Birdie's suit never turned up. Tok figure the Quarr took off with it before we got to the base. Commander Cer was pissed off, bigtime. Says we didn't do enough to get it back."

"Sounds about right. Offer's still out there. I'm going to need a team. Don't tell me you can't take orders from a woman," she said.

"Been doing it all my life," AJ said. "Shoot me the details. I'll take a look."

But of course, that's another story entirely.

ABOUT THE AUTHOR

Jamie McFarlane is happily married, the father of three and lives in Lincoln, Nebraska. He spends his days engaged in a hi-tech career and his nights and weekends writing works of fiction.

Word-of-mouth is crucial for any author to succeed. If you enjoyed this book, please consider leaving a review, even if it's only a line or two; it would make all the difference and would be very much appreciated.

FREE DOWNLOAD

If you'd like to receive automatic email when Jamie's next book is available, please visit http://fickledragon.com. Your email address will never be shared and you can unsubscribe at any time.

For more information
www.fickledragon.com
jamie@fickledragon.com

ACKNOWLEDGMENTS

To Diane Greenwood Muir for excellence in editing and wordsmithery.

To my beta readers: Carol Greenwood, Kelli Whyte, and John Donigan for wonderful and thoughtful suggestions. It is a joy to work with this intelligent and considerate group of people. Also, to my advanced reading team, you're a zany, fun group who I look forward to bouncing ideas off.

Finally, to Elias Stern, cover artist extraordinaire.

ALSO BY JAMIE MCFARLANE

Junkyard Pirate Series

1. Junkyard Pirate
2. Old Dogs, Older Tricks
3. Junkyard Spaceship
4. Junkyard Veterans
5. Junkyard Raiders
6. Junkyard Ghost Ship
7. Junkyard Commandos

Privateer Tales Series

1. Rookie Privateer
2. Fool Me Once
3. Parley
4. Big Pete
5. Smuggler's Dilemma
6. Cutpurse
7. Out of the Tank
8. Buccaneers
9. A Matter of Honor
10. Give No Quarter
11. Blockade Runner
12. Corsair Menace
13. Pursuit of the Bold
14. Fury of the Bold
15. Judgment of the Bold
16. Privateers in Exile
17. Incursion at Elea Station
18. Freebooter's Hold

19. Black Cutlass
20. Privateer's Supremacy

Space Troopers Series

1. Rebel's Call
2. Rebel's Run
3. Rebel's Strike

Privateer Tales Universe

1. Pete, Popeye and Olive
2. Life of a Miner
3. Uncommon Bravery
4. On a Pale Ship

Henry Biggston Thrillers

1. When Justice Calls
2. Deputy in the Crosshairs
3. Manhunt at Sage Creek

Witchy World

1. Wizard in a Witchy World
2. Wicked Folk: An Urban Wizard's Tale
3. Wizard Unleashed

Guardians of Gaeland

1. Lesser Prince

Made in the USA
Middletown, DE
09 January 2024